Reluctantly, she retreated and sank down on a pile of bricks, watching anxiously. There were about half a dozen men, all digging carefully, removing bricks and lumps of rubble one by one and setting them aside. The hole was growing larger, soon someone would be able to get down. Now and then, during the occasional brief lull in the crackling of the fires further along the street, mixed with the noise of people, running and calling, rising above the racket of fire engines and ambulances, she was sure she could hear voices coming from down below. If only I could tell who it is, she thought, straining her ears. If it's Mum, or Gran, or our Ginnie. Or one of the others. Or even all of them, all shouting together.

Oblivious of the cold, unaware of fatigue or hunger or of her burning thirst, she sat watching as the dawn crept slowly across the sky, pallid beside the rage of the still burning fires, and laid a dull, grey light over the smouldering ruins of the city of London.

Lilian Harry's grandfather hailed from Devon and Lilian always longed to return to her roots, so moving from Hampshire to a small Dartmoor town in her early twenties was a dream come true. She quickly absorbed herself in local life, learning the fascinating folklore and history of the moors, joining the church bell-ringers and a country dance club, and meeting people who are still her friends today. Although she later moved north, living first in Herefordshire and then in the Lake District, she returned in the 1990s and now lives on the edge of the moor with her ginger cat and two miniature schnauzers. She is still an active bell-ringer and member of the local drama group, and loves to walk on the moors. Her daughter and two grandchildren live nearby. Visit her website at www.lilianharry.co.uk or you can follow her on Twitter @LilianHarry.

By Lilian Harry

Goodbye Sweetheart
The Girls They Left Behind
Keep Smiling Through
Moonlight & Lovesongs
Love & Laughter
Wives & Sweethearts
Corner House Girls
Kiss the Girls Goodbye
PS I Love You
A Girl Called Thursday
Tuppence to Spend
A Promise to Keep
Under the Apple Tree
Dance Little Lady
A Farthing Will Do

Kiss the Girls Goodbye

LILIAN HARRY

An Orion paperback

First published in Great Britain in 2001
by Orion Books
This paperback edition published in 2001
by Orion Books,
an imprint of The Orion Publishing Group Ltd,
Orion House, 5 Upper St Martin's Lane,
London WC2H 9EA

An Hachette UK company

1 3 5 7 9 10 8 6 4 2

Reissued 2003

A CIP catalogue record for this book
is available from the British Library.

ISBN: 978-0-7528-4448-0

Typeset at The Spartan Press Ltd,
Lymington, Hants
Printed and bound in Great Britain by
Clays Ltd, St Ives plc

The Orion Publishing Group's policy is to use papers
that are natural, renewable and recyclable products and
made from wood grown in sustainable forests. The logging
and manufacturing processes are expected to conform to
the environmental regulations of the country of origin.

www.orionbooks.co.uk

For Brenda Courtie,
for her courage and humour

Chapter One

Thirty-first December, 1939.

It was the first New Year's Eve that anyone could remember when there hadn't been crowds celebrating at midnight in Trafalgar Square.

'It's like a blooming churchyard,' Phyl Jennings whispered to her cousin Jo as they trudged through the snowy streets on their way to report for the late-night shift at the Marble Arch Corner House. 'I mean, any other New Year's Eve there'd be gangs of people dancing and singing in the streets, the pubs'd be packed full and the Square'd be one big party. *Now* look at it – no Christmas lights, no music, nothing nice happening at all.'

They stopped for a moment and stood looking about them. The streets were covered in frozen slush and newly fallen snow but, for the moment, the skies were clear and above the looming buildings the girls could see the shimmer of stars.

'Well, that's something you never used to see in London,' Jo said softly. 'There were always too many lights on.' She paused, tilting her head. 'Listen, Phyl – hear that noise? It's people laughing, surely – laughing and shouting. Sounds like there's something happening in Piccadilly. Perhaps there *is* a party after all!'

'Let's go and see!' Phyl caught her arm and they stumbled through the icy, rutted slush. The noise was louder now, and Jo was right, people were laughing – laughing and calling to each other. There were flashes of light, too, and the girls glanced at each other in surprise.

1

Nobody flashed lights these days, with the blackout restrictions so severe. Then they heard the shrill pierce of a police whistle and their excitement turned to alarm.

'What is it? An invasion?' But Phyl's voice was lost in the uproar as they burst into Piccadilly Circus and skidded to a halt, staring in astonishment at the scene before them.

The Circus was crowded with roistering young men, just as it might have been on any normal New Year's Eve. Shouting and laughing, they were milling around the stone plinth, trampling the snow as they flashed their torches at the statue of Eros, poised with his bow and arrow above them. One was already trying to climb up, egged on by his mates, and the girls began to laugh, too, as they watched. But almost at once their laughter was stilled as, in the brilliant white light reflected by the snow, they saw policemen converging from all sides and what had been a party scene became suddenly ugly.

'Let's get away,' Phyl said, her voice trembling. 'Let's get out of here, Jo.'

Jo nodded and gripped her arm to pull her away. But their escape was barred by a mêlée of struggling bodies. Like a rugger scrum, it shifted from side to side across the road and the girls dared not get too near. Terrified, they pressed against a wall, clutching each other's hands.

They could hear the youths swearing and the police snarling back. 'We was only trying to see Eros . . . We wasn't doing nothing wrong . . . It's New Year's *Eve*, for Gawd's sake, can't a bloke 'ave a few beers and a bit of a party on New Year's Eve? Gawd knows, there ain't much ter sing about these days . . . Leave off, mate, can't yer? We could be dead this time next week . . .'

'Quick!' Jo dragged at Phyl's arm and they scurried through a gap and along a dark, narrow side street. To their relief, the noise of the fighting dwindled behind them. They paused and stared at each other.

'That's awful,' Jo said shakily. 'I mean, they only wanted

2

to look at Eros. Something like that never ought to be a crime.'

'It was because of the lights. They shouldn't have been showing lights.'

'I know, but still . . . To think of them ending up in prison just for showing a light on New Year's Eve . . .' They walked on slowly, shaken by what had happened. 'I tell you what, Phyl – this war's making everything nasty. I mean, I know we haven't been bombed yet or nothing, but there's other things happened – things like all the kiddies being sent off to the country and ships being sunk, and soldiers going off to France and Belgium . . . It's horrible. Horrible.'

Phyl squeezed her hand. 'Don't let's think about it any more, Jo. We'll be in the Corner House soon and we've got to smile at the customers and make them feel happy to be there. We've got to make sure they have a good time. That's what Nippies are for, remember? And you know what Mr Carter'd say. He'd say it was more important now than ever.'

Jo gave her a wry grin and nodded. 'I know. And it is, I suppose. So – let's take a deep breath and pretend everything's just like it used to be. Even though we all know it's not, nor ever will be again.'

The other girls had heard about the commotion in Piccadilly and were discussing it as Jo and Phyl walked into the dressing-room where they were getting into their uniforms. Someone had echoed Jo's feelings that it was dreadful for young men, full of nothing worse than high spirits and a few beers, to be arrested for shining a light at Eros. Others didn't agree.

'You wouldn't say that if some German bomber up in the sky saw the lights and dropped a packet of dynamite on Piccadilly,' Maggie Wheeler declared. She was at the mirror, trying to push her thick yellow hair under her cap.

3

'Mind you, it's as light as day out there anyway, what with all that snow laying about. I dunno why they even bothered to use torches.' She turned her back on the mirror and craned her neck to look down at the backs of her legs. 'These seams just won't stay straight tonight. I dunno what's the matter with 'em.'

'Maybe your legs have got twisted,' Shirley Woods suggested solemnly. Slender and neat, she was ready, with her cloudy dark hair rolled under her cap where it would stay all through the shift, unlike Maggie's unruly mane which needed to be continually pushed back. 'I heard about a girl that happened to. Woke up one morning with her knees on back to front and they had to put her in a—'

'Oh, for goodness' sake!' Maggie, who had been staring at her as if half-inclined to believe the ridiculous tale, grimaced with mock exasperation. 'Honestly, Shirl, you get worse instead of better. I wonder they don't employ you to go behind the German lines and tell 'em lies about what our boys are doing. You could be our secret weapon.'

Her grin faded and she looked sober. The other girls glanced at her, knowing what was going through her mind. Maggie's husband Tommy had been sent to France only days after their wedding in September on the day before war had been declared, and although she got regular letters from him Maggie didn't really know where he was or when she would see him again. There were times when her normally cheerful face looked really sad, Jo Mason thought sympathetically, and she shivered at the idea that she might herself soon be fretting over the absence of her own man. Nick was training to be a pilot and sometimes, when Jo lay unable to sleep, her mind was filled with images of him in the sky, being attacked by flocks of black planes, like a cloud of starlings.

The door to the dressing-room burst open and Etty Brown shot in, flushed and anxious. 'I'm late!' she cried. 'I'm late! Oh, goodness, where are my things – I'll never be

4

ready in time – there was that many people trying to catch the bus, I had to wait for another one and I only just managed to scramble on that – where's my other shoe – and then an old woman slipped in the snow just outside and hurt herself and I had to stop and help pick her up, she was all right, thank goodness, but she was a bit shook up and you can't just dash off and leave someone like that, can you – oh, now my cap's disappeared, I'll never be ready in time – Maggie, help me with my hair, would you?' She found her cap and stood still while Maggie pinned it on. 'Oh, dear, I hate being late for things.'

'It's all right, there's loads of time,' Jo comforted her. 'Just calm down a bit. You looked like the White Rabbit in *Alice in Wonderland*, rushing in like that. Anyway, even dear Irene's not here yet, and you know *she'd* never be late.'

'I suppose you were out with our Jim,' Maggie said, her mouth full of pins, and Etty blushed. 'You'll have to do your courting a bit nearer Marble Arch. There's a few nice spots in Hyde Park.' She winked and Etty blushed deeper. 'Me and Tommy don't need 'em no more,' Maggie concluded, the sad note back in her voice, and she finished pinning Etty's cap on and turned away, biting her lip.

'Course you don't,' Phyl said stoutly. 'You got a nice big double bed at home waiting for when he gets a bit of leave.' She came over and put her arm round Maggie's shoulders. 'He's bound to get some soon. There's nothing much going on over there, anyway. All that shouting and waving and talk about air raids and gas attacks, and practically nothing's happened. Half the kids in our street are back from evacuation already, just as if they'd been on holiday, and our air-raid shelter's turning into a cats' home. They dished out all these gas masks . . . .' she glanced over at the row of brown cardboard boxes hanging on the wall '. . . and give us shelters to build in the back gardens and told us all thousands of people would be killed by bombs, and there's been nothing at all. *I* don't think they know what's going to happen.'

'Well, I suppose they don't, not really.' Jo went over to the door to the underground passage that led through to the Corner House itself. 'There's never been a war like this before, has there?' She glanced at the wall clock. 'You know, it's practically time to go – if that Irene don't get here soon she really is going to be late, and then there'll be trouble. There might not be much going on outside but it's New Year's Eve in the Corner House all right, and we're going to be rushed off our feet.'

The door opened as she spoke and Irene sauntered in. Smart as always in her black winter coat and little fur hat, she looked as if she were on her way to the theatre or a cocktail party rather than to do a late-night shift as a waitress. Her sharp-featured face was made up to look rosily pink, her lips red and her green eyes shadowed. She gave the other girls a contemptuous glance as she slipped out of her coat and hung it up, taking care to separate it from the others.

'What are you all staring at, then? Know me next time, will you?'

Phyl turned away without speaking. Jo said, 'We're not staring. We were just saying if you didn't turn up soon you'd be late, that's all.'

'And I suppose you'd like that, wouldn't you? You'd like to see me get into trouble.' Irene slipped out of her fur boots, damp with slush, and began to get into her uniform. 'Well, hard cheese, because I'm not going to. I'm one of the favourites here, and don't you forget it. Supervisor, that's what I'll be, and then manageress. *I'm* not going to stay a common waitress like the rest of you will.'

'Come on,' Phyl muttered, moving closer to her cousin. 'She's not worth talking to. Don't start a row.'

'I heard that, Phyl Jennings,' Irene called out. 'Not worth talking to, am I? I'll remember that when I'm a supervisor

6

and you're still a stupid little Nippy. You'll have to watch your words then, I can tell you.'

'Oh, I will, will I?' Phyl whipped back, her eyes flaming. 'Well, let me tell you this, Lady Muck – if *you* ever get to be a supervisor, *I'll* be putting in for a transfer! And I bet a lot of the other Nippies'll be doing just the same. Nobody's going to want to work here with *you* chucking your weight about.'

Irene started forward, her face red with fury, but Maggie grabbed her arm and dragged her back. Jo tugged at Phyl's sleeve and muttered in her ear.

'Come on, Phyl. I thought you said not to start a row.'

'I'm not. It's just that she gets my goat, the way she queens it over the rest of us. She's nothing more than a spiteful cat.'

'I know. I feel the same – and I can't forget what she did to you, telling Mike those lies about you that time. But it don't do no good to let her get your rag out.'

Phyl shrugged and nodded. 'Well, it didn't work, did it? Mike and me got together just the same.' Phyl pursed her lips ruefully. Mike, Tommy and their mate Charlie had all joined the army together and had been sent across the Channel at the same time. It was as important to Phyl as it was to Maggie that they get some leave soon.

There was no more chatter. It was time to go through to the Corner House, and the girls wrapped their cloaks around them and scurried through the dank underground passage. It was colder than ever down there tonight, as the snow had started two or three days earlier. And nobody knew how long it might be expected to last now that there weren't any weather forecasts.

All the same, Jo thought as they came through the tunnel from the dressing-room, the Corner House was making a good job of New Year's Eve. Despite the bad weather, the blackout, the looming threat of rationing and the lack of festivities outside, once inside the brightly lit restaurant

7

with its decorations and the band playing at one end you'd have thought there was nothing wrong at all. People were smiling and enjoying their food, the Nippies were dashing to and fro with their big silver trays and the war seemed suddenly far away.

I'm really glad we work here, Phyl and me, she thought, making her way over to the cluster of tables that formed her 'station' with her warm smile in place, ready to welcome her first customers of the evening.

'That's a happy face,' a man greeted her as she came to his table. He was sitting with a pretty woman, obviously his wife, and they were dressed up, he in a dark suit and she in a red silk dress with a low-cut neckline. 'I told you, didn't I?' he said to the woman. 'I told you we'd get a warm welcome at a Lyons Corner House.'

'You didn't have to tell me,' she said, laughing, and looked up at Jo. 'He's an awful tease. We always come here on New Year's Eve – and on our wedding anniversary, too.' She blushed. 'We met at a Corner House, you see.'

'Did you really?' Jo gazed at them. 'How long ago was that?'

'You shouldn't ask,' the man told her, grinning. 'It gives away too much! But I'll tell you this – she's as pretty now as she was fifteen years ago, so work it out for yourself. Now, what special dishes have you got for us tonight?'

Jo made a face. 'Nothing as special as you ought to have. Not with this war on. Everything's going to be rationed now, same as at home. Only two lumps of sugar each, and one sixth of an ounce of butter! I don't even know how they manage to measure it out in the kitchens. And you won't be able to have two lots of protein at the same meal, so it's no use asking for ham and eggs!'

'I dare say we'll manage to have a good time.' They studied the menu. 'It's being in here that counts. All the decorations and the chandeliers, and the music. They can't ration that, can they?'

8

Jo took their order and hurried back to the kitchen. The band was playing a selection of tunes, from Ivor Novello's 'We'll Gather Lilacs' to some of the new Ambrose tunes that the girl singers like Anne Shelton and Vera Lynn were making so popular, and the lively dance music of Glenn Miller. Now and then there was a different selection, something from Gilbert and Sullivan or a bit of light classical stuff, but as midnight grew closer the music became softer and more romantic, nostalgic tunes that made the eyes grow moist and the heart begin to yearn.

'I wish my Tommy was here,' Maggie whispered as the band swung into a Scottish dance tune. 'I keep thinking about him and wondering where he is now and what he's doing. It's breaking my heart, all this separation.'

'I know. It's like half of you's not here.' Jo and Phyl stood one each side of her as they linked arms for 'Auld Lang Syne'. Three girls, all thinking of three men who were just as close friends. Tommy Wheeler and Mike Bennett, in the army somewhere behind the Maginot Line. Nick, learning to fly his Spitfire somewhere in Sussex.

Where would they be this time next year? Jo wondered as every customer in the place surged forward to the strains of the traditional tune. What would happen to them all during this coming twelve months?

What would 1940 bring, to the girls of the Corner House and the men and the families they loved?

Maggie got home late that night, but not as late as she'd have liked on New Year's Eve – or New Year's Day as it was by then. Any other year she wouldn't have been going indoors till the small hours – she would have been out in the streets, maybe joining the crowds in Trafalgar Square or maybe with her own family and some of the other Pearlies, dressed to the nines in glittering finery and banging on each other's doors to offer lumps of coal and crusts of bread.

ind bread! she thought wryly as she fitted her key into
ront door. You'd think twice about giving them away
e days.

The house was in darkness except for the glimmer of a
nt from under the kitchen door. Everyone else had gone
bed. There was going to be a bit of a knees-up in the
treet, she knew, but what with not being able to show a
ight without a yell from some nosy copper or ARP twerp,
and half the young blokes having already joined up and
gone away, it must have finished early. Maggie sighed. It
was an anticlimax, coming home like this after the brightness and cheer of the Corner House, but she was lucky to
have had that. No use in grumbling.

She opened the kitchen door, hoping that Mum had left
her a bite to eat, and jumped with surprise as her brother
Jim looked up from the newspaper he had spread out on the
table. He nodded and got up to put the kettle on. The match
wouldn't strike, and he muttered and used his cigarette
lighter instead. It was the one Etty had given him for
Christmas.

'Cor, you gave me a shock,' Maggie said, shutting the
door behind her. 'I thought everyone was in bed.'

'You gave me a bit of a surprise yourself,' he said, getting
cups from the dresser. 'Creeping in like that. I never heard a
thing till you opened the door. Training to be a cat-burglar,
are you?'

'Trying to be considerate and not wake the whole house,
that's all. Anyway, what are you doing down here? Don't
you have to go to work in the morning?'

'Course I do. It's Monday, isn't it? Not that we'll get
much done – I bet half the blokes will come in with thick
heads.' He grinned. 'We had a good time up the Dog and
Duck. Ivy Parrish come in with some of her mates and gave
us a song. Got things going a bit.'

'So why aren't you in bed?' Maggie mixed cocoa and
sugar with a small amount of milk in the cups and filled

10

them with boiling water. 'I'd have thought you wanted a bit of shut-eye.'

'Oh, well . . .' Jim shrugged. 'I just thought you might be bringing Etty back with you.'

'Oh, Jim.' Maggie set his cocoa before him. 'You know she said she'd be going back to the hostel tonight. She's been here all over Christmas, after all.'

'I don't see why she can't move in here,' he said, repeating an argument they'd had several times already. 'I mean, she's just miserable in that hostel. And it's daft, her having to trail back all that way on Saturdays and Sundays when she's been over here.'

'Well, I don't mind her stopping the night at weekends, and I don't suppose Mum would either. But you've got to see, Jim, it's my room she's sharing and when my Tommy comes home it's him I'll want with me, not Etty. And what's she going to do then if she's given up her place in the hostel?'

'Maybe we'll be married by then,' Jim said, 'and she can share my room.'

Maggie looked at him. 'I didn't know you were planning to get married that soon. You're not even properly engaged yet.'

'We are, to all intents and purposes. We got an understanding.'

'You haven't given her a ring.'

'No, because we're saving up. I want to be able to give her something decent. She's never had anything nice, you know that. I want her to have something she can be proud to show off at that Corner House of yours.'

'Well, all right, but if you've got to save up for a ring when are you thinking of getting married? It'll take a lot longer to save up for that.'

Jim shrugged with exasperation. '*I* don't know, for goodness' sake! Why are you keeping on at me about getting married? Who said anything about that?'

'You did. You said you and Etty might be married by the

11

time my Tom comes home, and I said I didn't know you were planning it so soon. So when—'

'I don't *know*! I didn't mean anything like that. I just meant—'

'You meant you think it's going to be a long time before Tom comes back here to live,' Maggie said heavily. She sat down suddenly and rested one hand against her forehead. 'Oh, Jim, I feel real fed up. Our first Christmas and New Year and I don't even know where he is, not properly. I don't know when I'm going to see him again, or what'll have happened to us by then, and all we had of being married was an hour. One *hour*.'

'I know, Mags. I suppose that's why I'd like Etty to be over here more. I dare say I'll be joining up myself soon and then it'll be the same for us. It seems as if we're wasting our time, being apart.' He stared moodily at his cocoa. 'Anyway, it was daft, what I said. We couldn't share my room if we did get married – not with our Gerald and George in it as well!'

Maggie giggled. 'A bit embarrassing way to start married life! And *I'm* not moving out to share with them, so you needn't even bother to ask.' She gave him another look. 'D'you mean that? About joining up?'

'Well, it's either join up or be called up, isn't it? We're all going to have to go one way or another. Better to jump than wait and be pushed.'

Tommy had said almost the same thing, Maggie remembered. And now he was over the Channel in France, or maybe Belgium, digging trenches and waiting to fight. 'It might be better to wait, all the same,' she said. 'All the time you're at home, you're safe. I bet our Mum don't want you to go.'

'Nobody's mum wants them to go,' Jim said soberly. 'But they don't ask people's mums when they decide to have a war, do they? They don't ask anyone. They just go ahead and have it – and *we* has to do the fighting.'

*

12

Etty, catching a late bus back to the hostel, was just as miserable as Jim. Despite all the restrictions, she'd had a Christmas with the Pratts such as she'd never had before, and leaving that big, sprawling warm-hearted family to go back to the chilly hostel with its mixture of rough girls and standoffish businesswomen was like being sent into exile. In the Antarctic, she thought bitterly as the bus drew up at her stop and she stepped down into a gutter full of slush. All we need is a crowd of penguins.

There were no penguins in the hostel, but a gaggle of young women came in from a nearby pub at the same time, and they didn't sound very different. Their squawking voices grated on Etty's ears and when they saw her in the hallway with its cracked linoleum and dark brown anaglypta walls they cackled with drunken laughter.

'Well, if it ain't our little Nippy! Bin nippin' about all night, have yer? Bet you had a great time down the Corner House, sittin' on all them soldiers' knees. All the fellers go there now, hopin' to pick up a nice little bit of fluff, so I hear.'

'Ow, my *dear!*' screeched another girl, affecting what she evidently thought to be a 'posh' accent. 'I 'ear it's the *ownly* plyce to go to meet a young man these days, my dear! *Nowbody* goes ter the Ritz these days, doncherknow.'

''Ow many soldiers bin after you, then, Etty? Bet *you've* 'ad a few behind the bushes down 'yde Park, aincher?'

'Bet she hasn't,' someone else said abruptly. 'No bloke with an ounce of decency would lower hisself to touch her – dirty little Jew. It's people like her what's caused all this war. Jews! Oughter be sent back where they come from and made to stop there, so's the rest of us can live in peace.'

Etty's face burned. She had heard sentiments like this often enough, from people in the street, from people at the orphanage where she had spent her childhood, even from people like Irene Bond at work, but although she'd been aware of the other girls' animosity nobody at the hostel had

13

ever said so quite so offensively. She thought of the newspaper reports, the cinema newsreels, the stories of Jews in Germany, forced to wear yellow stars on their sleeves, forced to live behind high brick walls in ghettos, forced to leave their jobs, their homes, even their country.

'You're a bitch!' she told the girl. 'A nasty, horrible bitch. And you're unpatriotic, too, what's more. We're supposed to be fighting a war against Hitler, but you're on his side.'

'*Ow!* Did you 'ear that? She good as called me a traitor. Look 'ere, you.' The girl pushed her face close to Etty's. She had small, spiteful eyes like hard little toffees and a thick nose and sullen lips. 'At least I'm British. Not like you, come from Gawd knows where. Not like a nasty, dirty little *Jew*.'

The other girls were beginning to look uncomfortable. One of them pulled at the toffee-eyed girl's sleeve, muttering at her to come away, leave the kid alone, she couldn't help being what she was. But she was shaken off and Etty found herself being pushed against the wall.

'What I wants to know is, why 'aven't you bin interned? I thought they was doing that to all the aliens, puttin' 'em in prison where they belongs? Why 'aven't they done it to you, eh?' She stared at Etty, her face so close that Etty could feel her beery breath on her cheek. The girl's nose was almost touching hers and Etty shrank away, revolted.

'Maybe it's because nobody's told 'em you're 'ere,' the girl said slowly. 'Maybe it's time someone woke the orthorities up a bit.'

'Come on, Dotty,' the friend urged, pulling again at her sleeve. 'You'll 'ave Mrs Denton down 'ere in a minute, wanting to know what all the racket's about. Let the kid go and let's get up to bed. I'm dead beat and we got to get up early in the morning.'

This time, Dotty allowed herself to be pulled away. The threat of the hostel manageress being brought down in her dressing-gown and curlers was enough to subdue most of

14

the hostel inmates. Mrs Denton wielded absolute power, and any girl who annoyed her was likely to find herself turned out, with nowhere else to go. Nobody wanted that, least of all in the middle of winter and with a war on to make everything worse.

The girls staggered upstairs, leaving Etty in the hall alone. She leant against the wall, waiting for them to disappear. They'd go to the lavatory first, she thought drearily, all of them, one at a time, so she had a wait of several minutes before the coast was clear.

As she stood there under the dim lamp, struggling to get her breath back, the front door opened again and one of the businesswomen came in, pulling it shut hurriedly behind her. You didn't dare show even the smallest chink of light these days – or these nights, rather – for fear of being shouted at or reported to the police. Every week the papers had columns of names of people who were hauled up in court for blackout offences. Most of them got off with a small fine, but one chap who had flashed his torch in a policeman's face, saying it was better than getting run over, had found himself in jail for a month, and Etty had heard of a girl who'd got six months' hard labour for swearing at a copper who'd told her to put out her torch. And look at what had happened in Piccadilly Circus that very night. Just a bit of fun, and now there were a couple of dozen young chaps in prison for it.

The newcomer stopped and stared at Etty. She was one of the older women, who had rooms on the top floor and a bathroom and lavatory between only five of them. She worked in one of the big stores; Etty thought she was a buyer or something.

'Hullo. What's up with you, lurking there? Here, you haven't had a boy in, have you?' Her voice was Streatham, overlaid with a more refined accent that she had probably learned at work and which occasionally slipped, and she used words that marked her out as 'posh'. She dressed smartly, too, wearing a black business suit by day and, tonight, a red silk jacket and black frock, and her dark brown hair was cut short and set in sharp, gleaming waves.

'No, I haven't,' Etty answered wearily. 'I've just got in from work. Some of the others came in at the same time – I was just waiting for them to go to bed.'

'Oh.' The woman looked at her thoughtfully. Etty remembered her name now. She was called Miss Chalk. 'Giving you a bit of trouble, were they?'

Etty flushed. 'Not really.'

'Oh, come on,' Miss Chalk said, her tone more friendly, 'I've heard them getting at you. Especially that one with the hair like a woolly bear. Dotty, she's called, isn't she? Dotty by name and dotty by nature, that's what I think about her.'

Etty giggled, almost as much in surprise at being talked to like a human being as because what Miss Chalk had said was funny. The sudden release brought tears to her eyes. She'd been trying to hold them back, but someone being kind was just too much for her.

'They're not so bad,' she said, sniffing and searching in her pockets for a hanky. 'They don't really mean it.'

'They do,' Miss Chalk said. 'But you don't want to take any notice of them. They haven't got the brains to know what they're saying. You're a different class to them, Etty – it is Etty, isn't it? Look at the job you do, working in a Corner House. I go into them myself for my lunch. Those others are nothing but common factory sluts.'

Etty smiled waveringly and put away her hanky. 'I'd better go to bed,' she said. 'They'll have finished by now.'

'Why not come and have a cup of cocoa with me?' Miss Chalk suggested. 'I've got a gas ring in my room and a drop of milk. It'll settle you down.' She smiled. 'I haven't even wished you a happy New Year.'

'Oh . . .' Etty was nonplussed. None of the business-women had taken any notice of her before, and she was surprised that Miss Chalk even knew her name, let alone thought her 'different' from the other girls and worth asking to her room. 'I ought to be going to bed,' she said uncertainly. 'It's nearly two in the morning.'

'You'll sleep all the better for a hot drink,' the older woman said firmly. 'Those other gels have upset you, I can see that. You won't sleep a wink if you go to bed now.'

Etty thought she would probably sleep like a log, but she followed her new friend up the stairs to the top floor, waiting just inside the door while the gas lamp was lit and cast its yellow glow. She had never been up here before and looked around with interest at the wide attic with its sloping ceiling. It was bigger than any of the downstairs rooms.

'You're surprised, aren't you?' Miss Chalk said with amusement. 'It's more like a little flatlet really. I've got my own little kitchenette, see?' She drew back a curtain at one end of the room to reveal a small table with a gas ring standing on it, beside a washbasin. 'I have to share the bathroom and conveniences, of course, but since it's only temporary I don't mind that.'

To Etty's knowledge, Miss Chalk had lived at the hostel for five years. She watched as the kettle was filled and set on the gas ring, and cups and saucers brought out of a cupboard. 'Are you moving out soon, then?' she enquired timidly.

Miss Chalk gave a short laugh. 'Well, I would have been if Hitler hadn't poked his nose in! He's altered all our lives, that man has, and not for the better either. I had my eye on a nice little flat, completely self-contained, you know, and in a nice district, too. But he's put a stop to all those sorts of plans.'

'He's upset a lot of people's lives,' Etty said, thinking again of the German Jews.

Miss Chalk brought the cocoa over, with a plate of Nice biscuits. Her black frock had a white collar, the sort you could pin on, and a thin red bow tied at the neck. Her short,

17

stiffly waved hair and the red tie gave her a mannish look. She gave Etty a smile with lips as red as the tie.

'I dare say you'll be thinking of joining one of the women's services. You and the other young gels in the Corner House.'

'I don't know,' Etty said, sipping the cocoa. Miss Chalk was right, it did make her feel better. There was a curious taste to it, reminding her of the smell of Sam Pratt's tea when he added a drop of whisky to keep out the cold. She felt the warmth run down into her stomach. 'Some of them are talking about it. But we all like being at the Corner House – we don't really want to go away.'

'They're a good company to work for, Lyons,' Miss Chalk observed. 'And they employ a nice class of girl. More refined than the usual type of waitress.' She lit a cigarette and let the smoke curl round her head. 'I've been in your place a few times. Seen you working. I haven't sat at your table, though. There's a tall gel and a small one with dark curly hair and big brown eyes. And another one – rather a smart-looking gel – with green eyes.'

'That's Irene Bond. And the other two are Jo and Phyl – they're cousins. Their mothers are identical twins, but you wouldn't know it to look at Jo and Phyl, they're nothing alike at all. Phyl's the one who takes after them.'

'Well, isn't that interesting? And there's a big gel, with yellow hair – a bit vulgar, I've always thought, not really Lyons' type at all.'

'That's Maggie. She's really nice. Got a heart of gold.' Etty dipped her eyes, wondering whether to tell Miss Chalk she was going steady with Maggie's brother. But she didn't think the older woman would be that interested in her – why should she be? Before she could say anything, Miss Chalk was speaking again.

'What's your proper name? I've only ever heard you called Etty.'

'It's Esther. Nobody ever calls me that now, except the

supervisors at Lyons.' Etty's mother had called her Esther, but Etty could barely remember it. It seemed too grand for her now.

'Esther. Now, that's a pretty name. And you know, you're quite a pretty gel, too.' Miss Chalk looked at her consideringly. 'I suppose you have young men after you all the time, especially now there's so many servicemen about. All you gels do, I dare say.'

It was almost what the other girls had said, but this time it didn't seem to have anything to do with the fact that Etty was half-Jewish. She shook her head.

'Not really. A lot are going steady. And Maggie's married. She and Tommy got married the day before war broke out. He had to go away straight after and she hasn't seen him since. I think it's ever so sad. The others are engaged, too, but Irene doesn't seem to have a boyfriend. She doesn't even seem to like men all that much.'

'Doesn't like men?' Miss Chalk raised her eyebrows. 'Well, that's unusual! And Irene's the one with green eyes, is that right?'

'Yes.' Etty was beginning to feel sleepy. The cocoa had warmed her and now her eyes were heavy and she felt very slightly dizzy. She stood up. 'I'll have to go now, I'm dead on my feet. Thank you ever so much for the cocoa, Miss Chalk, and—'

'Oh, please! Call me Muriel.' The older woman's voice had warmed again. She stood up as well and laid her hand on Etty's arm. 'We hostel gels must stick together in these difficult times, don't you agree? I'll tell you what, I'll come into your Corner House for my lunch some time, or maybe for a bite of supper, and you can introduce me to your pals. They sound a nice, friendly bunch.'

'They are.' Except for Irene, who scarcely spoke a word to any of them these days unless it was to sneer. But Irene always had thought herself a cut above the rest of them. Reckoned she'd been picked out at the very first interview as the right type for a manageress, and she meant to be one, too. I just hope I'm not there when she is, Etty thought as she slipped down the stairs to the room she shared with two other girls.

Pat and Cora were in bed, fast asleep, and Etty undressed in the dark and scrambled between the cold sheets. There was no heating in the bedrooms and only this morning she had woken to find the water in her stone hot-water bottle frozen. It probably hadn't thawed all day, and it was too late now to start boiling kettles so she just pulled on a pair of thick woolly socks and kept her old jumper wrapped round her. If it goes on like this, she thought, trying to will herself to get warm, we'll be putting on more clothes to go to bed than we do when we get up.

She lay for a few minutes staring into the darkness, wondering what this new year would bring. The bombs they had been warned to expect? A German invasion, like Poland? She thought of hearing the wail of the siren on a bitterly cold night like tonight, with snow and slush outside, and having to turn out and go down to the shelter no matter how tired you were. Or spending the night on the Corner House roof as they'd been told they would have to do, watching for bombs and ready to tackle fires.

I don't see how we're going to manage, she thought. I just don't see how anyone's going to manage.

Chapter Two

It was another week before Phyl and Jo were able to get home again.

By then, everyone knew this must be the coldest winter of the century so far. Nobody could remember one as bad as this since the late 1890s, when there had been a series of bitter winters, with the Thames freezing and people skating on the Serpentine. Now it looked as if the January of 1940 was going to be the same.

'They reckon another few days like this and the ice will be thick enough,' Jo said as she and Phyl sat on the top of the Woolwich bus. Most of the main streets were kept pretty clear so that the traffic could keep moving, but the side streets were filled with piles of snow, grimy from soot and dirt from the few vehicles that were managing to get about, and even the main roads were thick with ice. People shuffled along in wellington boots with thick socks over the top to give them some grip. The girls looked down at an old woman, creeping along the pavement with a heavy shopping basket hanging from one hand while the other kept a steadying hold on the wall. 'Mind, it's not much fun for people like her, poor old soul. I bet the hospitals are full of people with broken arms and legs.'

They got off the bus at last and walked down the road to their own street. Like other side streets, it was a muddle of piled snow, frozen slush and thick, bumpy ice. The baker's van was at the top of the street and the baker was trudging to and fro with a basket piled with loaves, while his horse waited patiently, his legs wet with slush and his mane sprinkled with frozen droplets.

'Poor thing,' Jo said, stopping to give him a pat on the neck. 'You must be so cold and miserable. Look, Phyl, his poor legs are frozen and there's icicles on his harness.' The horse turned his head and nuzzled her. 'Oh, look, he knows me, even though he hasn't seen me for ages!'

'You always were soppy about those horses. You're as bad as your Alice with that cat of hers.' Phyl wrapped her arms around her body, grinning. 'I remember that row you had once with the coalman because you said he was being cruel to old Dobbin. He wouldn't come down our street for a month and everyone had to collect their coal from the top of the road. *You* weren't the most popular person in the street, I can tell you!'

'Well, he *was* being cruel. And poor old Dobbin dropped dead the next week, so I was right.' Jo gave the baker's horse a last pat. 'I tell you what, Phyl, I wouldn't mind being a land-girl if we have to get called up. I've always fancied living in the country.'

'Better you than me, then, in this weather. I bet it's horrible, working out in the fields in the freezing cold. Come on, Jo, I'll turn into a block of ice myself if we stand here much longer.'

They walked on down the street. There were people outside, clearing fresh snow from the pavement in front of their houses with shovels and piling it up on the dirty mounds already there. A few chimneys had smoke curling from them but most people didn't have enough coal to light fires during the day and the girls knew the houses were almost as cold inside as out.

'I tell you what,' Phyl said as she rang the doorbell, 'we're blooming lucky to have jobs in a nice warm Corner House. I don't reckon I'll be joining up in a hurry – 'specially to work on a farm!'

Jo grinned and opened the front door of the Masons'

house, next door. She'd complained about not having a key and her father had agreed she might as well be given one, even though she wasn't yet twenty-one. It's only a few months to go now, she'd argued, and had been delighted to find one amongst her Christmas presents. It was a lot nicer to be able to let herself in than have to wait for someone to answer the door.

Not that she'd have had to wait long. Her younger sister Alice was already on the way to the door, with the big ginger cat Robertson close behind her. They were inseparable, those two, and it had caused a lot of trouble when Alice was supposed to be evacuated last September but had refused to go without him. She'd got her way and had stayed at home, and now half the other kids who'd been sent to the country were drifting back as well. They were mooching round the streets now, messing about with the grubby snow, half of them with no schools to go to since they'd been requisitioned for first-aid posts and rationing offices and so on.

'Jo!' Alice wound her arms around Jo's body. She had fair hair like her brother Eric, who had been evacuated to Kent but had come back for Christmas and was still at home. 'We didn't think you'd get here, with all the snow. It's three feet deep in the back garden! Next door's pipes burst when Mr Hawkins tried to thaw them out with a blowtorch, and they had floods all over the mat. And we didn't have any electricity all last Saturday, the power was cut off everywhere. What do they do in the Corner House when the power's cut off, Jo?'

'It hasn't been yet.' Jo had been wondering that herself until someone told her the Corner Houses had their own generators which would take over if the mains failed. 'I bet the people who've still got gas lights were laughing.'

'My friend Annie's still got gas,' Alice said. 'She says her dad'll never change, he doesn't believe in electricity, he says it's dangerous. You can't see it, that's what he says.'

'Well, you can't see gas either.' Jo unwound her scarf and

23

unbuttoned her coat. The fire was burning in the grate and she knew it had probably been lit just because she was coming home. 'And electricity can't leak and kill you like gas can.'

'How do they know that, if you can't see it? It might be leaking all over the place.' Alice looked around the room, as if the floor might be awash with invisible electricity.

Jo was saved from answering by the appearance of her mother from the kitchen. Carrie Mason was small and dark, like her twin sister and like Phyl. Jo, like Eric and Alice, took after their father but her hair was darker than theirs, a rich chestnut that seemed to have taken its colouring from both sides and mixed it in a pot, like paint. She was taller than her mother by several inches, and had to bend slightly to give her a hug and kiss her cheek.

'Sit yourself down by the fire and I'll fetch you a cup of tea,' Carrie said. 'You must be shrammed with cold. What sort of a journey did you have?'

'Slow and freezing.' Jo held out her hands to the flames. 'Mum, you didn't need to have lit this specially for me. I know you can't have much coal, everyone's saying how short it is. Mrs Holt's only lighting her fire after tea now.'

'Don't be daft. You're not home often enough to have to sit in your coat when you are here.' Carrie disappeared for a minute and came back with a tray of tea and a plate of broken biscuits. 'Look at these, they were selling them cheap up at the shop, there's some really nice sorts and some are nearly whole.'

'Our Eric's had all the custard creams,' Alice complained. 'It's not fair. He took three yesterday.'

'Well, he won't get any more, then, will he? Stop moaning, Alice, and have one of the rich teas instead. Or – look – there's one with pink icing on, you like those.' Carrie settled down in the chair opposite Jo. 'So how's London? Was it busy on New Year's Eve?'

'We were busy in the restaurant, but the streets were

24

pretty quiet. A few blokes got arrested for shining lights at Eros.' The sight of the youths being grabbed and knocked about by the police had upset Jo, but she didn't want to tell her mother about that. 'I hear they're going to take it away soon anyway, for safety if there are air raids.'

'What, Eros? Piccadilly'll seem funny without him.' Carrie stirred her tea, although Jo noticed that she'd stopped taking sugar. 'They're not going to try and move *all* the statues, are they? Old Nelson, up on top of his column in Trafalgar Square? And all those others, with soldiers on horses? It'll take them years – the war'll be over before they've finished.'

'I don't think so. I suppose Eros is easier to move and they think they might as well.' Jo took another bit of biscuit. 'Have you seen those barrage balloons? They're like great big whales up in the sky. Apparently the idea's to make enemy planes fly higher, so they don't get tangled up in the lines, and then they can be shot down. I just hope they don't get loose and fly off by themselves, that'll cause a bit of a hoo-ha.'

Carrie smiled, but her smile faded quickly and Jo noticed some new lines of worry between her brows. She glanced at Alice, who was now lying on the floor cuddling Robertson, and leant forward.

'What's up, Mum? You look a bit upset.'

Carrie made a little face. 'Oh, it's our Freddy. He's talking about joining up. Says he'll have to soon anyway, so why wait? I think he *wants* to go, Jo. He seems all excited, not at all like his normal self.'

'Well, that's what men are like, isn't it? They like fighting. Look at the way he collected up all them toy guns when he was little, and all those swords he made out of bits of plywood. He's no different from the rest.'

'Toy guns is one thing,' Carrie said. 'Seeing him march off in army uniform with a real gun's another. I don't want him to get killed, Jo.'

Jo looked at her mother and saw the distress in her eyes. She felt helpless. How could she say that her brother wouldn't get killed, when she knew that once this war really got going hundreds, perhaps thousands, of soldiers, sailors, airmen like her Nick and even civilians living in their own homes certainly would be killed? Nobody could be sure of being safe these days.

She reached across and laid her hand on Carrie's. 'I know, Mum.' It was the only thing she could think of, to acknowledge her mother's fears and share them. 'I know. It's awful for everyone, and there's not a blessed thing we can do about it, except just keep our peckers up and hope for the best.'

'It's like our lives have been taken over,' Carrie said, her voice trembling. 'We used to think we had some sort of control over what we did and the way our kids would go. Now we've got none at all. We just have to wait to be told what to do and then do it.'

'Yes, but it's either that or let Hitler tell us what to do, and that'd be even worse. We can't let him ride roughshod over everything, Mum. We've got to stand up to him.'

'I know. I know.' Carrie wiped her eyes and tried to smile. 'I just don't want it to be my Freddy who's got to stand up to him, that's all! I'm just selfish about it.'

'You're not selfish.' Jo gave her hand a pat. 'I bet there's not a mother in the country who doesn't feel just the same. Or a wife or sweetheart,' she added, thinking of Maggie and her Tom, of Phyl and Mike, of herself and Nick. 'We've all got men we're going to have to worry about.'

'Oh, now I feel even worse! Thinking about myself as usual—'

'Mum, you're not! We're all bound to think about the ones that matter most to us. What we've got to do is help each other through it.' She was quiet for a moment or two. 'There's plenty of poor souls already lost their men at sea. And you're doing your best to help them, aren't you?' She nodded towards the little heap of knitting that lay by Carrie's chair. Navy blue, it was obviously a Balaclava helmet. 'Some chap's going to be glad of that, and his mum's going to bless you for knitting it for him.'

'I expect she's knitting one herself,' Carrie said, and then smiled at herself. 'Well, no, obviously she can't be or I wouldn't be doing it – this is for someone who hasn't got a mum, or whose mum can't knit – oh, Jo, I don't know what I'm saying! I don't care who has it so long as it keeps his ears warm. And our Alice is knitting one, too – for her sailor, she says – and having the leftover bits to make pompoms for Robbie.' She glanced out of the window and shivered. 'It's awful to think of those poor men, isn't it, tossing around at sea in this bitter weather.'

Jo decided her mother needed cheering up. She began to talk about the Corner House, describing the meal they'd served on New Year's Eve and the customers who had been there. 'And we had a lovely band, with a girl singer and all the latest songs – "Somewhere Over the Rainbow", from that Judy Garland picture, and "We'll Meet Again". And then there was a couple of chaps dressed up like Flanagan and Allen, doing "We're Gonna Hang Out the Washing On the Siegfried Line" and "Run, Rabbit, Run". They were really good, ever so funny. Honestly, you just forgot there was a war on, or a blackout. I reckon it did everyone good.'

'Well, it wasn't so bad here either,' Carrie said, laughing at Jo's description. 'Your auntie and uncle came in, and the boys, of course, and we had quite a nice party. Nothing very much, of course – just a few songs round the piano and then a glass of port to see the New Year in. No conga up and down the street like we used to do.' She fell silent again and Jo sought for something else to say that would keep the smile on her mother's face.

'I bet you're sorry now you didn't go away to the country,' she said, turning to Alice. 'You could have had a nice little holiday and come back now with all the others. I wonder how many of them will go back.'

'Not many,' Carrie said. 'They all say there's been no bombing, so what's the point? Your dad says it's daft, the bombs are sure to come and then they'll have to do it all over again. If he had his way, our Alice would be going now just the same.'

'I'm not going,' Alice said from the floor. 'Not without Robbie.'

She had heard stories from the other children about life in the country as evacuees. Some had, as Jo had said, looked on it as a holiday – 'better than picking 'ops,' one boy had told her. 'We only went to school in the mornings and the rest of the time we could do what we liked. We could go anywhere in the fields. Here, did you know milk comes out of cows' bums? They got these bags hung under 'em, see, where the farmer keeps the milk till he's ready for it, and then he squeezes it out into a bucket. It's true! I done it meself one day. All warm and bubbly, it is, not like stuff in bottles. And there was chickings, too, laying eggs all over the place. *They* comes out of their bums, too, all covered in shit.'

Alice hadn't known whether to believe him or not, but her father had told her it was, more or less, true. After that, she hadn't fancied milk for several days and wouldn't have fancied a boiled egg either, if one had been offered to her – fortunately, she thought, despite what the boy had told her about eggs being laid 'all over the place', there didn't seem to be many in London these days.

Other children had told different stories. 'Stuck in the scullery, we was, and had to do all the washing-up, and just lived on scraps.' 'That's nuffin' – *I* had to live in the kennel with the dog and chew his bones!' 'The lady said we was dirty, just 'cause we didn't take our boots off to go to bed. I told her, we'd never had a bed before, so how should we know?' 'I had to scrub the kitchen floor every day, and our Jacky got hit because he let the pig out – it run all round the yard and knocked over a churn of milk and the farmer said it was Jacky's fault and he couldn't be doing with evacuees no more, so after that we was sent to a bloke down the other end of the village and he hit us every day, even if we didn't do nothing at all.'

It didn't sound very enticing to Alice, who was as determined as ever to stay at home. One boy had even told her that they ate cats out in the country. She stared up at her mother, her mouth set tight with defiance.

'All right! We've been through that, time and time again.' Carrie's voice was sharp. She still hadn't forgiven Alice for giving them all such worry when she'd run away rather than be evacuated without her beloved cat. And Bill had made it clear that the minute there was any bombing, Alice was going, and no more argument about it. Robertson would just have to take his chance, same as the rest of them that stayed behind. But they all knew it was going to be a tussle to part them.

The back door opened at that moment, and Phyl and her mother came in from next door. May was Carrie's double, and it always gave strangers a surprise to see them together – and an even bigger one, sometimes, to come across them separately, like when a new neighbour, admiring the new baby Phyl in her pram one afternoon, had almost fainted on encountering a still heavily pregnant Carrie the very next day. Today, however, Jo noticed a definite difference in them. The lines of worry that she could see on her mother's face were less deep on her aunt's. Like Phyl, May Jennings was always able to take a lighter view of life.

Carrie's face brightened at once on seeing her twin sister. 'May! And Phyl – you're looking well. Life in London obviously suits you.'

'Well, you know how much I wanted to be a Nippy.' Phyl sat down on a small stool, leaving the remaining chair for her mother. 'I'm not so sure about Jo, though, wanting to go off and work on a farm.'

29

'On a farm? You never said nothing to me about this, Jo.'

'Well, there hasn't been much chance,' Jo said, glowering at Phyl. 'Anyway, it's just an idea – I just said if they call us up I'd rather choose the Land Army, that's all. I don't suppose it'll come to anything.'

'I suppose it's not such a bad idea,' Carrie said. 'At least you'd be safe out in the country. And you might get somewhere near our Alice – if she goes,' she added hastily as Alice sat up from her sprawled position on the floor. 'You know what your dad said,' she told her warningly. 'If there's so much as a sniff of any bombs . . .'

Jo got up and went to make more tea. Before long, it would be time to start cooking the supper ready for the men when they came in, tired, dirty and hungry from work in the docks. Then the two families would spend their evening separately in their own homes and Jo and Phyl would go back to London next morning on the bus.

They loved these short visits home. Lodging with 'Auntie' Holt was almost as homely as you could get, but the warmth of life with your own family was something you couldn't get anywhere else – something special. The brotherly insults and jokes that Freddy and Eric would toss across the supper-table – the game of Ludo or Sorry after tea – the silent quarter of an hour when they all listened to the nine o'clock news on the wireless – all were part of something that Jo was coming to realise was very precious. As she stood in the doorway, waiting for the kettle to boil and watching the little group in the back room – her mother and her aunt, so alike, her cousin Phyl who could have been a copy of either of them, and her sister Alice once again engrossed with her big ginger cat – she felt a glow of love reach out and encompass them all.

I want you to stay safe, she thought silently. All of you. Stay safe for me, until this war's over.

The next morning, there was panic.

30

'It's gone! I must have had it when I came in. I must have put it down somewhere and now it's gone. Someone must have taken it – our Freddy, or Eric. They must have taken it in mistake for theirs.'

'They can't have done,' Carrie said. 'Theirs would be here instead, and they've all gone. Nobody's taken it, Jo.'

'They've hidden it, then. It's just the sort of thing our Fred would do, hide it for a joke. Alice, do you know what he's done with it? Have you seen it?'

Alice shook her head and her plaits flew. 'I never saw it at all. I don't think you had it with you when you came in.'

Jo stared at her. 'I must have had it with me.'

'You didn't. You just had your bag. I remember you putting it down on the piano—' she nodded towards the instrument, with Jo's shoulder-bag still lying on top '—but I never saw your gas mask. Honest, Jo, I don't think you had it.'

Jo stared at her, then at her mother. Her hand went to her mouth.

'Oh, lor. Don't say I've lost it.'

They looked at each other in dismay.

'I don't see that it matters,' Alice said, trying to be helpful. 'I don't suppose there'll be any gas attacks today. Willy Crewe from up the road says those masks won't be any good anyway.'

'That Willy Crewe's got altogether too much to say about everything,' Carrie said smartly. 'And it isn't that, Alice. You know we're all supposed to carry our gas masks everywhere we go. Jo could get into trouble if a policeman stops her and she hasn't got it.'

'Hardly anybody carries them anyway,' Alice said, undeterred. 'Willy Crewe's dad takes his sandwiches to work in his gas-mask box.'

Carrie drew in a deep breath, but Jo interrupted her. 'Never mind that. What am I going to do? That's what I

31

want to know. I think she's right, Mum, I didn't have it with me when I came in, or I'd have remembered where I put it. I must have left it on the bus, that's what.'

'You'll have to go to the lost-property office at the depot. Someone's bound to have handed it in. Nobody's going to pinch a gas mask, after all, and we all know how important they are. It'll be all right, Jo.'

Jo nodded, hoping her mother was right. At least it had her name on it. Lyons insisted that all their staff put their names on their gas masks so that they wouldn't get mixed up at work. It should be easy enough to find if anyone had handed it in, and no doubt the bus conductor himself would have made sure of that.

It was a nuisance, though, having to stay on the bus all the way to the depot, and Jo told Phyl to go back to Elmbury Street without her. 'You don't want to trail all the way there and back with me.'

'Don't be a twerp,' Phyl said cheerfully. 'It's as much my fault as yours. I ought to have noticed you'd left it on the seat. Anyway, we're not due on shift till three, so we've got plenty of time.'

They arrived at the depot and found the lost-property office. There were all kinds of things there that people had left on buses – umbrellas, suitcases, handbags, even good stuff like cameras and binoculars. And on a separate bench, all piled up in a heap, were hundreds of the cardboard boxes that contained gas masks.

'Coo-er!' Phyl said, staring at them. 'Look at that lot. You'll never find yours amongst all those, Jo.'

'Well, I ought to be able to,' Jo said, hoping she was right. 'It's got my name on it.'

'It's just about the first one that has, then,' said the little man who was in charge of the lost property. 'Look at 'em!' He went across and fished about amongst the heap, holding them up so that the girls could see the names scrawled on the cardboard. ' "Fred's Gas Mask". "Mum". "Our Jean".

32

"Dad". And look at this one! "*Mine*"! I suppose there's another one somewhere with "Yours" writ on it. I mean, 'ave you ever 'eard anything so bloomin' stupid?'

Phyl was convulsed with giggles and even Jo couldn't help smiling. 'Haven't you got one with "Jo Mason" written on it?' she asked. 'It should be on top, I only lost it yesterday.'

'It'd be easier if yer name was "Mum",' he said wearily. 'There's plenty of those. And I bin through this 'eap a dozen times already this mornin', stirrin' 'em up like a pan of cockles. Yours is as likely to be down the bottom as on top by now. You can 'ave a look for yourself if you like, ducks, I don't mind.'

The girls went behind the counter and began to sort through the boxes. One or two of them were stained with grease and smelt a bit funny, and Phyl opened one and peered inside, jerking her head back with a squeak of disgust.

'Yuk! There's old sandwiches in here, fish paste by the smell of it, and all gone green. Your Alice's friend was right, half of them probably haven't got gas masks in at all.'

'I don't know what to do,' Jo said despondently, staring at the pile. 'We could look through these for weeks and still not find it. Can we get new ones, Phyl? Will I have to pay for it?'

'Well, why not take one of these anyway? Nobody else is claiming them – by the look of those sandwiches, they've been here for weeks. Look, here's one that looks okay. Take that.'

'It's got "Mum" written on the side,' Jo objected. 'I can't go round with a gas mask with "Mum" on it.'

'Well, cross it out and write "Jo" instead,' Phyl said. 'Look, Jo, whoever "Mum" is she obviously isn't too bothered about her gas mask or she'd have been in for it by now. Anyway, she's not going to spend hours searching through the pile, is she? She'll just take the first one she comes to with "Mum" on it. She won't even notice the difference.'

'I don't know. It feels like stealing somehow.'

'Even if *everyone* whose gas mask is here comes in and collects them, there'll still be one left over for "Mum",' Phyl said impatiently. 'Yours! So she can have that, can't she? Come on, Jo, it's freezing in here, I don't know how that man stands it.'

'I'm not sure. I don't like the idea of using someone else's things.' Jo took the box and looked inside at the ugly black mask. It stared back at her with blank eyes, its snout thrusting aggressively upwards, and she made a face at the rubbery smell. 'You don't know where it's been—'

'I can tell you where it's been. It's been in that box. Look, Jo, she's not been wearing it to the pub. She's probably never had it out, except maybe once to try it on when she first got it. And if you ever have to put it on yourself, you'll have more to worry about than who wore it before you. Come on. Take it. Nobody's going to know or care, and Mr Chamberlain would rather you had a gas mask belonging to "Mum" than didn't have one at all.'

'All right.' Jo slung the box over her shoulder and called out to the man. 'I've got it! Thanks. I tell you what, though,' she said to Phyl as they made their way out and found a bus stop to go back to Elmbury Street. 'Soon as we get home, I'm going to make sure my name *and* my address are on this one. I'm not risking losing it again.'

Like Maggie Wheeler, Shirley Woods lived at home. Mostly, she and her father were alone, for Shirley's brother Donald was in the army and her mother and younger brother Jack in Wales. Donald had got home for Christmas, but Annie Woods and Jack had stayed in Wales and now they were probably snowed up, halfway up the mountain as they were.

'I hope they've got enough food in,' Shirley's father said

34

anxiously. 'Young Owen told me they're snowed up almost till Easter sometimes. I don't know how your mother's going to manage, stuck in a farmhouse all that time.'

'She'll be all right. And I bet Jack's loving it. Country snow's different from London snow, Dad. It's clean and white. He'll be making snowmen and playing snowballs and all sorts.'

Jack was too old for such games really, but although he was nearly twenty years old he was still like a little boy, happiest when he was playing games or helping to look after the animals. Annie had taken him to Wales to stay with Owen Prosser's aunt back in September, worrying that he wouldn't settle in the country, but he had taken to it like a duck to water and had his own jobs to do about the farm now, and did them well.

'Well, I know he's best off where he is,' Alf agreed. 'He wouldn't have understood about bombs and blackouts and all that. It's your mum I worry about. She's never been so far away from shops, and she's always been used to having neighbours. I don't like to think of her being lonely.' He stared into the small, flickering fire and rubbed his hands against each other, twining his fingers together.

It's you that's lonely, Shirley thought, gazing at him. Her mother's letters gave a picture of a tiny but active community up there in the Welsh hills, with everyone visiting each other regularly and helping out whenever needed. The farmhouse was always busy, and there was surely no time to be lonely. But for Alf Woods it was different. Accustomed to having his wife and son at home all the time, he must find the house very quiet and empty, especially when Shirley was on late shift at the Corner House. And Christmas with just her and Donald, who had now gone back to camp, must have seemed like a travesty of the Christmases he had known ever since his marriage.

'Mum's all right,' she said comfortingly. 'And you know you're happier knowing that she and Jack are safe up there.'

'I know. It just seems such a long way away, though. And it seems such a long time since she went.' He sighed heavily. 'And God knows how long till she comes back again.' He lifted his head and looked at her. 'I tell you what it is, Shirl. It's our lives ticking away, that's what it is. Weeks and months – maybe even years – when we can't do the things we wanted to do, can't even live with the people we ought to be living with. Our Donald having to go and fight, your mother and our Jack sent off to live with strangers when they ought to be at home with us. And we bin through it all before. Twice in one lifetime! It's too much.'

'It won't be very long, Dad,' she said. 'It'll be all over by next Christmas and we'll all be together again.'

Alf shook his head. 'They said that in September, when it all started. And they said it in the Great War, and *that* lasted four years. I don't think I can manage to live four years without your mother, Shirl. I just don't think I can manage.'

His head drooped again and Shirley moved to sit beside him, laying her arm across the broad, bowed shoulders. But what else can we do? she thought. If it takes four years – or even five – we're just going to *have* to manage, aren't we? We won't have any choice.

Four years. Could it possibly take that long?

Chapter Three

As if the bitter weather and the anxiety of evacuation and having your men away weren't enough, rationing began. The few ounces of meat and bacon, the scrap of butter and small amount of sugar that was allowed each week didn't seem enough to keep a bird alive. The housewives and mothers who were expected to feed their families were almost at their wits' end.

'Thank goodness my mum had the sense to get a good stock in as soon as she knew it was going to happen,' Irene Bond remarked one day in the canteen. The girls were always ravenous, eating every scrap Lyons provided for their meals. 'It'll be a long time before *we* need to depend on the rations.'

'That's hoarding,' Shirley said, shocked. 'You could get into trouble for that.'

Irene gave her a contemptuous glance. 'Don't be daft. Anyone who's got any sense at all must have been putting a few tins by. I bet your mum did, too. *And* the rest of you.' She looked defiantly round the table.

'A few tins, yes,' Phyl said uncomfortably. 'But not so much that we can live on it for months. Or even weeks.'

'Well, what's the difference? Your mum just put by a few tins, mine put by a few more. It's the same thing.'

'It's not.' Jo spoke up angrily. 'It's not a bit the same. Everyone has a bit of a store cupboard for emergencies. It's people like you, buying up all you can, that's made them have to bring in rationing at all. I bet you've got a room full of tins and stuff, and Shirley's right, that's *hoarding*

37

and you could get into trouble for it, and I hope you do, too!'

'Well,' Irene said, her eyes bright and two spots of angry red burning in her cheeks, 'if we finds a policeman on our doorstep we'll know just who split on us, won't we?'

Jo stood up and gave her a withering glare. 'I'm not a hoarder, but I'm not a tell-tale either. And I don't have to sit at a meal table with someone who thinks more of her own belly than her country, so if you don't mind I'll take my plate over to the other table.'

There was a moment's silence. The others watched Jo's stiff back as she marched across the canteen. Then Phyl picked up her own plate and cutlery.

'I'll go with her. I think the air'll be a bit fresher over there.'

Nobody else said a word. The other girls glanced at each other uncomfortably. Then Etty took up her own plate and crossed the room, while Maggie and Shirley stared at the table.

'Well, I've finished anyway,' Maggie said rather loudly. 'I'll go to the lav. See you in a minute.' She got up and walked out of the canteen.

Irene looked at Shirley.

'They're all a lot of twerps. Pretending to be so patriotic, when really they're just jealous of people who had the sense to see what was coming. It's not really hoarding like you said, it's just being careful, that's all.'

'I don't know what it is,' Shirley said. 'I don't know how much you've got. All I know is you were the one who kept saying there wasn't going to be a war, and now you're the one who's talking about having enough food to last for months. And I'd rather not talk about it any more, if you don't mind. I don't like hearing my friends called twerps.'

'Oh, come on,' Irene said, giving her a smile, 'you know they are. Just common, the lot of 'em – I don't know how

38

they got to be Nippies in the first place. Now you and me, we've both got a bit more class, you know that. We could be real pals.'

Shirley looked at her coldly. 'I don't think so. I've got all the pals I want, thank you very much – real pals.' She stood up. 'You're a fool to yourself, Irene Bond. You could have some real friends, too, if you didn't go out of your way to aggravate people.'

'Me?' Irene said, opening her eyes wide. 'Me, aggravate people? It's you lot that's aggravating, not me. Common, that's what you are. I tell you what, I was really surprised when I found out what kind of girls Lyons took on. I thought I was going to be working with girls who were a bit more refined.'

'Oh, so we're common now? And a minute ago you were trying to butter me up, saying I had class,' Shirley reminded her contemptuously. 'Well, common we may be, but at least we're patriotic and we *don't* hoard food. And we don't much want to be friends with them who do.'

She walked away to join the others, who were now gathering up their things ready to go and start work. It wasn't so much the hoarding itself, she thought, quivering with anger, it was Irene's whole attitude. Always out for number one. Always so sure she was the one who was right. Always looking down on the rest of them.

We won't win the war if there's many like her, she thought.

Jo gave her a grin. 'You didn't manage to put her right, then? I don't reckon anyone ever will. Too full of herself, that one is. Don't take any notice.'

'I'm not,' Shirley said, clenching her fists. 'She just riles me, that's all.'

'Tell you what,' Phyl said as they went back to the dressing-room to get into their uniforms, 'we're going round to Hyde Park after work. They say the ice on the Serpentine is two feet thick – we'll be able to walk right out

39

to the middle. And there's people skating. Why don't you come with us?'

Shirley hesitated. Her father would be wanting a hot dinner when he came home. But she'd have time, if she didn't stop too long. She nodded and smiled. The bitter weather might make things difficult – 'specially with the blackout and everything else – but you might as well get a bit of fun out of it while you could.

The girls went into Hyde Park later in the afternoon and slithered on the ice, holding each other and shrieking. Maggie slipped over and sat on her bottom, yelping with laughter. 'It's a good job I'm well padded,' she declared, struggling to her feet and almost bringing Shirley down with her. 'This ice don't give way much!'

'It's really peculiar, being out here in the middle,' Phyl said. 'I mean, we know it's a sheet of water really. I wonder how deep it is underneath us now?'

'You've been out here before,' Jo reminded her. 'When we hired that rowing-boat last summer.'

'I know, but it seems different to actually walk out here. Like walking on water!' Phyl giggled and then watched admiringly as several skaters whizzed past them. 'Oh, I wish I could skate properly. You know, if we keep on getting winters like this, we could learn.'

'I don't suppose we will. Anyway, ice skates are expensive.' Jo stared out across the park. She had always loved the expanse of grass and trees but it looked so different now. It looked magical. There had been more snow during the night and it lay fresh and sparkling on the roofs of London. The wind had scooped it up and flung it down in billowing drifts, and the bare black branches of the trees were bowed with exuberant eiderdowns or starkly rimed with glittering white. The surface of the lake had been partially cleared for skating, but much of the ice was also covered with snow criss-crossed with footprints. A flock of sparrows descended like scrappy brown leaves to poke about looking for food, their tiny prints scattered among the broad plod of webbed footprints where ducks and geese had waddled.

'One of the customers told me yesterday the Thames is frozen,' she remarked, shoving her hands deep into her coat pockets. 'All the way between Sunbury and Teddington. And that girl Jean who's just started working as a Sally, she told me her auntie lives in Bognor and she says the sea's frozen.'

Phyl stared at her. 'I thought salt water couldn't freeze.'

'Well, it can if it's cold enough. Think of the Arctic, Phyl. That's salt, isn't it? And lots of places are cut off. Nothing can get through, not even trains.'

'Well, at least it saves us from being bombed.' They picked their way back to the edge of the lake and began to trudge across the park. It was almost impossible to see where the paths were, and they had to go carefully to avoid falling into the trenches that had been dug before the war started. 'I bet it'll all get going again as soon as spring comes, though.'

It wasn't a cheerful thought, that with the daffodils and primroses would also come the bombs. The girls walked back to the tube station in silence. All were thinking of the young men they knew who were either already in the forces or would soon be called up – their brothers, cousins, neighbours and, most of all, the boys they hoped to marry. And Maggie's young husband Tommy and his mate Charlie, who was so shy he'd never really had a proper girlfriend. And all the others they knew, and all those they didn't know, who were being sent away from their homes and jobs and families to fight in a strange country against young men just like themselves.

All the Nippies went out of their way to be nice to the servicemen who came into their restaurant. Some had already been in action, at sea where ships were being sunk every day, or in Scandinavia. You only had to look at them

41

to know. As for those who hadn't yet seen action, some were arrogant and swaggering, certain that it needed only their contribution for the war to be virtually over. Others were scared. You could see the fear in their eyes, like cobwebs.

'Poor buggers,' Maggie said. 'They never asked for this and they don't want it. But they got to go all the same.'

'Most of the boys can't wait to go and punch Jerry's nose for him,' Phyl said stoutly. 'What I can't understand is why the Germans are doing it at all. We beat them last time, they must know we'll do it again.'

'They didn't have Hitler last time,' Jo said soberly. 'He's the one what's caused all this – taking over Czechoslovakia and all them other places. And making the Jews out to be all bad. He thinks he can walk all over everyone.'

'Well, he'll soon find out he can't,' Maggie declared. 'It'll be a different story when he tries it on with us. Not even Hitler's going to be allowed to take over the Land of Hope and Glory.'

They parted at the underground station to go their different ways home. Shirley glanced at the station clock. Just nice time for her to get something at the corner shop for her father's supper. She'd get something a bit special tonight. He'd seemed so low lately, he needed a bit of cheering up. Perhaps the fish and chip shop would have a nice bit of haddock. Dad was partial to haddock.

The platform was filling with people, all shivering with cold and stamping their feet. Outside, the cold wasn't so bad, it was at least fresh air – as fresh as London air ever got – and in the Park it had been lovely, kicking their way through the snow and slithering on the frozen lake. Down here it was all icy draughts that sliced their way through the tunnels. What her mother had always called a 'lazy wind' that went straight through you instead of taking the trouble to go round.

The train was a long time coming. More and more people

came and the platform got crowded. Shirley glanced at the clock again, a little more anxiously. At this rate, she wouldn't get home in time to have Dad's tea on the table, or even light the fire. I shouldn't have gone to the Park, she thought. Mum's always had a warm fire and a hot meal waiting for Dad to come in to, and now he's going to come home to a cold house and nothing in the oven, and he'll miss her more than ever.

The man standing next to her stamped his feet and blew into his hands. 'Bloomin' trains,' he said, catching her eye. 'Never know where you are with 'em these days. Be quicker to walk. What a way to run a railway!'

'I'd have caught a bus if I'd known it was going to be as late as this,' Shirley said. 'I suppose there's been a breakdown.'

'Bloody trains are always breaking down,' he said morosely, shoving his hands deep into his pockets. He wore an old greatcoat and had a scarf wound tightly round his neck. 'They want Mussolini in charge, that's what they want. Look what he done for Italy.'

Shirley said nothing. Nobody was quite sure whose side Italy was on. Mussolini seemed to have more in common with Hitler than with Mr Churchill, but that didn't mean he'd join forces with the Germans. He might have his own ideas about ruling the world.

There was a general movement of relief as the rumble of the approaching train was heard at last and everyone pushed forward, anxious to scramble on first. Shirley found herself squashed between a fat lady laden with shopping bags and two men who grabbed the swinging handles and stared fixedly over her head. There was a strong smell of cigarette smoke and general grubbiness. I hate this, Shirley thought, too crammed against the men even to sway with the movement of the train. I'm going on the bus from now on, however long it takes. She thought longingly of the Park and the fresh, cold air and the sparkle of the snow and ice, but she knew that she wouldn't go there again after work and risk being home too late to get Dad's tea ready.

It was dark by the time she turned the corner. She hurried along the street, feeling her way with one hand on the wall, touching the front doors as she passed them and counting. Number one, number three, number five . . . seven, nine, eleven, thirteen . . . Not a chink of light showed in any of the windows; all had their blackout firmly in place. Seventeen, nineteen – twenty-one! She was home at last. With a sigh of relief she fitted her key in the lock and pushed it open.

The house was in darkness.

Shirley frowned. Dad ought to be home by now. He'd be in the back room and there ought to be a line of light showing under the door at the end of the passage. She pulled the front door shut behind her and switched on the light, looking at the row of hooks where everyone hung their coats when they came in.

Dad's wasn't there.

He must be working overtime, she thought, pulling off her own coat. Well, that was all right, then. She'd be able to get his tea on the table after all. And light the fire, so that the back room was cosy and welcoming. Swiftly, she set about doing that first, putting a match to the paper and kindling she'd laid that morning. The room was chilly now but it would soon warm up. Now to get the kettle on – Dad liked a cup of tea when he came in – and start the potatoes.

By the time the meal was ready, the fire burning brightly, the table laid and an appetising smell of mince and vegetables wafting from the little kitchen, Shirley had drunk two cups of tea and put the kettle on again for a fresh pot. She looked at the clock. Where on earth *was* he?

Alf Woods quite often worked overtime, although he usually knew in advance that he'd be doing it. Once or twice

44

before he'd worked late unexpectedly, but he'd always been home by half past seven. Now it was nearly eight o'clock. Shirley sat down, stood up again and went out to the kitchen. Should she wait or start her own supper? She stood irresolute and then went back to the living-room and sat down, staring into the fire.

Dad would be starving. He only ever took sandwiches to work, and he was always hungry for his supper. Now he was nearly two hours late, and he'd had nothing but bread and fish paste all day.

Her stomach rumbled. There was no point in going without herself, she thought ruefully. Just as likely, the minute she got her own meal on the table and picked up her knife and fork, in he'd walk. That was the way things always did happen. As if it would speed his return, she went back to the kitchen and began to dish up a plate of mince, carrots and potatoes.

Her father didn't come walking in the minute she began to eat. In fact, she was halfway through the meal when she heard the ring of the doorbell.

Shirley stopped eating, her fork halfway to her mouth. He must have forgotten his key. With a little grimace of fond exasperation, she laid down her knife and fork and jumped up to open the front door, careful to close the inner door behind her to stop any light from showing.

'Dad! I thought you were never coming home. I've started my tea. What happened, did you have to work overtime? And what about your—' Her voice trailed away as she took in the shape that was silhouetted against the sky and she finished, in a whisper, 'key?'

'I'm sorry, miss,' the policeman said. His helmet blotted out the stars and made him look tall, an immense and suddenly frightening figure. 'You are Miss Woods, aren't you? Miss Shirley Woods?'

'Yes,' Shirley whispered, staring at him. 'What's happened? Is it my dad? Where is he?'

'He's in the hospital. Look, can I come in for a minute or two? You don't want to be standing out here on the doorstep in this cold.'

'In the *hospital*?' Shirley's voice ended on a squeal. 'But – oh, yes, come in – come in and tell me what's happened.' In the lighted hallway she stared at the policeman. 'Is he hurt? Is it bad? He's not – he's not—'

'He's not dead, miss,' the policeman said quickly. 'He's still alive. He's just—'

'*Still alive?* You mean he's hurt – badly hurt?' Shirley reached behind her to grab her coat from the hook. 'Where is he? I've got to go—'

'It's all right, miss. That's what I've come for. I'll take you there. Now, there's no need to look like that. Your dad's going to be all right. He's just had a bit of an accident—'

'What sort of accident? What's *happened* to him?' Shirley would never have believed that she could find herself shouting, actually shouting, at a policeman, that she could shake his arm and try to push him out of the door. 'Why won't you tell me what's happened to him?'

'Because you're not giving me a chance, miss.' The policeman was big and solid, a fatherly sort, a bit like her own father. He looked down at her hand and put his own over it, giving it a little pat, and then steered her gently back into the living-room. 'Now, look, the best thing is for you to have a nice cup of tea before we set off. You've got a long night ahead of you and you've had a nasty shock. And – look at this! You were halfway through your supper! Now, why don't you just sit down and finish it while I puts the kettle on for a cuppa? It'll do you good.'

Shirley stared at the unfinished meal. 'Eat? I can't *eat*! I just want to go and see my dad. You still haven't told me what's happened to him. How did he get hurt? How bad is he?'

The policeman put his hand on her shoulder and she

found herself sitting down. He gave her another little pat and went out into the kitchen. Shirley could hear him filling the kettle and moving things about. Without thinking, she picked up her fork and poked it about in the congealing mince. Then she dropped it again and leant her head on one hand. What was he *doing*, for heaven's sake? Why couldn't he just tell her what had happened and then take her to the hospital? He hadn't even told her which hospital her father was in!

She was almost on her feet again when the policeman came back with two steaming cups of tea. He set one in front of her and sat opposite her at the table, stirring his own cup thoughtfully with a dessert spoon.

'I couldn't find no teaspoons,' he said apologetically as he caught her staring at him.

'For goodness' sake! You can stir your tea with a garden spade for all I care!' Shirley exclaimed. 'Just tell me what's happened to my dad.'

'It's not so very bad. He got knocked down by a car—'

'This blackout!' Shirley exclaimed. 'Nobody can see their way about any more. It's *stupid*.'

'It's for a good purpose, miss. But I know it doesn't make life any easier.' The poilceman sighed. 'We get more people killed in traffic accidents now than are being killed in action . . . Not that your dad's one of 'em, miss. He's going to be all right.'

'But where *is* he? What happened to him? How badly hurt *is* he?'

'The doctors'll tell you more about that, miss. I've just been sent to fetch you along. Far as I know, it's just a broken arm and a bit of a knock on the napper. They might want to keep 'im in for a bit, but he'll be home soon, right as ninepence. Now, you finish up your tea and get your coat on and we'll make a start.'

Shirley gulped down half the tea and stood up. 'I'm ready now.'

'You oughter finish your food,' he said disapprovingly, but she shook her head impatiently.

'It's gone cold anyway. I want to go now.'

He sighed but said no more and they went out together into the darkness. To Shirley's surprise, there was a car waiting at the corner and she got in and found herself being driven through the dark streets to the local hospital. I hope we don't have another accident on the way, she thought nervously, wondering how the driver could see his way with only two narrow slivers of light to guide him. It's no wonder people get knocked over. And all the ice and snow made it all the more hazardous.

Oh, Dad, she thought, Dad, what's happened to you?

As the policeman had said, he had broken his arm and been knocked on the head. The arm wasn't too serious, the doctor told her, but the bang on the head needed watching and they wanted to keep him in till they were sure he was all right. He'd been unconscious for at least a quarter of an hour and that meant he probably had concussion and there might even be a fracture. They were going to take some X-rays.

'Oh, *Dad*,' Shirley whispered, staring at the white face on the hospital pillow. An arm, plastered and bandaged, lay stiffly on top of the covers. 'Dad, it's me, Shirley. Can you hear me?'

Alf lay very still. He looked very small and flat under the white sheets. Shirley stared at him and then gave the nurse beside her an agonised look. 'He – he can't hear me!'

'He's had a nasty knock,' the nurse said quietly. She was a young girl, not much older than Shirley. 'He's been awake, but he's just sort of drifting. Try again.'

Shirley's eyes filled with tears. She knelt beside the bed and took the good hand, holding it lightly between her cold fingers. 'Dad,' she said into his ear, 'Dad, it's Shirley. Can you hear me? Oh, *Dad*, what have you been and gone and done?'

The hand she was holding moved slightly and the fingers curled around hers and gave a faint squeeze. She took in a gasp of relief and glanced up at the nurse. The girl nodded and Shirley looked back to see her father's eyelids flickering and then stay half-open. She smiled, tears streaming down her face, and squeezed his hand in return.

'Dad, you're going to be all right. You had a bit of a barney with a car, remember? You shouldn't argue with people bigger than you! You're in hospital and you're going to stay here till they think you're safe to be let out again, and I'll come and see you every day, and – oh, *Dad* . . .' Her sobs overcame her and she struggled to speak again. 'You ought to take more care,' she scolded him in a shaking voice. 'You just ought to take more *care*.'

A faint grin crossed her father's face. His lips moved but no words came out and they twisted again in an expression of wryness. His fingers tightened again and he managed a thread of a whisper.

'Nothing but a blooming nuisance.'

'Yes,' Shirley told him severely, 'that's just what you are. Nothing but a blooming nuisance. So just get yourself better and come home, see?'

The nurse touched her shoulder. 'Better leave him to sleep now. He'll be all the better for seeing you.'

'D'you think so?' Reluctantly, Shirley stood up and looked down at the still figure. 'He really will be all right?'

'Oh, yes. He's in shock now, of course, but we'll take good care of him and he'll wake up in the morning with nothing worse than a thumping headache. And a broken arm, of course – that won't heal overnight!' The girl grinned. 'People like your dad are tough, they don't give way easy.'

'Pity he didn't give way when that car come along and hit him,' Shirley said tartly. She was quivering with shock herself, and feeling a bit sick. Suddenly, the room began to sway around her and she reached out and grabbed the nurse's arm. 'I'm sorry – I feel a bit queer . . .'

'Sit down.' The nurse pushed her into the wooden chair standing beside the bed. 'Put your head between your knees. That's right. Now, just take a few deep breaths and you'll be right as rain.'

Shirley did as she was told and the sick feeling receded. She looked up and gave the nurse a wry grin that was more like her father's than she knew. 'Sorry about that.'

'It's all right. It's natural.' The girl gave a look round the busy ward. 'I'm sorry – I'll have to go. Can you get home all right?'

'Oh – yes.' The policeman had gone as soon as he'd delivered Shirley to the ward. She missed his big, comforting presence and the thought of going home to an empty house and her father's supper, unwanted now, made her feel cold and empty. She wanted her mother, or Owen – anyone to whom she could turn. But her mother was far away in Wales and Owen was at home with his own family. It was too late to go there now.

Finding her way out of the big hospital with its stone corridors and blank, impersonal walls and setting off yet again through the blacked-out streets, Shirley felt very alone.

'We've got to save all the waste paper we can,' Mrs Holt said. She already had a pile of newspapers, kept for lighting the fire, but she was trying to use a page less each day. 'They need it to pulp and make more paper, to save having to get it from abroad. And it's not just paper, it's everything – scrap iron, bedsteads, bikes, old tools – anything at all. I'll ask you two girls to help me get up in the attic after dinner and bring down all the stuff that's been mouldering away there for the past ten years, if you don't mind. And we don't just chuck everything in the dustbin any more, it's all got to be kept separate. Kitchen waste is going to pigs, though where they're going to find pigs in the middle of London I don't know!'

'Perhaps they're going to send it over and drop it on Germany,' Jo said. Nick had told her that the RAF had been dropping leaflets with anti-war propaganda on German cities. If they could do that, she thought, what was stopping the Germans from coming over here and dropping bombs? But apparently they were too busy getting ready to invade Holland and Belgium. More little countries going under the iron heel.

'The iron railings round people's gardens are all going,' Auntie Holt continued. 'They're going to make aeroplanes and ships and tanks out of them. Waste not, want not, that's the word now.'

'It's going to be real, isn't it?' Phyl said. 'This "phoney war" – once the weather gets better, it's going to be really happening.'

She'd had a letter from Mike that morning. He had hinted that there might be a spot of leave coming soon. Phyl hugged the letter to her and dreamed of seeing him again. They'd had such a short time together – split up for so many months over a silly misunderstanding and then only coming together again at the last minute, before he went off across the Channel. They had a lot of catching up to do.

Maggie had heard the same news and was even more excited. 'My Tom's coming home!' she told her mother when she read the letter that evening. 'He says he thinks they're getting leave. He can't say when, but he thinks it'll be soon.'

'About time, too!' Ivy Pratt said. 'You'd have thought they'd have let them home for Christmas, wouldn't you, since there's bin nothing much going on? Well, you'll be pleased to see him when he does come.'

More than pleased, Maggie agreed. They'd only had an hour of married life in the whole five months they'd been married. Mind you, she remembered with a secret giggle,

51

we did have quite a bit before . . . But behind the bushes in Hyde Park wasn't quite the same as in a nice double bed. And they'd never had a whole night, really sleeping together. She wondered how long his leave would be. A week? A fortnight? Seven or even fourteen whole days and nights before he had to go back again? I'll never be able to let him go, she thought. They'll have to take me, too, packed away in his kitbag.

Nobody knew when the men would arrive. They weren't allowed to say – they'd just turn up on the doorstep, more than likely when you were in your oldest frock and had got your curlers in. For Maggie, it was when she was kneeling in front of the hearth cleaning out the fireplace, and she hurried to the door covered in soot and coal dust, thinking it was probably the baker.

'Well!' exclaimed the tall, grinning soldier standing on the step, a canvas haversack on his back and his kitbag dumped down beside him. 'If it ain't Betty Grable in person!'

'*Tommy!*' Maggie's shriek was like a train whistle. She flung her arms around him. 'Oh, my God! I never thought – I was just going to ask you for a cottage loaf and a dozen penny buns! Oh, and here I am all covered in dirt and looking like a dog's dinner! Oh, you ought to have let me know you were coming!'

'I couldn't, not unless you wanted me to hang about while the letter was delivered. I just wanted to get here as fast as I could.' He held her tightly and kissed her hard. 'Oh, Maggie, if you only knew how much I've been looking forward to this.'

'I have, too. I've missed you so much.' She pressed her face against his shoulder, tears soaking into the khaki. 'I'm making you all wet. And dirty. Honestly, your uniform's going to be all mucky.'

'Better take it off, then. But not here on the step. Aren't you going to ask me in?' He followed her into the house.

52

Gerald's bike was in the passage and he struggled to get the bulky kitbag past it, and then hit his knee against Queenie's tricycle. 'Just the same as ever, I see.'

'Well, there's a lot of us. Our Evie's here most of the time with Mum, and Queenie keeps half her things round here. They're out shopping now – or queueing, I should say – so it's just me and Gran.' She led him into the back room where her grandmother was sitting in the corner by the range, her teeth in their usual spot on a shelf beside her. They seemed to grin at Tommy as he came in. 'Look, Gran, look who's here.'

Old Granny Pratt looked up. Her eyes were faded but her mind and tongue were as sharp as ever and she knew Tommy straight away. Her old lips widened in the smile she always seemed to have for him, even when she was sparing with smiles for her own family, and she nodded.

'So they've sent you 'ome, 'ave they? Didn't 'ave no more use for you, then? Or did Hitler take one look and give in?'

'I dare say he would have if he'd come close enough,' Tommy said cheerfully. 'But he never came near us. Tell you what, though, I'll be a big help digging for victory – that's what we've been doing, digging trenches all along the Maginot Line to stop Hitler getting through. There's a song about it – George Formby came out himself to sing it to us.'

'George Formby? You've seen George Formby?' Maggie gazed at him.

'Seen him, heard him and shook his hand. And we've had Gracie Fields over, and Billy Cotton and his band.' Tommy shrugged off his haversack. 'Tell you what, Mags, I'm dying for a cup of tea. I've been on the train half the night. What's the matter with them? They're so slow it would've been quicker to hoof it.'

'Everyone's complaining about how slow the trains are.' Maggie ran out to the scullery to fill the kettle. She came back and set it on the range. 'It's the same with everything – buses, trams, trolley-buses. Everything takes three times as

53

long as it used to. If you ask why, they just say, "Don't you know there's a war on?" I think they just use it as an excuse half the time.' She sat down suddenly, trembling. Tommy's sudden arrival had knocked her right off balance. If Gran hadn't been here, she thought, he'd have swept me straight upstairs to bed, but now we've got to sit and drink tea and behave like civilised human beings. And I don't *want* to be civilised!

She got up to take cups and saucers from the cupboard by the range, and found a bit of Christmas cake in the tin, saved for this very occasion. There was just enough milk to go round. The milkman would be along later and she hastily scribbled a note to ask for two more pints, and scurried along the passage to stick it in one of the empty bottles standing on the step. When she came back the kettle was boiling and she made the tea and took it in on the old tin tray.

'Christmas cake!' Tommy said. 'At nine o'clock in the morning, too. Blimey, now, that's what I call a welcome home.'

'You wouldn't believe what a job we've had stopping our twins from eating it,' Maggie said, sitting down close beside him. 'Oh, Tom, it *is* good to have you back.'

'It's good to *be* back, I can tell you. I mean to say, I never even went camping when I was a nipper – we didn't have no Boy Scouts round our way – and sleeping under canvas in the weather we've had's no joke. You've had a bit of snow here, too, I see.'

'It's been awful,' Maggie said. 'But not as bad as you've had. At least we've had houses to stay dry and warm in.'

'Warm? I 'aven't noticed it being warm,' Gran said. 'The few bits of coal our Ivy puts on the fire wouldn't warm a gnat's backside. And now it's rationed it's going to be worse. If your dad hadn't bin able to bring home a few bits of wood from the market, we'd have froze to death.'

54

'Well, it's not as bad as living in a tent,' Maggie told her sharply. 'And you can stop looking at that cake, Gran, you know we've been keeping it for Tom. You had your share at Christmas.'

'I never. I only had one tiny little bit, that's all, and near broke me teeth on the icing, too. No, you 'ave it and enjoy it,' she said to Tommy as he held out his plate, grinning. 'I knows me patriotic duty. See that knitting? That's socks, that is, for our boys at sea. Twelve pairs I made so far, and there's many a mother's son thanking me for it out there in the North Atlantic, I'll be bound. I may be old and useless but I can still turn a good heel.'

'You're not useless, Gran,' Tommy said, finishing his cake. 'Not while you can turn a fancy heel and knit socks for sailors. Here, isn't there a song about that from the first war?'

'You mean "Sister Susie's Sewing Shirts for Soldiers",' Gran said, and to their astonishment she began to sing, her voice cracking on the higher notes and her toothless gums lisping over the s's until Maggie and Tommy were convulsed with laughter.

'Sister Susie's sewing shirts for soldiers.
Such skill at sewing shirts our shy young sister Susie shows.
Some soldiers send epistles, say they'd sooner sleep in thistles
Than the saucy, soft short shirts for soldiers sister Susie sews!'

'Oh, Gran,' Maggie cried, wiping her eyes, 'you're good enough to go out and entertain the troops yourself! How many other songs d'you know?'

'Hundreds,' the old woman said. 'But I ain't going to sing them now. That chap of yours is 'alf asleep where he's sitting. He needs to get up them stairs to bed, and if you got any sense you'll go with him while the 'ouse is quiet. I'm

55

going to 'ave a bit of shut-eye meself – all this excitement's fair wore me out.'

She leant her head against the back of her chair and closed her eyes. Maggie and Tommy looked at each other.

'She's right,' Maggie whispered. 'We won't have another chance once Mum and our Evie come back from the shops. But they'll be gone for a good hour yet. What d'you say, Tom? You been on the train all night, you must be tired out.'

'I am,' he said, pulling her against him. 'But not too tired to have a few words with my missus first. Come on, Maggie. We've only tried out that bed of yours once. Let's see if it's as good as I remember.'

They crept over to the door leading to the staircase and closed it quietly behind them. At the sound of their footsteps, going as softly as possible up the creaking stairs, Ada Pratt opened one eye and grinned to herself.

'That's right,' she murmured, sitting up and reaching for her knitting. 'You make the most of it while you has the chance.' She peered at the sock that hung from her needles and began the tricky business of turning the heel. 'Funny thing about youngsters, they all thinks us old ones have either never done it or forgotten all about it. But I 'aven't forgot.' A reminiscent smile crinkled her thin, dried lips. 'No, I 'aven't forgot nothing.'

It was like stepping back in time for Phyl when she came on duty later that day and walked over to her station to see the young soldier sitting there. It was like going back to that first day, when Tommy and Mike and Charlie had come into the Corner House and sat at Maggie's table, giving her lip. Only it couldn't be, of course. It couldn't be at all the same, because the soldier was at her table, not Maggie's, and the young men that day hadn't been in uniform, they'd been smartly dressed as the shopwalkers they'd been from the gents' outfitters along the road. And she hadn't felt this sudden dizziness, this sensation as though the world were falling away from beneath her . . .

'Hello, Phyl,' he said, grinning, and she heard the shake in his voice as if this moment meant as much to him as it did to her. 'Oh, Phyl – I'm back, I'm back.'

'*Mike*,' she whispered. 'Mike – oh, *Mike* . . .'

He jumped up and threw his arms around her. Phyl gasped and closed her eyes for his kiss, then squealed and pulled herself away.

'Mike! You mustn't – not here! You'll get me the sack.' She glanced swiftly around the restaurant and then looked up at him, scarcely able to believe that he was really here. 'Why ever did you do this? I thought you'd come round to Mrs Holt's. Fancy giving me a shock like that!'

'A nice shock, though.' He grinned. 'Come on, Phyl, there's a war on. Nobody'll mind you kissing your fiancé when you haven't seen him for five months.'

'They won't know that, will they?' Phyl pointed out, twisting away from him. 'They'll just think I'm a Nippy getting off with a soldier. Honestly, you'll get me into trouble. Look, are you going to have something to eat? I've got work to do, you know.'

Her heart was beating fast despite her severe words, and she could feel the colour in her cheeks. She gazed at him, wanting to feast on the mere fact that she could see him, reach out and touch him . . . Sternly, she resisted the temptation. 'Why couldn't you get here earlier?' she asked. 'Maggie says Tommy got back early this morning.'

'I had to go and see my mum first, didn't I? I wanted to come straight round to you, but it wouldn't have been right.'

Phyl caught sight of the floor supervisor looking her way. 'Order something, for goodness' sake,' she whispered. 'Honestly, Mike, I can't stand here talking, I've got customers waiting.'

57

'All right.' He glanced at the menu and dropped it again. 'Are you still doing Adam and Eve on a Raft?'

'Two poached eggs on toast,' Phyl said, scribbling. The Nippies hadn't been allowed to write down orders to start with, but it had proved impossible to remember all the varying requirements and they were now allowed to use very small, discreet pads. 'Only it's one now. Just Adam, all by himself. And a pot of tea?'

'A bottle of champagne'd be more appropriate. Phyl, when d'you get off duty? I can't wait to see you properly.'

'Not for hours yet.' The time seemed to stretch ahead for ever. 'You'd better go home to your mum for a bit. Meet me outside at eleven, you can walk me home.'

Mike groaned. 'Is that all a poor soldier gets after five months, digging trenches? All right, Phyl, but I've only got a week, we'll have to make up for lost time somehow. Can't you get a few days off?'

'I don't know. I'll try.' She scurried back to the kitchen with his order, her mind in a whirl. Mike was home, he was really home – but for such a cruelly short time. A week. Not time to get married, she thought ruefully, not time to do anything but just see as much of each other as they could, to make the most of every minute.

'A few days off?' Mr Carter repeated when she went to him with her request. 'Well, I don't know, Phyllis. Margaret's already asked, you see, and she's a married woman . . . We're busy enough as it is, with all these servicemen coming in. And there's Shirley, too, having to take time off to look after her father. I don't know that we can manage without you.'

'Some of the others say they'll take over some of my tables with their own,' Phyl said. 'Jo and Etty will take two each, and Brenda Walters said she'd help as well. I'm sure they'd be able to manage.'

'You'll talk yourself out of a job if you're not careful, young lady,' Mr Carter said with a smile. 'Well, all right, if they're happy to help out, you can have three days. Will that do?'

'Three days!' With her regular day off, that would take her up to the weekend, Phyl thought joyfully. Mike had to go back next Monday, and they could spend Saturday and Sunday evenings together. 'Oh, Mr Carter, thank you!'

'Don't do it too often, mind,' he warned her, and Phyl shook her head vigorously.

'I don't suppose we'll get the chance to do it very often,' she said ruefully. 'If the fighting really starts soon, they might not be back for ages.'

Or ever at all, Mr Carter thought, watching her bright face. He sighed. He remembered the 1914–18 war – the Great War, which was now beginning to be called the 'First World War'. He had fought in that himself and knew how lucky he was to have returned. So many of his friends and comrades had been left there, dead in the fields of Flanders.

'You go off and have a good time,' he said to Phyl. 'Make the most of it. Give yourself and your young chap some good memories to get you through.'

Phyl looked at him and saw the understanding in his eyes. She felt the sting of sudden tears in her own. 'We will,' she said. 'We will. And thanks, Mr Carter, thanks ever so much.'

When Mike met her outside at eleven o'clock that night, she flung herself into his arms. It didn't matter who saw them now. She wasn't a Nippy any more, she was just a girl meeting her sweetheart after work.

'Oh, Mike!' she exclaimed. 'Oh, Mike, I thought the time would never go!'

'Your shifts are too long,' he told her, hugging her tightly and covering her face with kisses. 'Eight hours too long! Phyl, I'm not going to want to let you go. It's such a waste of time.'

Phyl laughed. 'I can't stop out all night. It's too flipping cold for one thing. Mike, Mr Carter's let me have three days

59

off. Three whole days! And Friday's my day off anyway, so that's four. We can have all that time together. The others are going to cover for me – Jo, and Etty and one of the others. Maggie's having time off, too. Irene Bond isn't too pleased, I can tell you – she's been walking about with a nasty smell under her nose all day long, and you don't need me to tell you *she* didn't offer to help. But who cares about Irene Bond?'

'Not me, I can tell you.' Mike didn't care all that much about the others either. He was too pleased to be home and have Phyl to himself for a while. And four days was more than he'd dared hope for. 'What shall we do, Phyl? What would you like to do?'

'I dunno. There's not all that much we can do, in the middle of winter.' Phyl shivered and pulled her coat more tightly around her. She hugged Mike's arm against her side as they began to walk down the street. 'Go for walks, I suppose. Auntie Holt might let us stop indoors some of the time, but I don't think she'll be able to light a fire. Coal's rationed now, and you can only get it when they've got some down at the depot, and even then you can't always get it delivered.'

'I know. My mum told me she had to use our Joanie's old pram to collect some last week. We'd better spend some time at our place, Phyl. She'd like to see you and she won't like it much if I'm never home. Maybe I could ask if you could sleep there for a couple of nights.'

'Have you got room?' Phyl knew that Mike's home was small and crowded. He had two sisters, and as there were only two bedrooms Mike slept downstairs in the front room on a Put-U-Up.

'Well, I could doss down in the back room. I'll ask Mum. It'll save me trailing all the way over to your place every day, and mean I can spend more time at home anyway.'

They walked briskly through the streets – it was too cold to linger. There were still piles of dirty snow in the gutters and the pavements were still icy, but at least there was a moon to show them the way. On moonless nights it was almost impossible to find your way. She told him about Shirley's father.

'He had bad concussion but he's coming out of hospital tomorrow. There's been ever so many people run over since the blackout started. Someone said Hitler was going to win the war through road accidents alone! It was awful before they let us use torches with tissue paper over them.' Mike didn't answer, and she felt a stab of guilt. 'It can't have been as awful as it's been for you, though,' she added swiftly. 'It must have been horrible over there in France.'

'We were in Belgium. On the border, anyway. It wasn't much fun, but at least we weren't fighting. Wished we could have been really – we were just navvies, digging in freezing mud. At least if we could have got a sight of Jerry we'd have felt we were doing something.'

'They must have thought it was worth doing.' Phyl pressed his arm. 'It's so lovely to have you back, Mike.'

He stopped and pulled her into his arms. 'Phyl, I've missed you so much. It didn't seem real over there, and yet sometimes it seemed as if it was the only thing that was real. I used to lay awake thinking about you and wondering if you were just a dream. Maybe everything was a dream except for the mud and the trench and having to blanco your bloody belt . . . Sometimes I thought I was just going mad, Phyl.'

'Oh, Mike. Mike.' They clung together in the shadow of a building. 'Mike, I love you.'

'I love you, too, Phyl.' He bent to kiss her. 'I wish to God we could get married.'

'So do I. But there isn't time. It takes three weeks—'

'You can get special licences. They don't take so long. I could find out – what d'you say?' He tightened his arms about her. 'Just think – we could have a few days together, married, and then when I go away again we'll know we really and truly belong to each other—'

'We can't, Mike. I'd have to talk Dad into it for a start, and he'd never agree. And even if he did, it's bound to take at least a week. There just isn't time.'

Mike's body sagged a little. 'I suppose not. Oh, Phyl . . . It's having to go away, without ever – I mean, I want to *show* you how much I love you. I want to make love to you, properly, like Tom can make love to Maggie. I want to go away feeling that we've been properly together. Oh, *Phyl*.'

'I want it, too,' she whispered. 'But I just don't see how . . . I don't want to hide in the bushes like some girls do.' Like Maggie probably did, she thought, though no one had ever been quite sure about Maggie and Tom.

'Nor do I. Anyway, it's too flipping cold!' They walked on, their arms around each other's waists. 'Oh, well, I dare say I'll get another leave before too long. And the minute I do I'll let you know and you can see about getting a licence. After all, you'll be twenty-one in May and you won't have to get your dad's say-so.'

'Yes,' Phyl said with relief. 'Yes, it'll be all right then – though I think he'd still like you to ask him, mind. A summer wedding, Mike – that'd be nice. And I can start getting things together – not that there's much to get just now, with everything so short. But it'd be nice to think I'd got a bottom drawer.'

'That's settled, then. A summer wedding, the first minute I can get home again.' He squeezed her waist. 'And till then we'll just have to wait.'

62

Chapter Four

Alf Woods stayed in hospital for four days and then came home, still shaky and a bit weak. He leant on Shirley's arm as she opened the front door, and once inside the living-room sank into his chair with a sigh of relief. She looked at him anxiously.

'You all right, Dad?'

'I been better.' He gave her a wavering smile. 'I never even knew it was there, Shirl. It come out of nowhere and just knocked me for six. First I knew, I was in hospital with all these people peering down at me – gave me a proper scare, I can tell you. I thought I was in heaven and they was angels, all dressed up in white.'

'It's going to be a long while before you go to heaven, Dad. I'm not sure they'll have you anyway!' Shirley felt the tears coming again and turned away quickly. 'I'll make a cup of tea. You'll feel better once you've had a hot drink.'

'I just wish your mother could've come home,' he said, looking into the fire Shirley had lit before going to fetch him. 'It don't seem right, being here without my Annie.'

'It's the weather, Dad. They're more or less stuck on that mountain, and the trains are never on time. She couldn't have managed the journey with Jack and she couldn't leave him behind.' She went out into the kitchen and lit the gas under the kettle. She missed her mother, too. Looking after Dad when they were both fit and well was one thing, taking care of him when he was ill was a different matter. His broken arm made everything so difficult – he needed help with dressing and undressing, and with eating his food, and she didn't know what he was going to do about the lavatory. And his head wasn't right either. The doctors had said he'd have headaches for a while, but to Shirley's mind there was more wrong than that. His eyes didn't seem properly focused and he didn't always follow the conversation properly. Sometimes he repeated things over and over again, and sometimes he just didn't seem to be with you at all.

She made the tea and took it into the room. Her father was leaning back in his chair, his eyes half-closed and his jaw sagging. Her heart lurched. For a moment, she thought he was dead – and then he emitted a loud snore and she gave a sigh of relief and put the cups down on the table quickly, before she dropped them. A moment later her father was staring at her, a bemused expression on his face.

'Shirley? Shirl? What was that – what happened?' He wrinkled his nose. 'There's a funny smell. What you got cooking?'

'Nothing. I haven't started the supper yet.' She stared at him. 'I can't smell anything. Are you all right, Dad? You look a bit queer.'

'Queer? What d'you mean, queer?' His eyes were blurred, as if he couldn't quite get her in focus. Then they sharpened and he shook his head a little and frowned. Shirley watched anxiously. She made a move to hand him his cup of tea.

'Thanks, girl,' he said in a more normal tone, and then added fretfully, 'I wish your mother was here. It don't seem right, my Annie not being here.' He looked up at Shirley, his eyes filled with tears of weakness. 'It just come out of nowhere. I never even heard it . . . First I knew, I was in hospital, staring at all these people peering down at me. I thought I was in heaven and they was angels, all dressed in white . . .'

'I know, Dad,' Shirley said quietly, her heart sinking. 'I know . . .'

*

Muriel Chalk kept her word and came into the Corner House for lunch one day. It was her afternoon off, she explained to Etty as she sat down at her table, and she'd thought of going to the pictures.

'Why don't you come with me? You're off at two, aren't you?' She lit a cigarette.

'Well, yes.' Etty was working the early shift that week, and Jim was working late, so her evenings were rather empty. 'But . . . I can't really afford—'

'Don't be silly. This is my treat. I'll enjoy having company.' Miss Chalk's eye roved casually about the restaurant. 'Perhaps one of your friends would like to come, too.'

'I don't know. Maggie and Phyl have both got a few days off – Maggie's husband and Phyl's chap are on leave. Jo or Shirley might, I suppose, but Shirley's dad's poorly, he got knocked over by a car one night.'

But Jo shook her head. She'd promised to help Mrs Holt go through her attic looking for more waste. They wanted rags now as well as paper and old iron, and Auntie Holt had said there was a whole boxful of old clothes up in the loft. Shirley, too, declined the invitation. Her dad still needed a lot of help and, even though their next-door neighbour popped in and out during the day, she didn't like leaving him any more than she had to.

'What about the other girl?' Muriel asked when Etty returned with her order of egg and chips with a pot of tea. 'The smart one with the dark hair. Irene, did you say she was called?'

Etty looked uncomfortable. 'Well, Irene and me's not really friends. She's not really friends with any of us. She's different, you see – her dad's in the civil service. And she doesn't like me because – well, because I'm part Jewish.'

'I see.' Muriel Chalk looked thoughtful. She blew out a cloud of smoke and then stubbed out her cigarette and gave Etty a smile. 'Well, it'll just be the two of us, then. I thought you might like to have one of your own friends along, that's all.'

Since New Year's Eve, Miss Chalk had gone out of her way to be friendly towards Etty. She had invited her upstairs for a cup of cocoa two or three times, and although she didn't sit with her at meals she always gave her a special smile. The other girls had noticed it and her room-mate Pat had warned her to be careful. 'It doesn't work, them getting friendly with us,' she said, meaning the older business-women and the ordinary working girls. 'You don't want to get hurt.'

Etty had already made up her mind to take care – she'd suffered enough when Irene Bond had taken up with her when they'd first been Nippies together, and then dropped her once she'd found out all she'd wanted to know. But Muriel Chalk didn't seem to be like that. She didn't ask a lot of questions, just behaved in a friendly manner, and it seemed quite natural for Etty to confide in her.

They went to see *The Wizard of Oz*, with Judy Garland as Dorothy, and came out humming 'Somewhere, Over the Rainbow . . .' Etty had already seen it but enjoyed it just as much the second time, laughing at the cowardly Lion and cheering for him when he proved he really could be brave, and weeping for the poor Tin Man, who longed to have a heart.

'Like going to the pictures, do you?' Miss Chalk asked as they came out.

'Oh, yes,' Etty sighed. 'It really takes you out of yourself. Makes you forget all about what's happening outside.' It was dark as they emerged and the streets were cold and unwelcoming. 'And I love the Technicolor films, they're so cheery.'

'We'll go to see *Gone With The Wind* when it comes,' Muriel said. 'They say that's really good. Three and a half hours long! Of course, Vivien Leigh's a wonderful actress.'

66

'Clark Gable's in that, isn't he? I think he's gorgeous.'

Miss Chalk made no comment. They came within sight of the Coventry Street Corner House and she stopped. 'Let's have something to eat before we go back to the hostel. We'll be late for supper there anyway. And it'll be interesting to see the new restaurant.'

'Oh . . .' Once again, Etty wanted to explain that she couldn't afford it – even a Corner House meal – but her companion took her by the arm and ushered her through the door. They paused, looking at the signs to the Brasserie, down in the basement, and went up to the Old Vienna which had opened only a few days ago.

'Now, don't worry about the cost. I told you, it's my treat. Table for two, please,' she said to the seater who came forward, smiling at them. 'Not too near the band.'

The band was playing soft waltzes. Etty sat down, thinking how strange it was to be a customer instead of a Nippy, dashing backwards and forwards with her silver tray. She gazed around at the new décor. It seemed very flamboyant for wartime and it seemed queer, too, to have called their new restaurant after an Austrian city.

'I quite often come here,' Muriel said, gazing around. 'It's quite smart. I must admit, a gel always knows she's going to be well looked after in a Corner House. And I don't mind coming in by myself. I wouldn't go into a public house by myself.'

The Nippy came and took their order. Etty knew her slightly from the Lyons Club at Sudbury and the girl nodded in a friendly manner. But there wasn't time to chat – the restaurant was full of people, many of them service personnel.

'So your friends have got their sweethearts home on leave,' Muriel said. 'Army boys, are they?'

'Yes. Tommy and Mike are both in the same unit, and so's their friend Charlie. They've been over in France somewhere. I think they're going back next week.'

'Shame,' Muriel said. 'I dare say your friends will soon find other company, though.'

'Oh, no! Maggie and Tom are married, and Phyl and Mike are almost engaged. They wouldn't dream of going out with anyone else.'

'They're going to have a lonely time, then.' Muriel offered Etty a cigarette. 'Oh, no, you don't, do you?' She took out a small, silver lighter. 'Although I dare say the boys will get leave now and then.'

'I hope so. Maggie was ever so upset when Tom had to go away on the day of their wedding.'

'I'm sure she was.' Their order arrived. Meals were smaller than they used to be, and the range of cakes and pastries on the trolleys that were being pushed around by the Trippies wasn't as wide. But the atmosphere in the restaurant was just the same, with the smart décor, the soft murmur of voices and the background music. It made you feel you were somewhere special, yet almost anyone could afford to eat there.

'Bit of a busman's holiday for you, this,' Muriel said, watching Etty. 'Perhaps you'd rather have gone somewhere else.'

'Oh, no! It's lovely. After all, I didn't expect to be going anywhere at all.' Etty smiled at her companion. 'And it's ever so good of you to treat me.'

'Nonsense. It's nice for me to have a pretty young gel to take about. We must do it again.'

Etty smiled, though she didn't think it was very likely. Miss Chalk couldn't really be interested in going about with a young girl, and once Jim's and her shifts coincided again her evenings would be taken up with him. For some reason, she still hadn't mentioned him to Miss Chalk, who seemed to have assumed Etty had no boyfriend. Their conversation was usually confined to matters of interest to the older woman, and Etty's own life didn't appear to come into that category.

They ate their meal and then caught the trolley-bus back to the hostel. The lights inside were very dim, even though there were blinds on the windows, and Etty and Muriel sat close together. Muriel shivered and pressed against her.

'Ugh. It's freezing. Lucky we've got each other to keep ourselves warm.'

Etty smiled diffidently. She wasn't used to having another person touching her. Ever since she had gone into the orphanage as a small child, she'd only ever been touched either as a punishment – a smack from one of the nurses, or a pinch from another spiteful child – or in order to have some necessary ministration carried out – her hair examined for nits or a plaster stuck on a cut finger. Even when she'd been persuaded to go to the pictures with Charlie and had sat close to him in the cinema, he hadn't touched her. Either he'd been as shy as she was, or he just hadn't found her attractive, she was never sure which.

Of course, Muriel was only sitting close because it was so cold on the trolley-bus. But it felt odd all the same. Almost like the boy and girl who had got on before them and were now cuddling on the front seat.

Muriel was watching them, too. 'Look at those two,' she said disapprovingly. 'Behaving like that in public. Disgusting, I call it. I'm glad you're not that sort of girl, Esther.'

'Oh, but—' Etty's face flamed. She and Jim didn't go as far in public as these two were doing, kissing as if there was nobody else about, but they certainly walked arm in arm and held hands and sat with Jim's arm around Etty's shoulders. 'I've never told you—' she began, but already Miss Chalk had lost interest.

'I wonder where we are. It's impossible to tell with this awful blackout. Mind, it must be worse out in the country – did you hear they've taken down all the signposts? I don't know how anyone can find their way about. Conductor! Where are we? We don't want to go too far.'

69

'It's all right, ducks, you're safe with me,' the man shouted saucily from his little cubbyhole under the stairs. 'I only go too far on Saturdays when the missus has had a couple of port and lemons.' He caught sight of Muriel's expression and added, 'You got three more stops to go.'

'Cheeky devil,' Muriel said with a sniff. 'It doesn't matter what you say to some people, they'll find a double meaning in it. You'd think he'd be a bit more careful of his tongue, with decent young women like you and me.'

The bus arrived at the hostel at last and they got off and went inside. Like the other businesswomen who had the better rooms, Miss Chalk had her own key, but Etty had to ask for one if she wanted to stay out late. There was nobody about in the hallway and they went up to the top floor for a last cup of cocoa.

'It's not fair, you treating me to everything,' Etty said, taking her coat off. 'I ought to pay you back.'

'I've told you, you're not to be so silly. I like having a young gel with me.' Muriel looked at her thoughtfully. 'You know, you could be really pretty if you had your hair set in waves instead of pulled back like that. And a touch of pink lipstick, to brighten your face up. You've got unusual looks.'

'Jim likes me as I am.'

The words came out quite naturally and Etty was glad she'd said them. Now she'd be able to tell Miss Chalk about Maggie's brother, and how much they thought of one another, and she would realise that Etty was just an ordinary girl with a boyfriend. And she'd realise that Etty wouldn't always be able to go to the pictures or have tea out with her – she had her own life to lead. She'd begun to talk as if Etty were her own special property.

Muriel stared at her. 'Jim?'

'My boyfriend. He's Maggie's brother – you know, the Nippy with the yellow hair? I told you she's married and her husband's home on leave. He and Mike—'

70

'Never mind that! This Jim – you never told me you had a boyfriend.'

'It never came up,' Etty said uncomfortably. 'You never asked me.'

'I didn't think I needed to ask!' Miss Chalk's voice was icy. 'I imagined, for some reason, that you would tell me anything of that sort.'

They stood looking at each other. I don't know why you should have thought that, Etty thought, but she didn't say so. And what did Miss Chalk mean – *'anything of that sort'*?

'There's nothing wrong in it,' she said defensively. 'We're going steady. We're getting married one day. His mum and dad know, and they like me – it's all above board. I don't know why you're looking at me like that.'

Muriel Chalk turned away. Her back was stiff, as if she were deeply offended. Etty couldn't understand why.

'Well, never mind,' the older woman said at last. 'I suppose I should have realised. I shouldn't have expected anything different. You gels are all the same, after all.'

'There's nothing wrong with it,' Etty persisted. 'It's natural.'

Miss Chalk turned and looked at her. Her eyes were like chips of stone. 'Natural. Of course it is. Absolutely natural, to go about behaving in a filthy manner, like animals. Like those two on the bus tonight – kissing and touching each other for all the world as if they were home in bed. Of course it's *natural*. I just happen to find it rather disgusting, that's all. And what I don't understand is why you never said a word to imply that you didn't, too. Why you sat there and let me spend money on you, without ever mentioning the fact that you were just as bad. That you had a *boyfriend*.'

'It just never seemed to come up,' Etty said miserably. 'I didn't think you'd be interested.'

'Well, you thought wrong.' Miss Chalk walked to the door and opened it. 'I think you'd better go, Esther. It's too late for cocoa now.'

71

Etty looked at her. 'I didn't ask you to spend money on me. I didn't want you to. I'll pay you back—'

'Oh,' Miss Chalk said furiously, 'don't be so *stupid*!' And she pushed Etty through the door and slammed it behind her.

Etty stood for a moment, shaking too much to move. Tears of shock welled from her eyes. She felt bewildered, hurt and confused. Why did it matter to Muriel Chalk that Etty had a boyfriend? Why did it matter so much?

She must be ever so lonely, she thought, beginning to stumble down the stairs. She must be really, really lonely if she wants to be friends with someone like me, and not want them to have any other friends. I ought to be sorry for her.

A little bit of her was. But much more was hurt. She remembered her determination not to let herself be hurt again. It seemed sometimes as if the only way to avoid getting hurt was not to make friends.

She let herself quietly into the bedroom and undressed quickly in the cold darkness. At least Jim will never hurt me, she thought, slipping between the chilly sheets. I'll always be able to depend on Jim.

Mike's mother made no objection to Phyl staying overnight. She'd been half afraid he would want to stay at Mrs Holt's house, and was only too thankful to know he'd be at home for his leave. She borrowed a camp bed from a neighbour and said he could put it up in the back room at night while Phyl had the Put-U-Up.

Mike's two sisters, Joan and Peggy, were delighted to have Phyl staying there. Working in one of London's big Corner Houses seemed the height of glamour to them, and they plied her with questions about film stars and the Royal Family. Phyl laughed and told them that such people didn't often come into Corner Houses. 'Although the King and Queen did once, before the war,' she said. 'But only to look round, they didn't really sit down like proper customers.'

'You'd think they'd let the princesses come in some-times,' Joan said. At eleven, she followed their fortunes with avid interest. 'They'd like it.'

'I'm not so sure about that,' Mike's mother said. 'I know what I'd pick if I had the choice between a Lyons Corner House and Buckingham Palace!'

Phyl liked being at Mike's house. It wasn't so very different from her own home, and the family banter that went on reminded her of the cheerful insults that flew between herself and her brothers. All the same, she felt restless sitting with them all through the evening, and glanced once or twice at Mike, wishing they could be alone.

Mike's mother saw her glance and after they'd finished listening to ITMA she said casually, 'I suppose you two have got a few things to talk about. You'd better go in the front room for a bit. I'll knock when supper's ready.'

Mike stood up quickly. 'Good idea. Come on, Phyl.' She rose and followed him, feeling self-conscious, and even more so when she caught sight of Peggy's smirk. Once inside the front room, however, she forgot the slight embarrassment and went into his arms, lifting her face for his kiss. By the time he had finished, she was breathless.

'Oh, Mike. I was wondering how we'd ever get a minute to ourselves!'

'Mum's pretty understanding. And she's too glad to have me home to stand in our way.' He nuzzled her neck. 'Phyl, I do love you.'

'I love you, too.' They moved over to the settee that would become a bed later on, and sat down. It was so marvellous to be here together like this, Phyl thought, scarcely able to believe that it was really true that Mike was here beside her, that she could feel the warmth of his body against hers, the strength of his arms about her, that she could run her fingers through his springy hair and kiss his lips. 'Mike, I can't bear to think you're going away again so soon—'

'Don't think about it. Think about this. Just be here, now – don't think about anything else at all.' His kisses were fervent. They took her breath away and her own passion rose to meet his. She lay back in his arms, letting him kiss her lips, her face, her throat. He slid one hand down her neck and covered her breast with his palm. Even through the layers of jumper, blouse and bra, the feeling of it made her jump and gasp. He had never touched her there before. She ought to stop him. She ought to say no.

'Oh, Mike . . . that's lovely . . .'

'You're lovely, Phyl. Oh, when I think of all the time we've wasted . . . That Eileen—'

'Irene. Her name's Irene.'

'Eileen, Irene, what's it matter? I can't tell you what I call her in my mind! She nearly split us up, Phyl.'

'I know. She's a cow. Nobody likes her.'

'I'm not surprised. But we don't have to talk about her. Let's talk about us.' He hugged her close. 'Phyl, you will find out about getting that licence, won't you, so that we can get married the minute I get another leave? I tell you, I won't want to wait. I want you to be my wife the first minute it's possible.' He slid his hand down her body and then up underneath her jumper. 'I'd like you to be my wife now.'

'Mike . . .' Her breath quickened. His fingers were busy unbuttoning her blouse. She could feel them against her skin, just at the top of her breast. I'll tell him to stop in a minute, she thought. I'll just let him do it for a minute or two and then I'll say he's got to stop. But it's so nice . . .

The knock startled them both. Phyl sat up swiftly and pulled down her rucked jumper and tucked her blouse back into her waistband, her fingers shaking. Mike grinned.

'It's all right. She won't come in. Just coming, Mum,' he called out, and then turned back to Phyl. 'I – I didn't go too far, did I?'

Phyl had recovered some of her composure. 'You know

74

you did,' she told him sternly, and then smiled. 'But I liked it. Oh, Mike, I wish we could be married now.'

Tidy again, she stood up and he took her in his arms again and kissed her gently. 'I don't know how I'm going to sleep on that old camp bed tonight, knowing you're here in the next room,' he whispered in her ear.

'Come on,' Phyl said, removing herself. 'Your mum's knocked once. Next time, she'll be coming in to see what's keeping us. Anyway – I'm hungry.'

Tom and Maggie also had to divide their time between two families, but since they were married and could spend all their time together it didn't matter so much. They decided to stay the first few days at the Pratts' house and then go to Tommy's parents, staying there when Maggie went back to work so that Tommy could spend the time with his mother.

'Well, I'll go to sea in a pea-green boat,' Sam Pratt said when he saw Tommy that evening. 'If it ain't the soldier's return. Got chucked out of the daft and barmy already, have yer?'

Tommy grinned. He was accustomed to Sam's Cockney rhyming slang and even managed to top it occasionally with his own. Somebody had to make it up after all, he said, and he reckoned Sam himself did quite a bit. No reason why he couldn't as well.

'Only if you're a real Cockney,' Maggie told him. 'Born within sound of Bow bells.'

Tommy stood up when Sam came into the room. It was something he'd learned to do in the army when an officer came into the mess. Sam wasn't an officer but he was Maggie's dad and this was his house, and it didn't do any harm to show a bit of respect.

'They didn't sling me out,' he said. 'Sent me home for a spot of would-you-believe. We've dug up half Belgium in the past few months, now I reckon they're waiting for the seeds to be delivered.'

'Well, let's hope they're seeds the Jerries can harvest. A few land-mines planted here and there'd give 'em summat to think about.' Sam shifted the big tabby cat off his armchair and sat down, bending to untie his bootlaces. 'Cor, my plates of meat are giving me gyp today. Freezing brass monkeys it is, down the market, and hardly a bit of fruit or veg in the place. Carrots and parsnips frozen in the ground so's you'd need a pneumatic drill to dig 'em out, and anything from overseas, well, you can forget that. I don't reckon young Queenie's going to see a banana for the duration.'

'It's a shame,' Maggie's sister Evie said. 'Kiddies didn't ought to have to suffer. What about oranges, did you manage to get any like I asked?'

Her father shook his head. 'Someone said there might be some coming in tomorrow. Don't you worry, gal, I ain't going to let me own grandchild go without, no more'n I can help.'

Queenie was playing on the rag rug in front of the fire with Maggie's youngest sister, Ginnie. Properly, Ginnie was her auntie but it would have been daft to make Queenie call her that, when there were only six years between them. They were organising a family of dolls of various kinds and degrees of decrepitude, from a china doll that could close its eyes when you tipped it on its back to a smart gollywog with a red jacket and blue trousers. Two teddy bears that looked as if they'd been loved almost bare and a purple knitted elephant completed the family.

'What in Gawd's name are you doing with that lot?' Sam asked the two girls. 'You looks as if you're organising a war of your own down there.'

'They're being evacuated,' Ginnie told him with dignity. Each of the little family had a label made from brown paper tied round its neck. 'They're going to the countryside to milk cows and pick 'ops.'

'Pick 'ops? Well, that's a useful sort of a job – keep the

beer flowing. I can see you got your 'ead sewed on the right way round.' Sam looked up. 'Tell you what I 'eard today, them blokes from the *Exeter* and *Ajax* are going to march down Westminster tomorrow, and 'ave their dinner with the Lord Mayor. Making heroes of them, they are.'

'So they should,' Tommy said. 'They did a good job down in the River Plate. That *Graf Spee* was a real thorn in the merchant navy's side. That's the trouble with us being an island, see, we can keep invaders out but they can stop supplies getting in. It's like being under siege.'

'That's right. That's why there ain't no bananas or oranges.' Sam leant back in his chair and sighed. 'A cup of Rosy Lee'd go down a treat, Ive.'

'It's ready now,' Ivy Pratt said, filling the teapot from the kettle that was always humming on the range. 'And there's a bit of bread and jam to go with it. I'm doing a toad-in-the-hole for supper.'

'And cabbage? That was a good hearty one I brought home yesterday.'

'And cabbage,' Ivy said, smiling. 'It's all right, Sam, You won't go short of your vittles, not as long as I'm here to cook 'em for you.'

He lay back in his chair and the tabby climbed up on his lap. Sam stroked the furry back contentedly, and looked across the fireplace at his mother, ensconced in her own corner with her knitting.

'This is what life oughter be, ain't it, Ma?' he said, sipping his tea. 'Warm and cosy by the fire with yer family all around and a good hot meal in the oven. This is what we works and slaves for. And I bet there's plenty of good, ordinary men and women over in Germany what feels the same. Why do we have to go to war, eh? Tell me that.'

'You knows as well as I do, Sam Pratt,' his mother told him. 'Because there's greedy, wicked men in the world, and too many who won't stand up to 'em. Too many as greedy as they are. They got to be wiped out, and we never done the job proper the last time. Well, let's hope we can now, otherwise there's nobody going to be able to live like this, warm an' comfortable at home, 'cause that bleedin' Hitler won't let us.'

Her voice shook. Maggie glanced at her, remembering that her own husband, Maggie's grandfather, had been killed in the Boer War, forty years ago, leaving Ada Pratt with four young children and another on the way. And then she'd lost two sons in the Great War of 1914–18. Ada had had plenty of experience of what war could do, and it was no wonder she was sometimes bitter and sour about life.

'Don't worry, Gran,' she said, laying her hand on the old woman's knee. 'We'll send him packing this time. We won't let that man take over the world.' She turned to Tommy and touched his cheek with her other hand. 'Men like my Tom here'll see to that.'

Chapter Five

Sleeping in the next room to each other had proved just as impossible for Phyl and Mike as he had forecast.

The first night, after hearing his parents go upstairs to bed, the knowledge that he was just the other side of a thin partition wall kept Phyl awake for hours. Now and then she heard movements and started up, staring towards the door and half expecting the door to open softly. But Mike stayed where he was and she fell eventually into an uneasy doze, sleeping heavily at last and waking with a dull headache and eyes that felt too big for their sockets.

Mike looked at her as she opened the door. The camp bed had been folded up and put behind a chair, and breakfast was on the table. He was eating Weetabix soaked in milk and hot water. Peggy and Joan were there, too, with mugs of cocoa beside them.

'Hullo, Phyl.'

'Hullo.' She felt awkward and shy, appearing like this in an old dressing-gown of her father's. Up till now, she'd always tried to smarten herself up a bit for Mike, but you couldn't do that when you were staying in the same house. She went through to the kitchen and outside to the lavatory, then had a wash at the sink, hoping he wouldn't come through. But she was left alone in the small kitchen – even Joan and Peggy didn't interrupt her.

'We've got to go to school now,' Joan informed her as she went back to get dressed. 'They've opened some classrooms in the church hall, now that the school's been requisitioned.

It's only for the morning, though, the boys are going in the afternoon.'

'It's not fair,' Peggy said. 'Why couldn't it be the boys who go in the morning?'

'Because boys can't get out of bed like girls can.' Joan swallowed the last of her cocoa. 'Come on, we'll be late.'

They ran out of the house and Mike looked at Phyl and grinned.

'Sit down and have some breakfast. Mum's gone up to the shops.'

'I ought to get dressed first,' she said nervously.

'No, don't. I like you in your dressing-gown.'

'This thing?' She looked down at the camel-coloured wool fabric. 'It's Dad's really. Nobody else has got one and we're not sure where he got this one from. He's had it about a hundred years!'

'I like it. It makes me feel – well, sort of married, seeing you like that.'

Phyl blushed. Mike looked at her and smiled. He leant across the table and kissed her nose.

'Good morning, Phyl.'

'Good morning, Mike,' she whispered back.

'Did you sleep all right in the Put-U-Up?'

She shook her head. 'No. I couldn't sleep for ages.'

'Nor could I. I kept thinking of you in there all on your own. I nearly came in to you once or twice.'

'I thought you were going to, once or twice.'

They looked at each other.

'I don't think I can manage three nights like that,' he said. 'Without any sleep.'

'D'you want me to go back to Auntie Holt's?' Phyl asked innocently.

'No!' He caught her look and grinned. 'You little devil! Mind you, I don't think I would've slept any better if I had come in. Do you?'

'I don't know,' Phyl said demurely.

80

'Am I going to find out?'

'Mike! I don't know what you're suggesting—'

'Yes, you do.' His grin faded and he reached across the table to hold her hands. 'Phyl, I didn't mean to ask you this. But being next door like that – and knowing I'm going away again soon and don't know when I'll be back . . . . It's awful, Phyl. I love you so much. I'll always love you. And – and I'd be really careful. I mean, there wouldn't be anything to worry about.'

Phyl was silent. Her heart was beating fast. She felt scared and excited and uncertain. All her upbringing had been against doing as Mike wanted. Keep yourself for the boy you marry, her mother had told her, keep yourself decent. And there had been grimmer warnings. Don't you never bring trouble to this house. We've never had nothing like that in this family.

She didn't think her parents would actually turn her out of the house if she 'got into trouble', like a girl along the street had been turned out. But she'd probably have to go away somewhere to have the baby, and then it would have to be adopted, and she'd never know what had happened to it, or where it was . . . Her eyes stung.

'Phyl?' Mike said, and she jumped and looked at him, startled. I don't know what I'm thinking of, she thought. What baby? There isn't going to be a baby!

'What's the matter?' He stroked her fingers. 'Are you frightened of letting me love you? Don't be frightened, Phyl. Please.'

'Oh, Mike—'

'We love each other. We'd be getting married if only we could. We *will* be getting married, the first chance we get.' He tightened his hand on hers. 'I don't want to go away, not knowing what it's like to love you properly, Phyl. I can't bear to.'

'Oh, Mike,' she whispered. 'Mike . . . .'

81

'You love me, too. I know you do. You want it as much as I do.'

She dropped her eyes. She knew that if he had come to her last night she would have not only given in to him, she would have welcomed him.

'Say it,' he urged her. 'Say you love me. Say you want me, too.'

'I love you, Mike. I – I want you, too.' She cast a quick, nervous glance towards the door, as if expecting to see the accusing figures of her mother and father there, of his mother and father. 'Oh, Mike, I don't know . . .'

'I could be gone a long time,' he said soberly. 'It was five months this time. Next time, it might be longer.' He lifted his eyes to hers. 'I might not come back at all.'

'Don't say that!'

'It's true. You know it's true. Some of us aren't going to come back.'

Phyl was silent. She knew he was right. Suppose he was one of those who didn't come back. Suppose he got killed, and died not ever having done what he wanted most; suppose she had to live her life without him, knowing that she'd refused him; never knowing, herself, what it would have been like to love him . . .

She took a deep, deep breath.

'All right, Mike. Tonight.' And now you've done it, she told herself. You've promised him now. You can't go back on it.

'Phyl. Oh, Phyl, you really mean it!' His face was alight and he got up and came round the table to take her in his arms. 'I didn't think you would. I didn't even mean to try – I know you wanted to wait – but I couldn't help myself. I'll be careful, I promise I will. I won't hurt you, or – or – you know. Oh, Phyl, I love you, I love you, I love you!'

He kissed her wildly, passionately, and she forgot her doubts and let herself be caught up in his kisses. For several minutes they clung to each other and then she said a little shakily, 'We ought to get on with our breakfast. Your mum'll be back any minute.'

Mike went back to his chair and Phyl took two Weetabix out of the box. Her hand shaking, she poured cold milk on them and measured out a teaspoonful of sugar. After a moment, she said, 'Mike?'

'Mmm?' He was gazing at her with dreamy eyes. She blushed, wondering what he was thinking about, fairly sure that she knew.

'Mike . . . Is this your first – I mean, have you ever—?' The blush was so fierce it was almost painful.

He looked away and spoke awkwardly. 'Well, you know how it is, Phyl. A bloke needs to get a bit of experience. And there's always a few girls willing to give it to him. Not many,' he added hastily, seeing her face. 'Well – one, actually. And it was before I met you. Once you came along I never wanted anyone else.' He reached for her hand again. 'It doesn't make any difference, Phyl. It'll be like the first time, for me. It'll be our first time together.'

'That's nice.' She paused and ate a spoonful of cereal, then added, uncomfortably, 'So you do know what to do? I mean – you won't get sort of – carried away, or anything – and forget – well . . .' She floundered to a stop and looked at him with big eyes. 'I don't know much about it myself, actually,' she confessed.

Mike laughed. 'Don't you girls talk about it? I'd have thought Maggie would have passed on a few tips!'

'I didn't know I was going to want any,' Phyl said with some dignity. 'I know what happens, of course. I'm not that daft. But, well, all *that* side of it – it's the man's responsibility, isn't it?'

'Yes, it is,' he said. 'And I'm sorry I laughed. You don't need to worry, Phyl. I'll get something today. I've got to get my hair cut anyway.'

The back door opened and his mother came in and

83

dumped two shopping bags on the kitchen table. She looked round the door and gave Phyl a comfortable smile.

'Well, there you are, then. That dressing-gown looks nice and warm, I must say. Did you get a good night's sleep on that Put-U-Up? I always say, that's a good piece of furniture, good as a proper bed that is. Everyone sleeps well on that Put-U-Up.'

'Yes, Mrs Bennett,' Phyl said demurely. 'I bet they do. And I'm already looking forward to tonight.'

Irene Bond didn't offer to take over any of the tables that had been shared out amongst the other girls. She didn't approve of Phyl and Maggie being given leave and she wasn't going to put herself out to help them. Mr Carter remarked on it as they lined up on the first afternoon, holding their hands out to be inspected.

'I'd have thought you'd be eager to take on extra work, Irene. You're keen to become a supervisor, aren't you?'

'Yes, Mr Carter. I'd like to become a manageress eventually.'

'Supervisors have to be able to cover any table in an emergency,' he said, looking at her. 'And we have to feel confident in sending them to other Corner Houses, too. It's not enough to be smart and quick in your own work, Irene. We need extra qualities before we think about promotion to the more responsible jobs.'

Irene coloured. It had been a mistake not to offer, she saw now. Mr Carter already knew that she didn't get on well with the other Nippies, and she didn't want him to think she was mean or spiteful. 'I didn't know if I'd be able to work myself this week,' she invented swiftly. 'My mum's been poorly and what with having to look after my dad and little brother . . . I'd have offered straight away if I could have.'

'I see. And how's your mother now?'

'Oh, she's a bit better, but she's still in bed.' Irene hoped her mother wouldn't take it into her head to come into the Corner House this week, as she sometimes did. She'd have to warn her the minute she got home. 'I'm having to do all the shopping and cooking – not that I mind that, of course. We've all got to pull together these days, haven't we?'

'We certainly have,' he agreed, and went on to the next girl, pointing out a loose thread on one of her buttons. Irene smiled. It had been a tricky moment, but she'd come out of it okay. He probably thought all the more of her now, knowing that she was looking after all the family as well as doing her job . . . Irene chuckled softly. She'd almost had herself believing her own story!

The restaurant was busy, and without Phyl and Maggie the girls were kept on the run. Irene, with no extra tables to worry about, sailed smoothly through her orders. She kept a bright smile pinned to her face and was gratified to see that a number of customers were obviously asking to be seated at her tables.

'Hullo,' said a rather smart-looking woman who had come in alone. 'I've seen you before. You're Irene, aren't you?'

'Yes.' Irene looked at her in surprise. 'How do you know my name?'

'Oh, I know most of you young gels. I've noticed you quite a lot. You're a cut above the others, aren't you?'

Irene coloured with pleasure. 'I'm glad you think so, madam. What can I get for you?'

'I'll just have a pot of tea, a buttered teacake and a plate of fancies. Some of that Battenberg, if you've got any, and an Eccles cake.' She smiled and Irene hurried away, pink with delight at having been noticed.

'My, that was speedy,' the woman said when she came back and unloaded her tray. 'I'm sure my usual Nippy isn't as quick as that.'

'We do our best to please,' Irene simpered.

'But some bests are better than others, is that right?'

85

'Well – maybe.'

'And you've brought me the nicest fancies, too. I'll sit at your table again.'

'I hope you do, madam.' Irene smiled at her and sped away. She sensed that the woman would have liked her to stop and chat but, apart from the fact that she wanted to reinforce the impression of being swift and efficient, she was aware that Mr Carter was watching her more than usual this afternoon. I ought to have offered to take on those extra tables, she thought. That was a mistake.

She didn't have a chance to say anything more to the customer. When she gave her the bill, her other tables were all full of people needing attention, and there was time for no more than a quick smile. Still, maybe the woman would pass some favourable comment about her to Mr Carter. People sometimes did, and occasionally someone would write a complimentary letter which would be pinned up on the staff noticeboard for all to see. It would be nice if this woman did that.

She saw the woman again next day. The seater made to show her to one of Etty's tables, but she shook her head and pointed towards Irene. Irene pretended not to notice, but hurried forward at once as soon as the woman had sat down.

'Good morning, madam. It's nice to see you again.'

The customer looked pleased. 'You remember me?'

'Of course, madam. We always remember our nicest customers.'

There was a glimmer of a smile. 'And your nastiest ones, too, I'll be bound!'

'Well – yes.' Irene returned the smile. 'What can I bring you today? We've some very nice snacks, or would you like a proper lunch?'

'Oh, a snack, I think. Do you have Welsh rarebit?'

'Of course we do, madam. And a pot of tea, or would you prefer coffee?'

'Tea, thank you. I think it goes better with cheese, don't you?'

Irene smiled at her and sped off to the kitchen. There was already a long queue of Nippies waiting for their orders and she tapped her foot impatiently as she stood by the counter. Etty was immediately in front of her.

'Let me go first, will you, Etty?' she said commandingly. 'I've got rather a special customer and she's in a hurry.'

Etty turned. It was the first time Irene had spoken to her for weeks. 'My customers are in a hurry, too.'

'It won't matter – they'll never know.' Irene tried to push in front of her. 'One Welsh rarebit,' she called along the counter. 'And make it a nice, thick one.'

'Excuse me. I haven't given my order yet.' Etty stood her ground, but Irene shoved her aside. 'Look, if you don't mind—'

'No, I don't mind at all.' Irene was ahead of her now and already collecting a pot of tea and cup, saucer and cutlery. 'In fact, it's a pleasure!' She gave Etty a swift, spiteful smile and held out her hand for the Welsh rarebit. 'There, you see, it hardly took a minute and your customers will still think what a nice, quick little waitress you are.'

Etty gasped with indignation, but Irene was already stalking out of the kitchens with her laden tray. Etty collected her own orders and then followed her out. She glanced across the restaurant towards Irene's station.

Well! So that was who all the fuss was about. Muriel Chalk. And just why was she so interested in Irene – or Irene so interested in her?

All day, the expectation had been there, the knowledge that they were going to discard all their upbringing along with their clothes, go against all they'd both been taught about not 'anticipating' marriage and go to bed together. It had coloured all their thoughts, their words and many of their actions. The first thing they'd done had been to go to the local high street.

'Had a haircut, Mike?' his mother asked in surprise when they came in for dinner at midday. 'I thought it was short enough already. You look as if you've been scalped.'

'Well, you know what the army's like,' he muttered, brushing a self-conscious hand across the back of his neck. 'They don't call it a short back and sides until you've been just about shaved to the skin.' He glanced at Phyl and she felt her colour rise. Mike had only gone to the barber because it was the only place he knew where he could get a French letter. Well, you could get them at a chemist's shop but you didn't know who might be behind you in the queue listening, and you'd probably have to ask a girl assistant or one of those frosty-faced women. In the barber's it was all casual and matter-of-fact. 'Something for the weekend, sir?' And you nodded and were handed a small packet and paid at the same time as you paid for your haircut.

'I'll never be able to pass a barber's shop without blushing again,' Phyl giggled when he came out, red-faced. 'I'll look at all them chaps with short hair and think, I wonder if you've got something for the weekend. Anyway, why's it the weekend? Can't you do it during the week? Is it illegal on Wednesdays, or something?'

'Don't be daft. It's just what they say, isn't it? Anyway, never mind all that. We're all right now, whatever night of the week it is.' He looked at her seriously. 'You really are sure, Phyl?'

Phyl smiled at him. 'Of course I'm sure. I said so, didn't I? You know, Mike, you've changed. When we first started going out together you never stopped trying to get me to go all the way. I thought you were a real Casanova.'

'Oh, that was all talk,' he said. 'I knew you weren't that sort of girl. But a bloke's got to give it a go, hasn't he?'

Phyl stared at him, then began to laugh. 'And they say

88

women are illogical! And I suppose if I had given in, you'd have put me down as a common tart.'

'No, I wouldn't,' he said quietly. 'I knew that if you'd given in, it would have been serious. And it was serious with me, too.'

The day seemed endless. Before supper, the family played cards together but Phyl couldn't keep her mind on the game. She won one game by a fluke and then lost all the rest. She could see that Mike's dad thought she was hopeless.

'You've got to try to work out what the other players have got in their hands,' he told her. 'It's easy then.'

'Phyl's got more to think about than playing cards,' his mother said, and Phyl shot her a startled look. Surely she hadn't guessed. But Mrs Bennett looked quite unconcerned as she put the cards back into their box and got out the tablecloth for supper. 'You two can go into the front room for a while,' she said. 'Say your goodnights. We'll have to be getting to bed as soon as we've had our cocoa.'

Mrs Bennett always made a snack for supper – cheese on toast, or a few chips. It was the last hot meal Mr Bennett would have before next evening. There wasn't time for a cooked breakfast, even if you'd been able to get the bacon and eggs these days, and he took sandwiches to work.

Tonight it was sardines on toast. Phyl usually enjoyed her supper and sardines were a favourite of hers, but she could only toy with them tonight and finally slipped the last bit on to Mike's plate when his mother went out to the kitchen for the biscuit tin. Once again, when she caught Mrs Bennett's eye on her, she wondered if the older woman had guessed what was going on, but once again no comment was made and she told herself she was imagining it. Guilty conscience, she thought ruefully.

At last supper was over. Phyl said goodnight and went into the front room. Mike followed her for a 'last' kiss.

'Don't you fall asleep, now,' he whispered. 'I'll be in as soon as I think Mum and Dad have settled down.'

'You're the one who's got to stay awake,' she retorted. 'All I've got to do is wait.'

'Don't worry. There's no chance I'll drop off.' He hugged her. 'I'm too excited.'

'Mike!' his mother called from the back room. 'Your dad and me are going up now.'

'Just coming,' he called back, and kissed Phyl hard. 'See you soon, sweetheart.'

Left alone, Phyl looked nervously around the room. The Put-U-Up was unfolded and made up. It was a double bed, not very soft but quite comfortable. It was hard to imagine that in a short time she and Mike would be in it together. She could hear him now, getting his camp bed ready. Above her the creaking floorboards told her that his parents were getting ready for bed. Suppose they hear us, she thought. Suppose they hear us and come downstairs . . .

There was silence from next door. Phyl undressed swiftly, suddenly terrified that Mike would come in before she was ready. She folded her clothes neatly, putting her skirt and jumper on top of her petticoat, knickers and bra, and pulled her nightdress over her head. I wish it was a bit more romantic, she thought. Plain pink cotton, and it's not even new. She slipped into bed and pulled the covers to her chin, lying there watching the door with wide eyes.

It seemed an age before the sounds from above ceased, and another age before the door opened softly and Mike appeared. He was wearing striped pyjamas. He closed the door without a sound and stood there looking down at her.

'Phyl.'

'Ssh,' she whispered. 'I'm sure they can hear every sound upstairs. We'd better be as quiet as mice.'

'I wasn't thinking of yelling out a running commentary,' he murmured, and came and sat on the side of the bed. He pulled the sheets down. 'Let me see you, Phyl.'

90

'You'll have to put the light out. They'll see the shine in their window.'

'Don't be daft. There's a blackout, remember? First time I've been glad about that.' He touched the soft mound of her breast. 'Oh, Phyl. That's so much nicer without that thing you wear during the day . . . Can I take off your nightdress?'

Phyl stared at him. 'Take it off?'

'Of course. I want to see what you look like. I want to be able to remember every bit of you.' He began to scoop the material up with his hands and Phyl sat up quickly, pushing his hands away.

'I'll do it.'

'No,' he said, 'let me. Please, Phyl.' He ran his hands up her body, bringing the thin cotton with it. Phyl shivered at the touch of his fingers against her skin, and closed her eyes. He lifted her arms and she held them up, letting him pull the nightdress over her head. Like a baby thinking that if she couldn't see she couldn't be seen, she kept her eyes closed, and Mike laughed softly.

'Look at me, Phyl. Look at me.' He moved away from her and when she opened her eyes he, too, was naked, still sitting on the edge of the bed and gazing at her.

Phyl felt as if she were blushing all over. She sat in the bed, her skin on fire, watching as his eyes moved over her. She looked at him as well, noticing the muscles of his arms and shoulders, the sturdiness of his chest and thighs. His skin was white and there were hairs on his chest, not a thick mat of them but just a nice covering. The hairs in a line down to his navel were short and soft, like fur. She glanced lower and caught her breath.

'Mike—'

'It's all right,' he said, but his voice was hoarse and trembling. 'It's all right. There's nothing to be scared of.'

'I don't think I—'

'It's all right,' he said again, and put his arms around her.

91

'Darling, it's all right. We'll take it nice and easy. We won't rush.' His lips were tender as he kissed her, but she could feel the taut passion in them. 'Phyl, I love you so much.'

'I love you, too.' The words seemed to bring a kind of comfort, a relaxation of tension. She clung to him, her hands on his naked back, aware of every particle of his skin pressed against hers. 'Oh, Mike, I really do love you.'

He pressed her back gently and they lay together. Phyl wound her legs about his and held him tightly. Her eyes were closed again. We might as well have had the light out, she thought, and then opened them to find Mike gazing at her and knew that she wouldn't have wanted to miss the expression in his eyes. The passion, the love, the deep, deep tenderness.

After that, it all seemed quite natural and easy. All Phyl's worries about not knowing what to do vanished as she responded to Mike's caressing hands, to the pressure of his body against hers, to the ardour of his kisses. It was as silly as wondering how to breathe, she thought as he rose on his elbows above her and looked down deep into her eyes. Of course I know what to do.

She waited as he moved away slightly and fumbled with the French letter. It would be nice not to have to bother, but she knew that it would be taking far too great a risk. At last it was on and secure and Mike came back. Once again, he lifted himself above her.

'Now?' he whispered, and she nodded very slightly. 'Phyl . . .'

There was a moment of sharp, unexpected pain, and she almost cried out, then remembered his mother and father in the room above. And then the pang was over and it was smooth, and warm, and comforting, and exciting, all at once, and she was swept away by the force of Mike's passion, swept high on a mounting tide of joyous sensation, swept as if on a huge wave that rose to massive heights before thundering to the shore . . . I can't, she thought, I can't, it's too much – oh, *Mike* . . . And then, clinging to him as if to a lifeline, she felt the crescendo attain its climax and the wave crash, and the thundering in her ears went on as they lay together, breathless and panting in each other's arms.

It was her heart thundering, she realised slowly. Or maybe Mike's. Or both. His parents could probably hear the noise in the room above. They probably thought it was traffic outside. Tanks coming down the street. Or a runaway train. Her confused thoughts jumbled together and she giggled.

'So you thought it was funny, did you?' Mike whispered. He had seemed completely exhausted, but now he lifted himself on his elbows again and looked down at her.

'No. It was lovely. I was just thinking – I wonder how much noise we made.'

'Not too much, I hope. It doesn't seem to have woken anyone up, anyway.' The house was still silent. He bent his head and kissed her lips. 'Phyl, I love you. I love you more than ever.'

'I feel warm all over,' she whispered. 'It's a lovely feeling, Mike. I never knew it would be this lovely.'

'Nor did I.' He rolled over and lay beside her, sliding one arm under her neck. Phyl rested her head on his chest. 'I ought to put the light out.'

'You're not staying here? Your dad comes down at six in the morning – he'll see you're not in the camp bed.'

'Oh, blast. So he will.' Mike pulled her close again. 'Phyl, I can't just go off and leave you. I want to stay here. I want to sleep with you – I want to wake up with you.'

'Tell you what,' she said, 'I've got my alarm clock in my bag. I'll set it for five. Then you can nip back next door before your dad comes down.'

'You're a little minx. I bet you had this all planned.'

'I didn't! You know I didn't.' They began to giggle softly as she sat up and found her bag, scrabbling in it for the alarm clock. She set it for five and wound it up, and it stood beside the bed, ticking loudly. Mike got out, too, and went to switch off the light.

Getting into bed together in the dark was another new experience. They slid down between the sheets and lay close, softly stroking each other's skin. The darkness folded itself about them. And gradually, inevitably, their passion began to flower again, and this time Phyl thought of nothing else but what was happening. Waves at sea, the thunder of her heart, all were lost in the soaring delight of being with Mike, of being a part of him, of the two of them united in love and making a memory that would last them through the coming months, a memory that would last them a lifetime.

It was a memory already, she thought as she heard the train let off steam. For a moment, she was dazed, jolted back from the memory of those few days and those all-too-few blissful nights, to the reality of today and the crowded station platform, the men in khaki and the tear-stained faces of the women. Her control trembled and gave way, and the tears poured down her cheeks.

Maggie and Phyl had come together to the station to see Tom and Mike off. The platform was filled with men in khaki, humping kitbags over their shoulders, and girls and women dressed in their best clothes to see them off.

'All the blokes are here,' Mike said, glancing around. 'There's old Charlie. And Nobby Clarke, and Knocker White . . . I can see the sarge, too. Don't look, Phyl. Make out you don't know he's there.'

'I don't care if he is.' Phyl hugged his arm against her side. 'I don't want to let you go, Mike.'

'I know.' They came to an open carriage door and he dropped his kitbag and put his arms around her. They clung to each other. Phyl was trembling. She could feel the ache in her throat, the sting in her eyes, that meant she was

94

going to cry. I mustn't, she thought. I mustn't make it worse for him.

'It's been wonderful being with you,' Mike whispered in her ear. 'These past few days . . . and nights . . . Oh, Phyl, I've never known anything so marvellous.'

Phyl blushed and hid her face against the rough material of his tunic. She still couldn't quite believe that she'd done what she'd done – let Mike come into her bedroom (well, his bedroom really) and slip into bed beside her and make love to her.

'Phyl, Phyl . . .' Mike held her against him, rocking her in his arms. 'I'll be back the first minute they let me go. And then we'll be married. You'll find out about the licence, won't you? And you'll start collecting that bottom drawer.'

'Yes, yes, of course. I'm going down the shops tomorrow. Mum told me there's a nice teaset in Gamages . . . Oh, Mike! You'll take care, won't you?'

He gave her a wry look, but didn't say what was obviously in his mind. Phyl bent her head, recognising the futility of such a warning.

'You know what I mean,' she whispered. 'I don't want anything to happen to you, Mike. I want you to come back to me, safe and sound.'

'Don't you worry,' he said. 'I mean to. I'm going to marry you, Phyl Jennings, and it'll take more than Hitler's army to stop me.' The train let off steam again and they heard the guard's whistle. 'Oh, God,' he said, 'that's it. I'll have to get aboard, Phyl.'

'Yes.' She held him tightly once more and they kissed a last, desperate kiss. It was almost impossible to let him go, but he was out of her arms, out of her reach, and climbing into the train. She watched him in misery and despair, and he slammed the door and leant out. Half a dozen other soldiers tried to lean out with him, each of them jostling for the best position, leaning down, reaching out their hands. Tommy was amongst them, she saw through her tears, and

Maggie beside her, and the little knot of women on the platform reached their hands up and gripped the first fingers they could touch. Mike's fingers, Tommy's, the hand of some stranger she had never met, would never see again – it didn't seem to matter. What mattered was that everyone could feel the touch of a hand, the tingle of love and pain and promises that all those hands and fingers held. What mattered was that last moment of contact, that final communication.

The guard whistled once more and waved his flag. The engine began its rhythmic thunder, and the train began to move slowly out of the station.

'Well, that's it,' Maggie said quietly. 'Gawd, Phyl, it don't half feel rotten, don't it?'

'It's awful,' Phyl said, mopping at her tears. 'It's horrible. I don't know how I'm going to bear it.'

'I dunno how we're going to bear any of it,' Maggie said as they watched the train out of sight. 'But we don't seem to have no choice, do we? So I suppose we will.'

They turned and walked along the platform. All the other women were walking away, too, their heads bowed, many of them crying. The great arched roof of the station echoed to the muted weeping, and even the cooing of the pigeons flying high overhead seemed subdued.

'Come on,' Maggie said, taking a deep breath. 'Let's get back to work. There'll be plenty more soldiers and sailors coming in, wanting to see a friendly face and a cheery grin. That's our job, remember? We're Nippies, and Nippies are always willing to serve.' She gave another small sigh. 'We'll call it our bit of war work.'

Chapter Six

'They reckon the Jerries'll start bombing London soon,' Jo said as she and Phyl walked to work one day in the middle of April. Preparations had started again as soon as the bad weather was over, and now there were sandbags stacked in front of every shop window and doorway, and piled in mounds around every statue. In Piccadilly, the advertising lights that had blazed and glittered all around the Circus at night – the Bovril sign, the Wrigley's, the Schweppes Tonic Water – remained unlit, and Eros had been removed from his plinth, the empty space surrounded by hoardings advertising National Savings. Most of the Nippies bought a sixpenny savings stamp every week and stuck it into a little book, wondering what the money would be spent on. A fighter plane, perhaps, or a new tank. How many sixpences would that be? 'And then I suppose we'll start bombing them back.'

'I suppose your Nick'll be going over there.' Phyl shuddered. 'I don't know which is worse, to think of your chap going off to bomb Germany or to think of mine fighting in trenches.'

'Nick's flying Spitfires. They're fighters, not bombers. Not that that makes it any better. He could still get killed.'

They walked along the side of Hyde Park. The middle was fenced off now with barbed wire, with soldiers standing guard over the anti-aircraft gun emplacements and barrage balloons inside, and there were shelters for people to go into during an air raid. London was a different city now from the flag-strewn, decorated city that Jo and Phyl had seen at the coronation of George the Sixth. It seemed impossible to look back at that joyous day and believe that it had been barely three years ago.

'The one thing that's nicer is the balloons,' Phyl remarked, looking up. They floated overhead, a school of huge pearly whales that glittered in the light and turned rosy pink with the sunset. 'It'd be nice if they kept them once the war's over, just for decoration.'

'They could put adverts on the sides,' Jo agreed. 'Here, d'you remember Airship on a Cloud that we used to have on the menu? It'd be good to have that again. Topical.'

'London's a miserable place these days, all the same,' Phyl said. 'I'll be glad to go to the pictures tonight and forget it for a few hours. They say that picture's ever so good – I'm really looking forward to it.'

They were going to see *Gone With The Wind* that night. It had just opened and Maggie had suggested going as a group. Shirley's father was well enough to be left for a while now and she'd already promised to go with Owen, but Etty said Jim was working late that week, and the four of them agreed to go after work. The idea of three and a half hours of romantic Technicolor, and a story that was as far removed from wartime London as could be imagined, was a cheering one and they looked forward to it all day.

'Why don't you come along, too?' Jo asked Irene. Every now and then one of them would be assailed with pity for the aloof girl who didn't seem able to make friends, but as usual the well-meant approach was met with a rebuff. Irene looked down her nose.

'No, thanks, I've got company already.'

'Oh, well, that's all right, then,' Jo said, and went back to her table with a tray laden with plates of egg and chips. 'Pardon me for speaking.'

Irene sniffed. She was irritated to find that the others were also going to the pictures that evening. The film was on at three different cinemas – why did they have to choose

98

the one she was going to? She comforted herself with the thought that they'd probably all be downstairs, whereas she and her friend would be in the circle.

The queue was halfway round Leicester Square. Jo, Phyl and Maggie arrived early, Phyl carrying a box of chocolates from the Corner House sweet counter. The counter was less well stocked these days but you could still get a nice box if you had enough coupons. The girls, deciding this was to be a proper night out, had clubbed together their points.

'Where's Etty? Wasn't she coming with you?'

Maggie shook her head. 'She had to go back to the hostel first. She'll be along soon – said to save her place in the queue.'

Phyl nudged her. 'Look, there's Lady Muck in front of us. Not so posh she doesn't have to queue like the rest of us, I see! The way she spoke to Jo, you'd think she was coming with the Queen herself. I wonder who that is with her.'

'I've seen her before,' Maggie said. 'Sits at Irene's table and talks ever so posh. Only she's not really posh, you know what I mean? Just pretending. She dresses smart, though.'

'D'you think she's a – you know?' Jo whispered. 'A streetwalker.'

'Gawd, no! They don't dress like that – they show what they've got. She does her best to hide it. No, I reckon she's a buyer in a shop or maybe a civil servant. I dunno what she sees in our Irene, though, she must be thirty if she's a day.'

'Well, let's just hope they don't sit near us,' Phyl commented. 'I can do without her sniffing like there's a bad smell all through the picture. Here comes Etty now.'

Etty was hurrying along the street, her eyes searching the queue. The girls waved, but before she saw them her glance lit on Irene and her companion. She stopped short, her face flaming, and then walked swiftly past and caught sight of Maggie and the others.

'Oh, there you are. I was frightened I'd missed you.' She slipped into the queue beside them, ignoring the mutterings of the people immediately behind. 'The trolley-bus was late and then there was some sort of alarm in the street and I had to walk a different way round, and—'

'Never mind that,' Maggie interrupted. 'What did that Irene say to you as you come past? You looked all upset.'

Etty looked at her in surprise. 'She didn't say anything. It was just—' Her colour rose. 'The woman she's with – she lives at the hostel. She's a buyer at Selfridges. She – she used to be quite friendly with me, and ask me up for cocoa and that sort of thing, and then I told her about Jim and she sort of didn't want to know me any more. As if there was something wrong with me having a chap. And now she always sits at Irene's table, but I didn't know she was taking her to the pictures.'

The other girls stared at her.

'Did she used to take you to the pictures, then?' Phyl asked curiously.

Etty flushed. 'Well, once. She was nice to me. I thought she was my friend.'

Maggie put her arm around Etty's shoulders. '*We're* your friends. You know that. You don't need no stuck-up store buyer. You let Irene have her, and good luck to 'em. I wouldn't mind betting they deserve each other!'

The others laughed and agreed. The queue began to move forward and soon they were standing at the box office, buying their tickets. 'Four seats in the stalls, not too near the front,' Maggie said. 'We don't want to get stiff necks, craning up at the screen.'

Etty glanced around and caught sight of Irene and Muriel Chalk ascending the stairs to the circle. She breathed a sigh of relief. They wouldn't be in front, so that she couldn't help seeing them, and they wouldn't be behind so that she felt as if she was being watched. They'd be quite out of sight and she could put them out of her mind and enjoy the film.

They came out of the cinema nearly four hours later, sighing.

'Wasn't it *gorgeous*? Vivien Leigh's a real smasher, isn't she? And as for Clark Gable . . . When he said, "Frankly, my dear, I don't give a damn," my spine went all shivery. And when he carried her up the stairs . . .'

'I liked Leslie Howard best myself,' Etty observed. 'He's so nice and gentle.'

The others laughed at her.

'Gentle!' Maggie snorted. 'I bet he'd be just as much a pig as Rhett Butler if he got the chance. Men are all the same.'

'Maggie!' Etty said, shocked. 'You can't say that. What about your Tommy? And Jim?'

'Well, maybe not all men,' Maggie allowed. 'The trouble is, you probably won't know what sort you've got till it's too late! Anyway, Scarlett lost 'em both in the end, didn't she, so she wasn't so clever.'

'It was a lovely picture, though,' Phyl said as they climbed aboard a bus. 'It really took my mind off all this.'

'It took mine off it, too,' Maggie said, and then added, 'Mind you, I've got something else to think about these days anyway.'

The other girls turned to stare at her. There had been something odd in her tone and in the dim glow of the bus lights she looked half laughing, half embarrassed.

'What d'you mean?' Etty began, but her question was drowned by the cry that went up from the rest of the girls.

'Maggie, you're *not*! Don't tell us you're in the family way! Honestly?'

Maggie nodded, almost shyly. 'Looks like it. I mean, I haven't been to the doctor yet, but all the signs are there. Or not there!' She attempted her usual saucy grin but couldn't prevent it widening until it seemed as if her face would split in two. 'Must have bin that port and lemon I had the last night Tom was home.'

101

'If it was, I'm never going to drink port and lemon again,' Jo declared. 'Are you sure it couldn't have been something else, Maggie?'

Maggie dug her in the ribs. 'Want the details?'

'Oh, Maggie – fancy you expecting a baby!' Phyl gazed at her, aware that her own colour had risen. Despite Mike's care, she had been anxious after he'd gone back off leave, and deeply relieved to find that she wasn't pregnant. But for Maggie, it was quite all right – Maggie and Tom had been married for months, so nobody could possibly suppose the baby had been started till after the wedding.

'Are you pleased?' Etty asked curiously, and Maggie almost turned on her.

'Of course I'm pleased! And Tom is, too – I told him I thought I might be, and he wrote back to say he was over the moon. He says he hopes the baby looks just like me, but I want it to look like him. I want a little boy, just like my Tom. It'll make up a bit for him being away.'

'When's it due?' Jo asked, thinking back to when Tommy had been home. February, she thought. That would make it due in November.

Maggie confirmed her thoughts. 'It'll be our little Christmas present. I'm going to call it Noel.'

'That's nice,' Phyl approved. 'Noel can be a boy's or a girl's name.' A thought struck her. 'Here – how long are you going to keep on working?'

'As long as I can, so don't you breathe a word. They've let me stop on after getting married because Tom's away, but they won't want me once I start getting fat.' Everyone laughed at this. Maggie was already several sizes larger than the average Nippy. 'All right, you funny lot,' she said, grinning. 'Anyway, they probably won't notice – just think I'm putting on more weight. That's the advantage of not being like a yard of pumpwater like our Jo.'

'Yes, but you shouldn't be on your feet too much,' Phyl told her. 'You'll get veins.'

102

'I'll get veins anyway. They run in the family – you should see our Mum's, like bunches of grapes they are. And our Evie got them with her Queenie, straight off. Anyway, veins or no veins, I want to keep working as long as possible, get a bit of money put by. D'you know what the army separation allowance is? Three and six a day! That's one pound four and six a week, for letting your man go off and risk his life. That won't buy the baby many bonnets, I can tell you.'

'Oh, Maggie,' Etty sighed, 'it's lovely to think of you with a baby. I'll help look after it.'

Maggie grinned. 'You'll have your own soon enough, once you and our Jim gets yourselves sorted out. Still, it'll be good practice for you.'

'You'll bring it up the Corner House and show us, won't you?' Phyl said. 'We'll all want to see it.'

'Crikey, give us a chance! It ain't due till November. That's over six months away. There's a lot of spilt milk can flow under the bridge before then.'

'Not the way this rationing malarkey's going, there won't be,' Jo remarked, and they all turned to belabour her over the head. She crouched in her seat, protesting, until the conductor came along to demand their fares and they sat back, laughing and looking so bright and happy that he didn't have the heart to tell them to quieten down.

'A baby,' Etty whispered again, looking at Maggie with shining eyes. 'A real little baby. D'you know, Maggie, I've never seen a really small baby before. Not close to, I mean, not to actually *know* it.'

Maggie smiled at her. 'Well, you'll get to know this one all right,' she promised her. 'After all, you're going to be its auntie, aren't you? You're going to know it really well.'

Irene and Muriel Chalk were also discussing the film as they came out into the cold, dark streets.

'It was quite well acted, really,' Muriel said. 'I don't like

103

American films all that much but I must say this one is quite good. Much too long, of course.'

Irene had been so wrapped up in it that she had hardly noticed how long it was. 'I thought it went quite quickly. It didn't seem like three and a half hours.'

'I suppose you fell in love with Rhett, like all the other gels.'

'No, I didn't! I didn't like the way he treated her at all. And that soppy smile on her face the morning after he'd – well, you know. I could have smacked her.'

'Really?' Muriel glanced at her. 'What kind of man do you like, then, Irene? I dare say you've had plenty of boyfriends, a nice pretty girl like you.'

'Me? Oh, I'm fussy.' Irene remembered Herbert Lennox, who had been greasy and pushy and pretended he was something he wasn't, and Richard Godwin who had seemed to be a gentleman and then tried to go too far in Hyde Park. 'I don't go out with many men. I prefer a nice gentlemanly sort of chap, someone who'll respect me. Someone with a decent sort of job that can provide a good home.'

'I see. But surely you'd like a good-looking chap as well. Like Clark Gable. I mean, all the gels seem to like his sort of looks.'

'Well, I'd like someone I was proud to be seen with, naturally. But I don't go for all that lovey-dovey stuff.' Irene made a little grimace of distaste. 'I think it's all a bit overrated, if you ask me.'

'Well, it's nice to come across a gel with a bit of sense. Too many let themselves get carried away with all this romantic nonsense. Especially just now, with all these servicemen about. You get a lot of them in the Corner House, don't you?'

'Oh, yes. They come in a lot when they're on leave – give their girls a bit of a night out. Or to get a bite to eat before they go round the pubs. It's good for business, I suppose.'

'Didn't you say that Maggie's hubby's gone back now?'

Irene nodded. 'He and Phyl's boy together. They were in Belgium for a while, working on the Maginot Line, but they're in France now, so Maggie says.'

'I dare say they're looking forward to a scrap,' Muriel observed. 'The Germans are sure to go into France pretty soon. I've heard they're about to invade Holland. They've knocked Norway into a cocked hat, there's no stopping them now.'

They reached the Strand Corner House and joined the queue. Irene had seldom seen a Corner House without a queue, but nobody minded waiting to get into the warm, light luxury of a Lyons. Tonight the queue moved quickly and soon she and Muriel were seated near a potted palm, studying the menu.

'Mind, I ought to know it off by heart anyway,' Irene remarked. 'So should you, the number of times you come into Marble Arch.'

'That's to see you as much as have a meal,' Muriel said lightly. 'I'm not all that hungry, after those sweets you brought to the cinema. I'll just have a toasted teacake.'

Irene stared at her. 'What d'you mean?'

'What do you think I mean? A round bun, toasted and buttered. Oh, and a pot of tea, of course, and maybe—'

'No, not that. Saying you came in to see me.'

'Well, of course I do,' Muriel said. 'You're my friend. Of course I want to see you.'

'Yes, but . . .' Irene looked puzzled. 'You see me when we go out together. Like tonight.'

'We wouldn't ever have done that if I hadn't met you at the Corner House,' Muriel pointed out.

'Well, no, but . . .' Irene frowned, trying to put her meaning into words. 'I suppose it just sounds funny – coming from a girl. I mean, it's more like what a chap would say, isn't it?'

Muriel regarded her amusedly. 'And are "chaps" the

only ones who can feel like that about a gel? Can't another woman?'

Their Nippy brought their order – teacakes for both and a plate of fancies. She set the teapot in front of Muriel, who began to pour milk into the cups.

'Feel like what?' Irene asked cautiously.

Muriel Chalk shrugged. 'Friendly. Fond of each other. Wanting to see each other – spend time with each other. That's all.'

'Oh. Well, I suppose so. It's just that girls don't usually say it.' Irene took the cup Muriel was holding out to her, and helped herself to a teacake.

'Well, I believe in saying what I think,' Muriel said breezily. 'I like you, Irene. I'm fond of you. There. It doesn't sound too awful, does it?'

Irene smiled. 'No. And I like you, too, Muriel. I'm fond of you.' She sipped her tea, little finger elegantly crooked. 'I'll tell you something else. It's really nice to have a proper friend like you. Those other girls – well, they're not my class. I can't talk to them like I can talk to you.'

'I'm surprised you're a Nippy at all.' Muriel lit a cigarette and fitted it into a long green holder. 'Anyone can see you're cut out for better things than that.'

'I know, but you got to work your way up, you see. Start at the bottom. I don't mean to be a Nippy for long.'

They ate and drank companionably. Muriel rested her cigarette on the ashtray and puffed it occasionally between mouthfuls. Irene watched her and thought she ought to start smoking. It looked so sophisticated. But her mother didn't like it in the house, she said it made the furnishings smell, and her father had to go down the garden to the shed when he wanted to puff his pipe.

She glanced around the restaurant. It was still brightly lit and glamorous, but the war had brought changes. Some of the pictures that had hung on the walls had gone, to be replaced by posters exhorting young men to join the forces.

There were ones for women as well – a smart-looking young girl at the salute in a khaki uniform, extolling life in the ATS, and another for the Wrens. Then there were the warnings – *Careless Talk Costs Lives*, with two city men chatting in comfortable armchairs, or *Be Like Dad – Keep Mum*.

'I dare say you hear a lot of talk when you're at work,' Muriel said, noticing what she was looking at. 'Soldiers bragging about where they've been and what they've done. Some of them don't know how to keep a button on their lips. They don't realise what harm it can do, dropping hints about what's going on.'

'That's right. You don't know who might be a fifth columnist,' Irene agreed sagely. 'You'd be surprised the things I hear. I mean, Maggie's chap Tommy, he's a bit free with what he says. Told her all about the Maginot Line, he did, and they've got a code now so that he can tell her where he is when he writes. Something for France, and something else for Belgium, that sort of thing. Song titles, I think it is they use.'

'Really? That's rather clever. What are they?'

Irene wrinkled her forehead. 'What was the last one? Oh, yes – "The Bells Are Ringing" – that means France. She read it out to us in the canteen. He asked her if she remembered being in the Park one day and hearing it played on the bandstand. And if he mentions "A Long Way To Tipperary", it's Belgium, but he hasn't said that yet.'

'He shouldn't be doing it at all,' Muriel said disapprovingly. 'And she's as bad, reading the letters out to you. You don't know who might be in that canteen.'

'Oh, I don't think there's any fifth columnists in Lyons,' Irene said. 'Though I'd be careful what I said in front of that Etty, mind, her being a Jew and all.'

They finished their meal and went out again. It was getting late, so they walked to the nearest bus stop. In a moment a bus or a tram would come along and they would part to go their separate ways. To Irene's surprise, Muriel leant forward and gave her a quick hug and a kiss on the cheek.

'There,' she said as a trolley-bus came round the corner, 'that's for being my friend. I'll pop in and see you again soon.'

'All right,' Irene said, taken aback but oddly pleased. 'I'll look out for you.'

She watched as the bus disappeared along the road. It was funny how she hadn't minded Muriel kissing her, whereas if a man had done it she would have slapped his face. But it wasn't the same with a woman. You knew it was just meant in a friendly way, and that there were no strings attached.

I wish I didn't have to bother with men at all, Irene thought as she peered into the darkness. I'd just as soon be friends with nice women like Muriel, women with a bit of class and sophistication about them.

The bus arrived and she climbed aboard, making up her mind that the first chance she got, she'd buy herself a packet of cigarettes and a long green holder.

Those who had foretold that the war would begin in earnest once the weather improved were proved right. By the beginning of May, Hitler had defeated Scandinavia and poured his troops into the Low Countries. Everyone knew that France must be next.

'It's awful,' Maggie said as the girls ate their lunch in the canteen. 'We just don't know what's happening any more. I haven't heard from my Tom for a week.'

'I haven't had a letter from Mike either,' Phyl agreed despondently. 'I don't think they're sending letters out. It's so cruel. They must know we're all out of our minds with worry.'

'Perhaps it'll be better now Mr Churchill's in control,'

Shirley suggested. 'Everyone thinks he'll get things sorted out.'

'Even he can't stop the war just like that,' Maggie said dispiritedly. 'He can't stop people being killed now.'

Many of the Lyons staff were affected by the bad news. Some of the older members had sons in the forces, the younger women had sweethearts. Until now, most women employees had left on getting married, but since the war had started a few, like Maggie, had asked if they could stay on. They had no man at home to cook for and look after, and no children yet. It didn't make sense to stay at home – especially when so many men were being called up. Just as in the last war, women would be required to take over the jobs that men had to leave.

'Mind, they're calling girls up as well,' Jo said. 'I've made up my mind. If it comes to it, I'm definitely volunteering for the Land Army. What d'you reckon you'd like to be in, Phyl?'

'Don't know. I quite fancy the Wrens' uniform, but I expect if I go into anything it'll be the ATS. It'd make me feel a bit closer to Mike, being in the army. I don't really see what they'd expect girls to do, though. I mean, we wouldn't go and fight, would we?'

'It'll be mostly office work,' Irene said. Once again, she was back on their table. 'It's to set the ones who do the administration free to go and fight. It'd be more like being in the civil service.'

'I'm not sure I could do figure work,' Phyl said. 'I was never any good at arithmetic at school.'

'Oh, there'll be other jobs for people like you. Packing uniforms and parachutes and things. Ordinary sorts of jobs.'

Phyl looked down at her plate. It was amazing how Irene could always make you feel small. 'I suppose we could get jobs in the canteens,' she said. 'Waiting on officers – we ought to be good at that.'

'They have their own orderlies,' Irene told her. 'And it's a mess, not a canteen. I'd have thought you'd know that.'

'Well, I've heard they're going to give the girls more interesting jobs than that,' Jo said assertively. 'Looking after barrage balloons and even manning the anti-aircraft guns. It won't all be sitting in offices or working in factories.'

Mr Churchill had made his first broadcast, promising nothing but 'blood, toil, tears and sweat'. It was a gloomy outlook, yet somehow his words, and the way he spoke them, gave everyone a fresh determination. 'Victory,' he declaimed in his slurred, growling tones. 'Victory at all costs, for without victory there can be no survival . . .' And then, with a determination in his voice that you couldn't help but follow, 'Come, then, let us go forward together, with our united strength.'

'He talks like a prayer-book,' Shirley said. 'He really makes you feel we can do it. He makes you feel that, however bad it's going to be, we'll win in the end.'

She had sat and listened to the broadcast with her father. Alf was back at work now, even though his arm was still in plaster, but he still had headaches and he still had those queer moments when his eyes would roll upwards and he'd seem almost to fall asleep for a moment or two and then come to with a jerk, complaining about a funny smell. They passed so quickly, however, that it didn't seem worth mentioning them to the doctor, and he did seem better in himself, though he missed Annie badly. If it hadn't been for Jack, Shirley knew that her mother would have come home immediately, however bad the weather.

Maggie nodded. 'And you know, I reckon with him to lead us, we *will* do it. I tell you what, the way Hitler's been riding roughshod over all those other countries, I'd begun to think we hadn't a hope. But listening to him's made me feel better somehow.'

She was still worried sick about Tommy, though, and Phyl was equally anxious about Mike. A few letters had got through, but they were short and scrappy, with little information. Letters were censored anyway, and anything that might have given the slightest clue to where the unit was, or what they were doing, was covered with blue pencil.

'I hate thinking someone's had his paws all over my letters,' Maggie said. 'Reading private things and sniggering.'

'They have to do it, though,' Irene commented. 'Especially when they know people are using codes. I bet they've found out all about them.'

'Don't be daft,' Maggie said, but her colour was high and she told Phyl later that she was sure some of Tommy's references to songs had been obliterated. 'I just hope he hasn't got into trouble for it.'

'I don't suppose he has. They probably know some of the men do it and scratch them all out, just in case. They can't be sure.'

'It's nearly as bad when they're still in England,' Jo said. 'My Nick's not allowed to tell me anything about what he's doing, down near Chichester. Flying, that's all I know, and the wireless says the Luftwaffe is sending raiders all along the south coast. He might be in the air any minute and I just wouldn't know. There was a raid right up as far as Yorkshire the other day.'

'It's the army I'm worried about,' Maggie said. 'We've still got Calais, but they say the army's being driven back into a corner. I'm scared.'

'So am I,' Phyl agreed soberly. The two girls had become very close in their anxiety. Mike and Tommy had been friends for years, and with their mate Charlie had managed to stay together throughout their recruitment, basic training and service. What happened to one would happen to the other two. The girls tried not to think the worst, but with such bad news coming daily it was hard to stay optimistic.

'What'll happen if they push them right back to the

111

coast?' Jo asked her father when she and Phyl went home
for a night off. 'They can't expect them to swim home!'

'The Germans won't expect anything. They'll just mow
'em down.' Bill had fought in the last war and knew how
ruthless the enemy could be. Jo stared at him in horror.

'But surely we'll do something. We can't just stand by
and let that happen.'

Bill shook his head. 'I dunno, girl. See, they can send the
navy over but them ships are too big to get close in to the
shore. It's getting the blokes from the beach to the ships
that's the problem. And the Germans won't be serving ice
cream while they're doing it neither. They'll be giving 'em
all the trouble they can.'

'Dad, it's awful,' Jo said in a small voice, and he looked at
her gravely.

'It's war, love. It's war.'

The first that was known of the rescue was a massing of
naval ships in the Channel. Then the smaller boats began to
join them – the ferries and holiday steamers, the pleasure
boats and cruisers. And, finally, the smallest of all – the
fishing boats, the yachts and sailing boats, the family
weekend boats and even the little dinghies that could carry
no more than a few people, yet could still be taken across the
Channel and on to the beaches of Dunkirk to bring the
trapped soldiers back to the ships.

'They're coming back,' Maggie said in hushed tones.
'Phyl, they're coming back. All those left alive . . .'

They stared at each other. 'All those left alive . . .' Phyl
whispered. 'Maggie—'

'Don't say it,' Maggie said roughly. 'Tom and Mike'll
come back. And Charlie, too. It'd take more than a few
cowardly Jerries to do for them.'

No matter how worried and anxious they were, the
Nippies still had to do their work, and they still had to be
bright and cheerful about it. Mr Carter gave them a little

pep talk every morning, pointing out that their customers needed more than ever to see a smiling face.

'They've got husbands and sweethearts in the forces, too. And a lot of them are servicemen themselves, going back off leave. It's your patriotic duty to give them something pleasant to remember.'

'Our patriotic duty!' Irene said with a sniff. 'Anyone'd think they were all saints. Half them soldiers would be in jail if they hadn't got called up – a lot of thugs, they are.'

'Irene! You could get into trouble, saying things like that,' Shirley exclaimed in horror. 'They're brave boys, they might get killed any minute.'

'There was a bloke in here yesterday, he used to live in our street,' Irene said defensively. 'He got had up for pinching an old woman's purse out of her shopping basket. Four weeks' hard labour they give him, and a good thing, too. Now he's joined up and he's strutting around in a uniform making out he's cock of the walk.'

'You don't say!' Maggie said, her eyes round. 'And I always thought you lived in such a nice neighbourhood, Irene.'

Irene flushed and turned away. She regretted having spoken, but that was just like those other girls. She couldn't say a word these days without one of them biting her head off. It was best to say nothing at all.

Anyway, now that she had Muriel Chalk, there wasn't really any need to talk to anyone else. Muriel and she were really good friends. They saw each other several times a week and Muriel had started coming out to Irene's home on Sundays for tea. She had made friends with Mrs Bond, talked to Mr Bond almost as if she were another man, and didn't pay too much attention to Bobby. Irene didn't like too much attention to be paid to her younger brother.

Muriel understood that Irene was different from the other Nippies. She knew that, whereas to the other girls being a Nippy was an end in itself, to Irene it was a stepping stone to better things. A job as manageress or – although Irene had never told her this – a way to find a good husband. Irene hadn't mentioned the husband because she sensed that Muriel wouldn't have approved. Muriel had no desire to get married and looked on men as a nuisance.

'They're the ones who cause all the trouble,' she said. 'We wouldn't have this war now if it wasn't for men. We'd be a lot better off without them, that's what I say.'

Irene agreed, but she still thought you needed a man to provide you with a comfortable home. She had no wish to spend her whole life working in Lyons. Being a manageress would show everyone how much better she was, but she didn't want to be one for ever.

Their shift finished, the girls were preparing to go home when Mr Carter came back into the restaurant, walking hurriedly as if he had something urgent to say. Phyl, kneeling on the floor polishing table-legs, looked up in surprise. Jo, still cleaning cutlery, laid down a knife as she saw his expression and Maggie felt her heart plummet and let salt run over the top of the salt cellar she was filling.

Mr Carter gave a sharp clap of his hands and everyone turned towards him. Phyl stayed in her kneeling position. If she tried to stand now, she thought, her legs just wouldn't hold her up.

It's bad news, Jo thought with a swift glance towards her cousin. I can tell from his face, it's bad news.

'Girls.' Mr Carter's voice was sombre and a little gasp ran round the big, quiet restaurant. Many of the Nippies had brothers, fathers and boyfriends in the forces. 'Girls, I have some news for you. The British Expeditionary Force is retreating from Dunkirk. Many thousands of soldiers are being brought across the Channel at this very moment. They'll soon start arriving in Dover, and from there they'll be brought by train to London ready to be dispersed to their own camps.' He paused and looked round at the silent faces. 'They're going to be tired, hungry and thirsty,' he said quietly. 'Some of them will be wounded. We at Lyons are going to do all we can to welcome them back. Their trains will stop at Addison Road Station which, as you know, is quite close to Cadby Hall. The Hall is to be opened up as a feeding station, all the bakery goods are going to be used for the returning soldiers and I'm asking now for as many Nippies as possible to come and help feed them.'

There was an instant outcry. Phyl leapt to her feet, waving her duster. Nearby, Maggie had dropped her salt cellar and Jo was gathering her cutlery together with shaking fingers. Other girls, too, were working as swiftly as possible to finish their work and leave the restaurant bright and clean, and Mr Carter was soon almost engulfed by a crowd of volunteers.

'We're all going!' Maggie exclaimed. 'Oh, Phyl – Jo – just think, we could be seeing our own chaps soon, coming back from Dunkirk. They'll be here – on their way home – I can't hardly believe it!'

Mr Carter heard her and looked grave. 'Don't expect too much, Maggie,' he warned her. 'They're coming back from a nasty battle. They won't be looking smart and clean like they did when they went away. They may even be hurt.'

'I'll soon kiss it better!' Maggie laughed at him. 'Don't you worry, Mr Carter. My Tom's as tough as old boots. He'll be all right.' She turned back to her table and her face paled. 'Oh, my Gawd – look at all that salt I've spilt. Oh, *Phyl . . .*'

'Don't be daft,' Phyl said briskly. 'You're not that superstitious. Just throw some over your shoulder and then let's change the tablecloth as quick as we can. I want to get to Cadby Hall!'

Chapter Seven

'Owen!' Shirley spotted him the minute they arrived at Cadby Hall. Normally he worked in the offices, well away from the kitchens, but tonight he was mucking in just like everyone else and she felt a pang of love at the sight of a large dab of flour on his nose.

'Hello, Shirley, *cariad*,' he greeted her, shouting above the clatter of trays and the hubbub of voices. 'Got me cooking now, see. They reckon there'll be thousands of men coming through, all wanting a penny bun and a cup of tea.'

'Poor chaps,' Shirley said feelingly. 'I've heard they were getting bombed on the beaches while they waited to be rescued. It's horrible.'

'Well, they're safe again – for a while.' There was no more time to talk. The bakers and cooks were rushing about with great trays of freshly prepared pies and cakes, slamming them into the huge ovens as fast as the hot ones were removed. There were already massive piles of pies and cakes ready to be carried out to the station on big trolleys and the squeaking of their wheels added to the noise. Outside, on the station, people were unloading the trolleys, piling the food on the long tables that had been set up, and there were big urns already steaming with boiling water. The first train was expected at any moment. The girls stood behind their tables, waiting anxiously.

The noise of an approaching train drowned all the other sounds. It came round the corner and steamed slowly to a halt beside the platform. The girls stared at the faces that crowded the windows. Shirley put a hand to her mouth.

'Oh, my *Gawd* . . .' Maggie breathed. 'Oh, my Gawd. Them poor, poor devils . . .'

The train was crowded with soldiers. You could see them through the windows, packed tightly on the seats, sitting on the floor, standing in the corridors. Some hung out of the doorways, and others could be seen behind them, pressing forward for a glimpse of friendly British faces, a glimpse of home.

The girls gazed at them unbelievingly, trying to recognise the men who had marched off so bravely through the London streets, who had boarded these same trains with such cheerful courage. Now they looked weary beyond belief, their eyes hollowed with fatigue, their skins dull and grimy. Their hair was lank, their uniforms filthy and caked with salt, and many of them wore bandages – some around their heads, some on their hands and arms, some – as could be seen when they climbed stiffly down from the train – around their legs and feet. The bandages were as filthy as the rest of them, and dark with dried, clotted blood.

'They look so *tired*,' Phyl whispered. 'And so dirty . . . And Mr Carter was right – some of them have been hurt. Oh, Maggie . . .'

The girls looked at each other. Suddenly the invincibility of their own men seemed less likely – unreal. A dream – a silly, romantic dream.

'Come on,' Jo said, pulling herself together. 'Let's get serving this stuff out. They look as if they need a really good meal, but a couple of buns and mug of tea will help set them up.'

'Oh, Gawd,' Maggie muttered again, and then drew a deep breath and stationed herself behind a trolley to serve out tea and buns.

The queue seemed never-ending. They went past in a long, shuffling line, their eyes blank and staring from the grimed faces. Their hands shook as mugs of tea and sandwiches, buns, doughnuts or fruit cake were pressed into them. They tore at the food with their teeth, swallowing great lumps of unchewed dough, and when the more able of them grinned their thanks, the pity of it tore at Maggie's heart. She wondered how long it was since they had eaten, what they had suffered between then and now, and she thought of the reports they had heard of men massing on the beaches while German planes strafed them from above, of men running and hiding, fighting like cornered rats in the ruined town of Dunkirk before they could reach those beaches; of men standing waist-deep in water under a smoke-blackened sky waiting for the rescue boats, the tide rising and falling about their bodies as the hours dragged by.

Tommy . . . where was Tommy? Her eyes searched for him but he didn't come. Now and then her heart kicked as she thought she saw him. A turn of a head, a flicker of a grin, a sudden glance – but it was never Tom. She laid her hand on her stomach and thought of the moment when she would first see him.

'You okay, Mag?' Phyl stood beside her, giving her an anxious glance. 'You're not doing too much? Maybe you ought to go and have a rest—'

'I'm all right,' Maggie cut in sharply. 'I can't go and leave the rest of you to manage.'

'I don't want you getting ill. You've already done a full shift at work—'

'I told you, I'm all right! Stop fussing.' Maggie's tone softened. 'Sorry, Phyl, but I can't go off now and risk missing Tommy when he comes through. I want to be the one he sees first – like on St Valentine's Day!' Her grin was crooked. 'I just hope he still fancies me.'

'He'll fancy you all right.' A new batch of buns arrived and Phyl turned back to the tea-urn. There wasn't time to chat. A soldier with a wide, bloody bandage round his forehead leant on the trolley and took the mug she handed him. He drank it as if it were stone cold.

118

'You'll burn yourself,' she said. 'And I'm sorry, but you'll have to move on, there's a queue behind you.'

'First hot drink I've had in days,' he said, through cracked, dry lips. 'You're an angel.'

'I'm a Nippy,' she said with a smile. 'We're all angels. Now, please go on.'

'A Nippy from one of them Corner Houses?'

'Yes. Now, please—'

'I'll come in and see you soon as I've had a bit of a kip,' he said. 'I'll take you on a date.'

Phyl opened her mouth to tell him she was engaged, but knew there was no need. The soldier was swaying on his feet, about to pass out. He would never remember what he had said, never even remember who she was. He collapsed in front of her and two men came forward to half carry, half drag him away. She watched in pity and distress, and forgot the queue that had built up behind him.

'Come on, miss. Don't we get no tea?'

Phyl jerked back to awareness and hastily filled a large mug. She held it out with a bun wrapped in paper, glanced up and met a pair of eyes that she knew.

Mike . . .!

'Phyl,' he said. 'Phyl, what the hell are you doing here?'

'Waiting for you,' she said shakily. 'Giving out tea and buns. Oh, Mike, *Mike* . . .'

'God, Phyl. I never thought I'd see you—'

'Are you all right?' she interrupted him. 'Are you really all right? You're not hurt? There's been lots of boys coming through all bandaged . . .'

He made a face. 'They're the lucky ones. God, Phyl, it's been a nightmare.' He hesitated. 'Is – is Maggie—?'

'She's here – look.' Phyl turned away and caught at Maggie's arm. Maggie was busy changing an empty tray for a new one piled with meat pies and didn't respond at once. 'Maggie, look – it's Mike. Mike's here.'

'Mike?' Maggie whipped round. 'Gawd – so it is! Oh,

119

thank Gawd, thank Gawd you're all right.' She reached across the trolley toward him, her face alight, and laughed shakily. 'Blimey, you're a sight for sore eyes, you are. So where's Tom, then? Where's my Tom?' Her eyes went past Mike to the line of men behind him, slow-moving, dispirited men, men who were battered and bruised and bloody, men who were weary to the bone. 'Where's my Tom?'

Mike's eyes darkened. He glanced from Maggie's face to Phyl's, and Phyl felt her heart drop.

'Maggie . . .' he said painfully, 'it's bad news about Tom. I'm sorry—' He caught his breath, his eyes miserable, his mouth twisting a little. 'He's dead, Maggie,' he blurted out, and the tears ran down his grimy cheeks, leaving white, salty tracks. 'He was shot on the beach. We were just getting on board a rowing-boat – there wasn't nothing anyone could do. I'm sorry, Mag, I'm really, really sorry.'

'Dead?' she whispered, staring at him. 'My Tom's *dead*?' Slowly, she shook her head and Phyl, watching with alarm, saw her face whiten and her hands move to cover her stomach. Her voice was raw and husky with disbelief. 'My Tom's been shot dead by a bloody German? No. I won't believe it. I won't *let* him be dead. No. No . . . *No* . . .'

Phyl moved swiftly, just in time to catch her as she sagged and fell. Helplessly, Phyl staggered, unable to hold the bigger girl's weight for long, and Mike came quickly round the trestle table and helped her lower Maggie gently to the cold concrete of the station platform.

Mr Carter was beside them at once.

'What's wrong? Is Maggie ill?'

Phyl, kneeling beside her friend, raised a tear-streaked face. 'Oh, Mr Carter, it's awful. Mike here's just told us – her hubby's been killed. Just as he was getting on the boat at Dunkirk. And she's expecting, too—'

'*Expecting?* Oh, my God!' Mr Carter knelt beside them, feeling for Maggie's pulse. Her eyelids fluttered and she

120

stared blearily at him for a moment, bemused. Then comprehension flashed across her face and, with it, pain. Her mouth crumpled, and she turned her head away.

'It's not true! Say it's not true.' She clutched Mr Carter's hand and turned her head again to stare at him piteously. 'Mr Carter, tell me it isn't true, tell me it's all a mistake. My Tommy's *not* dead! He *can't* be.'

'My poor child.' He glanced round swiftly. 'We'll have to get her out of here. You,' he addressed Mike, 'can you help me carry her? We'll get her into the fresh air and then take her over to the Hall. Phyllis, you'd better come, too.' He looked about, harassed. The queue of weary soldiers was building up and those who hadn't seen Maggie's collapse were beginning to mutter and call out. 'No, stay here for a moment and serve these poor men. I'll get a nurse to see to Maggie, there's bound to be one about somewhere . . .'

Phyl scarcely knew what to do. All her instincts were to go with Maggie and Mike. It seemed almost a betrayal to turn away from them and start serving out tea and buns again. Yet as soon as she did so, as soon as she looked into the first pair of exhausted eyes, she knew that she must. Maggie would be looked after, Mike was safe, these men were the ones that needed her now. These men who had suffered God knew what horrors and now longed for no more than a cup of tea, something to fill their bellies and journey's end in a warm, dry bed. She poured tea, handed over fresh, warm buns and gave them her warmest smile.

Underneath the smile, however, she knew the tears were waiting, along with the pain. Mike was safe, but Tommy was dead. Cheery, cheeky Tommy, who had promised to love and cherish Maggie till death them did part.

As it had now done.

'It was absolute bloody hell,' Mike said. He lay back in his father's armchair, with Phyl sitting on a stool by his knee. He had had a bath, shaved and slept for sixteen hours without stirring, and now he was looking more like the Mike she remembered. But his face was thin and pale, the bruises livid still, and the haunted look was still there in the dark hollows of his eyes. There was a difference in him, the deep, marked difference of a man who has now seen action, a man who has fought and run and hidden from his enemies, who has been forced to retreat and has watched his friends die and been compelled to leave them where they'd fallen. 'It was a bloody nightmare.'

'Do you want to tell me?' she whispered.

'I dunno. It's not the sort of thing I like telling you about. But – oh, Phyl . . .' He sat up suddenly and pulled her close. 'I can't get it out of my mind. The Germans pushing us back into the town – if you can call it a town any more, it's just about ruined, Phyl, hardly a building left standing. They were just too much for us. There was too many of them – we just had to give way. We had to run and hide in them ruins, like rats in holes. We had to make for the beaches – it was our only chance – and yet the beaches were a trap, too, because once we'd got there where else was there to go? And they were sending planes as well, to strafe and bomb us . . . The weather was bloody awful and that stopped them doing too much damage, and once our ships got across it was better because they put up a smoke screen to stop the planes getting through, but even so . . . And we had to walk out into the sea, just walk out in the water and queue up for the boats. All sorts of boats – little dinghies like we go rowing in on the Serpentine, and funny old tubs you wouldn't think'd cross Dover harbour, let alone the Channel. The ships couldn't get in close enough, see. Then there was ferries – I saw that one they called the *Gracie Fields*, it went round in circles and then sank, it seemed like an omen . . . And then they got us to the ships and we come home. Packed like sardines – on the decks, below decks, wherever there was a corner, and men screaming and dying and bleeding . . .' He buried his face against Phyl's neck and she felt him shudder.

'And what happened to Tommy?' she whispered after a long silence. 'Tell me about Tommy.' She felt his head shake. 'Please, Mike. Maggie'll want to know. She's entitled to know.'

'We were together,' he said at last. He raised his head and looked at her. 'We kept together all the while. I lost him for a bit in the town – I thought he was dead then – but on the beach we found each other again. We were queueing up in the water together and a boat came and we just started to climb over the gunwale, and then – then a plane got down through the smoke, flying low. There was a machine-gun strafing us. And Tommy got hit. That's all there was to it.' His voice shook and rose a little. 'He just let go and fell back in the water. There wasn't anything I could do. The blokes on the boat dragged me aboard and I turned round to help him and – and the water was all red. I saw his face just as he went under.' He raised his head and stared at Phyl. She saw the tears in his eyes, understood the anguish of the moment when he had seen his friend die and hadn't been able to lift a finger to help him. 'He looked straight at me,' he whispered, and dropped his head against her shoulder again.

Phyl held him tightly, her own tears flowing. The horror was as real to her as it was to Mike, as vivid as if she had been there herself. She saw the long lines of desperate men, waiting either to die or be rescued. She saw the beaches, massed with those who had no hope of reaching the boats until thousands had been rescued before them. She saw, as if looking down from above, the implacable advance of the enemy, and she saw the aircraft gathering to attack them from the air. And she saw the thousands of boats sent across the Channel to bring the soldiers back to safety – the ships of the Royal Navy, the ferries from all around the coast, the yachts and cruisers and pleasure boats, the tiny dinghies and rowing-boats.

Men were dying there at this moment, she thought. But

123

other men were still being rescued, and what a rescue it was – surely the greatest that had ever been known.

'Oh, Mike, I'm so sorry,' she whispered. 'It's awful about Tommy. It's awful about all those who've been killed. But you're back – and so are lots of others. We won't let this beat us. We're still going to win the war.'

She hugged him tightly, trying to give him hope. Even though, she thought, it was hard to believe what she was saying; even though she felt sick at the thought of letting him go again; even though she knew that they had no choice, just as the soldiers in Dunkirk had no choice; that the war they had gone into was proving a trap in itself, a corner into which the whole of Europe had been driven and now could not escape.

Maggie had no hope at all. She had lost her husband, and now she was losing her baby.

'Don't let him die,' she begged the nurses at the hospital where she had been taken the next day after the pain had started and the blood had begun to flow. 'Don't let our baby die.'

The nurse looked at her compassionately. 'I'm sorry, love. He's already dead. It's just a matter of making you comfortable now.'

'Comfortable?' Maggie cried. 'I don't want to be bloody comfortable! I just want to be pregnant again – and I want my Tom.' She dissolved in uncontrollable weeping. 'I want my baby, and I want my Tom.'

The nurse's face twisted a little. Her own man was away at sea and she had suffered many sleepless nights worrying about him. She held Maggie's hand a little more tightly.

'I'm sorry. We did our best.'

'It ain't your fault.' Maggie turned her face on the pillow and let the tears soak in. 'It's that bloody Hitler. Why don't someone kill him, eh? Tell me that. Why don't they send someone over and do to him what he's doing to our boys? Why do they let him live, for Gawd's sake?'

'I don't know. I don't know.' The nurse felt almost as miserable as Maggie. You weren't supposed to let this happen, you were supposed to stay detached and not get too upset about what happened to your patients – but she knew that what was happening to Maggie now was going to be repeated many, many times. She knew that in other parts of the hospital men were being treated who had come home horribly wounded, and that this, too, was going to happen over and over again. You would have to be very hard not to feel it yourself.

'Did you say he's dead?' Maggie whispered after a while. 'My baby . . .? He's dead?'

'I'm afraid so, yes. He was still very small, you know. He wouldn't have known anything.' They weren't even sure it had been a boy, but there was no need to tell this poor young mother – who wasn't going to be a mother after all – that.

'He didn't even know me.' She lay quiet for a while and then said, 'I was going to call him Noel.'

'That's a nice name,' the nurse said quietly. 'It means Christmas, doesn't it?'

'He was going to be our Christmas present,' Maggie said in a small, lost voice, and she turned her head on the pillow and stared at the wall.

'Oh, Maggie.' Etty's face was white, her eyes red. 'Maggie. It's awful. I just don't know what to say.'

'There's nothing nobody can say.' Maggie came slowly into the living-room. She stood for a moment looking around her. It was the same as ever, yet looked different and unfamiliar, as if it had shrunk while she was away, and the furniture subtly changed. She sighed and sat down heavily in her father's armchair, opposite her gran. Etty looked at her helplessly and then went out to the scullery to fill the kettle for a pot of tea.

The old woman looked across at her granddaughter. For the occasion she had put in her teeth, but they were so uncomfortable that her words were more difficult to understand than ever. Her lips, stretched over the ill-fitting gums, tried to smile but it looked more like a grimace.

'You've 'ad a bad time, girl. I knows what it's like – I lost me own man when I wasn't much older than you, only I 'ad kids to look after.'

'I wish I had kids to look after,' Maggie said bitterly. 'I wish I had just one kid to look after. My little Noel. I even had to lose him, Gran. Why? Can you tell me that? Why'd I have to lose the baby as well? Wasn't my Tom enough?'

'I dunno, girl. 'T ain't no good asking me questions like that – 't ain't no good asking nobody, if you asks me. All I can tell you is, it ain't no good expecting life to be fair. It ain't.'

'I know, Gran. I know. But it don't have to be as unfair as it is, surely. The bad luck could be shared around a bit.'

She leant her head back. She was pretty well recovered from the miscarriage now, if only it weren't for this awful tiredness that swept over her without warning. She'd been in hospital for almost a fortnight, kept in bed for a week and then allowed up for a few hours each day. She felt as if she had been out of the world for months.

During that time the men who had passed through London from Dunkirk had gone back to their camps and were preparing for the next stage of the war. Nobody had any doubt that the British Government, led now by Mr Churchill, would – as he declared in his most stirring speech yet – 'go on to the end'. 'We shall fight on the beaches,' he declaimed, 'we shall fight on the landing grounds, we shall fight in the fields and in the streets, we shall fight in the hills . . . we shall never surrender.' His deep, rolling tones sounded from every wireless set in the land and stiffened the backbone of the nation. The returning soldiers were greeted as heroes, feted and fussed over, as if they had scored a famous victory rather than suffered a crushing defeat, and it was this perhaps that helped more than anything else. A country which ought to have felt humiliated and afraid was instead defiant and filled with new valour. Any exultant foe would be totally baffled.

Maggie felt out of tune with it all. She felt as if the world had taken a sudden twist in its path, leaving her floundering behind. Her Tommy had died – thousands of men had died, enough to populate a whole town – yet people were talking as if it had been a triumph. It's all a big lie, she thought. Why does anyone believe it?

'It ain't no good us asking why it all 'appens,' her grandmother said suddenly, and Maggie had to think for a minute to remember what question the old woman was answering; for a moment, it had been almost as if she were reading Maggie's mind. 'But I can tell you this, girl. It don't do no good to let yourself get bitter about it. It don't do no good to let things get you down. Always make the best of things as they are, and don't waste time grumbling, that's bin my motto.'

Maggie stared at her in astonishment, then glanced up to catch Etty's eye as she came in with the tray of tea. For a moment the two girls gazed at each other, and then Maggie gave way and burst into hysterical laughter.

'Don't waste time grumbling!' she exclaimed. 'Don't let things get you down! Oh, Gran, you're a marvel, you really are!'

Ada Pratt stared at her indignantly. 'I don't see why, young Mag. I don't know what you're laughing at, I'm sure. I've always bin cheerful, I 'ave, you knows that. I've always kept a smile on me face, no matter what I 'ad to put up with.'

Etty handed her a cup of sweet tea. Her lips were pressed tightly together, her eyes dancing. She turned to Maggie and began to giggle.

Maggie was lying back in her chair, wiping her eyes and

127

shaking with laughter. 'Our Gran!' she gasped. 'Our *Gran*, talking to me about making the best of things. Oh, that's rich, that's really, really rich.'

Ada snorted and took a broken biscuit from the plate to dunk in her tea.

'You never knew me when I 'ad kids to bring up and ninety shirts a week to wash and iron,' she said darkly. 'I never 'ad time to grumble in those days. There was always too much to do.'

'Well, Gran, you've got time now,' Maggie said, sitting up and taking her own cup of tea. 'And you ain't half making the most of it, that's all I can say!'

Phyl and Mike came in to see Maggie later that evening. Etty had told them she was coming home and Mike was due to go back to barracks the next day. He and Phyl would have liked to spend this last night alone, but he'd agreed with Phyl that he couldn't go off without seeing Maggie. The four of them went into the front room by themselves.

'They reckon you're all heroes,' Maggie said, trying to smile. 'What's it feel like, then, to be a hero?' Her fit of giggles had turned into the tears that came all too quickly these days, but her grandmother had soothed and stroked her with surprising effect, and she was beginning to feel a little better.

Mike twisted his mouth. 'It don't feel much like being a hero, I'll tell you that. I felt bloody frightened at the time, and so did everyone else. You'd have to be mad not to.'

'Was my Tom frightened?' Maggie asked quietly, and Mike gave her a quick look.

'I don't know. Honest, Mag, I don't know. Up till then we'd been so busy just keeping one jump ahead – there wasn't time to be scared. It was afterwards, when we were on the boats – that's when I felt it, when there wasn't nothing more we could do about it. So maybe he didn't. Maybe he really was a hero.'

'He'll always be a hero to me,' Maggie said, and Mike nodded.

'He will be to me, too.' He hesitated, then went on, 'I want to tell you about something that happened in Dunkirk – the town – before we got to the beach. We were all over the place, us army blokes and the Jerries, chasing in and out of ruined buildings. All the people who lived there had gone. The place was just about wrecked – houses bombed and burnt out, walls falling down, floors all broken up. None of it was safe but we didn't have much choice, we just had to go in them. We hid by windows – no glass, of course – and tried to pick off Jerries as they went by, but there was so many of them and we knew we had to get to the beach. We'd all got separated, but Tom and me managed to stay together. So we decided to make a break for it.'

He paused. The three girls watched him without speaking. Mike's eyes were distant, as if he were back in that ruined township, skulking in shattered houses and trying to kill the enemy passing by. In his face was the taut, grim determination of a soldier who knows he must kill or be killed, who knows that he has been trained towards this moment and that his training would overcome his fear.

'We got about three houses down the road when we heard machine-gun fire. You don't argue with machine-guns, and we dodged into another house. There was no door but it wasn't as badly damaged as the others. There were chairs and a table in the room, and a pile of children's toys – a doll, a few carved wooden animals and a stuffed bear, like a teddy bear.'

'Oh, Mike,' Phyl said softly. 'Some little kiddy's toys, and she couldn't even take them away with her.'

'The teddy bear looked almost new,' Mike went on quietly. 'Tom picked it up and said, "This'd do for my Mag's little 'un." And then he put it down again, and said, "No – the poor little bugger that left it here might come back. She'll want her teddy then." And then half a dozen

129

Jerries went by and we nipped out the back way and found a way down to the beach.'

There was a small silence.

'A teddy bear,' Maggie said. 'Some little French kiddy's teddy bear. And my Tom was thinking of me and our little 'un even then.' She wiped her eyes and Phyl and Etty, one on each side of her, moved closer and slipped their arms about her shoulders. 'I wonder if that little girl will ever come back for her toys. Oh, what a horrible, cruel war this is!'

'Yes,' Mike said. 'It's worse than people in England realise. And it's not going to get any better.'

Phyl looked at him, her face full of fear. 'Do you think we're going to be invaded?'

Invasion was the great fear now. Hitler had marched across Scandinavia and the Low Countries. Since Dunkirk, he had driven into the heart of France and taken over Paris. The swastika was flying from the Eiffel Tower, and the Champs Elysées echoed to the tramp of jackboots and the rumble of tanks. He had fresh support, too – Mussolini had brought Italy to join him against the Allies. Europe was being overrun, and without France to protect her shores Britain would be a lonely force indeed.

'It's on the cards,' Mike said gravely. 'They're bringing back all the troops from Norway. Churchill's been talking about the Battle of Britain. They think the Germans will try anything – ships, planes, parachutes, spies—'

'What they're calling the "fifth column"?' Phyl broke in.

'That's right.' He looked gravely at the girls. 'We've all got to be careful. Those posters – *Walls Have Ears*, *Be Like Dad, Keep Mum* – they're not jokes. Anyone could be a fifth columnist.'

'But we don't know anything worth spying on,' Etty said.

'You don't know what you know,' Mike told her. He glanced at Phyl. 'We ought to be going.'

130

'Yes.' Phyl glanced at her friends. 'Are you coming back to the Corner House when you feel better, Maggie?'

Maggie shrugged. 'What else can I do? I got no man to wait for, no baby on the way . . .' Her voice trembled. 'I might as well come and cheer up some poor bloke going back to be cannon-fodder. They got nothing to look forward to, neither.'

'Don't talk like that, Maggie,' Mike said. 'We're fighting for a new world, haven't you heard? We're fighting for freedom. Isn't that something to look forward to?'

'The way you say that,' Maggie said, 'you might almost believe it.'

'I do believe it,' Mike said. 'I have to believe it.'

He stood up and Phyl rose with him. He slipped his arm around her shoulders and shook Maggie's hand while Phyl bent to give her an awkward kiss. They all looked at each other, wordless.

'Good luck, Mike,' Maggie said quietly. 'Good luck, and come back soon.' She flashed him a watery grin. 'Our Phyl's a proper pain in the backside when you're not around.'

'I'll remember that,' Phyl said, 'the next time you want me to cover one of your tables. Cheerio for now, Maggie. See you back at work. Cheerio, Etty. See you tomorrow.'

They walked out into the cool evening air. It was still light and the streets were full of people – women sitting at their front doors gossiping, children playing on the pavements. Maggie's little sister Ginnie was playing two-ball against the house wall with a couple of other small girls. They waved as Phyl and Mike went by, and one of them ran to touch his uniform 'for luck'.

'Let's just hope it really is a lucky uniform,' Phyl said. 'You will take care, won't you, Mike?'

'As much as I can. But soldiers aren't meant to take too much care, Phyl.'

She was silent for a moment, then burst out angrily, 'I don't see why you had to be a soldier! You had a good job at

Burton's – you never wanted to go and fight. Who is it decides these things? What *right* do they have to make ordinary people like us get caught up in a war?'

'What right do *we* have to say we won't help fight a man like Hitler?' he asked. 'What right do we have to sit back and let him overrun all Europe – including us? And then maybe the rest of the world as well? And can you imagine what the world'd be like if we did? We've got to do it, Phyl. We don't have any choice.'

She sighed. 'I know. I know. I'm being selfish – I don't want you to go, that's all. I don't want to be like Maggie, grieving over you and knowing we'll never be together and I'll never have your baby. Oh, Mike – if we'd just had time to get married like we planned, but it all happened so sudden.'

'We will,' he said, and stopped on a corner to take her in his arms. 'Next time I come back, we will. And there will be a next time, Phyl. There'll be a baby, too – more than one. Lots. And we'll have our life to live, when all this is over, you and me and the kids. There.' He kissed her. 'Don't that sound good?'

'Oh, yes, Mike,' she said, and leant her head against him. 'It sounds very, very good.'

Chapter Eight

France had surrendered. Everyone was now expecting the invasion. Sandbags appeared again, piled up around doors and windows. The whole country seemed to hold its breath.

'There's barbed wire all along the beaches,' Jean, the 'Sally Salesgirl' whose aunt lived in Bognor, told Jo as she served chocolates and flowers from her counter. It looked pitifully bare these days, with none of the glamorous silver caskets or pretty boxes that had been piled so high before the war started. 'Nobody's allowed to go down there. And they're building pillboxes to put guns in—'

'Pillboxes?' Jo broke in. 'What are they?'

'Little square buildings made of concrete. Like boxes with holes in the sides. Soldiers can get inside with their guns. They're putting them everywhere but they're making them look like something else – haystacks and teashops and things. So that the Germans won't suspect there are guns inside.'

'I should think they'd be a bit suspicious if they came across a haystack on the beach,' Jo remarked. 'I know I would.'

'Well, I don't suppose they put haystacks on the *beach*. They'd make them look like ice-cream stalls or beach huts there. But they're afraid the Germans might fly in, see, not just come by sea, so these pillbox things are out in the fields as well. And there's a golf course nearby, all messed up with old cars and stuff, in case they try to land gliders—'

'I don't think you ought to be talking about all this,' Jo

interrupted again. 'You don't know who might be listening. You know what all the notices say.'

'Well, it's common knowledge, isn't it? Everybody knows what's going on.'

'We still don't have to talk about it,' Irene Bond butted in. She had been waiting impatiently to collect a cake in a box for one of her customers. '*We* might know all about it, but someone who'd only just got here from Germany wouldn't. That's just the sort of thing they're listening out for.' She frowned at Jean. '*Careless Talk Costs Lives.*'

The girl flushed. 'I was only passing a remark.'

'Well, don't. You're here to work, not pass remarks – especially with Nippies who ought to be getting on with their own work.' Irene picked up her cake, gave Jo a withering look and stalked away. Jo and the Sally looked at each other and made a face.

'Bossy cow,' Jean said. 'Anyone'd think she was a manageress already.'

'That's what she wants to be,' Jo said. 'I just hope I'm not working here when she is. All the same, Jean, she's right – we didn't ought to be talking about things like that.'

She went back to her tables. The defiant spirit of Dunkirk which had carried them all through those days and nights when they had worked so hard at Addison Road, handing out buns, pies and mugs of tea to the returning soldiers, had stiffened everyone's resolve not to be beaten. It was queer when you thought about it – they *had* been beaten at Dunkirk, they'd been driven out of France, chased into the sea itself and harried across the Channel, yet in some strange way it had become a triumph rather than a defeat.

It was like when our Alice refused to be evacuated without Robbie, she thought. She didn't exactly win, because she lost Robbie and then got lost herself – but we were all so pleased to see her when she came back that she got her own way after all, and now most of the other kids have come home, too. It's a bit like that. We've been chased away and now there's every chance the Germans will invade us as well, but we're damned if we're going to let them. Not without a jolly good fight, anyway. We'll fight them on the beaches, we'll fight in the fields, in the streets and in the hills . . . we'll never surrender.

She glanced out of the window at the London street and tried to imagine German tanks rumbling down the road and German soldiers goose-stepping into London as they had goose-stepped into Paris, and she felt a surge of anger within her. He's right, she thought. Mr Churchill's right. We won't give in – just like our Alice wouldn't give in – and just when they think we're beaten, we'll turn round and give 'em the biggest surprise they've ever had in their lives.

Alf Woods was restless and anxious. He stared at his meal as if he'd never seen such food in his life, and pushed his plate away still half-full. Shirley gazed at him in consternation.

'What's the matter, Dad? You're not sickening for something, are you?' She'd been hoping that now the plaster was off his arm he'd pick up a bit, but he still seemed low-spirited and miserable. Not that you could blame him, but he'd always been one for getting on with things, not sitting about and brooding.

Alf sighed. 'No, I don't reckon so, Shirley, love. Tell you the truth, I'm just fed up with being here on me own. Oh, I know you do your best, girl, but it's your mother, see.' His face screwed up as if he were about to cry and he said in a choking voice, 'I miss her, Shirl, I miss her something awful.'

'Dad.' Shirley got up quickly and went round the table to put her arms round his neck. 'Oh, Dad. I know. It's so quiet here without her and our Jack. But, honestly, they're in the best place. They're safe in Wales with Owen's uncle and auntie. Even if there's an invasion—'

'I know that. I'm not saying they should come back. It's

135

not safe enough, 'specially for Jack. It's just that I miss them. And when she couldn't get home because of the weather and all when I had that accident – and then at Easter our Jack was poorly . . .' He looked at her piteously. 'Well, it just seems to go on and on. We'd never bin apart a single night since we were married, till all this started. I don't seem to know how to go on without your mother.'

Shirley hugged him wordlessly. After a few moments she said, 'Why not go and see them? You could get a few days off work for that, couldn't you?'

'I dunno. I don't think so. She'd have to be ill or something.'

'Why ask? Perhaps I could come, too. And Owen. We could all go together, have a family reunion.'

'All the way to Wales?' He looked doubtful and Shirley went back to her chair and smiled.

'Well, there wouldn't be much point in only going halfway, would there? Look, Dad, if it's the fare I've got a bit saved up. There hasn't been much to spend money on just lately. I'm sure we could manage.' Her eyes sparkled suddenly. 'It must be lovely there at this time of year! Let's try, Dad. Let's see if we can both get a few days' holiday and I'll ask Owen, too.'

'Well . . . I did put in for some days in July. You know we usually have a few days at Southend then. It's my regular time and I never altered it, but I'm not sure they'd let me have it now, what with the war and everything.'

'I bet they would, when they know what it's for. They're trying to let people have time to see their families. Come to think of it, I think I'm down for that week, too – I'd forgotten all about that.' Shirley gave a little jump of excitement. 'Let's do it, Dad! Let's go to Wales and see Mum and our Jack.'

Alf was still looking doubtful. 'You know what they say. *Is Your Journey Really Necessary?* We're not supposed to be cavorting about all over the country without good reason.'

136

'Well, this *is* good reason. And it *is* necessary – just as necessary as soldiers going on leave. It's months since we saw them. Families have to stick together – isn't that what this war's all about?'

Alf didn't quite follow her reasoning, but he felt dimly that there was some logic in what she was saying. Anyway, you didn't really expect to follow a woman's reasoning, did you? And the idea of seeing his wife again, even if she wasn't coming back home with him, was too appealing to reject. He made up his mind to see about his holiday tomorrow.

'Perhaps you could find out about the trains in your lunch hour,' he said. 'See what the times are and how much it'd be and all that. I must say, it'd do us a power of good to get out in the countryside for a couple of days.'

The next day was a busy one for Shirley. She did as he'd asked and went to Euston railway station to find out about trains, and straight after work she went to Cadby Hall to catch Owen as he came out. He looked surprised to see her and caught her in his arms.

'Shirley, *cariad*! What's wrong? Is it your da', or have you had bad news from the farm?'

'Nothing's wrong,' she laughed, kissing him. 'It's just that me and Dad have decided to go and see Mum and Jack and we want you to come, too!'

He stared at her. 'Go to the farm? To Wales? When?'

'Well, we've both got our holidays booked for the week after next, and Mr Carter says it'll be all right for me to go. I'll find out about Dad tonight. But what about you? Could you get off?'

'I might be able to.' He thought for a moment. 'We're short-staffed, of course, but we always are these days. I'll try anyway.' He caught her about the waist again and whirled her off her feet. '*Cariad*, it's a marvellous idea! I wonder if I could get Mam and Dad to come as well. They haven't been home since before the war. It'd do them so much good.'

'That's what I thought about Dad. He's missing Mum so much, it's really getting him down. She wanted to come back when everything went quiet, you know, but the weather was so awful and then things started getting bad again – and then they started to talk about invasion . . . It's Jack really, she won't take any chances with him.' They walked quickly along the street, Shirley chattering nineteen to the dozen in her excitement. 'Owen, it'll be so lovely. All of us going off on holiday together, and seeing all the others at the same time. Your Auntie Mair and Uncle Dafydd . . . And the farm. Mum says it's beautiful now and Jack loves it, he knows all the lambs by their own names—'

'Their own *names*?' Owen broke in. 'Lambs don't have their own names!'

'These do. Jack knows all the nursery rhymes and fairy-tales and he's given them all names. There's Boy Blue and Bo-Peep and Marymaryquitecontrary and Cinderella, and Mum says he really does know them all. And she says they know him!'

'They probably do. Sheep are very intelligent creatures,' Owen said.

Shirley gave him a disbelieving glance. 'Anyway, he'll love showing it all off to us. You know,' she said thoughtfully, 'I don't think we're going to find it very easy to get him back home when the war ends. He's turning into a real farmer's boy.'

For once, everything went as planned. Timetables were consulted and train tickets bought. Letters were written and telegrams sent. Owen's father shook his head and said he wasn't up to the journey, but his mother decided to come and the little party set off in great style, their shopping bags bulging with sandwiches and buns and their clothes packed into suitcases borrowed from neighbours.

The journey took almost an entire day. The train mean-dered through the countryside, stopping at tiny stations or sometimes in the middle of nowhere and waiting for what seemed like hours, for no apparent reason. Sometimes an express train would thunder past them filled with soldiers, sometimes nothing at all would happen and the engine would finally heave a great sigh, as if wondering itself what the delay had been, and set off again with an air of resignation. It was a beautiful summer's day and the countryside looked as if it were in the middle of a deep and slumbrous dream. Now and then you could see people working in the fields, or the train would pass through a village and people standing in gardens unpegging washing or digging their vegetable plots would pause and wave. Sometimes a crowd of children playing in a school yard would cheer as if the train were carrying heroes back from the war. Sometimes there was nothing to be seen but cattle, up to their knees in deep green grass or cooling themselves under a spreading oak tree.

'You wouldn't think there was a war on at all,' Owen's mother said, gazing out. 'It all looks so peaceful.'

'That's how it ought to look,' Alf said. 'No guns and shelters, no barrage balloons or sandbags . . . That's how life ought to be. And it'll be like it again, once we've given Hitler a bloody nose,' he added forcibly. 'That's what our boys are fighting for and we all ought to come out and see it now and then, just so we remember.'

Shirley smiled. He was sounding more like his old self already. Even the thought of being with his Annie again was doing him good.

They reached the farm late that evening. Dafydd came and fetched them in his rattling old van and took them on the hair-raising drive up the twisting mountain track. They left behind the village, with its narrow streets grimed with coal dust and its towering slag-heaps, and climbed high up the valley to a softer, greener landscape. Here, sheltered on every side by the towering sides of the rocky hills, they stopped at last in the little secret hollow where Dafydd and Mair had their farm.

'Oh, Owen,' Shirley said, clambering stiffly from the van, 'it's even more beautiful than I remembered.'

She stood for a moment breathing in the fresh, cool air. The yard was as she had seen it last autumn, but greener and fresher. The gold and brown of September had been blown away and replaced by lush grass and leaves. The little stream still ran down the side of the yard into the pond, and as she watched a little family of half-grown ducklings scrambled out of the water and came waddling towards them.

The farmhouse was covered in honeysuckle, its scent drifting towards them on the breeze. And as Shirley took in her second deep breath the door opened suddenly and her brother Jack tumbled out and came running towards her, his flat, round face beaming, his slanted eyes dancing with pleasure.

'*Shirley*. It's my *Shirley*.' He flung his arms around her and hugged her tightly, and she hugged him back, wondering how she had ever managed without him all these months. She felt the tears spring hot to her eyes and her deep breath of pleasure turned into a sudden gasping sob.

And then her mother was there, too, flinging herself into her husband's arms, laughing and crying all at once, breaking away to hug Shirley close and then drawing them all into her embrace. They stretched their arms about each other, their tears mingling on their cheeks, and anyone would have thought, as Owen remarked a few minutes later, that it was a funeral they'd come for, not a reunion.

'No, they wouldn't,' Shirley said, treading on his toe to teach him a lesson. 'You haven't seen us in action yet. We can cry a *lot* more than that at funerals.'

There was a tiny silence. Then Owen's Aunt Mair said in her lilting voice, which always sounded as if she were about to break into song, 'Well, let's go indoors, shall we? I've got the tea brewing and there's a nice piece of bara brith to go with it. No use standing out here and letting it all go cold, now, is it?'

The funniest thing was discovering that Jack had begun to acquire a Welsh accent.

It was only slight, and he'd always had a sing-song kind of voice anyway, but Shirley and her father noticed it immediately. Annie looked put out when they remarked on it.

'He never has. *I* don't notice anything different.'

'Well, you wouldn't,' Shirley said. 'You're with him all the time and you hear Welsh accents every day. But he has, Mum, honest. It's quite nice, really.'

'I don't know about that. Jack's a Cockney, he shouldn't be talking Welsh. No offence to you, Mair and Dafydd, but I don't hold with people changing their accents, they're part of what we're brought up to.'

'I reckon there'll be a lot of youngsters going home with different ways of talking when this war's over,' her husband said. 'And not only talking. They're being brought up in a different way altogether. Look at our Jack, now, going out to feed chickens and cows as if he was born to it. How's he ever going to settle in a London street again?'

'He can do more than feed them,' Dafydd said proudly. 'He can milk them, too. The cows, I mean,' he added, in case these city-dwellers might misunderstand. 'Not the chickens, you know!'

They all laughed but Alf looked alarmed. 'My Jack, milking cows? He won't get hurt, will he, with those horns?'

'No, no,' Dafydd assured him. 'Love him, they do, and he loves them. Gentle as a lamb, he is, see. And cows are docile creatures, unless you get between them and their calf and then they're worse than a bull. But we'd never let any harm come to our Jack.'

Our Jack. They all looked at him. Shirley saw her father flush a deep red. He glanced at his wife and she caught a brief glimpse of his feelings in the look. He's afraid he's going to lose them, she thought. Jack, settling down as a farmer's boy and Mum looking so well and happy. He's afraid they won't want to come back.

Annie was certainly looking much better than when they had first arrived here. Her thin cheeks had filled out and she seemed to have lost the cough that had almost crippled her in London. Funny, really, that the Welsh air should have improved her health whereas poor Rhys Prosser, Owen's father, had lived here all his life and got that terrible lung disease that was slowly killing him. But that was from going down the mines, of course, not from living and working up here in the clean air above the dust-ridden valleys.

After supper, they went out and looked around the farm. It was poor enough, with the harsh winter weather and the thin soil making crop-growing almost impossible, but there was plenty of grazing for the sheep and the half-dozen cows that were kept to supply the farm and a few neighbours with milk. There were a couple of goats, too, who came trustingly up to Jack and butted him gently with their hard little heads, and the chickens who filled the yard with their soft clucking and occasional fierce squawk as they scuffled over a scrap of food. But the lambs were obviously Jack's delight. He took his father and sister to a nearby gate and uttered an odd, bleating little call, and at once a dozen lambs tore across the field towards him and jostled for his attention. He turned, beaming with pride, and Alf's face softened.

'You'd think he'd been on a farm all his life. I hope he's not a trouble to you.'

'Trouble?' Dafydd said. 'Why, he's the best little farm-hand I've ever had! Do anything, he will, never a sour look or a grumbling word, and you can see the animals love him. He's got a real way with them.'

Alf nodded and turned to watch again as the lambs suddenly broke away from the gate and galloped off across the field again. They reached a large boulder and leapt on

142

top of it, one by one, before turning to hurtle back across the pasture. The onlookers laughed.

'They're racing!' Shirley exclaimed, and Jack nodded at her, his slanted eyes crinkled with delight.

'They like racing. They always race after supper.'

'That's right, they do,' Owen said. 'They seem to want to play then. Look at them, jumping on that rock, playing King of the Castle.'

They watched the lambs for almost half an hour, then wandered back to the house. Although it was the beginning of July, it was cool up here in the mountains as evening approached, but the farmhouse kitchen was warmed by the big iron range and Mair moved the kettle over to the hottest part so that it would soon boil. She made them all cocoa and they sat around the big table nibbling home-made biscuits and Welsh cakes.

Alf sat beside his wife. Tonight, he was to share the room she slept in, with the window open to the evening air and the scent of honeysuckle, the only sounds those of the chuckling stream and the lambs and the cows. It seemed to be a different world from the anxious, hurrying streets of London, with the barrage balloons floating above and the constant fear of invasion. It was impossible to imagine such a thing here, in this quiet place.

'I'm glad you're here,' he said to her under cover of the general chatter. 'I've been missing you something awful, but I'm glad you're here, you and our Jack. I just hope – I hope you're going to want to come back home when it's all over.'

Annie looked at him. She heard the plea in his voice and recognised the fear in his eyes. She knew now that the accident had been more serious than she'd been led to believe, and that he hadn't recovered as well as he should have – and she'd have a few words to say to both him and Shirley about that, for if she'd known the truth she'd have been on the first train back to London, snow or no snow –

but for tonight she was just thankful that they were all together again. All, that was, except for Donald, and she sighed at the thought of her son in the army. Then, determined not to let anything spoil this evening, she smiled and put her hand over his.

'Of course I will, Alf. It's lovely here and the Prossers are really kind, and it's good to have Jack safe if anything does happen, but it isn't *home*. Home's where you are, you and our Shirley. And that's where we'll be, all together – even if we do have to get our Jack a cow of his own to keep in the back yard!'

The short holiday did them all good. Alf, who had been unable to go when Annie and Jack had first gone to Wales, was comforted by the warmth of the welcome he had received in the farmhouse and he got on well with Dafydd, even though he could only understand one word in ten that the Welshman spoke. The two men trudged about the mountainside with Jack at their heels like an eager puppy, inspecting the sheep and the skipping lambs, doing repairs that had been waiting during the severe winter and sawing logs for next year. You did something every day for next winter, Dafydd said, and then you wouldn't be caught napping, see.

Annie had her own tasks to do, too, but she and Alf managed to find plenty of spare moments to spend together and it was almost like a new courtship, or maybe a second honeymoon, as they wandered the paths in the sunshine or sat together on the old bench before the farmhouse door, watching the sun set. Sometimes they would catch a glimpse of Shirley and Owen slipping through the fields to the little patch of woodland they had chosen as their own special place. Above them, the sky was bubbling with the long, whistling call of the curlew, or the sweet, high song of a lark, and from indoors came the strains of Jack's mouth organ, playing some of the Welsh tunes he had learned – 'Bread of Heaven', 'Myfanwy' and 'Land of My Fathers'.

'It's like a little bit of heaven here,' Alf said quietly. 'You'll never want to come home again.'

Annie felt for his hand. 'I will, Alf. I will. As long as you're in London, that's where I'll want to be.' She smiled and then said, 'Remember that song we used to sing? "I'll see you again, Whenever spring breaks through again . . ." Well, that's a promise from me to you. I'll be coming home, but I won't necessarily wait till next spring to do it. It'll be just the first moment it's safe for our Jack.'

She glanced down the field to where Owen and Shirley were strolling up the meadow towards them. 'I'm not so sure about our Shirley, mind. She and Owen look so settled here, and so free. I wouldn't be surprised if they wanted to come back here when it's all over.'

They were silent for a moment, then Alf squeezed her hand and said, 'Well, we can't stand in our children's way, not once they're grown up. And it'll be good to have somewhere like this to come when we want a bit of a holiday, won't it? Better than Southend!'

'Oh, yes,' she said with a smile, 'much better than Southend.'

Shirley and Owen, far below, looked up and saw them there and waved. Owen grinned and said, 'They look as if they've been put there as ornaments, like.'

'They're enjoying it,' Shirley said. 'I'm really glad we came, Owen. It's so beautiful and so peaceful.'

'It is up here. Not down in the valleys, though.' He frowned. 'You saw what it was like when we drove through the villages. All grey and gloomy, and full of coal dust. I wouldn't ever want to go back to that, Shirley, *cariad*.'

'No. That would be awful.' Shirley thought of Owen's father, crippled by the disease of the coal dust that had got into his lungs. 'I should hate that to happen to you.'

'Well, it's not likely to,' he said, and drew her into the shadow of a tree, out of sight of the farmhouse. 'Once this war's over, *cariad*, we're going to have a good life together, you and me. And it won't be in the valleys.'

Maggie came back to work at the beginning of July. She was still pale and had lost weight, so that her uniform had to be taken in, and her smile was less saucy than before, but she was determined not to let her loss interfere with her work. 'People come into Corner Houses to see cheerful faces, not miserable ones,' she had told Etty. 'There's plenty had just as bad a time as me, and plenty more got it to come. At least I know it's over as far as I'm concerned,' she had added sadly. Then she had tightened her shoulders and given Etty a severe look. 'If you hears me being sorry for myself, you just give me a smack, all right? And I don't want nobody treating me like a china doll, or going on about how sorry they are about Tom or — or about the baby, see? It'll just start me off, and I don't want to be started off.'

Etty had passed the message on and Maggie came back to work to find everyone behaving as if she had never been away. It wasn't easy at first, and the atmosphere was a little strained, but once they were all busy, dashing about with their trays held above their heads, they stopped worrying about it. Maggie herself did her best to be her old ebullient self, cracking jokes with the customers and flirting with the servicemen, and although nobody forgot what had happened to her they were able to put it behind them — perhaps, as she said, because equally bad things were happening to so many people now, and because the fear of invasion left little room for other worries.

'You'll have to come and eat at the Corner House every day now,' she told one couple who came in regularly once a week. 'You won't have nothing to cook with at home. My mum's giving all her saucepans to the Spitfire Appeal.'

The man grinned. 'Mr Eden didn't say *all* our pots and pans. We got to have something to make Lord Woolton's recipes in. And they've already had all our railings and iron fences.'

'That was for ships,' Maggie said. 'They wants aluminium now, for aeroplanes. One of our Nippies' boys is a pilot so we're saving as much as we can for him. Anyway, have you decided yet what you're having?'

'Poached eggs,' the woman said at once. 'It's a treat to have an egg these days, we can't spare them at home. You've got to make them go as far as you can.'

Half a dozen soldiers came in and sat at the last vacant table in Maggie's station. She saw them when she came out of the kitchen, and hesitated. Determined though she was not to let her tragedy affect her work, the sight of the little group caught at her heart. Spruce and smart, their hair gleaming and buttons polished, they looked so like her Tommy and his mates just before they'd gone off to war. And so unlike Mike and the others when they'd come back, without Tom – dirty and bedraggled, their uniforms caked with dried salt and mud, their faces grimy and eyes bewildered. I can't do it, she thought, I can't go and talk to them just like nothing's happened . . .

'D'you want me to serve them?' Phyl asked quietly, just behind her.

Maggie turned. Only Phyl truly understood, she thought, and shook her head.

'No. I got to do it. It's not their fault. They've never even been away yet by the look of them, poor blighters. Look at 'em – not a clue what it's all about. Think they'll just go over and kick Hitler's backside for him. I tell you what, Phyl, it's up to us to give 'em something to remember, something worth fighting for.'

She walked over to the young men, her head high and a broad smile on her lips. They watched her with admiration and nudged each other.

'Looks like our lucky day, lads,' one of them said. He was big and broad, with dark, curly hair and full red lips.

'Didn't know they were getting film stars to wait on us these days.'

'You can cut your cheek,' Maggie told him severely. 'I'm a Nippy, and Nippies are respectable girls, so you needn't think you can try any funny stuff here.'

The dark-haired boy pouted and the others laughed. 'You come to the wrong shop, Andy. She's not going to fall for your charms.'

'Don't you be too sure.' He gave Maggie a dazzling smile. 'Did I say anything about you not being respectable? I wouldn't have bothered speaking to you if I'd thought you weren't.'

At this, the others whooped. Maggie could hardly bear it. Tommy and his mates had behaved in just the same way when they'd first come into the Corner House. But, then, so did most young men, and if she couldn't take it she'd have to give up, and to give up being a Nippy was something she just wouldn't do. She gave the young soldier a haughty look.

'It's none of your business whether I'm respectable or not. All you got to do is tell me what you want—' she ignored the inevitable crow of laughter '—and as long as it's on our menu I'll get it for you. Don't forget it's against the law now to have more than one course with protein in. And don't take all night making up your minds because there's a queue out the door halfway down Oxford Street and plenty of other people out there wanting to eat, if you don't.'

'Do as you're told, Andy,' one of the others said. He had ginger hair and freckles and a ready grin. 'It'll be good practice for when the sergeant gets us back in barracks.'

They looked at the menu and Maggie watched them, her heart filled with pity. They were so young – young like Tommy had been when he first went away – and full of laughter and jokes and excitement at the adventure that lay ahead. She wondered if they would come back as he had done that first time, sobered by what he had seen, the shine of his youth dimmed. She wondered if they would come back at all.

They made up their minds what they wanted and turned their faces towards her again, and in that moment she was struck by an emotion that was more powerful than pity, deeper than sadness. You poor, poor loves, she thought, and she wanted to take them all in her arms and hug them to her and give them whatever comfort she could. She wanted, as she had said to Phyl, to give them something to remember – something to fight for.

'So that's egg and chips three times, sausage and chips twice and one cottage pie,' she said. 'And tea all round. Right, boys, it'll be with you as soon as I can get the kitchen staff to cook it.' She gave them all a stern glare. 'And just you behave yourselves while I'm gone, see? No getting off with any of the other Nippies.'

'No chance,' the dark boy said, flashing his smile at her again. 'We're going to wait for you – aren't we, lads?'

Maggie made her way back to the kitchen and stood in the queue that formed permanently along the serving counter. She felt a little sick and shaky inside. Looking at the soldiers, as new and shiny as if they'd just been taken out of a box, she'd felt as though she could see into the future – a dark, unhappy future. What was going to happen to them – where would they be in a few months' time, a few weeks? Would they even be alive?

'So what did you lot do in civvy street?' she enquired carelessly when she returned to the table with a tray full of food. 'If anything!'

'We all had jobs,' Andy told her indignantly. 'What d'you think we are, layabouts? I was a motor mechanic, and my brother here, Ted, he was a dockie. Gordon, that's the one with the ginger hair, he delivered coal and Mick was a bus driver. And Tom and Len—'

'*Tom?*' The name broke out of Maggie as sharply as if she had been slapped. She stared across the table at the young soldier. He was thin and dark, with a sallow skin and olive eyes. He looked a bit foreign – Spanish or Italian, perhaps. But Italy was in the war now, they were enemies on Germany's side, so he couldn't be Italian or he'd have been interned. The thoughts jumbled confusedly in her head. 'You don't look like Tommy,' she said blankly, and could have bitten off her tongue. 'No – I don't mean that – it's just that I know – *knew* – someone called Tom.' She bent her head, fighting the sudden tears, and fumbled with the plates.

The young men were silent for a moment. Then Andy said, quite quietly, 'We don't think he looks much like a Tom either. More like a Twerp. Or a Dope. Don't we?'

The olive-skinned boy grinned awkwardly. 'They call me that all the time,' he told Maggie, and she gave him a tremulous smile and straightened up

'Eat it while it's hot,' she told them, and turned swiftly away, unable to look at any of them again. But she could feel their eyes on her as she hurried to the next table to clear away used plates and cups.

I don't know if I can stand this, she thought, taking advantage of a moment's quiet to lean her head on the wall in the kitchen, out of sight of the customers. Seeing these boys, knowing half of them are going off to be killed or wounded . . . remembering Tommy. I don't know if I can manage.

Phyl was beside her again. 'You all right, Mag?'

Maggie opened her eyes and looked at her. 'I dunno. It's harder than I thought it'd be, Phyl.'

'I know. I keep looking at them, too, and thinking – wondering . . .' They stood silent for a few seconds, and then Phyl went on more briskly, 'But we can't give in, can we? Every little thing we give in to's another bit of victory for Hitler. And I for one don't mean to let him have any at all. I don't reckon you do either.'

Maggie didn't answer immediately. Then she looked

150

Phyl in the eye and her voice was stronger as she said slowly, 'No, I don't. It'd feel wrong – a sort of betrayal of what my Tommy did. I can't do that, Phyl.' She straightened up and glanced about her at the busy kitchen. 'I tell you what I think. We got to do as much as we can for these poor blighters. As much as we flipping well can.'

Bill Mason, Stan Jennings and Sam Pratt all joined the Home Guard. There were over a million members, mostly men who were too old or perhaps too young to be called up. Their job was to be ready to resist an invasion, whether it came by sea or air. Those around the coast felt important because they would be in the front line if attack came from the sea, and those near airfields or open countryside were convinced that they would soon have to deal with huge numbers of armed parachutists.

Londoners took Mr Churchill's words 'we shall fight them in the streets' as their motto. Some of the schoolboys who had not been evacuated formed themselves into little gangs and marched up and down, saluting and parading, staging mock battles in and out of the alleyways.

The girls were all to be firewatchers on the roof of the Corner House, ready to put out incendiary bombs if they landed. Instead of learning how to treat their customers, they were taught to handle fire extinguishers and sandbags.

'Won't you be too scared?' Etty asked rather timidly, lugging a bucket of sand across to where Mr Carter was demonstrating with a small fire made out of paper and a few sticks. Shirley took the shovel and threw sand on the fire, which promptly and obediently went out. 'I mean, the fires are going to be a lot bigger than that, aren't they?'

'You won't have time to be frightened.' Mr Carter looked kindly at the two girls. Etty was as thin as a reed and really didn't look strong, despite the fact that he knew she could carry heavy trays in the restaurant. And Shirley, too, was slim and dainty-looking. It didn't seem right that they were going to have to do men's work, fighting fires in the midst of a lot of bombing which nobody could yet really imagine. But there was nothing else for it. Many of the younger men at Lyons had already left to join up, and the girls were just having to move over into their jobs, both at work and in preparation for the invasion.

The weeks wore on. It was hard to stay defiant when there didn't seem to be anything to defy. People began to wonder if they could really resist an invasion after all. The barbed wire that now surrounded the coastline seemed a feeble barrier against determined troops and tanks. Worst of all, the Government announced a new evacuation scheme for children. They were now to be sent, not to the country-side of England and Wales but overseas. To Canada, to South Africa, to Australia or New Zealand, and even to America.

'That's awful,' Carrie said. 'They must think nowhere in England's going to be safe.'

'They're sending a hundred thousand to America alone,' Bill said, reading the newspaper. 'A hundred thousand! They don't do that sort of thing for nothing, Carrie.'

They stared at each other in consternation.

'What are we going to do about our Alice?'

There was a short silence. Bill stared down at his newspaper, then folded it neatly and sighed. He looked at her again.

'I dunno, love. I just dunno. What do you think?'

'She'll never go willingly.'

'We had all that bother last time,' he said with a touch of irritation. 'That girl expects her own way far too much. If things are going to get as bad as they say they will, she'll have to do what we decide's best for her. There'll be no running off, and no fuss about that cat.'

Robertson, who seemed to know the word 'cat', stopped washing his back leg and looked up warily, his foot stuck in the air. His green eyes regarded Bill steadily.

'Look at that,' Carrie said, diverted despite her worry. 'He knows we're talking about him.'

'We're *not* talking about him,' Bill said impatiently. 'You're as bad as our Alice is. Sometimes I wish I'd never brought him home for her.'

'You don't mean that, Bill. You know how much she thinks of him.'

'We all know how much she thinks of him, and that's half the trouble in this house. She thinks everything ought to revolve around him. Well, you know I'd never do him any harm and I wouldn't have him put to sleep at the beginning of the war like they said we ought to, but I can't let him rule the roost. If we decide our Alice has got to be evacuated, then evacuated she'll be and that cat will stop here with us. She ought to know we'll take care of him.'

'So are we going to see about this American business?' Carrie asked. 'Honestly, Bill, I don't like the idea of her going off so far. I mean, when they went to the countryside you could at least go and visit them once in a while. If she went to America we might not see her again for years.' Her lips trembled as she thought about it. 'If the Germans invade, we might never see her again.'

'I know. It's a hard one. But look at it this way, Carrie, at least she'd have a decent life. She wouldn't be living under the jackboot like we might be.'

'Oh, Bill,' Carrie said, the tears brimming over and running down her cheeks, 'what's going wrong with the world? What's happened to let it come to this? We used to have such a nice life, even if we never had much money. I don't reckon we knew how lucky we were.'

'Well, we know now,' he said heavily. He lifted the folded newspaper and beat it against his knee. 'I dunno, Carrie. It's not something we can make up our minds about all at once. It wants thinking about.'

He thought about it for perhaps a little too long, for only a few weeks later it was announced that the French fleet had been scuttled to prevent it falling into German hands. Convoys were now needed for the merchant ships bringing in desperately needed supplies, and only those children whose passage had been booked by parents who could afford to pay their own fares were able to go to the dominions and America.

'It's not fair,' Carrie complained, forgetting that she hadn't wanted to send Alice at all. 'It's always those who got money who can get the privileges. It says here that they paid so that poorer kiddies could have the free places – but they're the ones what're going, aren't they? And now our Alice isn't going to have a chance.'

'Don't get yourself all upset, lovey. They'll get it going again. Anyway, I'm not sure those ships are all that safe, with all the U-boats prowling about under the sea and letting off torpedoes.' Bill put his arm around his wife's shoulders. 'We'll look after Alice ourselves. We'll send her to the country, like we should have done in the first place.'

'I don't know what to do, and that's the top and bottom of it.' Carrie leant her head against his shoulder. 'I'm worn out just thinking about it all. And nothing's really happened yet! What's it going to be like when they do start bombing us, or invading? How on earth are we going to manage, Bill?'

Maggie threw herself into anything to do with the war. She would do anything, from firewatching to fighting, and declared that any German who dared land on the Corner House roof would have her to reckon with. 'He'll find himself decorating the pavement before he can say Jack Robinson,' she said pugnaciously.

'I don't think Germans do say Jack Robinson,' Shirley observed solemnly. 'They probably say something like Hans Schmidt instead.'

'Or Hans Up,' Jo said with a grin. 'No, that's what we'll

be saying to them. Like on that daft poster we saw, with the German for things like "Hand over your weapons. Left march!"' She put on a mock German accent. '"Your veapons or your life!"'

'I shan't be bothering with conversation,' Maggie said grimly. 'And they won't get no choice neither. One hard push, that's what they'll get, and look out down below.'

She grieved for Tommy every night, and for their lost baby, too. She lay awake, longing for his arms about her, thinking of the times they had been together in Hyde Park, nestled amongst the bushes. I'm glad we did that, she thought, I'm glad we went together before we got married. I'd have precious little to remember now if we hadn't. And he'd have had hardly anything before he died – just that once on our wedding day, and those few days in February. Poor Tom.

She thought of those other boys who had come into the restaurant, so bright and polished, looking forward to fighting for their country. She hoped they were making the most of their last days and nights in England. It was all wrong that young blokes like that should have to go away without even knowing what it was like to go with a girl, without having felt soft arms around them and soft lips pressed to theirs. They ought to have something to look back on, something to keep them going through the fighting, something to look forward to when they came back.

If they came back.

Maggie turned over and thumped her pillow as hard as if it were the German she had threatened to push off the roof. She couldn't bear to think of it. All those bright young men, their smart uniforms torn and muddy, crawling through mud, dodging and hiding in ruined buildings, shooting and being shot at . . . dying in a strange land, hundreds of miles from their homes.

All those boys, just like her Tommy. All with Tommy's face, staring back at her, turning to reach out for her, longing to hold her in their arms and to know what love could be.

Phyl, too, lay awake at night. But she was worrying rather than grieving, for Mike was still alive and still safe enough in barracks on the south coast, awaiting the next operation of the war. If the Germans invaded, there would be plenty of fighting to do at home; if they didn't, presumably the army would be sent overseas again to defeat them abroad.

She was also wondering whether to join up herself. There were notices everywhere exhorting women to join the ATS, the WRNS or the WAAFs. Army, navy or air force – there was a women's branch for each of the services. There was even, as Jo pointed out a shade indignantly whenever she thought it had been forgotten, the Women's Land Army for those who wanted to serve their country with spades and forks rather than guns.

'You don't even have to join up,' she said as they discussed it far into the night. 'There's plenty of jobs for girls now that the men are going. Driving buses or lorries – maybe even trains – or working in munitions. Nick says some women are even being trained as pilots, to transport planes.'

'Why do planes need transporting?'

'Well, when they're built they've got to get from the factory to the airfields, haven't they? Or maybe they need more in the south and they're all up north. All sorts of reasons. Anyway, he says there's a lot of people against it, they say the women are being used just for publicity and they're taking the jobs away from real pilots.'

'But they *are* real pilots!'

'Men, he means. Mind you, Nick doesn't agree with that – he says the men need to be ready for real action, they shouldn't be used as delivery boys.'

'People will grumble at anything,' Phyl said. 'I heard a bloke going on at a clippie on the bus the other day, saying

156

she was taking a man's job away. She told him the chap she'd replaced had joined the army but he wouldn't have it, said there were plenty over forty who needed jobs and she ought to be at home being a good wife to her own man.'

'Who's probably not there anyway,' Jo said. 'I tell you what, Phyl, it's just a muddle and all we can do is what seems right to us at the time. And if anyone else doesn't like it, well, they can just lump it, that's all.'

'Trouble is, I don't know what is right. They're crying out for girls in the forces one minute, then saying they've got enough the next. They've stopped recruiting for the Wrens now, you know. And Maggie reckons we're doing good war work by staying as Nippies – she says the people who come in need to see a happy face, and it's as important as anything else we could be doing. Maybe she's right.'

'I dunno. I'm a bit worried about Maggie, to tell you the truth. She's a bit *too* bright and cheerful. It doesn't seem natural, after what she's been through.'

Phyl was silent for a moment. Then she said quietly, 'I reckon it's the only way she can manage, Jo. It's the only way she can get through the days.'

Chapter Nine

Shirley let herself into the house and put the kettle on. A quick cup of tea, and then she'd have to start getting Dad's dinner ready. He'd be in at seven, and she wanted him to come in to a table with a good meal on it.

No – that wasn't all he wanted. What he really wanted was to have his wife waiting for him with a meal she'd cooked herself, and his son Jack beaming like a six-year-old, thrilled to have his daddy back home again.

At first, Shirley had thought the holiday in Wales had done her father good. He'd seemed just like his old self at the farm, wandering the meadows and lanes with his wife at his side. But on the day that he and Shirley had left, he had looked white and drawn, and he had grown more and more silent as the train had taken them further away from the valleys. When Shirley had tried to comfort him, he'd shaken her off and she'd sat back in her corner, watching him with anxious eyes. Perhaps he would cheer up once he got back home, she'd thought, amongst his own things.

But he hadn't. He'd seemed to withdraw into himself, going silently about his tasks at home, speaking only when spoken to, and sitting in his armchair of an evening, the newspaper open but unread on his lap. Shirley tried to interest him in the wireless, in the records he used to enjoy playing on the gramophone, in the doings at the Corner House. She suggested a game of cards or dominoes. He simply shook his head. Nothing, it seemed, would shake him out of his apathy.

He'd even started to lose interest in his food. The last

three nights, he'd pushed away his meal only half-eaten. Shirley was almost at her wits' end. At this rate he would be ill again, and although the strange episodes when he lost concentration and complained of an odd smell were growing fewer they still worried her.

Tonight, she'd managed to get a bit of liver, which she was going to fry with a rasher of bacon and some onions to pep it up a bit. She mashed some potatoes and then poured some boiling water into the frying-pan with the cooked liver and bacon, and crumbled an Oxo cube in it. It was simmering when her father came in, spot on time.

'That smells tasty,' he said, coming into the kitchen and sitting down to take off his boots. 'Liver and bacon, eh? One of my favourites.'

Shirley looked at him, surprised. He sounded almost cheerful.

'I know, Dad. I was lucky to get it.' She dished it out while he washed at the kitchen sink. 'Come and eat it while it's hot.'

They sat down together. The wireless was on, playing a selection of ballads. Alf Woods gave her a rueful smile.

'That's your mum's favourite, that what they're playing now. "I'll see you again, Whenever spring breaks through again . . ." She always liked it.' He ate silently for a moment or two, then added quietly, 'I don't half miss our Jack and his mouth-organ.'

'Oh, Dad.' His face was screwed up like a middle-aged baby about to cry. She wished she hadn't put the wireless on. Just when he seemed to be getting a bit brighter, too. 'I know. I miss them, too, and you're right, it wouldn't have mattered a bit if they'd been home all this time. But you know what the Government's saying, we've got to really prepare ourselves for the worst now. The Germans have beaten our chaps once and they're not going to give up. They'll be trying an invasion, and they'll be sending their bombers over. It's really going to start now.'

'Send their bombers over? With the RAF all down the south coast, and all those barrage balloons in the sky? And you know what our Donald said, they got the best part of the BEF out of Dunkirk, and they're all raring to go again. I don't reckon the Germans'll get a sniff of our coast, by sea or air.'

'They already have,' Shirley said quietly. 'You know that. There've been air raids already, over on the east coast. They'll get through to London next. It's going to be bad, and our Mum and Jack are better off where they are. You know it's true.'

Alf sighed heavily and stared at his plate. Then he folded his lips together and nodded. 'I know, girl, I know. I just hope sometimes that if we says it enough we can make it different. I just wish I knew what we done to get into this mess.'

'We stood up for someone weaker than ourselves,' she said, 'just like you used to tell me and Donald to do when we were kids. Dad, your dinner's going cold. Finish it up. It's your favourite, remember?'

'Is it?' He stared at the plate as if he had never seen such a thing before. Then he frowned and sniffed. 'It smells funny. Here, our Shirl, what are you—?' His arms shot out in front of him and he pushed the plate violently across the table. Shirley cried out in shock as it toppled to the floor, scattering liver and bacon and onion everywhere, and then the table itself tilted and there was a loud crash as Alf jerked out of his chair and fell to the floor in a writhing, convulsing heap.

'The doctor said it was an epileptic fit,' Shirley told the others a few days later. Once again she had had to take time off to look after her father on his return from hospital. They hadn't kept him in long this time – there wasn't much they could do for him now, except give him some sort of tablets that were supposed to quieten him down. 'It could happen again, any time.'

'That's awful. Your poor dad. How're you going to manage?'

'I don't know. Mrs Jackson next door said she'd pop in, like she did when he had his arm broken, but I can't expect her to look after him all the time. I don't know how long it'll take him to get better either. The doctor wouldn't say much.'

'People don't get better of epileptic fits,' Irene remarked. 'It goes on all through their lives. Mostly, they end up in an asylum.'

'Irene! That's a horrible thing to say. Shirley's dad's not mad!'

Shirley looked close to tears and Maggie was red with anger. The rest of the girls glared at Irene, who sniffed. 'I'm only saying what's true.'

'It's that knock on the head, that's what the doctor said. And all those other times, when he looked as if he was going to sleep and said there was a funny smell, that was part of it, too. The doctor says he'll be able to tell when he's getting one of these – these turns because he'll get that smell again. So he'll know to get himself somewhere safe.'

'He'll have to carry a cork around with him to put in his mouth,' Irene said. 'I knew someone in our street bit his tongue almost off when he was like that. And they took him off to an asylum in the end,' she finished defiantly.

'You just like upsetting people,' Maggie told her. 'You're a spiteful cat, you are, Irene Bond.'

The other girl tossed her head. 'Only trying to help. Shirley won't thank anyone if her dad bites his tongue off and nobody's told her about the cork.'

'Yes, and it's a pity nobody ever told you to put a cork in *your* mouth.' Maggie turned her back. 'It's a shame your mum can't be there. Couldn't she come back now? There don't seem to be any bombing after all, and if they're going to invade they're taking their time about it.'

'Only because of boys like my Nick,' Jo broke in.

'Fighting in the air to stop 'em. They'd be in like a shot if it wasn't for the air force.'

Nick was in the air every day, flying his Spitfire against German bombers and fighter planes. Dover, situated nearest to the French coast, was subjected to an almost incessant wailing from the banshee sirens, and people were forever having to drop whatever they were doing and run for the shelters. So far, the enemy's missiles had been aimed at shipping, but when they bombed the harbour itself you could feel the buildings tremble and windows were smashed all along the seafront.

'We have to be ready to scramble at any moment,' Nick said when he managed to wangle a rare evening off and came up to London to see Jo. They sat close together on the settee in Mrs Holt's front room. 'It's like a race to see who gets in the air first. Then we go and hunt out the raiders and shoot 'em down, if we can. Some of those German flyers are pretty good – they can make their crates do almost anything in the air. But we're good, too.' He smiled. 'I copped three of 'em last week.'

'You mean you shot them down?'

'That's right. Straight into the drink. Put the flames out a treat.'

He described the fight to her. It had been early one morning, when raiders weren't normally expected. The pilots, torn from their beds by the call to scramble, raced still half-asleep to their planes and climbed into the cockpits, yelling to the flight mechanics to get the crates moving. The men stood at the propellers, giving them a swing to start the engine, and then jumped aside as the planes began to move. Ripping the chocks from beneath the wheels, they ducked out of the way of the blunt-ended wings and watched as the aircraft lifted into the clear sky. Some of them would come back damaged, some unscathed. Some wouldn't come back at all.

Nick loved flying, but when the Spitfire lifted its nose at

the call to scramble, all that was in his mind was the need to find and defeat the enemy. The call meant that German raiders were on their way to bomb London. To bomb his family and friends. To bomb Jo. His mind was clear and cold, and he didn't think of killing another young man such as himself, he thought simply of shooting down an enemy aircraft, a malignant force which would kill his own people if he didn't stop it. The war was a very personal thing to Nick.

That morning they'd encountered the raiders quickly, almost as soon as they'd flown over the Sussex coast. There was a huge cloud of them, flying straight out of the morning sun. Somebody yelled 'Bandits!' into his radio, shrieking in Nick's ear. The squadron leader shouted orders, but in the end it was every man for himself, and if you were heading for the drink, take as many of the bastards with you as you could. But Nick didn't intend going anywhere but home.

He flew steadily, aware as always of the hundred gallons of pure octane in the tanks right in front of him. Catch a bullet in them and he'd have the skin burnt off his face before he could blink. That had happened to more than one bloke, and it wasn't pretty. But there was no time to think of that now, and there wasn't anything you could do about it anyway.

The enemy planes were Messerschmitt Me109s, fighters sent to protect the Junkers and Heinkels which carried the bombs. Me109s could only stay for about twenty minutes before having to turn back to Germany, but they were like mosquitoes, darting in and distracting you while the bombers ploughed on with their deadly cargo. You could get them as they came in or chase them on their way back, but you couldn't let the bigger planes go by while you were doing it. The squadron had to be properly organised.

At the same time, allowance had to be made for the pilots to use their own initiative. Each one might be caught up in his own private battle and unable to help the rest. And the squadron never had a chance to learn each other's ways, because it changed from day to day as pilots were shot down and lost, and new ones, barely trained, came to take their place.

Nick scored his first hit of the day against an Me109 whose pilot had been looking the other way, and grinned with triumph. Then he gave a grunt of dismay. One of the squadron was just ahead of him and on fire. He saw the pilot bale out just as he jerked at the controls to evade the ball of flame, and recognised him as one of the new chaps, a nineteen-year-old boy called Kenny Harris. As the parachute opened he heard the rattle of machine-gun fire from above and saw another Messerschmitt hurtle past him. Kenny Harris kicked and jinked in his parachute and then hung still. The plane fell past him, a twisted mass of orange and black, and the smell of burning fuel and cordite filled Nick's cockpit.

Nick was suffused with a rage as hot and red as the burning plane. He turned his Spitfire on a sixpence and set off in pursuit of the Messerschmitt. It was on its way back and he ought to have targeted one of the bombers or another fighter, but he wasn't going to let the German pilot get away with what he'd just done. Kenny Harris had only been with them a day. This had been his first flight in action. It wasn't bloody fair.

He could hear his squadron leader screeching in his ear. 'Okay, okay,' he muttered, 'I'm coming back when I've dealt with this bastard.' He narrowed his eyes and set his jaw. The German pilot knew he was there. He was taking evading action, trying to escape, getting into the sun so that Nick couldn't see him – but Nick wasn't having any. This plane was going down, and there were no two ways about it.

It was almost as if the German pilot sensed his rage, almost as if he knew there was no escape. Coming out of the sun, he caught the full force of Nick's fury, and did nothing at all about it. The Messerschmitt, riddled with bullets, fell like a stone.

Nick watched it grimly. The only pity was that it hadn't burst into flames, he thought, so that the bastard could have felt a bit of what Kenny had felt in his last moments. But he was dead, there was no doubt of that, and Nick could turn for home now and rejoin the rest of the squadron. When he spotted another bandit coming at him, he felt almost casual about how easy it was to just shoot him down as well.

Jo listened to the story silently, imagining the enemy plane dropping like a ball of fire into the sea and then seeing the steam and smoke billowing like a huge, black cloud above the surface of the water. She shuddered.

'Nick, how horrible. I can't bear to think about it. Suppose it was you—'

'It won't be,' he said, his voice suddenly rough. 'Don't say things like that. Jo. It won't be me.'

'How can you say that? You can't know. It could be you tomorrow, just like it was poor Kenny Harris, just like it was that other friend of yours, Geoff, that you said "bought it" last week. How can you be so *casual* about it? Don't you ever think about what it's like for me and for your family?' She stared at him accusingly. 'I think you *enjoy* it!'

'It's not like that,' he said. 'We don't think about it. We don't talk about it. We make a joke of it. It's the only way we can manage, Jo, and you've got to understand that. We're fighting a war. It's the way things are when you fight a war.'

'But it's wrong. People shouldn't get like that – callous and uncaring. Those German pilots – they're young like you and Kenny Harris, they've got their lives before them. They were running races against us before the war in the Olympics. It's awful to think of you all up there killing each other and – and revelling in it.'

'Listen,' he said roughly, 'we can't afford to think like that. If we did, we wouldn't be able to fight any more. They're the enemy. They're not blokes like us, they're

165

German bastards, and if we didn't kill them they'd kill us, or go on to bomb people like you to bits. Is that what you want?' He stared at her, his face white, the muscles taut around his jaw. 'And we can't afford to get upset about the chaps who don't come back. We've just got to go on. It's no good you sitting at home and bleating about it being wrong. It's the way it *is*.'

'It's horrible,' she said again, shakily.

Nick was silent for a moment. Then he put his arms round her and pulled her close, his face against her hair. In his mind was the image of a plane falling like a ball of flame from the sky, but he couldn't tell her that. He'd told her too much already.

'Nick,' she said, 'I do love you. It's just that I – I'm so scared of losing you.'

He turned his head and kissed her lips. 'I love you, too, Jo,' he said. 'And I wish things were different. I wish we could get married and settle down in a house somewhere and have our kids in peace. And one day we will.'

'Is that a promise?' she asked with a tremulous smile.

'That's a promise,' he said, and kissed her again.

It was a shock when Jo and Phyl came home one evening to find the floors covered in sheets of brown paper and Mrs Holt busy cutting them into long strips and sticking them to the windows, carefully arranging them in a criss-cross pattern. In the hall, Jo nearly tripped over a bucket filled with sand and there was a stirrup-pump leaning against the wall.

'Blimey,' she said, standing in the door of the front room, 'you making next year's Christmas decorations, or getting ready for a siege?'

'We might be,' Mrs Holt said grimly, looking up from her cutting. 'This is the latest idea for protecting ourselves against air raids. The windows can all get blown in, see, and then there'd be glass like knives shooting all over the place –

cut you in half, they can. And the sand and stirrup-pump's for incendiaries. We're getting them in every sixth house in the street.'

'You mean to say they expect you to get out there and fight fires?' Phyl picked up one of the strips of paper. 'This don't seem strong enough to stop a window smashing.'

'I don't think so either, but it's all we got.' Auntie Holt put one hand on the settee and levered herself to her feet. 'I dunno, I'm sure. It comes to something when you got to stick bits of paper to your windows. I dunno what we're all coming to.'

She looked dispirited, standing there amongst all the brown paper, and Phyl felt a wave of pity for her. It wasn't fair, she thought, that old people like Auntie Holt, who'd already lived through one war and lost people they loved then, should have to go through all this. Until now, she'd been thinking more of people of her own age, just starting out in life, with all their hopes and dreams torn apart, but now she could see it was just as bad for those who were tired and old and ought to be looking forward to an easier life.

Phyl had never thought of Auntie Holt as being old and tired before, but now she saw the sagging skin, the crinkled lips and eyes, the grey hair pulled back into a bun. She noticed the way the older woman rubbed her knees as she came up from her kneeling position, and she tried to imagine her fighting an incendiary bomb with a stirrup-pump when she ought to be tucked up fast asleep in bed.

'We've got to clear the rest of the attic, too,' Mrs Holt went on. 'I know we got a lot of stuff down, but there's still a load of rubbish up there. Old letters and books and clothes and bits of wallpaper – all sorts. It's all inflammable, see, only wants a spark on the roof to set the whole lot off. Perhaps you two girls'll give me a hand with it after.'

'Of course we will,' Phyl said. 'Won't we, Jo? Now, you come and sit down and I'll make you a cup of tea. Me and Jo can finish doing these windows. You've done enough.'

It was usually Mrs Holt who made tea as soon as they came in, fussing about them as if they were princesses, but today she just nodded and went through to the back room, where she sank into her favourite armchair. Phyl watched as she leant her head back and closed her eyes, and drew Jo through to the little kitchen.

'She looks worn out. It's not fair, Jo. Old people didn't ought to have to worry about things like this.'

'I know, but there's not much we can do about it. We're all having to worry. Doesn't matter who we are or how old we are – we're all in the same boat, Phyl.'

'I know.' Phyl set the kettle on the gas ring and got the teapot out of its cupboard. 'Well, I suppose we'll just have to do whatever we can to help. But all these preparations, Jo – it means it's serious, doesn't it? They really do think we'll get these awful raids.'

'Yes, it does.' Jo was silent for a moment, then she turned to face her. 'Oh, Phyl, it's just getting worse and worse. Your Mike – my Nick – Norman and Fred and Ron – they're all going to be in the thick of it, and so are we. Maggie's already lost her Tommy – who else is going to go before it's all finished and done with? What's going to happen to us all?' She bit her lip and then burst out, 'I tell you what, I almost wish they'd just get started on some proper air raids, so that at least we'd know what we'd got to face. Let's get *on* with it, that's what I think.'

They stared at each other, half terrified, half defiant. And when the kettle boiled and suddenly began to whistle, they jumped as if it were an air-raid warning, and clutched each other.

'Come on,' Phyl said, pulling away. 'Let's all have a cup of tea. And then we'll see about making this house properly bombproof. You're right, Jo. Whatever happens, we're not going to give in quietly, so just let's remember what Mr Churchill said and get ready to fight 'em in the streets!'

*

Irene took as little notice as possible of the general anxiety. She was, like everyone else, afraid of invasion, but she didn't see why it should interfere with her own life. She listened to the other girls discussing call-up and made up her mind that she wouldn't volunteer for any of the women's services. If conscription came, she would go, of course, there would be no choice, but until then she would concentrate on furthering her career with Lyons. In many ways, it seemed as if the war would help with this, because Nippies were beginning to leave and it was a question of either employing new, younger ones who perhaps wouldn't be as good, or doing without them altogether.

'They're talking about doing away with waitresses,' she told Muriel Chalk. 'Make people serve themselves. I think it's an awful idea.'

'How would they do that, then?'

The two were sitting in a teashop – not a Lyons, for a wonder – and sampling some different and, Irene commented disparagingly, inferior fancies. Irene cut daintily into a little fairy cake with a thin smear of pink icing and wrinkled her nose fastidiously.

'Well, they'd have a long counter and customers would have to queue up and collect their food as they went along. It's the same as we do in the kitchens, but I think it'd be awful to make customers do that. They come into Corner Houses for a bit of attention, a bit of luxury. If they've got to do half the work themselves, they might as well stay at home.'

'Well, I suppose they'll only do it if they can't get the waitresses. They're afraid they'll all join up, I suppose.' Muriel gave Irene an assessing glance. 'You're not thinking of it, are you? Mind you, you'd look well in uniform.'

Irene preened a little. 'Yes, but that's not the main thing, is it? I don't want to go away and have to live in a hut with a lot of common girls. It might be different if I could be an officer, but I don't have the education, you see.' She sighed.

'My father's the old-fashioned sort, doesn't believe in girls being educated. I'd have liked to have gone into the civil service, like him, but I'd have had to have another year at school for that and he thought I'd be getting married young, you see.'

'Oh? Why did he think that?'

Irene looked down at her plate. 'Well, because I'm pretty, I suppose, and like to make the best of myself. He thought the boys would be after me in droves.'

'And have they been?'

Irene tossed her head. 'I wouldn't know. I'm not interested in boys. When I get married, it'll be to a man who knows what's what and how to treat a lady.'

'*When* you get married?' Muriel enquired softly.

Irene flushed. '*If* I get married. I've had one or two nasty experiences with men and I'm not at all keen on it, to tell you the truth. All that pawing and slobbering.' She shuddered. 'I'm happier as I am, to be honest.'

Muriel said nothing for a moment. Then she said delicately, 'It's difficult, though, isn't it? With so few careers open to a young gel, how can she have the life she's entitled to without a husband to provide for her? You're more or less forced to marry.'

'*You* haven't,' Irene said, and then, afraid that she might have been rude, 'Well, not yet, I mean.'

Muriel laughed and poured another cup of tea. 'Nor shall I. My job pays quite well, and I do have a little money from an uncle who's quite well-to-do. He looks after me. So I don't need a husband, you see, and, like you, I see no other reason to acquire one. I don't like all that "pawing and slobbering" any more than you do!'

They ate for a while in silence, then Irene said, 'Jo Mason had that chap of hers in the restaurant the other day. Pilot, he is. She says he's flying all hours against the Luftwaffe.'

'I suppose he is.' Muriel chose a slice of Battenberg cake. 'Where is it he's stationed? I forget.'

Irene didn't think she'd ever mentioned where Nick Laurence was stationed, but she said obligingly, 'Somewhere near Chichester. Tangmere, I think. He flies Spitfires. Jo thinks he's the bee's knees – the best pilot in the RAF!' She gave a small, contemptuous laugh.

'And does Jo see a lot of him?'

'Oh, no. He hardly ever gets any time off. He's only been in once in the past month or more.'

'Perhaps she goes down there. Stays near the airfield – you know.' Muriel gave her an arch look.

Irene shrugged. 'She goes down there sometimes, when she gets a day off. I don't know what they do and, quite honestly, I'm not very bothered. I'm not very interested in what Jo Mason gets up to with her boyfriend.'

'No, of course you're not.' Muriel smiled and then wiped her lips with a plain white handkerchief. She had given Irene a pair only last week, lace-edged, which she'd said she'd found in a drawer at the store. You couldn't get such things for love or money nowadays and Irene had been thrilled, even more so when she realised that Muriel had chosen not to keep them for herself. 'Well, shall we go? No – it's my treat today. And don't waste time arguing or we'll miss the start of the picture!'

Irene waited while Muriel paid the bill, and then took her arm as they went out into the street. It was nice to have a friend like Muriel, she thought appreciatively. Someone a bit older, with a bit of money – a private income as well as her own pay! – who was happy to treat a girl to tea out or a nice seat at the cinema. As good as having a man friend. Better, really.

You didn't have to put up with all that 'pawing and slobbering'.

Etty saw as little of Muriel Chalk as possible these days.

It was easy enough to avoid her most of the time. The businesswomen who lived at the top of the hostel kept very

171

much to themselves, coming down only for meals which they took at a separate table from the rest of the girls. Etty, nervous of the girls who had harried her on New Year's Eve, usually sat with her room-mates, Pat and Cora, and went to the smaller of the sitting-rooms where neither Muriel nor the other girls were likely to go. She spent as much time as possible at the Pratts' house near Covent Garden.

'I'm going to join up soon,' Jim told her. 'I can't stop at home when all these other blokes are going. They need as many men as they can get, and I'll be called up in the end anyway.'

'I know.' She didn't want him to go, but she knew it was inevitable. 'What will you go into?'

'Oh, the army, I expect. Most of the blokes round here do. I wouldn't mind the navy, but I even get seasick on the Woolwich ferry. And I wouldn't go up in one of them aeroplanes if you paid me.'

Etty smiled tremulously. 'They *would* be paying you, Jim.'

'Not enough,' he said. 'I'd want a blooming fortune!' He took Etty's hands. 'The worst bit'd be leaving you.'

Etty nodded. She looked down at their hands, hers small and slim in Jim's big paws. He was going to be as big as his dad, she thought. He was tall now, and broad, but he'd start filling out soon and be as big as a boxer. 'I wouldn't like to meet you on a dark night!' she said with a small laugh, and then giggled at herself. 'Well – maybe I would!'

'I hope you would.' He put his arms round her and squeezed. 'I like meeting you at any time, Et. You know that, don't you?'

Etty nodded again, or rather tried to against his chest. 'I know, Jim.'

'I think the world of you,' he said. 'You're my girl.'

'Oh, Jim.'

'We love each other, don't we? We're going to get married someday. That's right, isn't it?'

172

Etty pulled away and looked at him with shining eyes. 'Oh, Jim, yes. Yes, please.'

'You don't have to say please to me, girl,' he said. 'It's me that should be saying please.' He kissed her. 'You know, there was always summat special about you. Right from that first day when you come back with Maggie for our Ginnie's birthday party. I could see you were different.'

'You took me out to show me your motor bike,' she said. 'You were doing a de-coke.'

'That's right. And then we went out for a ride on the Sunday. It was nice, just riding along with your arms round my waist.' He hugged her again. 'I want it to be like that always for us, Etty. You with your arms round my waist – me with mine round yours. Both of us together for the rest of our lives.'

'I'd like that, too, Jim,' she said softly.

Jim kissed her again. Then he looked down at her and smiled.

'Well, that's it, then. We're properly engaged now, except for the ring. I reckon we'd better see about that next, don't you?'

'A ring?' she said. 'But I thought you were going to wait—'

'Till I could afford a decent one,' he agreed. 'Well, I've had a reckon-up and I think I can. As a matter of fact . . .' he fumbled in his pocket while Etty watched, bemused '. . . I been along to the shop and had a look, and I thought you might like this one. I think it'll fit,' he added rather shyly. 'I took that grass one I made for you when we were on a picnic once, and they measured it from that. I brought it back,' he added hastily, and when she opened the box the first thing she saw was the little scrap of dried grass, twisted on to her finger once as they lay in a sunny field, a hundred years ago before the war began, it seemed.

Etty took it out, smiling through sudden tears. She didn't even think Jim had known she'd kept the scrap, in a tiny box

173

in her handbag. He must have found it that day she'd asked him to fetch her hanky out for her. And I didn't even miss it, she thought guiltily.

'Is it all right?' he asked, a shade anxiously. 'D'you like it, Et?'

With shaking fingers, she removed the little scrap of grass, and gave a gasp of delight. 'Oh, Jim – it's lovely! It's *beautiful*.'

'It's a real diamond,' he said. 'I wouldn't get you a ring till I could afford a real diamond, but that is. The shop said so.'

Etty took the little ring out of its velvet nest. She held it to the light and it glittered. Jim took it from her and slipped it on to her third finger, where the tiny diamond winked up at her.

It was no bigger than a flake, minute in its setting, but to Etty and to Jim it was as fine as the crown jewels.

Chapter Ten

'I've made up my mind. I'm going to volunteer.'

The girls were sitting in Mrs Holt's back room after supper. Jo was doing a crossword and Phyl was altering one of her frocks to make a blouse. All of them were thoughtful after listening to one of Mr Churchill's speeches on the wireless.

'Phyl!' Jo exclaimed, and Mrs Holt dropped the Balaclava helmet she was knitting.

'Are you really sure? It's a big step – and you wanted to be a Nippy so much.'

'I know, and now I am one. But we've all got to do our bit. You've given up all those pots and pans and the railings out the front, and Nick and Mike and all those others have had to go away and fight. And people have been killed – hundreds of them – and there's more being killed all the time. I can't just stand by and watch it all, and go off to a nice, safe, comfortable job in a restaurant every day.'

'You know what Maggie says,' Jo reminded her. 'What we're doing is war work as well, in a way. We give people a bit of brightness to cheer them along. Mr Carter says that, too.'

'I know, but it's not enough. Not for me.' Phyl put down her sewing and got up to stare out of the window. It was still full daylight and the scene was peaceful – a few wives sitting out at their doors, gossiping, men doing a bit of work in their tiny front gardens. Nearly all of them had been dug up now in the Dig For Victory campaign and there were vegetables growing where once there had been tiny scraps of lawn. 'I want to do something more,' she continued, turning back to look at them. 'I want to feel I'm doing as much as I can. In the services, I will be.'

Jo was silent for a moment. Then she said quietly, 'You're right, Phyl. I've been thinking about it, too.'

'You mean you're going to go off and leave me? Both of you?'

The girls turned to their landlady. She had become so much more than that to them – an 'auntie' in truth, caring for them and making them comfortable just as if they were her own. They knew that it was their company that she valued, as much as the board and lodging they paid. Without them she would be lonely.

'It's not that we want to,' Phyl exclaimed. 'You know that, Auntie Holt. You've been as good as a mother to us.'

'Perhaps you could get another couple of girls,' Jo suggested. 'Lyons are always looking for places.'

'I don't know as I want anyone else. Not with all this going on. I wouldn't get used to them.' The blue eyes blurred a little. 'I'm getting too old for new things, that's what it is. I don't reckon I'll want anyone else if you two goes.'

The girls were silent for a few moments, then Phyl said quietly, 'Well, I don't suppose it'll be all that quick, anyway. Someone told me she'd volunteered weeks ago and she's still waiting for her papers.'

'You don't have to go in the forces,' Mrs Holt suggested. 'You could do some other war job – be a bus conductress, what they calls a clippie, or summat like that, and still live at home.'

Phyl smiled. 'From Nippy to Clippie, eh? Well, it's an idea, but somehow I'd feel better in a uniform – a real uniform, I mean. I want to feel I'm doing something to help Mike and the others. Just clipping tickets on a bus wouldn't be the same.'

'It's the Land Army for me,' Jo said. 'I made up my mind to that a long time ago.'

'What, out in the country?' their landlady exclaimed. 'With all those fields and owls and things?'

Jo grinned. 'Well, I can't do much farming in the middle of London. And I've always fancied living in the country, ever since we went hop-picking down in Kent. Phyl's right, we can't just stay safe in London while other people are doing all the work.'

'London – safe?' Auntie Holt said. 'I don't think anyone could say that, not now the bombing's started at last.'

The first bombs to fall on London had hit the airport at Croydon. They were followed by others, scattered over the whole city. Most of them fell during the day, and people were supposed to take shelter. At home, there were the Andersons in back gardens or the street shelters, but if you were out shopping it wasn't so easy to know where to go.

'What'll happen if we hear the siren while we're in here?' a worried-looking customer asked in the Corner House. 'Do we have to go out and look for a shelter? I tell you, I'm half-afraid to leave home these days.'

'You'll be all right,' Jo reassured her. 'We'll all go down to the shelter in the basement if there's a raid. We've done training for it. It's safe as houses down there.'

The woman gave her a look. 'But houses *ain't* safe, are they? That's why we all got shelters to go to.'

'Well, it's safe as shelters, then,' Jo said, feeling irritated. But maybe it wasn't the woman's fault. She looked really frightened and when she told Jo that she'd actually been in a raid, and the house next door had been bombed, Jo could see why.

'That's awful,' she agreed. 'What's happened to the people? Are they all right?'

The customer nodded. 'They weren't there, they'd gone round her sister's for the evening. When they got home and saw what had happened my neighbour nearly fainted. They

177

got in and saved quite a bit, but they can't live there no more, not till it's been shored up.'

Jo fetched her order, feeling subdued. The little story had brought home to her what was happening, and what would happen even more. People bombed out of their houses, with nowhere to live. Managing to save some of their possessions – or perhaps losing everything. People being killed, in their own homes.

Safe as houses. What a daft expression.

All the Lyons staff had been trained for firefighting and had their instructions as to what to do if they were bombed. Most of the staff and any customers who were in the restaurants were to go down to the basement, and those on fire duty would go up to the roof. They went up to see and stood, awed, gazing out over London.

'It's a smashing view,' Phyl said. 'They ought to have a restaurant up here. A roof-garden. In peacetime, I mean,' she added.

'This waiting,' Jo said in a low voice as they stood gazing out over Hyde Park with its barbed-wire barriers and trenches, 'it's getting me down. I want to get on with it.'

'I know what you mean.' Phyl slipped her arm through Jo's. 'There's plenty going on, but it's all a sort of skirting around, isn't it? The Germans trying to get at us and our boys fighting them off. You get the feeling that it's not going to end there – it's going to get a lot worse. But I can't say I'm looking forward to it.'

'I'm not looking forward to it. I don't mean that. I just want it to be *over*.' But even as she spoke, she knew deep down that it had scarcely begun.

It started at last on September the seventh.

It was a year and four days since war had been declared. A clear, sunny Saturday with a nip of autumn in the air. Phyl and Jo had worked all day and were looking forward to an evening off. They were going to the pictures.

'It'd be nice to go dancing,' Phyl said wistfully, 'but I don't fancy it without Mike. It don't seem right, dancing with another chap.'

'You wouldn't object to him having a dance, though,' Jo said. 'I mean, we know they do have them at barracks, and get the local girls along. Or even sometimes abroad.'

'Who said I wouldn't object?' Phyl enquired, bridling. 'He's my bloke and don't anyone forget it! No, you're right, though – I don't begrudge him a bit of fun when he's stuck in camp training all the time. But it don't seem right for *me*, that's all. I'm still living at home in comfort and I can go out and about when I like, that's what makes the difference.'

They were getting ready after tea when the air-raid warning sounded.

'Oh, dash it,' Phyl said, halfway through buttoning up her best blouse. 'I think he does it on purpose, Jo, to spoil our evening out. I suppose we'll have to go down the shelter.'

'It might be another false alarm.' There had been so many of them that people scarcely bothered any more. But since the hits on Stepney and Bethnal Green the shelters had begun to fill up a bit more. The reports of damage and deaths had reminded people that the war was real and bombs could kill.

Mrs Holt shouted up from the bottom of the stairs. 'Did you two girls hear that? You'd better come down straight away.'

Since the siren was still wailing its banshee call, it would have been difficult to miss it. But as the sound died away and Phyl and Jo looked round for books and knitting to take with them, they heard another sound. They stopped and stared at each other.

'That's aircraft,' Phyl said in a whisper, and they ran to the window to look. 'Oh, my God. *Jo* – look at that!'

They were coming in a wave of black dots, freckling the evening sky. High above the barrage balloons, silver and gold in the glow of the setting sun, they were like a flock of menacing black birds, and as the girls watched, transfixed, they saw the first small black dots fall away and drop steadily towards the earth.

'Bombs!' Jo gasped. 'Phyl – we got to get to the shelter. *Quick!*'

Panic-stricken now, they snatched up what they could and made for the stairs. Mrs Holt was waiting in a fever of impatience and terror. There could be no pretending now that this was a false alarm. They all knew the truth. This was bombing in earnest, and there would be people killed that night in London. The shelters were the only place to go.

'Quick! Quick!' Mrs Holt cried, pushing them out of the door. 'We'll have to go down the street to the shelter and they could bomb us any minute, before we even gets there! Oh, I knew it'd come to this, I knew it! Oh, Phyl, Jo – oh, what *would* my Bert say if he could see this?'

Bert's photograph stood on the sideboard in Mrs Holt's back room. He looked stern and forbidding, quite unlike his round-faced, smiling wife, and the girls thought he'd have had plenty to say about the bombing if he'd still been alive. But he wasn't and they didn't have time or inclination to speculate about his opinions. As far as they were concerned, this was none of his business.

'Don't get in a flap, Auntie,' Jo urged. 'We'll be all right. I'll carry your bag. My goodness, whatever have you got in here? I say, it looks as if we're going to have a real party in the shelter tonight – everyone's coming.'

People were pouring from their homes all along the street. Men, women, children, old folk who had scarcely ventured out of doors for months or even years – all were hurrying towards the big brick shelters at the end of the road. Mr and Mrs Hoskins were helping their old mother along, one on each side of her, guiding the trembling footsteps. The Browns had all their kids in tow, including two rammed into an old pram and almost hidden by the pile of possessions thrust on top of them. Ancient Mr Foster, who lived by himself and dared anyone to go into his house to help him, was hobbling along on two sticks, swearing and cursing the invaders. Some were carrying deckchairs or stools, most had a blanket or two or a cushion. False alarm or not, you never knew how long you'd be stuck in the shelter and there were no seats provided.

Mrs Holt had brought a pile of blankets and a cushion for each of them. Phyl took some of them while Jo carried the shopping bag and the few things she and Phyl had grabbed. They arrived at the shelter and crowded through the narrow doorway with the others.

It was dank and dark inside. Someone had brought a torch and flashed it about. Everyone began to search for a place to sit, and soon the corners were taken and all the sides. The last arrivals had to sit in the middle, wherever they could. The people who had brought deckchairs were cursed by the others.

'Take up too much room, they do. Selfish, that's what I call it.'

'Go on, Ma, you're only jealous 'cause you never thought of it yourself.'

Phyl, Jo and Mrs Holt found a spot against the wall and spread out their blankets. The floor wasn't overly clean and Phyl made up her mind to try to get a groundsheet from somewhere. Norman probably had one from his Scouting days. You didn't want to keep putting blankets on the floor in places like this.

'It's awful, isn't it?' a woman nearby said. Her voice was shaking. 'Like rats in a hole. I tell you what, this war's getting too much for me, all these alarms and my Arthur says there's planes coming over this very minute, we'll all be bombed to death—*Oh!*'

She screamed as a crash sounded not far away. The shelter trembled and everyone cried out. Someone near

181

Phyl began to cry. There was another crash – and another. This time they were nearer and the screams were louder.

'They're bombing us now! Oh, what are we going to do? All our houses are going – we'll have nowhere to live. Oh, my God, my *God* – what are we going to *do*?'

It sounded as if the entire street were falling to pieces about them. Mrs Holt and the two girls clutched each other. The girl next to Phyl scrabbled at her arm and Phyl put it around her, holding her tightly. Everyone was holding someone else. Some people were crying, others still screaming, some were silent. There was a lull in the explosions outside and everyone held their breath, waiting for the next.

'We're not going to have no homes to go back to,' a woman on the other side of the shelter moaned. 'It'll all be gone. All me photos and me best frock and our Brian's model aeroplane what he took so much trouble over – it'll all be gone.'

'Never mind model aeroplanes, what about our cat? My little girl'll break her heart if anything's happened to our Blackie. She's had him since she was a little girl, and he went out after tea and now I don't know where he'll be. He doesn't even like fireworks, he'll be going mad with this lot.'

Jo thought of Alice and Robertson. 'I hope everyone's all right at home,' she muttered to Phyl. 'I hope they've got into the shelters. Our dad's a firewatcher, you know, and so's yours, they'll have to stop outside. I hope they're all right.'

'They'll be okay. They got Andersons there. I reckon they're better than these shelters.' Phyl jumped and cringed as another explosion shook the small building. 'Oh, lor! I don't see how these can be safe, do you, not standing up above ground like this? Irene was right, they're no better than houses. Oh, there goes another one!'

'Stop crying!' a woman a few yards away was screaming at her children. 'Stop that bloody crying! What good d'you think that's going to do, eh? You think old Hitler's going to stop the bombing just 'cause of a few kids piping their eye?' Her voice, tight with hysteria, rose until she, too, was crying. She buried her head in her hands, weeping loudly, and the two children beside her watched with fear-stricken eyes. 'Oh, my God, my God, my God . . .'

There was a small commotion near the door and the crowd parted to let an ARP man through. ARP weren't popular – they were officious and self-important in their dark blue uniforms and tin helmets, forever yelling at people to put that light out or telling them off for not having their gas masks with them. This one had been running up and down the street as they headed for the shelter, blowing his whistle and waving his wooden rattle. Now he shouted for silence.

'Blimey,' he said when there were only a few people still whimpering, 'there's so much racket going on in here I should think old Hitler can hear it in Berlin. 'Ow about making a bit more cheerful noise? 'Ow about a bit of a song, eh? Mrs Foster, you're a one for getting a bit of a sing-song going down the Buller's Arms, why don't you start summat up?'

'There ain't much to sing about, that's why. Stuck here in this hole . . .'

'It'll keep your spirits up,' he urged. 'Come on. "It's a long way to Tipperary, It's a long way to go . . ." You got a good loud voice, Mrs Mitchell, you get 'em started, come on.'

A few voices rose in song. They tried 'Tipperary', they tried 'Roll Out the Barrel', they tried 'Run, Rabbit, Run', but it was no use. If a song did get started, a fresh explosion drowned it out, and nobody had any heart for it. The half-hearted efforts faded to nothing and people sat more or less in silence, listening tensely for the snarl of approaching aircraft, the whistle and roar of the bombs, the violent crash of buildings shattering and collapsing around them.

'What's happening outside?' someone asked the ARP man. 'What's left? They must've knocked it all to pieces.'

'Oh, there's plenty left,' he answered cheerfully. 'A bit of damage here and there, but nothing to write home about. Our boys are seeing 'em off, don't you worry.'

'So what's all that noise, then?' a man asked sceptically. 'Missing a few fireworks, are we?'

The ARP man didn't answer. He looked tired, Jo thought. Like the Home Guard, all ARP personnel were volunteers, working at ordinary jobs as well as taking on the responsibility of making sure blackout regulations were observed and looking after people during air raids. This was the first serious one, but there had been plenty of false alarms, as well as the attacks on Croydon and Stepney, and he and his colleagues would have been out most nights. They couldn't go home to look after their own families, and they certainly couldn't allow themselves to panic.

The night wore on. People grew tired and tried to sleep. They moaned with exhaustion, unable to do more than close their eyes. There was no comfort, even on a pile of blankets on the hard concrete floor. A deckchair, it was discovered, was nowhere near as comfortable in an air-raid shelter at night as it was in the garden in the sun. The noise kept them awake and in the lulls a few people who had managed to drop off kept the rest awake with their snoring. Fear and anxiety kept them awake more than anything else, and some dissolved into a steady, despairing weeping.

At last it was over. It was half past four in the morning; they had been in the shelter for over eight hours. The all-clear, a more comforting upward swoop of sound, brought a general sigh of relief. There was a scramble to fold up blankets and repack bags and cases. Rubbing their eyes and yawning, the girls climbed stiffly to their feet and helped Mrs Holt to stand up.

'I'm too old for this lark,' she panted, leaning stiffly against them. 'Spending the night on a hard floor . . . Oh,

God, I'm half-afraid to go outside. I'm half-afraid to look . . .'

They made their way to the door. It was dawn and the sky was beginning to colour faintly with pink. The air smelt smoky and dank.

The first people out of the door stopped dead. There was a gasp and a scream.

'What is it?' Those still inside pushed anxiously. 'Let us out. What's happened?'

'Oh, my *Gawd* . . .' someone muttered, and stood aside so that others could emerge. 'Oh, my Gawd . . .'

Phyl and Jo came out and stared about them. Their hearts sank.

'Oh, *Phyl* . . .'

'Jo – it's *awful*.'

Mrs Holt was beside them. 'What? What is it? What've they done?' She stopped, drawing in her breath in a gasp of dismay. 'Oh, my Gawd – *look* at it, look at our street what we kept so neat and clean – what a *mess*, what a terrible mess. Oh, who would have believed it? Those bloody, *bloody* Germans! They oughter be *shot*, that's what, they oughter be *shot*!'

They stared around. The dawn sky was smeared with black smoke, pouring across from the direction of the docks. Windows were smashed everywhere, doors blown in, roofs torn to pieces. Some houses were untouched, others had their walls ripped away. At the other end of the road was a vast crater, stretching from pavement to pavement. Two houses were on fire and already there was a fire engine on the scene, with firemen racing with hoses to control the flames.

The screaming had begun again. Not everyone had had all their family with them in the shelter and people were running to their houses, calling out names. 'Joe! Fred! Where's our Jacky? Where's our Joan?' One of the bombed houses was little more than a pile of rubble, and a woman

185

began to scrabble furiously with her bare hands at the smashed and tumbled bricks. 'My hubby's under there! He wouldn't come down the shelter, I *told* him to come and he wouldn't so I come without him – oh Perce, Perce, I'm sorry I shouted, I never oughter have left you – oh, be alive, Perce, be alive, *please* be alive . . .' She turned and stared up at those who had gathered around her. 'Help me! *Help* me!'

People helped her. They dropped their belongings and scrabbled with her. Jo and Phyl joined in, tearing at the tumble of broken floorboards. An ARP man pushed them aside.

'Get out. It's dangerous – it's got to be done proper.' He spoke to the woman. 'You're sure your hubby's in here, love?'

'I *know* he is,' she sobbed. 'We had a row – oh, I'm so sorry, Perce, I never meant those things – he said the shelter wasn't no safer than the house and I said I was going anyway – I wish I hadn't, I *wish* I hadn't!'

'Well, you were right, love, weren't you?' he pointed out. 'Now, you just stand out of the way, and me and the boys'll have him out in no time. The rest of you, better get back to your own places. We'll see the lady's all right.'

Phyl, Jo and Mrs Holt continued along the street, silent and sober. The road was cluttered with rubble – slates from roofs, broken glass from windows, bricks and lumps of concrete and planks of splintered wood. There were holes and craters in the road, and when they came to the corner there was a barrier up and people working carefully on the other side.

'Now what?' Phyl began, and a man turned and said, 'Unexploded bomb, love. Nobody can go past till it's been made safe.'

'Oh, my goodness.' Phyl stared at the pit in the road. There were men climbing down inside. 'But it could go off any minute.'

186

'That's right, so you'd all better get well back out of the way.' An army sergeant came forward, waving his arms. 'Get off home if you can, and if you can't there's a reception centre being set up in the church. There's cups of tea and buns there.'

'I want to go home,' Mrs Holt said, her lips trembling. 'I want to see my own house and make sure everything's all right.'

'We will. We'll go round the other way and cut through the alley.' Jo took her arm. 'Don't worry, Auntie, your house'll be all right and me and Phyl will make you some tea. And then you can go to bed for a bit.'

'Go to bed? It's Sunday morning – I've got a dinner to cook.' Her voice was suddenly indignant, and the girls looked at each other and smiled. 'And you two ought to be thinking about getting home to make sure your people are all right.'

Jo's smile faded. She had said nothing, but anxiety had been gnawing at her all night and even more since they had emerged from the shelter. How had they managed down in Woolwich, so near the docks? They had the Anderson shelter, but that smoke had been coming from the docks themselves and she had already heard rumours of huge fires down there. It was just the sort of target the Germans would go for, and the houses round about would hardly escape the damage.

And there was Nick, too. He must have been flying all night, fighting the invaders. How many Spitfires had been shot down? How many young pilots killed?

Nick, she thought. *Nick* . . .

187

Chapter Eleven

Except for a wall blown out of the corner house and a few windows blown in, Elmbury Street was undamaged, and they all breathed a sigh of relief. Mrs Holt unlocked the door and they went in and dumped their bags and blankets in the front room and looked at each other in silence.

'I don't think I can stand this,' Auntie Holt said, her voice beginning to tremble again. 'I mean, how long's it going to go on, eh? Now they've got through, they're going to keep on, ain't they? Are we going to have to spend every night like that, cooped up in that horrible shelter like monkeys in a zoo?'

'I don't know.' Jo went through to the kitchen to put on the kettle. 'Let's have a cup of tea and see if there's any news on the wireless.'

'There won't be, not for hours yet. It's only just gone five in the morning. It'll be another two hours before that starts up.' Mrs Holt shook her head. 'I dunno what to do. I'm so tired. I don't think I got a wink all night, with all the noise and disturbance.'

Jo started to get out plates and cups. 'I'll tell you what we're going to do. We're going to have a cup of tea and something hot for breakfast. A slice of toast and some baked beans. That'll make us feel a bit better. And then you're going to go to bed and have a rest, while me and Phyl see if we can get home and make sure everything's all right there. It doesn't *matter* about the Sunday dinner,' she said as Mrs Holt began to protest. 'You can cook it tomorrow. It's not as if you had a joint to roast, is it?'

'I'm beginning to forget what a joint looks like,' Auntie Holt said. 'But I did get a nice lamb chop each. With a few potatoes and some veg they'd have been just as good. And I can't keep them till tomorrow, not in this hot weather.'

'Well, let's have them tonight,' Phyl suggested. 'Jo and me have got to come back to be ready for work tomorrow. We'll be posh and have dinner in the evening, like the King and Queen do.'

The kettle began to whistle and Jo made the tea and took it into the back room. She started to cut bread for toast. Phyl got the tin of beans out of the cupboard. Mrs Holt sat in her chair, listening to the sounds from the kitchen, feeling weak and shaky.

'It's reaction,' Phyl said when she came in to lay the table. 'That's all it is. We're all feeling it. It's been a shock. And then coming out and seeing all that damage – it's enough to make anyone feel shaky.'

'I don't know what people are going to do.' They drew their chairs up to the table and began to eat. It was surprisingly hard to swallow the beans on toast. Mrs Holt took a gulp of tea. 'I mean, they can't live in those houses any more. They're just ruins. And that poor woman whose husband was buried, I wonder if they've got him out yet.' She laid down her knife and fork. 'I can't eat this. I just can't.'

'Try,' Jo said gently. 'It won't do anyone any good for us to starve ourselves. We'll feel better with something inside us.'

The tears began to roll down Mrs Holt's face. 'It's thinking about all them poor souls that have lost their homes. And maybe worse than that. I mean, it's not just people, it's cats and dogs as well. They said we ought to have them put to sleep but a lot of people didn't, and now they'll be out there terrified and lost, and perhaps hurt as well . . . It don't bear thinking of.' She leant her head on her hands and began to sob.

Phyl and Jo glanced at each other. Neither was far from tears herself, and in addition they were desperately anxious about their own families. They wanted nothing as much as to be on their way to Woolwich, but they knew that it was too early yet for the buses, even if the roads were clear, and they couldn't leave their landlady in this state. Jo reached across and patted the older woman's arm.

'Don't cry, Auntie. You went through the last war. You didn't give way then and you're not going to now.'

There was a small silence. Mrs Holt sniffed and felt in the sleeve of her cardigan for her hanky. She blew her nose and wiped her eyes and took a long, shuddering breath.

'You're right. I know you're right. I'll get over it. It was just the shock of it all – it seemed to come over me all of a sudden.' She looked at them both and managed a wavering smile. 'You're good girls. You're as good as daughters, the pair of you.'

The girls looked embarrassed. Phyl smiled at her.

'You wouldn't say that if you'd had us when we were kids! Come on, Auntie, eat your beans on toast before they get cold. And then we'll clean up a bit and then listen to the news at seven o'clock before me and Jo try to get home. And you'll go to bed and have a rest, just like you were told.'

The news, when it came at seven o'clock, was terrible and they listened in dismay to the catalogue of destruction.

'Over ten thousand tons of high-explosive bombs,' Phyl said in awe. '*Ten thousand tons*. How do they know that? And as many incendiaries. Why, they must have set fire to almost all of London.'

'We've got to get to Woolwich,' Jo cried, jumping up from her chair. 'Come on, Phyl – let's go straight away.'

'I shouldn't think there'd be any buses running at all,' Mrs Holt said. 'Nor no trams, nor trolley-buses neither. Not if all the roads are in as bad a state as Fulbury.'

'I don't care if we have to walk and it takes us all day – we've got to get there and make sure everyone's safe.' Jo was

190

in a fever of impatience, gathering up her bag, searching her purse to make sure she had some money. 'I'm sorry, Auntie, I don't like leaving you – but you do understand, don't you? We'll never get through the day, not knowing.'

'Of course I understand, ducks. I'm as worried as you are. And I bet your dad'll put his foot down over young Alice and that blessed cat now. They were right, you know, the kiddies ought to be out of it.' She pulled herself to her feet. 'Don't you worry about me, now. You get off home and set your minds at rest. But make sure you're back in good time in case they comes over again and gives us another walloping.'

'And you'll go to bed and have a bit of kip now, Auntie?' Phyl picked up her jacket and looked anxiously at the landlady. 'You look real tired.'

'Bed? Not me,' the older woman said robustly. 'Not while there's folk in trouble all around. No, now I've had a rest and a bite to eat I'm going out again, see what I can do to help. I still can't get that poor soul and her Percy out of my mind. I'd never rest easy, wondering what happened.'

The girls saw that she had made up her mind, and she did look better so they said no more. Together, the three of them went out and walked down the street again. There were still people milling about and at the corner of Elmbury and Fulbury Streets, where one house had lost an entire wall, a little crowd was staring and chattering amongst themselves. Phyl and Jo paused and looked, too.

'It's queer, isn't it? Like a doll's house with the front taken off. You can see all their wallpaper, and their furniture, and the man's dressing-gown where he took it off and hung it on the door—' Jo stopped abruptly and turned away. 'It don't seem right, staring like this, it feels like prying. Come on, Phyl.'

They picked their way down the next street. Some of the rubble was being cleared away and the house where Percy had lain buried was now deserted. Phyl stopped a man who was dragging furniture out of a house a few doors down and asked if he knew what had happened.

'They got him out,' he said, pausing and using the back of his hand to wipe his face. 'He was in a pretty bad way, though. Pinned under a beam he was and broke both his legs, from what I could gather. He's bin took off to hospital and his missus gone with him.'

There were people everywhere, digging in the ruins, going in and out of damaged houses, just standing in groups discussing the night's raid. Even where there had been little or no damage, there were still people about, walking like Phyl and Jo to check on their friends and families, or just out to see what the damage was. Everyone in London had heard the sirens and even if they hadn't gone to shelters they would have been kept awake all night. Now they had come out to see just what had happened to their city.

'It's not like a Sunday at all!' Phyl exclaimed. 'Look at them all – you'd think it was a weekday. Taxis, bikes – what are they all doing?'

'Same as us. Looking for people. Looking for somewhere to stop.' Jo watched a little family trudge past carrying a pitiful load of possessions, with more packed into an old pram. 'Look at them – I bet they've been bombed out. Where are they going to go? You'd think there'd be some sort of place fixed up for them, wouldn't you?'

'Maybe there is. That ARP man said something about the church hall, didn't he? But a lot of these have just come to stare, Jo. Like sightseers.' She gave a group of young men a withering look. 'It might be your turn next, then we'll all come and stare at you,' she said, leaving them to turn and stare after her instead.

Now and then the two girls managed to get on a bus that was going in their direction, but they were forced to walk a good deal of the way and by the time they reached Woolwich they were worn out. As they drew nearer to the docks, the sky grew darker with the smoke that was still streaming overhead, and their hearts grew heavy with dread.

To their huge relief, their own street was untouched. They turned the corner and saw their own front doors standing wide open, and their own mothers standing outside, talking to a group of neighbours. Phyl called out and they turned at once and saw them. Jo's mother gave a little cry and broke away from the group, with May close behind her.

'Jo – Phyl – thank God you're safe. Where were you when it all happened? Come indoors, you must be parched for a cup of tea.'

'We went down to the shelter at the corner of the street. It was all right.' Jo made a face. 'Not like your own place, though. I'd rather have been in our Anderson!'

'That's not exactly a palace,' Carrie said. 'Your dad's been keeping his garden tools in there and I'm sure Robbie's been using it for his own purposes. I gave it a good clear-out this morning and washed it down with Jeyes fluid.'

'It smells even worse now,' Alice said, wrinkling her nose. 'And it wasn't Robbie did that in the corner, Mum, he'd never do that. I bet it was that Tibs from up the street.'

Bill came in, covered in dust and looking tired, but his grimy face brightened when he saw the girls.

'Well, you're a sight for sore eyes, I will say! Come and give your dad a kiss, then.' He held Jo close for a moment, showing a rare emotion. 'Your mother's been fretting herself silly about you.'

'That's why we came – we knew you'd be wondering. And we were worried about you, too, 'specially when we saw the smoke in the sky.'

'You saw it all that way off?' He sank down in his chair. 'Well, I'll admit it was a pretty big fire. They're still down there working on it. Some oil tanks went up, and they'll just have to wait for them to burn themselves out.' He looked up as Phyl came in with a tray of tea. 'My, that looks good. And

193

a trained Nippy to serve it, too. How are they going to manage up at Lyons, then, if this lot goes on?'

'Same as ever, I expect,' Phyl said cheerfully. 'Proper service, silver trays and the customer's always right. What else d'you expect?'

Her uncle grinned. 'That's the spirit. Keep the old flag flying, eh? Show Hitler we won't be downtrodden.'

'That's right, Dad.' Jo sat down beside him. 'We'll show him, won't we? A few measly bombs and a fire or two aren't going to stop us winning this war.'

They didn't stay long at home. Everyone was on edge, wondering if there would be another raid that night, and although May and Carrie would have liked the girls to stay at home, they knew that they would be expected at work next morning. After a hasty meal, Phyl and Jo set off back to Elmbury Street, feeling as if they were departing for the other side of the world. Suddenly, London seemed a different place, strange and dangerous. Every crater and every damaged building reminded them of last night and foretold worse to come. By tomorrow, even the streets that were now clear might be blocked by debris. By tomorrow, there could be even more people dead.

'It's no good thinking about it,' Phyl said after a while. 'It just makes it all seem worse.'

'I know, but I can't help it. The look on Mum's face when she saw us . . . They'd been out of their minds with worry, Phyl. I can't bear to think of them feeling like that, night after night.'

'It's not just us. It's the boys.' Both Fred and Norman had now joined up and were in the army. 'And that's worse – they're being trained to fight. They're going to have to go where they're sent.' Phyl kicked despondently at a fragment of shattered brick. 'You know, I really do want to join up myself but Mum'd be so upset. I don't know what to do for the best.'

'I don't suppose we'll have the choice much longer.

194

They'll be bringing in conscription for women soon. I'm going to see about the Land Army, Phyl. I've made up my mind.'

'At least you'll be safe, out in the country,' Phyl remarked unthinkingly, and was astonished when her cousin rounded on her.

'That's not why I'm doing it! I want to help my country, same as anyone else – I just think I'll be best at farm work, that's all. Anyway, who's to say the country-side's going to be any safer? The Germans could still invade, and they can drop their bombs anywhere. There was that cottage down in Kent got hit, a whole family killed, and there wasn't another house for miles. I suppose *they* felt safe, too!'

'All right, all right,' Phyl said after a pause. 'No need to get your rag out, Jo. You know I didn't mean anything like that.'

Jo said nothing for a moment, then she sighed and said, 'No, I know. Sorry, Phyl. I'm just feeling a bit on edge. Tired, I suppose, after last night. Let's hope we get a bit of shut-eye tonight, eh?'

It was a faint hope. For a while, it seemed as if all was well. The skies stayed clear and no warnings sounded. The girls and Mrs Holt ate their supper with their ears cocked for the slightest sound. They debated whether to put the wireless on and decided that the siren was loud enough to drown anything the BBC might be offering. They listened to a church service and some music, and felt a little calmer. Perhaps nothing was going to happen after all.

The sun went down and Mrs Holt put up the blackout curtains and switched on the light. They looked at each other, unsure what to do.

'Well, I suppose we might as well go to bed. It's no good sitting here waiting for them. I'm just wondering whether to keep my clothes on and just lay on top. I mean, it's warm enough still. And I was thinking about filling up the

195

Thermos flask. I could have done with something in the middle of all that last night.'

Feeling more cheerful with something positive to do, they began to cut bread and make Marmite sandwiches. Phyl smoothed out a bit of greaseproof paper, only used once, and wrapped them up. Mrs Holt filled the flask with tea and put the whole lot into her shopping basket, with her knitting on top.

'Might as well do something useful while we're at it,' she remarked. 'And I bet after all this there won't be a raid at all. Next thing we know, it'll be seven o'clock and you'll be in a panic about getting to work.'

They took turns to wash at the kitchen sink and then went up the stairs. Mrs Holt said goodnight and the girls went into their own bedroom. They got undressed and slipped into bed and lay quiet for a while.

'I've hardly had a chance to think about Mike today,' Phyl said presently. 'There's been so much happening. I wonder what they're doing, Jo. They must be getting ready to fight, I should think, wouldn't you?'

'I should think so. And I expect Nick was flying all night.' Jo turned over to face her. 'I've been worrying all day, at the back of my mind. How long d'you think it'd take before I heard, Phyl? I mean, they'd let his mum know first, wouldn't they? But she'd send me a telegram, I know. I just don't know how long it'd take for it to get through.'

'Oh, Jo, I'm sorry. I never even thought . . .' Phyl shook her head on the pillow. 'I'm selfish, that's what I am. Look, you'd know by now if anything had happened. I'm sure you would.'

'Yes. Yes, I expect I would.' They lay silent for a while, thinking of all that might have happened, might happen yet. At last Jo heaved a deep sigh and said quietly, 'I'm going to say my prayers now, Phyl, and then I'm going to sleep. Goodnight.'

'Goodnight, Jo,' Phyl whispered, and closing her eyes

she, too, tried to pray. Please, God, take care of Mike and Nick and Norman and Fred and Mum and Dad and Auntie Carrie and Uncle Bill and Alice – and Robertson – and everyone we know. Please, God, take care of them and let this horrible war stop soon. And please don't let there be an air raid tonight.

But if God had wished to answer her prayer, he would have had to turn back the clock. For at that very moment the German bombers were heading for London, a black swarm, looking and sounding just then very like a swarm of angry bees. And soon after eleven o'clock, when both girls had fallen into their first deep sleep, the air-raid sirens began again to sound their chilling wail, and when they came stumbling down the stairs and ran out into the street they saw the shimmering network of searchlights criss-crossing the sky and heard the low, threatening snarl of German bombers approaching for the second raid on London.

Chapter Twelve

Shirley and Alf Woods spent the night in their Anderson shelter. They sat opposite each other on the narrow camp beds and listened to the racket going on outside. Alf's face was white and pinched in the flickering light from the hurricane lantern and, scared as she was, Shirley felt even more sorry for him.

After his fit, he had stayed at home for a while, afraid to go out in case it happened again. He imagined falling down in the middle of the road and getting knocked over again, or having a sudden convulsion in the middle of Woolworths. People would stare at him and move away, and think he was mad. 'Maybe I am,' he said to Shirley. 'Maybe that's what's happened. I've gone mad and I'll end up in a loony-bin.'

'Don't be silly, Dad!' Shirley spoke all the more sharply for remembering Irene saying almost exactly the same thing. 'You're not mad at all. It's just something in your brain got knocked a bit when you had that accident.'

'Well, it's your brain what goes wrong when you're mad, isn't it?' He held his head between his palms. '*Summat's* gone wrong up there, you can't deny that. And now the doctor says I can't go on the crane no more.'

Shirley didn't know how to answer him. Alf worked in the docks, unloading cargo ships. He'd operated the big crane for years and was proud of it. Now he was relegated to the ground, helping to shift the loads when they were dumped on the pontoons. It was a comedown in more ways than one and he felt ashamed and humiliated.

'I don't know, Dad. I suppose we just have to make the

198

best of things. There's a lot of people can't do what they want these days.'

'They ain't all been sent mad, though, have they?' he replied, setting his jaw tightly.

The planes roared overhead and they heard the crash of exploding bombs. Shirley put her head between her knees. Someone had told her this stopped your brain being shaken up by the blast. Alf lay down on his bunk and stared at the corrugated-iron roof. He seemed to retreat into himself, almost unaware of what was going on, and when Shirley glanced over at him during a lull in the noise, she saw that his eyes were open and staring fixedly above him. She sighed and swung her legs up on to her own bed to lie down more comfortably. You couldn't spend all night doubled over with your head on your knees.

If only Mum hadn't had to go away, she thought miserably. Dad's never been right without her. He never will be right till she and our Jack can come home again.

At the present rate, that looked like being a long, long time away.

Jo and Phyl came out of the shelter at dawn next morning, already half-prepared for what they would see, and stumbled through more rubble to reach Mrs Holt's house. Once again, it was untouched except that those windows which had survived the first raid had now been shattered. Mrs Holt, however, opened the door with a cry of dismay.

'Someone's bin in here!'

'No!' The girls crammed in behind her. In the hallway, the little half-moon table which had been Mrs Holt's pride and joy, with a lovely Staffordshire figure standing in pride of place upon it, was bare. The china figure had gone, and so had the little embroidered cloth on which it had stood.

'That's awful,' Jo said, staring at the blank space. 'That's *looting*.'

'Let's see what else has gone.' Mrs Holt pushed into the front room and stared wildly around. 'All me little ornaments! All me bits of china what my hubby give me on our anniversaries. And the pewter tankard I give him for our twenty-fifth, and the silver cup he won in the tug of war. Oh, it's not *fair*! As if there wasn't enough to put up with!'

'It's dreadful,' Phyl said. 'To think that anyone would be mean enough to come in during an air raid . . . . They ought to be bombed, they deserve it. You'll have to go to the police, Auntie.'

'What good will that do?' Their landlady sat down and began to cry helplessly. 'They'll never be able to find out who did it. Besides, they've got enough to do, with all that mess outside. They're not going to be interested in a few bits of china.'

'They'll be interested in looting, though,' Jo said grimly. 'Looters can be shot. Let's see if there's anything else gone and then we'll go straight down the station.'

Nothing else had been taken, however. Perhaps the looters had themselves been frightened into making for a shelter. The three of them made a thorough tour of the house and decided in the end that whoever the intruder had been, he – or they – had gone no further than the front room.

'How can we keep people out, with all the windows blown in?' Mrs Holt asked. 'I mean, what can I do with all my stuff? It's an open invitation.'

'We'll pack it all up and put it in the attic,' Jo decided. 'It'll be safer up there anyway. Perhaps we could get a padlock to put on the hatch.'

'They'll be like gold dust if anyone else has been looted, and I bet they have,' Phyl said. 'Look, I'll stay here and start packing stuff up and you two go down to the police station. Then me and Jo'll have to go to work, but we won't leave the house empty till it's all safe.'

'I'm not leaving it empty at all, not while there's no windows,' Mrs Holt declared. 'I'm not going down the shelter tonight, no matter how many bombs come. What's the point? No bombs have dropped on Elmbury Street anyway, except that one at the corner.'

Going to the police and packing Mrs Holt's remaining treasures took some time, and when the girls finally left for work they knew they were going to be late. Picking their way through the already depressingly familiar streets with their heaps of rubble, burst water mains, fire engines and general turmoil, they wondered how many customers there would be to serve anyway – and what food there would be to serve them.

'I bet there'll be lots of other people late, too,' Phyl remarked as they struggled past a pile of broken wood and bricks. She stopped dead as a thought struck her. 'Jo, I've only just thought – I hope the others are all right. Maggie, and Shirley and Etty and all the rest. When you think there's hundreds of people working at our Corner House alone, there's bound to have been some got caught, aren't there?'

Sobered again, they carried on, catching buses or trams where possible, and finishing their journey by underground. They emerged close to Marble Arch and saw to their relief that there didn't seem to have been any damage in the area. Anxious to meet their friends, they hurried through to the dressing-room.

'Oh, thank Gawd you're here!' Maggie rushed over and flung her arms around them. 'I bin that worried! What a weekend, eh? I'll never be scared of thunder again, not after that lot. I thought the whole world was going to cave in.'

'Is Etty here, too? Is Shirley all right?' They looked anxiously about and were relieved to see their friends. Irene was there as well, and the other Nippies. Nobody seemed to be missing. Jo sank down on a bench and bent her head, feeling suddenly dizzy and near to tears.

The cloakroom supervisor came in and started to count heads. 'Get ready as soon as you can, girls, we need you in the restaurant. We're late opening this morning and there are customers queueing already.' She gave them a friendly smile. 'You must all be feeling very tired – I don't suppose anyone got much sleep over the weekend. Now, there are a few rules we're going to wink at while this is going on. Don't worry about sewing your collars to your dresses, you can just pin them on for the time being. Obviously we'll expect your buttons to be sewn on correctly, but we won't be quite so strict as usual. And we'll understand if you're a bit late coming to work – we all know what a problem it is getting through the streets. I think you've all done well to have got here at all!'

'Well, that's good of them, isn't it?' Phyl commented as they scrambled into their uniforms. 'They've realised we can't manage to get everything done, what with all the bombing.'

'Did you go to a shelter?' Maggie enquired. 'Gran wouldn't shift! She said she's lived in that house all her life and it'd take more than a few Germans to push her out now. So our Dad felt he ought to stay with her, and Mum felt she ought to stay with Dad, and our Ginnie wouldn't go without Mum – so in the end, none of us went! Anyway, there wasn't no damage round our way so it was all right in the end, and we reckon we might as well just stop in bed if it happens again.'

They scurried through the tunnel to the main building and came out into the restaurant. With the sunshine flooding through the tall windows and the tables set as usual with clean tablecloths and shining cutlery, it looked almost bizarrely normal. Mr Carter smiled as he saw them and repeated the cloakroom supervisor's words.

'Well done, girls. We're winking at five minutes these days.' They were more than five minutes late, but everyone knew what he meant. They hurried to their posts and smiled as the doors were opened and customers began to flood in. Everyone was full of talk about the weekend.

'I ain't had a decent meal the whole time,' one man told Shirley as he ordered brunch and a pot of tea. 'We had a burst gas main down our street and no one could do any cooking. We had to get out and go down the church hall while they tried to repair it. It's still up. God knows when we'll be able to go home again.'

It was the same story the whole day. Yet there were others who took a different view. In the middle of the afternoon, Maggie found herself serving a couple of young men from Burton's, where Tommy and Mike had worked. They were full of excitement about the whole thing.

'D'you know, I really enjoyed it! I mean, you got to admit it's quite a thrill, listening to the planes coming over and seeing the searchlights all over the sky. And when a bomb drops – wow! You can see the whole thing go up, like a huge, great, giant bonfire.'

'You mean you stopped outside and *watched*?' Maggie asked, horrified. 'You could've been killed.'

'I know – that's half the thrill of it. Knowing they're trying to get you and not managing to do it. And everyone running about and yelling – I tell you, it was better than the flicks any day!'

Maggie had brought them a tray of coffee and a plate of toast each. She dumped it down rather heavily.

'P'raps if you find it so exciting you ought to join up and have a go at fighting back,' she said caustically. 'You might get a bit more than you'd bargained for. It's all very well talking like that when you got a nice handy shelter to dodge into – it's a bit different when you're stuck in some foreign town with a mob of Jerries after you, and nowhere to hide!'

The boys stared at her. 'Here, there's no need to take it like that. We were only talking—'

'Talk when you know what you're talking about,' she retorted crisply. 'Sitting there all done up like window-dresser's dummies in your smart floorwalkers' suits! You ought've bin at Dunkirk, that would have wiped the silly grins off your faces.'

'It's not our fault we weren't there,' one of them began argumentatively, and Maggie leant closer.

'Ain't it? Ain't it? You mean you tried to join up and they wouldn't take you? You mean you'd have *liked* to be there? And before you says anything else, let me tell you who I am. I'm Maggie Wheeler – Tommy Wheeler's wife. His *widow* now. You remember Tommy, don't you? You know what happened to him. Well, if you don't, just ask your boss, because *he'll* know. He was a hero, my Tommy was, and there ought to be a bloody plaque up to him in Burton's.'

She stood back and watched their expressions change. Their faces flushed and they glanced at each other and then looked down at their plates. One looked up at her, started to speak, then bit his lip and fell silent. Maggie felt a hand on her arm and turned to see Mr Carter. He looked at them worriedly.

'Are you having a problem, Margaret?'

'No, sir,' she said, turning away. 'No, it's all right. It was just something they couldn't understand, but I've put 'em right now.' She went back to the kitchen and leant against the wall for a minute. Perhaps it wasn't their fault they hadn't been at Dunkirk. Perhaps it wasn't their fault they'd been excited by the bombing. But in her grief and sudden despair, it seemed cruel that they should laugh and joke about it, and she knew that if they had been wearing service uniforms her feelings would have been very different.

Phyl was beside her. 'Maggie? Are you all right? Mr Carter says you ought to be at your station. There's a table full of soldiers and they're asking for you to serve them. One of them says to tell you his name's Andy.'

Maggie stared at her. Andy? Andy who? And then she remembered the young recruits, so bright and polished, so eager to serve, so innocent of what lay ahead.

She picked up her tray.

'Tell 'em I'll be right there, Phyl. They're the ones that *deserves* to be waited on.'

The soldiers were looking less bright and polished than the last time. They looked tired and a bit subdued. Maggie marched over to them, her head high, ignoring the two floorwalkers at the next table.

'So what are you lot doing in here again? I thought I'd managed to put you off last time.'

The one called Andy grinned. His dark, curly hair gleamed, as if he'd tried to tame it with Brylcreem. His cap looked dusty and a bit battered.

'We just came in to see if you were real. Ted reckoned we'd dreamed you. And I wanted to see if you were okay,' he added in a lower tone, and to her amazement his face coloured slightly.

'Been worrying about you all weekend,' the ginger-haired boy said with a wink. 'Couldn't get to sleep for the worry, could you, Andy?'

'If that was all that kept you awake, you done all right,' Maggie told them. 'Now, what are you going to have to eat? There's a lot of things off this afternoon – couldn't get supplies through. But we're doing our best.'

'We'll have whatever there is. So long as it's hot.'

She looked at them curiously. 'What have you been doing? You look proper done up.'

Andy shrugged. 'Helping fight fires, mostly, in Stepney. They copped it real bad down there. We've got a couple of hours off and then we're supposed to be getting some kip before the next lot. So we thought we'd just pop along here, have a bit of luxury before we go back to barracks.'

'You reckon they're coming back tonight, then?'

'Everyone thinks they will. Hitler's started now, he's not going to stop till he's smashed London into the ground. Or we've smashed him instead – which is what's going to happen.'

She looked at their faces. They were tired but determin-ed. There was a toughness about them, even though they'd not seen active service yet, even though they'd barely finished their basic training. They looked harder, more adult, than the floorwalkers with their smart suits and soft hands. These boys had been up for two nights, fighting fires, while bombs had dropped about them; they had risked their lives. The others had spent their time watching as if it were some kind of giant firework display, staged for their entertainment.

'Just you tell me what you want,' she said, and this time no one smiled or made any suggestive comment, 'and I'll see you get it, all right?'

Jo was serving a little huddle of women. They, too, were discussing the events of the weekend.

'A lot of people say they're coming up West to shelter. The basement at Dickins & Jones is going to be open and they're going down there – they reckon it's the safest place. I thought I'd get a picnic packed and come up early with the family.'

'That's a good idea. I'll do that, too. I came to get some food in from Selfridges. Wonder if they've got any Thermos flasks, we could do with a new one.'

The third woman shook her head. 'I've already tried. Can't get one for love nor money. Nor won't be able to neither, for the duration. There won't be nothing like that about for the rest of the war.'

The rest of the war. Nobody knew how long that would be – or what state the world would be in when it finally ended. Nobody could even tell what state Britain would be in. Still British – or a part of Hitler's empire? The thought made Jo shudder as she went back to the kitchen to collect their order.

The women were right. Huge numbers of people made their way to the West End that night, to find shelter in the basements of the big stores. Phyl and Jo, snatching a moment to peep out of one of the windows, saw them crowding out of the underground station, whole families complete with grandmothers, grandfathers and small children, all festooned with bags and blankets. They watched in awe.

'It's a bit like when we came up to see the Coronation,' Phyl whispered. 'Remember that fat woman next to us, with the Marmite sandwiches? And we gave her a bit of our fruit cake. It's nearly as crowded as it was then.'

There was no happy anticipation this time, however. People looked tired and harassed, as if they'd been travelling half the afternoon, as probably they had. Already tired out by two sleepless, terrifying nights, they looked half-dazed, and not quite sure where they were or why they were there. They stared about them uncertainly and trailed off down Oxford Street, dragging whining children and grumbling old men and women in their wake, their blankets and bags coming unwrapped and tangling in their legs.

'Poor things,' Phyl said. 'They look as if they've come from the slums, some of them. Look at those rags. It's a shame.'

'And look at the children,' Jo said. 'They don't know what's going on, poor little devils. They ought to be out in the country, away from all this. I'm going to tell our Mum and Dad the first chance I get – our Alice has got to be evacuated, never mind that blooming cat. It's past a joke now.'

Most of the refugees had come from the East End, down by the docks where the great fires were still raging. They had, as Phyl supposed, set off early in the afternoon to be sure of their places in the shelters, and the underground trains had been packed like sardine tins. The platforms had been jammed and the escalators crowded. It had been almost impossible to move at times, and there had been several scenes of panic when a child had got lost in the crowd or an old, feeble man or woman had been taken ill.

One old fellow had had a heart attack right there in the station and it had been impossible to get enough space round him to give him air. Eventually, he'd been carried into the ticket-seller's office and revived with a bottle of water, and an ambulance called.

'God knows how long they'd have to wait for it,' one of Jo's customers told Jo, as she sat reviving herself with a pot of tea. 'I dare say the poor old bloke's dead by now, still laying on that platform. I tell you, girl, it was 'ell down there, bleedin' 'ell.'

'I don't know how they're going to get everyone down into the shelters anyway,' Jo said. 'When me and my cousin looked out just now there was hundreds coming. It looked like January sale time.'

'Well, that's it, ennit. They *won't* get 'em all in. There'll be people roaming the streets all night with nowhere to go. A sitting target, that's what they'll be, a sitting target.' She finished her tea. 'I'll be all right. I left our Bert and our Emmy keeping a place for me. I'll go back now and they can pop along for a cuppa, and by then perhaps they'll be letting people in.' She wiped her lips. 'What a life, eh! What a bleeding life.'

She departed and there was an immediate surge in the waiting queue for her place. The seaters were having problems controlling them today – usually quiet and biddable, the customers were all on edge, anxious to be served quickly and get away again. Queueing had become such a part of everyday life that people were generally patient enough, but with nobody knowing when the next raid would come and where they would find shelter it was difficult to wait your turn.

The woman had only been gone a few minutes when the air was split by the scream of the siren. Everyone stopped in their tracks and stared at each other. Customers began to rise to their feet and snatch up their bags and one or two of the Nippies almost dropped their trays. Mr Carter came quickly forward to where everyone could see him and raised both hands.

The noise died slowly away. Nobody had moved. The customers stared anxiously around and the Nippies, who had been rehearsed for this, stayed still.

Mr Carter raised his voice. 'Ladies and gentlemen! There is no cause for alarm. We have watchers on the roof and if there appears to be any danger we shall hear three sharp blasts on a hooter. In that case, you will all be led down into our own basement, where you will be perfectly safe until the danger is past. Until then, please take your seats again and your waitresses will bring you your orders.'

The customers glanced at each other again and some of them sat down slowly. Those who had food already on their tables began to pick up sandwiches or cakes and nibble uncertainly, or took a grateful sip of tea. Others shook their heads and continued to gather their belongings together.

'I'm not stopping. My Stan's waiting for me in the Dickins & Jones queue. I'll pay my bill, but I'm not finishing.' A few cakes and sandwiches were hurriedly snatched up and pushed into pockets or bags. 'There. I'll leave the money for this lot . . .' A few didn't even do this. They took a swift look round and saw that in the general confusion they would not be challenged, and just slipped quickly to the door. After a few minutes, order was more or less restored and the Nippies continued with their work.

'Look at that!' Maggie was flushed with indignation. 'That couple on table number seven, they've just nipped off without paying. Didn't even leave a tip! Of all the cheek – and they looked a nice, respectable pair, too, not even young. I don't have to pay their bill, do I, Mr Carter?' she appealed. 'It's not my fault there was a warning.'

'No, Margaret, you needn't worry about that.' He looked harassed and worried. 'I'll explain at the end of the shift—' He was interrupted by the three blasts on the hooter for which they'd all been subconsciously waiting. 'They must be almost overhead,' he exclaimed. 'Get everyone on your tables down to the basement. In an orderly fashion, mind – there's plenty of time. We don't want any accidents.'

The Nippies all took charge of their own tables and ushered their customers towards the stairs. Slowly, the crowd moved down past the lower restaurants, where they were joined by other customers and staff, and eventually into the lowest part of the building. Here they found themselves in a vast underground labyrinth of stone passages, with thick iron pipes coiling like snakes along the walls and here and there a few wooden benches. Every now and then they passed an iron door, from which they could hear the rumbling and clanking of machinery, and at the far end was a huge double door marked FIRE ESCAPE, firmly chained and padlocked.

'Well, I wouldn't like to be caught in a fire down here,' Maggie muttered when she saw it. 'You'd need a flaming hacksaw to get through that. Why in Gawd's name is it padlocked?'

'To stop people getting in, I suppose,' Shirley replied. 'Seems a bit daft, though, doesn't it?'

The young soldiers had followed them down. Andy looked at the chain and padlock and frowned. 'That's not right. It'd be a deathtrap in here if anything happened upstairs. You ought to get something done about it.'

'I'll tell Mr Carter.' Maggie found a bench in a corner and sat down. 'I wonder how long we're going to be stuck down here.'

'Could be all night,' Andy said, settling himself on the floor beside her and indicating to Shirley to take the next seat on the bench. 'Don't know as I'd grumble if we were!'

'You needn't think this is a chance to get fresh,' Maggie warned him. 'This is an air raid, not the back row at the Odeon.'

'Oh, you know about back rows, then, do you?' he

210

enquired innocently. 'I wouldn't have thought a nice respectable girl like you would know about that sort of thing.'

'I know about a lot of things,' Maggie replied tersely, and looked down at her hands.

Andy's glance followed hers and he saw the wedding ring on her finger. She heard him draw in a breath.

'Sorry – I didn't realise you were married.'

Maggie didn't answer at once. Then she said quietly, 'My Tom was killed at Dunkirk. I'm a widow, only it seems a queer sort of word to me. We only ever had a few days' married life together. The war was declared the day after the wedding, see, and he went straight off and just had a bit of leave after Christmas.' She gave him a sudden, startled look. 'I dunno why I'm telling you this.'

Andy reached up a hand and touched hers. 'It's all right. I'm not a blabbermouth.'

'Don't matter if you are. I'm proud of what he did. His mate told me what happened – my Tom was a hero, he said so. He was shot just as they were getting aboard a boat.'

'I don't want to be shot,' Andy said quietly. 'But I'd rather be a dead hero than a live coward.'

Maggie looked at him. 'You dunno what you're saying. You dunno what it's like. You haven't bin abroad yet, have you? You haven't bin in any real fighting.'

'No, but I know a lot of blokes who have. Most of 'em were at Dunkirk, too – might've known your Tom. I've heard them talk and I've done the training. I'm ready to go. I want to go.'

Maggie looked down at his face. Her eyes filled with tears and she touched his cheek with her fingers. His eyes met hers steadily.

'Let me know before you go,' she whispered. 'And come and see me when you come back. I—'

They were interrupted by the voice of one of the managers. It wasn't Mr Carter, but another, higher up, whom Maggie knew only by sight. He called for silence and the crowd stopped chattering.

'It seems to be quiet up above now,' he said when he had their attention. 'Anyone who wishes may stay here, but the building will resume normal activity now unless there's any further danger.' He glanced at the staff in their uniforms, and they took their cue and began to move towards the stone stairs. Maggie stood up and smoothed down her skirt, and Andy stood up beside her.

'Can I see you again?' he asked in a low, urgent voice. 'Not just in the Corner House, I mean – outside. We could go for a drink, see a flick . . .'

Maggie looked at him. 'Oh, Andy . . .'

'I know it's not long since you lost your husband,' he said. 'But we don't have time to wait – not these days. I like you, Maggie.'

'I like you, too,' she said helplessly. 'But – Andy, I'm sorry, I just don't want to go out with anyone else, not just yet. I can't.'

They were moving with the crowd towards the stairs. People jostled against them; in a moment, they would be separated. He reached out and found her hand, and she stared at him, dismay and desire warring in her heart. I can't be feeling like this, she thought, I can't.

'I'll think about you,' he said. 'I'll think about you all the time.'

Maggie shook her head. Tears were in her eyes, blurring her vision. She felt someone push against her, and her fingers slipped from his grasp. A man and a woman, thrusting in their hurry, shoved between them and she lost sight of him. Irene was beside her, and then Mr Carter. She hesitated and, as she reached the top of the stairs, found herself propelled along to the restaurant.

'Well, thank goodness that's over,' Irene said crossly, dusting herself down. 'What a horrible place! All those nasty pipes squirming round like great big worms, and that

212

awful clanking noise . . . I'd rather be up here with the bombs. There haven't been any, anyway.' She marched off to her station and glowered at the unoccupied tables, as if blaming them for their lack of custom.

'Half the people have just skived off without paying,' Jo exclaimed indignantly. 'I call that a brass cheek, I really do. They don't deserve to be let in again, that's what I say.'

They set about clearing the tables of half-finished meals, fetching fresh tea and cakes for the customers who had returned and making out bills for those honest enough to have come back to pay. Outside there was a continuous rattle of ack-ack gunfire. Obviously the raiders were still about, but nobody was taking much notice.

'It's funny how soon you get used to a thing,' Jo remarked as she encountered Phyl in the kitchen. 'A few days ago we'd never have thought it possible we could stand here collecting beans on toast just as if nothing was happening when we can hear guns firing at German planes.'

'I feel as if I'm in some sort of dream,' Phyl confessed. 'We've had hardly any sleep for two nights and we're on firewatching duty on the roof tonight, so we won't get much then. But I don't feel exactly tired – more as if I'm walking a few inches above the floor.'

'Well, now they've been over during the afternoon, they might not bother us tonight.' Jo cocked her head and listened. 'There's the all-clear. Well, that wasn't so bad, was it? Maybe the Germans are giving up. I hope they were all right at home, and Auntie Holt, too.'

The shift ended at last. There was time now to have a rest, but the girls were restless, too 'strung up' as Jo put it, to sleep on the makeshift beds that had been provided at the top of the building, and too tired to read or knit. They had supper in the staff canteen, sitting round the table discussing the weekend, which had already been discussed so much that they were half-sick of it, yet unable to find anything else to talk about. It seemed impossible that this could go on for long, they agreed. Nobody would be able to stand it.

'That's what the Germans want,' Irene said. 'They'll hammer us till we drop and then walk in and take over.'

'They can try,' Maggie said grimly. 'They'll have me and a few million others to reckon with if they do. What are you, Irene Bond, a quisling or something, trying to lower morale?'

'Don't be more stupid than you can help,' Irene said, flushing with anger. 'I'm only saying what everyone knows. It's what they're *trying* to do, that's all I said, not what they're *going* to do.'

'Well, you'd be better off not saying it at all.' Maggie got up. 'I'm going to go and try to get a bit of kip. If the last two nights are anything to go by, we're going to be up till tomorrow morning, and then we got another day's work to do.'

The others followed and lay on the camp beds, dozing fitfully. Etty and Shirley had gone off duty and set off for home. Shirley was worried about her father.

'I don't like going off and leaving you to it,' she'd said anxiously. 'But Dad needs a good hot dinner when he gets home, 'specially now. He's still not really well but he would go into work this morning, says there's an awful lot of mess to be cleared up.'

'You go off while you got the chance,' Maggie advised her. 'Your turn'll come soon enough. You want to look after your old man, it's only natural.'

'I'd stay, too,' Etty said guiltily, 'but Mr Carter's put me on tomorrow's rota and he says he can't start altering it all round now.'

'Just get going, the pair of you! There's enough of us here to make sure the place don't catch fire tonight. Let's hope we gets a quiet night, wherever we are.' Maggie yawned suddenly and drew a weary hand across her brow. 'Go on, Shirl! I want to get some sleep.'

214

The girls hurried off at last. Inside the Corner House, things began to quieten down. The all-night restaurant was to stay open, but the staff were ready for an alert. At the top of the building, the firewatchers took turns to stay up on the roof while others tried to rest. As they looked down into the street, they could see the crowds diminish as people found shelter, until only a few brave or foolhardy souls were left, strolling in the September twilight.

As darkness fell, the siren sounded again, and once again the black swarm approached from the south and the east, and for the third night running London braced itself against the coming of the bombs.

'That's them,' Mr Carter said. 'That throbbing sound – that's German planes. Ours have a nice, steady note, but they throb and growl.'

The dusky sky was netted with the thin, white beams of the searchlights, moving slowly across the darkness. Now and then they caught the silver, floating shape of a barrage balloon, like a huge, eerie fish swimming high above. And as the throbbing planes drew nearer, you could see the bombers themselves, trapped in the beam, and hear the sudden burst of ack-ack as the guns in Hyde Park and other emplacements fired.

'What'll happen if they get them?' Phyl asked, sounding scared. 'We'll get a whole plane full of bombs dropping on us!'

Nobody answered her. Sometimes, you could see that a plane was hit, and flames would crawl across the fuselage or along a wing, but none of them were brought down. The small fires went out or the plane vanished into the darkness, perhaps to crash in the countryside on its way home, or in the sea. Jo knew from Nick that planes could be hit many times and survive. His own 'crate' was peppered with holes which were apparently a source of some pride.

The bombers had reached their targets, if indeed they had any specific targets at all, and were beginning to drop their bombs. The girls stared as the brilliant beams of the searchlights gave them brief, horrifying glimpses of bombs, falling from the bellies of the planes like droppings from huge birds. They dropped fast, with a whistling sound that tore the eardrums, a sound like that of chalk being scraped across a slate but far, far louder, and wherever they fell there was an earth-shaking explosion and as often as not a sudden burst of flame as a gas main ignited or a domestic fire or a furnace scattered its burning coals.

'My God,' Jo whispered, staring around as the explosions sounded on all sides and more fires were started by incendiary bombs falling on buildings or in the streets. 'Oh, my God . . .'

'Get *down*!' Nobby Clarke, one of the kitchen porters, grabbed her ankle and pulled her down beside him. Everyone else was lying flat. 'D'you want yer head blown off, you silly cow?' He flung his arm across her head and pinned her to the leaded roof. ''Strewth, we're in the thick of it up here, a bleeding deathtrap, that's what this is.'

A bomb screamed down close by and the whole of the great building rocked. Jo never knew whether she screamed as well. The air was filled with noise – the roar of the explosion, the crash of falling bricks and masonry, the harsh shattering of glass. Her nostrils were filled with dust and the acrid smell of smoke and cordite, and she gulped and choked. She felt Nobby's arm lift away and looked up, terrified, but he was on his feet and wielding a fire extinguisher.

Jo leapt up beside him. The bomb had not fallen on the Corner House, or as close as she had thought. It was several streets away, but it had sent debris flying over the whole area and some of it was in flames – lumps and gobbets of burning wood and other, indefinable, material. The fire-watchers were already working to prevent it setting fire to the Corner House. They snatched up buckets of sand and hurled them over the blaze, they pumped water from stirrup-pumps, they even threw their own blankets over the smaller outbreaks and scorched holes in them, but in the end they had defeated the fire and stood panting, wiping their brows and grinning at each other.

'All right,' Mr Carter exclaimed. 'Well done, everyone, but we haven't got time to congratulate ourselves. The raid's still on, in case you hadn't noticed – and we may need more sand and water. You porters, you'd better fetch some more, and you Nippies get down below the parapet and keep watch. My God, they're not letting up, are they?' he added, gazing out over the burning roofs. 'They're going to beat hell out of us at this rate.'

There were no more fires on the Corner House roof that night, but the raid continued until the small hours, with wave after wave of bombers swooping across the stricken city. If it hadn't been so horrifying, Jo thought, it would have been a fascinating show, and indeed she couldn't help feeling a kind of mad exhilaration. It was like the greatest firework display ever seen – but with every flash and every bang, there was the thought that someone might have been killed, and this was enough to quell her excitement. That someone might be her own family. She would never forgive herself if she had leapt and crowed, as one or two of the porters were doing, and then found out that her own mother and father were being blown to pieces at that very moment.

At last the droning of the planes faded and the sky was quiet. There were no more little black crosses caught in the beam of the searchlights and the rattle of ack-ack had ceased. It seemed as if they might, at last, have gone.

'We can't go off duty yet,' Mr Carter said. 'Not until the all-clear sounds. But I think some of you could go down and try to get a bit of sleep. We'll soon let you know if you're needed again.'

He blew his whistle and sounded the hooter to let the rest of the building know that the coast seemed now to be clear, and the girls stumbled down to the makeshift dormitory. In the dim light, they looked at each other and laughed weakly.

'Cor, what a sight!' Maggie said. 'You look like a piccaninny, Phyl, with your hair all curls and your black face. And Jo's not much better, she's striped like a blooming zebra.'

'You can't talk,' Jo retorted. 'I reckon we're all as bad as each other. But I'm too tired to bother about it now – I just want to get my head down on a pillow.' She wiped her face with one hand and looked at it, grimacing. 'It's not going to do the pillow much good, though!'

Irene pulled a mirror out of her bag and stared into it. 'Ugh, how disgusting! I've never been so filthy in my life. Well, *I'm* going to have a wash, anyway. The rest of you can go to bed dirty if you like, but *I* think we ought to keep up our standards. If the Germans do invade, they're not going to find *me* living like a pig!'

She stalked out, making for the staff washrooms, and the other girls looked at each other and made rueful faces.

'She's right,' Phyl said with a sigh. 'It hurts me to say it, but for once I agree with her. Come on, let's go and wash some of this muck off – we'll feel all the better for it.'

There were no more calls from above. The 'raiders passed' signal didn't sound until five-thirty and by then the girls, having washed as best as they could manage in the small basins that were only meant for washing hands, and only provided cold water, were fast asleep in their narrow camp beds. In the streets below, those who had sheltered in the basements emerged into another dawn of torn buildings and rubble, of death and destruction, of raging fires and burst water mains. Bleary-eyed and weary, laden with blankets and the remains of their night-time picnics, they made their slow way home. Some of them paused to help dig for missing people, buried under ruined houses, some went straight to work.

It was the third morning of the blitz over London.

Chapter Thirteen

It was surprising, Jo remarked, how you could get used to a thing. You got home from work and either ate early, before the siren went, or made up a picnic to take to the shelter with you. Thermos flasks, blankets and cushions were all packed ready in baskets and the whole thing turned into a kind of party, with people singing to drown out the drone of the planes and jeers and shouts directed at the German flyers as they let their bombs fall all around.

The determined cheerfulness flagged each time the shelterers emerged to find new destruction. The sight of so many ruined houses, so many fires and such awful desolation in the streets that had been their homes struck them all to silence. The craters in the roads, the shambles of smashed houses, the glass that lay knee-deep, the ambulances carrying away the dead and injured – none of these were things that could be laughed or joked away. The Londoners went to what was left of their homes sobered and in silence.

'I don't care what you say,' Bill Mason told his daughter Alice after a shelter in the next street had received a direct hit and a young couple and their three-year-old son had been dug out, all dead, 'you're going away. I'm not having you in London a minute longer. Carrie, you're to go down the offices today and see what can be done.'

Alice's face crumpled. She put out her hand automatically for Robertson. He had spent the night in the Anderson with them, miaowing persistently to be let out and almost mad with fear when the bombs fell nearby. In the end, they'd managed to cram him into a pillowcase and Alice had held him tightly on her lap all night long.

'I can't leave him. He'd die without me.'

'Well, that's better than dying *with* you,' her father retorted. 'Look, Alice, I've had enough of this nonsense. I know how much you think of him, but he's only a cat and he's just as likely to get run over in the street as hit by a bomb. You can't be with him all the time. Anyway, that's not the point. The point is, you matter more than a blood—*blooming* cat, and I want you safe in the country.'

Alice stared at him and he met her eyes steadily. Carrie, watching them both, thought how alike they were – and how stubborn. But when it came down to it, Bill had size and authority on his side, and Alice wasn't likely to try running away again. She put out her own hand and touched Robbie's orange fur.

'You know we'll look after him,' she said gently. 'I'll take him down the shelter every night. I won't let anything happen to him.'

'What if he runs away? He gets so frightened, he'd run for miles, he'd be lost and never find his way home . . .' The tears weren't far away, and she gathered the big cat against her as if afraid he would escape at that very minute.

Carrie sighed. 'Maybe your dad could make a cage to put him in, so that he can't run away.'

'A cage? You can't keep Robbie in a cage. He's used to being free – it'd be cruel.'

'Not all the time,' Carrie said. 'Just at nights, in the shelter. He can do what he likes the rest of the time.'

Alice didn't speak. Her head was bent and her hand stroked the cat's back hard. After a few minutes, Carrie saw a large tear fall on Alice's bare knee, and knew that they had won.

'I don't want to go away,' Alice muttered, snuffling. 'You know I don't want to go. I'll miss you,' she added belatedly.

Carrie's mouth twitched. 'Well, you'll just have to tell Robbie to look after us,' she said. 'I reckon we'll be all right with him, don't you? And he can remind us of you, too.' As if we'd be likely to forget our own daughter, she thought, but Alice was so wrapped up in the blessed cat she'd never see the joke. The great thing was that she'd agreed to go, and Carrie felt as if a great weight had been lifted from her shoulders.

'We'll make sure you get a nice place,' she said, without any idea as to how this could be done. 'We won't let you go off anywhere you don't like.'

It took a few days for the authorities to organise another evacuation, and it was less well prepared than the first. Alice would have to stay for a while longer and Bill started to make Robbie's cage, knowing she would never rest until he'd done it. They put a scrap of old blanket inside and the cat crept into it, seeming to understand that he'd be safe in there. Alice spent the next night curled up on the camp bed they'd put in the shelter, with one hand inside the cage and Robbie nestled against it, if not purring then at least content.

Getting to work in the morning was harder every day. There were no buses or trams, the underground was packed and the trains all to pot, and people had to walk to work, sometimes for several miles, picking their way through fresh rubble and being turned back by fires or barriers across the street. Phyl and Jo had to make a long diversion one morning to avoid a huge unexploded bomb. They paused for a few minutes, joining the crowd to watch what was going on. The army was there, digging a huge pit, and they'd roped off a large area.

'Come on, now, keep back,' a young soldier was saying, waving his hands at the craning heads. 'You don't want to get blowed to bits, do you? That'd make Jerry laugh.'

'I'd make 'im laugh the other side of his face if I could get hold of 'im,' a stout woman with a shopping bag said aggressively. 'Knocking down our 'ouses and spoiling everything. Blooming lot of nonsense.'

'Why is it dangerous?' Phyl asked. 'If it didn't go off when it dropped, why's it likely to blow up now?'

'Timing,' a man nearby told her. 'They all got clocks inside 'em, see, like alarm clocks, set to go off. When they does, it sets off the fuse and the bomb blows up.'

'So it might go at any minute?'

'That's it. I bet those soldiers down that pit are listening to it tick and wondering the same thing.' He paused for a few minutes while they all stared at the crater and the men working carefully around it. 'They has to dig it out, see, so they can get at the clock and stop it. Then it'll be safe.'

'So if it's not ticking, it's all right?'

'Well, not necessarily. Sometimes the clocks don't even start till they get jogged or something, or maybe the timer's not set to start going yet. So if it *starts* ticking all of a sudden, it's just as bad. And nobody knows how long it's set for. All you know is that if it ticks it's alive and might go off any second.'

'Coo-er.' Phyl shivered. 'And those soldiers down there – they might get blown up any time.'

'That's right.' The man shook his head. 'Heroes, they are, bloody heroes.'

One of the men crouching at the rim of the pit suddenly straightened and waved his arms. All the soldiers relaxed and let out a cheer. Phyl looked enquiringly at the man, who grinned back at her as if he'd just been given an extra birthday.

'That means it's safe. They've defused it.' He joined in the cheering and Phyl felt herself drag in a huge sigh of relief and realised she'd been holding her breath.

'Oh, thank goodness, thank goodness. Oh, Jo, isn't that smashing?' Phyl clapped her hands. Everyone was smiling and cheering, even the woman with the shopping bag. Jo had tears pouring down her face.

222

'I'm glad we saw that, Phyl. It would have been awful if it had gone off. But we'd better get a move on, we're going to be ever so late for work.'

They hurried on down the street and were thankful to find no more obstructions. As Jo had predicted, they were once again late for work, but this morning the supervisors were less sympathetic.

'It's the same for everyone,' Miss Trimble, in the cloakroom, said brusquely as they began their explanation. 'We've all been in the same raid. You'll just have to leave a bit earlier.'

'But we can't, not till the all-clear goes—'

'Well, it went round our way at half past five, same as usual,' she said sharply. 'That gives me plenty of time to get an hour or two's sleep and still get here on time, so I don't see why it's got to be any different for you. Dawdling through the streets, stopping to watch unexploded bombs . . . Don't tell me you couldn't have been here on time if you'd wanted to.'

Their faces colouring, the girls had to admit that they could at least have been a little less late. They hurried to put their uniforms on, aggrieved all the same. How could you be expected not to stop when you saw something like that? It wasn't as if it happened every day.

'It does now, though,' Maggie said when she asked them why they looked so down in the mouth. 'It's like she says, we all got the same tale to tell, but some people are taking advantage, that's what. They're just not bothering. They're coming in any old time and using the raids as an excuse.'

'Well, why shouldn't we?' Irene demanded, overhearing them. 'We put in all those extra hours firewatching when our turn comes round, and we don't get paid for that. Why shouldn't we get a bit of time off in lieu?'

Maggie and Phyl stared at her. 'Fancy you talking like that! I thought you was going to be a supervisor yourself by next Wednesday teatime. I'd have thought you'd be the one to be in sharp to time and holding your watch up to the rest of us.'

Irene flushed. 'I just want what's fair. They expect us to sweat blood and then tell us off for being a few minutes late. Anyway, your cap's crooked and you ought to get that yellow hair cut if you can't keep it tidy.'

She turned away and Maggie snorted with laughter. 'Always got to have the last word! I reckon she was sorry she spoke then. She wouldn't have said it if any of the high-ups had been around to hear her.'

Some of the others didn't bother who heard them. The newer Nippies, who didn't feel quite the same loyalty towards Lyons, were much more casual. Phyl and Jo, queueing in the canteen, heard a couple of trainees grumbling together.

'I'm not breaking my neck to get here on time. Not when I've been awake half the night in a shelter. I'll get some sleep and then I'll have my breakfast and *then* I'll come in, and just see what time it is when I gets here. They can't expect more than that, and I told her so.'

The friend she was talking to gazed at her in admiration. 'Coo. What did she say then?'

'What could she say? They won't sack us, not when all them older girls are joining up, they won't be able to do without us, see. Anyway, this won't go on all that long – the Germans'll run out of bombs soon and then we'll all be back to normal.'

Jo and Phyl glanced at each other, tempted to join in and give the two young trainees a piece of their mind. But since they'd been late themselves, they just shrugged and said nothing. The young ones hadn't had their advantages, Phyl remarked later. They hadn't had all those lovely days out at the club at Sudbury and all those sports and dances. The club was still there but hardly anything was happening these days. You couldn't expect it, in present circum-stances.

Not that people had stopped enjoying themselves. After the first few days, when everyone had scurried home as fast as possible to shelter from the bombs, people were starting to rebel.

'Let's go to the flicks tonight,' Maggie suggested. 'I'm fed up with all this hiding and skulking. I reckon you're just as safe in the cinema as in one of those shelters – anyway, they say if a bomb's got your name on it you'll get it wherever you are. No point in wasting the rest of our lives!'

'I can't,' Shirley said. 'Dad would be worried stiff if I wasn't there when he got home.'

'Mrs Holt would be, too,' Jo said. 'Why not go tomorrow, then we can let them know we'll be late?'

They agreed to this. Only Etty was free to stay out without anyone worrying about her, and even she would have to ask permission and get a key if she was going to be late. The hostel had a large basement where they could shelter, and no one would hear a knock at the front door.

'Suppose there is a raid?' she asked nervously. 'How would we get home, with all the bombs?'

'Oh, we'd just find somewhere to shelter,' Maggie said carelessly, and then added as an idea struck her, 'We could come back here! The restaurant's open all night and we could go down the basement anyway. That's what we'll do.'

It seemed almost dull to go back home and get ready for that night's raid, rather than go to the pictures. The girls were fed up with the confinement, with the tedious routine of filling flasks, making sandwiches and carting blankets to the shelters. They were irritated by their companions who took up too much room, or sang when others were trying to sleep, or fell asleep themselves and snored. The air was fetid with unwashed bodies, beer, smoke and farting. The noise of the guttural throb and snarl of the aircraft coming over, the rattle of ack-ack and the juddering explosions of the bombs were both frightening and aggravating. They were conscious of a desperate need to sleep.

'I'm not coming here again tomorrow, and that's definite,' Mrs Holt declared as they scrambled through the streets next morning. 'There's been no more hits round here, you can see that. They've done enough damage round this way, they're aiming at someone else now. Anyway, I'm worried about all my things. I'm stopping home tonight.'

She had managed to get her windows either mended or boarded up, and after much persuasion had agreed to use the shelter again after the looting. Now the girls had to admit that it did seem safer. Elmbury Street and its surrounding neighbourhood hadn't been struck again and perhaps Mrs Holt was right in saying that the Germans were attacking other parts of London. It made sense, after all.

'Well, we're going to the pictures tonight,' Jo said, 'and we'll stop at the Corner House if there's any trouble. So you don't need to worry about us. You can go to bed early and have a good night's sleep.'

It was quiet enough at work that day, too, almost as if things were getting back to normal. The nightly trek to safety had become a way of life, and people came in for breakfast before starting for home almost as a matter of course. It was like a club, with customers swapping experiences and sharing their memories of extra-loud explosions or funny things that had happened while they were sheltering. Dickins & Jones's basement shelter was especially popular, with refreshments being served and people getting up to do 'acts' as well as community singing. It sounded as though it was a party every night down there.

The girls had some spare time between finishing work and going to the cinema, and Maggie suggested they walk down Park Lane and then along Constitution Hill to Buckingham Palace.

'It's been hit twice this week. The King and Queen are still there, though, they say they won't leave London. They won't even send the princesses away. I think that's ever so brave.'

The road outside the Palace was in ruins, with craters and rubble all over the place. Some of the Palace railings had been torn away, too, and soldiers in khaki guarded the archways. The girls stopped and stared.

'It's nearly as bad as our street.'

'Whatever must they think when they look out of their windows? D'you think they're scared, like us?' Phyl giggled suddenly. 'D'you think they've got an Anderson in the back garden?'

'Silly twerp.' Maggie dug her in the ribs. 'They'll have a big basement. Probably got red carpets and chandeliers and all down there, too.'

They turned away and strolled along in the sunshine. Apart from the barricades and gun emplacements in the parks, you might have thought it was peacetime. People were milling about, some of them having their picnics early before going down the shelters, and in St James's Park the ducks were flocking for crumbs just the same as always. The girls leant over the bridge, watching their antics.

'They don't know there's a war on,' Phyl observed. 'I wonder what they make of it at night, though, with all the noise and explosions. You'd think they'd be frightened then, wouldn't you?'

Jo gazed at them thoughtfully. 'I'm more surprised a few people haven't caught them for food,' she said, and then added, after a short pause, 'I've done it, Phyl. I've volunteered.'

Phyl raised her head and stared at her cousin. Maggie and Etty turned their heads, too. There was a moment's silence.

'You mean you've joined up?'

'Well, I've put my name down. For the Land Army. I went along at dinnertime.'

'So that's where you slipped off to!' Phyl said. 'I thought you'd gone to get your mum a birthday present.'

'Well, I did that as well, but mostly it was to go to the recruitment office. They seemed to think I'd get in, too,' she finished, looking pleased in an embarrassed sort of way.

'Well, if that ain't a turn-up for the book!' Maggie exclaimed. 'Our Jo going for a ploughgirl! You sure you'll like it out there in the country, Jo? There's nothing there but owls and rabbits. Mind you, there's plenty to eat from what I hear.'

'Jo's always wanted to live on a farm,' Phyl said. 'You should see her with animals. The baker's horse, the coalman's horse, the milkman's horse – they all know Jo. And her Alice is just as bad.'

'Well, I thought it'd be nice if I could get somewhere where they'd take Alice as well,' Jo said. 'You know Dad's set on her being evacuated, only nothing's been done yet. I thought if I got sent off quick, I might be able to put a word in.'

'That's a good idea. Maybe she'd be a bit more willing to go then.' They turned away from the ducks and wended their way back. They were going to a small cinema not far from Marble Arch.

'It'll be handy for the underground if we can get home and handy for the Corner House if we can't,' Maggie said. 'And they're putting on a good picture, too – that one with Laurence Olivier and Joan Fontaine in, about Rebecca.'

'Oh, I like Laurence Olivier,' Phyl exclaimed. 'He's so romantic! I saw him in that other one, *Wuthering Heights* – I dreamt about him for weeks after that.'

'I don't know why they don't let people stop down the underground all night,' Jo remarked, as they got caught up in a crowd of people emerging with their baskets and blankets, looking for their night's shelter. 'I mean, they'd be safer there than anywhere and there's loads of room on the platforms. I heard one of the customers saying in the restaurant today they've been on at the authorities about it again.'

'Frightened of the electricity, I suppose,' Phyl said. 'You've only got to touch that live rail and you're a goner. I suppose they think someone might roll off the platform in their sleep.'

'Well, they could turn it off while the trains aren't running.' They came to the cinema. There was the usual queue and they joined it, moving forward slowly. A commissionaire in a dark red uniform came along at intervals to ask if anyone wanted the circle seats, or the front stalls, and eventually they reached the little box office and bought their shilling tickets. Inside, it was dark and stuffy, and they felt their way along to their seats, directed by the usherette's torch. It all felt reassuringly normal.

'I'm glad we came,' Phyl whispered to Jo as they settled themselves in their seats. 'It'll be nice to forget the war for a bit.'

Forgetting the war wasn't as easy as that, however. *Pathé News* reminded them forcibly, with shots of the bombing in London and the aircraft battle as the RAF fought the invaders in the skies. Watching all the damage, it seemed impossible that Britain could go on struggling against such terrible odds. The Germans seemed to have an unending supply of planes and men to fly them, of bombs and ammunition. Swarm after swarm blackened the skies, and the reverberations of gunfire and explosions shook the little cinema until it was difficult to know if they were simply on film or happening outside in reality.

Phyl was aware of Jo, sitting rigid beside her. She felt for her cousin's hand and squeezed it. They sat close together, staring at the pictures of RAF fighters in dogfights with the Luftwaffe. Spitfires and Hurricanes swooped and dived and darted between the heavier German planes, and you could see the splatter of gunfire and the rip of fabric as they found their mark. You could see the flames and the black, oily smoke as an aircraft spiralled down to destruction.

'Oh, *Phyl* . . .' Jo whispered.

'He'll be all right,' Phyl whispered back. 'Nick'll be all right. He's an ace flyer – you know he is.'

Jo nodded. But her eyes were still fixed to the screen above them, and in her mind she knew that even ace flyers could be shot down. Even Nick.

Nick was in the air at that very moment, high above the Channel. The call to scramble had come just as he was sitting down to his evening meal but he leapt up as usual without a second thought, pausing only to grab a handful of sausages and stuff them into his mouth. He was still chewing when the propeller started to whirr round and the plane rolled forward and lifted into the air.

The raiders were coming in as usual, a flock of them, all trying to get into the sun so that the RAF pilots wouldn't be able to see them. The trick was to get up high and come at them from behind, so that the tables were turned and they couldn't see you. Nick's squadron was well practised at this by now and needed hardly any instructions. They flew like a skein of geese, wheeling and turning as one.

Nick was never happy until he could see the enemy aircraft. You couldn't evade something you couldn't see, and his back tingled as if he expected a shell to come crashing through the plane at any moment – as indeed he knew it might. Once he had got above them, however, and had the grey planes with their black swastikas firmly in his sights, he felt better – powerful, elated, determined to shoot them down.

He was above them now and had the luxury of choosing which one to pick off. In his ears were the calls of his fellow pilots and the orders of the squadron leader. He listened and then targeted the Heinkel bomber in the middle of the flock. You'll not get my Jo this time, he thought as he settled on its tail and began to shoot.

He knew he was hitting the plane, but the first few bullets

did no more than rip the fabric. He saw the tears appear and swore to himself. It was no use sending a plane back with no more than a few holes in its side. He wanted it down, destroyed. He flew closer, his eyes intent, and fired another burst.

The Heinkel seemed to pause momentarily. Its outline shivered and, far more slowly than seemed natural, it flew into a million fragments in the air. At almost the same second, an explosion of flame seared from its centre and the fragments became burning stars of brightness. In the midst of it all Nick caught a tiny glimpse of a black, flailing figure which hurled itself from the ball of flame and kicked itself into a savage descent. The whole flaming mass descended into the sea, which received it with a surging, hissing cloud of steam.

Nick was entranced. The whole thing was over in seconds. Oh, wizard, he thought, wizard. And now for the next . . . He turned his aircraft and began to search the sky for his second victim.

He never saw it. A tremendous bang seemed to knock his head sideways and he felt the scorch of a shell brushing past his cheek. The instrument panel in front of him disintegrated and disappeared. The canopy was torn to shreds. He found himself riding alone and unprotected in the open air, the speed of the air blowing his cheeks out as tightly as a bullfrog's and the strap of his flying helmet almost cutting his throat.

Baling out wasn't a choice; it simply happened. In those first few seconds of wild tumbling Nick's mind was totally blank. He watched in bemusement as sea and sky whirled about him, then his training came to his rescue and he found the ripcord and jerked. There was a moment of fear as he thought the chute wasn't going to open after all, and then he felt a jolt and found himself wafting slowly down towards the sea. He hung there, staring about him, waiting to be shot as he floated helpless and vulnerable, but the sky was suddenly quiet. The raiders and the RAF had vanished to continue their battle further up the coast.

Oh, well, he thought philosophically, I suppose I'll just have to drown instead.

It would have been a surprise if the bombers hadn't come over that night. They'd been coming like clockwork ever since the beginning of September after all. The raid began while the film was still showing and they stopped the reels for a few minutes to give people a chance to leave if they wanted to. The girls glanced at each other and Maggie shook her head firmly.

'This is the first night out I've had for Gawd knows how long. I want to see what happens to that girl!'

'I'm not going either,' Phyl said, 'not while Laurence Olivier's up there.'

Jo and Etty were also determined to see the film through and after a few minutes it began again and they tried to immerse themselves in the story once more, ignoring the noise coming from outside.

It ended at last and they came out into the night. There were wardens ready to direct them into shelters, although nothing much was happening in this part of the city. The girls looked at each other, hesitating.

'What d'you reckon?' Phyl asked Jo. 'Shall we try and get back to Auntie Holt's?'

'I dunno. She'll be in the shelter anyway – I know she said she'd stop indoors, but I bet she won't, not when it comes to it. You know how full they get. I think we'd be better to stop here.'

'Well, I'm going down the Corner House,' Maggie declared. 'Etty, you come with me, you can't get back to the hostel tonight. We'll be all right there, down in the basement.'

Ducking their heads, they hurried through the streets. The activity from above was increasing now and they jumped as a bomb fell not far away and the ground shook and juddered beneath their feet. Wardens yelled at them to get under cover, and an old van converted to an ambulance tore by, its bell ringing frantically. There were few people in the streets now, but above the buildings they could see the red glow of fires and at one point they found themselves sprayed with water from a fireman's hose.

'Oh, quick, quick!' Etty cried in an agony of fear. 'Let's get inside somewhere! Let's go down the subway.'

The girls hesitated. The subways beneath the road should be as safe as any shelter. But even as they peered down the steps they could see that the tunnels were packed with people and the only room left was on the steps, hardly safer than the road above. Jo shook her head.

'It's all right. We're nearly there.' They were within sight of Marble Arch. The great façade of the Corner House reared above them, ornate and comforting in its familiarity. Jo looked up at it, feeling almost as if she had come home. She grabbed Phyl's hand and pulled her along.

'Come on, Phyl. We'll be safe inside. Come on—'

There was a screaming, whistling rush of sound. The explosion tore at the earth all around them. It wrenched at the surface of the road and ripped huge gashes in the pavement. The walls of the Corner House shuddered and seemed for a moment to turn to liquid, like jelly that had not quite set. For a moment, it seemed as if they would tumble, bringing down the entire edifice, and then they seemed to settle back and take on their normal shape, and only the road and the pavement remained damaged and twisted beneath their feet.

Jo felt Phyl's hand tugging at her wrist, the nails biting into her flesh. She dropped to the ground and they lay together, their arms covering their heads, while debris and dust and shrapnel rained all about them.

'Oh, blimey,' Maggie was muttering beside them. 'Oh, blimey, blimey, blimey, *blimey* . . .'

Another bomb dropped. Again, the rushing noise, like a train racing through a station; again the juddering of the earth, as if it would rise up and swallow them all. Again the swirling cloud of dust and smoke, filling the nostrils, choking the throat. Jo, momentarily lifting her head, caught a brief, horrifying glimpse of an entire wall falling away from a building somewhere down the road, lit up by flames and swaying as it seemed to hesitate before crashing down into the road.

'Get inside!' It was Etty who took charge now, hauling them to their feet and thrusting them towards the big glass doors. 'Quick, before there's another one.'

Nobody argued. They pushed their way in and scrambled for the stairs to the basement. Inside, there was pandemonium. Nobody knew if the House had received a direct hit, but the blast had brought down plaster and smashed windows. Broken glass lay in huge shards and tiny fragments. A few lights still burned and people had come from the basement or the roof to see what had happened. They stood staring at the wreckage, while a few ran about in a state of shock, shouting out to everyone to stay still, get down, take cover. And outside, the noise continued still, the throb of German aircraft, the clatter of ack-ack, the thunderous explosion of bomb after bomb after bomb . . . .

The raid had been directly over Oxford Street. The heaps of rubble were now directly in front of great shops and stores. The smashed glass was of windows filled with the goods of wartime – a pitiful array, even in the greatest stores of the country, now stuck all over with splinters like the spines of a hedgehog.

The bomb that had fallen so close to the Corner House had hit the subway under Marble Arch, where the girls had thought momentarily of sheltering. The blast had torn the tiles from the walls and twenty people had been killed. The girls looked at each other, horrified, when they heard.

'That could have been us . . .'

To those who had been in the Corner House all night, the word came from Nippies and other staff arriving for work. Other bombs had fallen in Oxford Street, hitting a number of the big shops. D. H. Evans and Bourne & Hollingsworth had both been damaged and John Lewis, one of the biggest stores of all, had caught fire and the firemen were still there, trying to put out the flames. No one knew how many people were trapped in the basement beneath. Bond Street and Burlington Arcade had been hit, too, the smart shops reduced to rubble just like anywhere else.

'They'll have to let people go down the underground now,' Phyl said, horrified. 'There's nowhere else safe.'

The girls had been lucky to escape injury from the Marble Arch bomb – perhaps, Mr Carter said later, they had been close enough to the building to escape the rain of debris, as you could be sheltered from ordinary rain when you were close enough to a wall. But a gas main had been broken and another bomb had come right down into the building and lay there without exploding. The bomb disposal unit had been called and the restaurants were closed.

'We're keeping just one floor open,' Mr Carter explained as more and more staff began to arrive for work. 'Quebec will be open as usual. The police assure us we'll be safe to work there while the bomb is being dealt with. It isn't a time-delayed bomb, so there's no danger that it will go off – it just needs to be removed.'

The girls looked at each other. Even with so many arriving late, there were still far too many to work in one restaurant. Jo shrugged and led the way upstairs.

'We might as well go and see what's what.'

'It's a mess, that's what,' Irene said aggrievedly. 'I mean, look at them all. They don't know what to do, and they don't know what to tell us to do.' She surveyed the turmoil in the restaurant. Nippies were thronging through the

235

doors, besieging the distraught supervisors with questions. A few of them were looking defiant and turning back to the doors, saying they were going home. What was the use of everyone stopping on when it was obvious there'd be hardly any customers and hardly anything to serve them anyway?

'Shut up,' Jo said as a girl pushed past her, grumbling loudly. 'Shut up and listen. Mr Carter's going to say something.'

The floor manager had climbed on to the platform where the band usually played. He had a sheet of paper in his hand. He raised the other for silence and the noise subsided to a mutter.

'We've decided to open this café to the public,' he said. 'Listen carefully to the following instructions. As you know, a bomb fell just outside last night and a gas main has been fractured. That means there will be very little cooking. There will be only the following hot items on the menu – soup, steak and kidney pie, and brunch. Salads are on as usual and, of course, there will be tea and coffee.' He paused as the girls rippled into laughter. The idea of there being no tea or coffee was quite ludicrous – there was *always* tea and coffee. 'This is an emergency,' he reminded them. 'Lyons are relying on you all to remember your training and your loyalty and do all you can to help us.'

'And what about *them* helping *us*?' Irene muttered. 'We struggled all the way here and we don't get so much as a thank you. Just told off for being late. I ask you!'

'Well, we got to do our job,' Jo told her. 'We can't expect to get paid if we don't work.'

'Yes, but there's too many of us. We'll be standing about doing nothing all day. We might just as well go home and get some rest. And you know what they're saying up in the canteen, don't you? We're only to take one dinner – no second helpings. When they know most of us don't have no gas at home neither and this is the only decent meal we'll get!'

236

'I'm surprised to hear you talking like that, Irene,' Miss Trimble said, materialising beside them. 'I always looked on you as a girl I could rely on. I thought you had ambitions to be a supervisor yourself.'

Irene flushed scarlet to the roots of her hair. 'I'm only repeating what some of the other girls are saying,' she said quickly. 'It's not what *I* think. I think we ought to be all pulling together.'

'I'm glad to hear it.' Miss Trimble moved on and Jo gave Irene a withering look.

'Liar. You'd be off this minute if you thought you could get away with it.'

'I wouldn't!' Irene was furious at having been overheard. 'Anyway, you know they're expecting too much. We've got other lives besides Lyons – it's not as if all we've got to do is think about work. You know that as well as I do.'

Jo had to admit she was right. Some of the supervisors didn't seem to give much thought to what went on outside the Corner House. It was as if the Nippies lived in boxes, to be taken out and wound up and set in motion for the day's work, then returned to their boxes for the rest of the time. Whereas they had to make their way home all over London, not knowing what might have happened while they were at work, and then struggle back next morning after a night in an air-raid shelter.

She thought of Elmbury Street and Mrs Holt. Apart from their firewatching duties, this had been the first night she and Phyl had spent away from their digs, and she felt a sudden anxiety about their landlady, who had looked after them so well. I wish we could get off early, she thought. I hope she did go to the shelter last night after all . . .

'Let's ask Mr Carter if we can slip off at dinnertime,' she suggested as the customers began to trickle in, most of them people who had been sheltering in the basements all night and were now about to go home again. 'Irene's right, there's plenty of staff here, they can't need us all.'

The floor manager agreed to them going. 'You were here last night, helping sort out the mess,' he said. 'You deserve a few hours off. Go along now, and I'll see you in the morning. Bright and early, mind!'

'We will,' Phyl promised with a flash of a smile. 'Thanks ever so much, Mr Carter. It's just that we're worried about our landlady.'

'Go on,' he said, smiling back with tired eyes. 'Go home and put your minds at rest. And if I were you, I should give the pictures a miss for the next few nights!'

'Some hope,' Phyl said cheerfully as they went outside and looked for a bus. 'Oh, well, I suppose it's shanks's pony again . . .' They set off, walking through the ruined streets. 'It won't take us all that long. And then we might even have time to slip home and see that they're all right there as well.'

There was, however, no time for slipping home, or for slipping anywhere else. For as they turned the corner into Elmbury Street they were shocked into rigidity by a scene of totally unexpected devastation.

It wouldn't have mattered whether Mrs Holt had gone to the shelter or not. Both the shelter and the entire row of houses had been demolished. They lay in scattered mounds of bricks and mortar and crumbled concrete, piled and splintered wood and smashed glass, and it was obvious that almost nobody could have survived.

Chapter Fourteen

'I've just about had enough of this,' Jo said bitterly as they trailed away from the church hall. The bodies of all those who could be found were laid out there, covered with sheets, and Jo and Phyl had been faced with half a dozen middle-aged women, some almost unmarked, some battered and bloody. Auntie Holt had been one of the less badly injured, but her back had been broken, they said, and her skull fractured. She lay as if asleep, her eyes closed and only a smear of dust across her cheek to show that anything was wrong.

'Thank God her face looked all right,' Phyl sobbed as they wandered aimlessly through the streets. 'I couldn't have took it if she'd been all knocked about, like those others, Jo. Oh, poor Auntie Holt, poor, poor Auntie Holt . . .'

'If only we'd come home,' Jo said wretchedly. 'I keep thinking if we'd been here we might have been able to do something . . .'

'We couldn't. You know we couldn't. It would have happened whoever was there – and we'd be laying on the floor covered in sheets, too.' The tears were streaming down Phyl's face. 'And we don't even know how they are at home. Suppose they copped it, too. What are we going to do?' A sudden thought struck her. 'Where are we going to sleep tonight? All our stuff's gone. And all those ornaments and things we put up in the attic last week – oh, it's just not *fair!*'

'They said for anyone homeless to go round the offices. I

suppose we could do that. But we were Lyons lodgers, so we ought to let them know.' Jo rubbed a weary hand across her forehead. It seemed like years since they'd sat in the cinema, caught up in the story of Maxim de Winter and his wife. 'Maybe we just ought to go back and tell them what's happened. At least we could stay there tonight.'

'I tell you what,' Phyl said, 'I'm scared to stay anywhere. Our own digs bombed and the Corner House as well, all in one night – Jo, I can't stick not knowing what's happened at home. For all we know, they might be bombed out as well. We've got to go and see.'

Once again they made the long journey home. It seemed to get more difficult each time, but eventually they turned the corner of the street and saw with a great surge of thankfulness that there had been no damage.

'You'll stay here tonight,' Carrie said when she heard what had happened, and May nodded her agreement. 'Lyons will manage without you tomorrow. You've had a bad shock and you need time to get over it.'

'We'll send a telegram to say you won't be in,' May added. 'Mr Carter'll understand. From what you say, they can't cope with all you girls anyway, the state they're in.'

'They'll be back to normal tomorrow,' Jo protested without much conviction. 'The bomb'll be gone and they'll have got temporary cookers in. They'll need us, Mum.'

'They don't need you looking like ghosts. Anyway, you've got to get some more lodgings sorted out – that's if you're going back at all.'

'Mum! Of course we're going back. We work there.'

'And there's been bombs there. I'm not sure I want you going back—'

'There's been bombs everywhere,' Jo said wearily. 'Anyway, it may not be for long. I've applied to join the Land Army. I'll be out on a farm soon, I dare say, and I'm going to see if our Alice can't come out there with me.'

'A farm?' Carrie stared at her, open-mouthed. 'You've

been and applied, without even talking it over with me and your dad?'

Jo nodded. It hadn't really occurred to her to discuss the plan with her parents. 'I'm twenty-one now,' she pointed out. 'And I'll be called up some time anyway, and not be able to choose what I do. It's what I want, Mum.'

'You know how she's always been about animals,' Phyl chimed in. 'And I'm going, too. I've made up my mind. I can't stand by in a nice comfy Corner House while there's people doing real war work.'

'*You're* going into the Land Army?' May's eyes rounded. 'You've never even been interested in the country!'

'Not the Land Army, no. I thought I'd try the Wrens. Fancy meself in navy blue, I do.' She grinned saucily. 'And you know what they say – every nice girl loves a sailor. Well, maybe every nice boy will love a sailor-girl!'

'Phyl! What a way to talk! And you engaged to a boy already.'

'I was only joking. You know I'd never look at anyone else. Anyway, I'm going down the offices tomorrow. I'd almost made up my mind before, but what with all that's happened . . .' Her eyes filled with tears again. 'Oh, Mum!' she sobbed. 'It's been so awful. And poor Auntie Holt, laying there on that floor – I can't get it out of me mind. I've just got to do *something*!'

May pulled her daughter close and folded her in her arms. 'I know, lovey, I know. It's bad for all of us. Well, you know me and your dad'll never stand in your light. You do whatever you feel you got to do, and with our blessing. Let's just do our best, all of us, to get this horrible war over.'

'It's going to take a bit more than just us,' Carrie remarked sadly, reaching out to stroke Robertson's ginger fur. 'It's going to take everyone in the land to beat that lot. But if spirit'll do it, Londoners will show them all. Londoners have got more spirit than all Germany put

241

together, and that's what'll beat 'em in the end. You mark my words.'

Nick came into the Corner House two days later and waited for Jo to come off duty. She found him at the door and her eyes filled with tears.

'Oh, *Nick* . . .'

'Hey,' he said, putting his arms round her. 'Hey, what's all this? You haven't been worrying about me, have you? I told you it's hard to get a chance to get away these days.'

She shook her head and rubbed at her eyes. 'It's not that. Well, it is – I'm always worried about you. Even when we were at the pictures the other day and saw the *Pathé News* . . . I couldn't help thinking about you. But it's been so awful here . . . Nick, Auntie Holt's been killed.'

'Auntie Holt?' He gripped her more tightly. 'You mean she's been bombed? When? What happened? You're all right, aren't you? Were you in it, too?'

'No. We were here. We'd been to the pictures and when we came out – well, it was so bad we just came straight back here.'

Nick lifted his head and stared around him. Some of the debris had been cleared away and tarpaulins stretched over the worst of the damage, but it was clear that Marble Arch and Oxford Street had been badly knocked about. 'You were *here*?'

'We got down in the basement. We were safe there.' They wouldn't have been if the building had caught fire, like some of the big stores, but neither of them said so aloud. 'But at home – almost all the houses in Elmbury Street have gone. Nick, and poor Auntie Holt . . . We had to go and see her body and say it was her.'

'*Jo*. You poor thing.' Nick became aware of Phyl standing beside them. He reached out and drew her into his embrace as well. 'I got the wrong bloke this time,' he said bitterly.

Jo looked up at him. 'What d'you mean?'

Nick twisted his lips in a wry grimace. 'I always reckon that if I manage to bring a Jerry down I'll be keeping you safe. It's like a sort of talisman. Some blokes take mascots with them, a teddy bear or something daft like that – they reckon it brings 'em good luck. I just think about you and my mum and dad, and try to keep you all safe by shooting down the bloke that would bomb you.'

Jo smiled shakily. 'Well, we are safe,' she pointed out.

'Only just. You could've been hit before you got here. And you could've been at home with poor old Mrs Holt.' He hesitated. He'd intended telling Jo about his own adventure, making a funny story of it, but now he decided not to. 'Let's go and have a drink. Where are you stopping now?'

'We've got to go round to the office now and get it sorted out. They're finding us some new digs.' Jo and Phyl fell in beside him and began to walk along the shattered street. On every side there was evidence of the raid. Shop windows were blasted in and boarded up, walls broken, the road filled with craters. 'All our stuff went, too – our clothes and books, everything. We'll get some money for new things, but not much. Oh, Nick – I've lost all your letters as well!' She began to cry again.

Nick stopped and took her in his arms again. 'Not to worry, sweetheart – I'll write you lots more. I was making one up all the way down—' He stopped.

Jo wiped her eyes again and frowned. 'All the way down where?'

'Nowhere. Forget I said it.'

She looked at him. 'What d'you mean? What should I forget?' She tugged at his sleeve. 'What is it you're not telling me, Nick? What's happened?'

'Oh, nothing. It was just that I had to bale out during that raid, probably while you were at the pictures – some bloody Messerschmitt got on my tail, my own fault, I was too busy

243

congratulating myself on shooting down your bomber – what I *thought* was your bomber – and he sneaked up behind me and blew the crate away from under me. Strange sort of experience, really—'

'*Nick!*' Jo shook his arm violently. 'Stop jabbering and tell me what you're talking about! You had to *bale out*? You mean *you* were shot down? Why didn't you tell me at once?'

'Because you had more important things to tell me,' he said reasonably. 'And anyway, I didn't want to upset you. You've been through enough.'

'Oh, Nick.' Jo hid her face against his sleeve. Her body shook with sobs. 'Nick, you've been shot down and I didn't know. *I didn't know* . . .'

He held her closely and met Phyl's eyes above her head. They gazed at each other wordlessly. There was nothing to be said, no comfort to give. Only a shock to be borne, one of a series of shocks. And they all knew that the shocks wouldn't end yet.

The air raids made it difficult for Irene and Muriel to go out together as often as they would have liked. Muriel popped into the Corner House for lunch whenever she could, but in the evenings Irene hurried home straight after work. Her parents were anxious to have everyone safely at home before the raids began, she explained.

'That's all very well,' Muriel remarked as Irene hovered by her table, ostensibly taking her order. 'I like to get into shelter in good time, too. But I can't go on for ever, never seeing you, Irene.'

Irene looked at her, startled. Once again, Muriel was behaving more like a young man talking to his sweetheart. She felt uneasy and flattered and slightly excited all at once. It's just her way, she thought, but it's nice to know someone thinks that much of me.

'I've missed our evenings out, too,' she said. 'And I tell

you what, a lot of the girls are getting fed up with having to rush home like this. They want to go to the pictures or out dancing and I don't blame them. I mean to say, stopping at home all night in an air-raid shelter with your knitting and a lot of old people, that's no life for a young girl, is it?'

'Indeed it's not,' Muriel agreed warmly. 'And if you ask me, it's selfish of them to want you to do it. They've had their youth, after all.'

'That's right. They don't see it that way, though. They just talk about us being *safe*.' Irene curled her lip. 'I told my mum yesterday, I'd be safer at the pictures than I am when I'm firewatching up on the roof here.'

'So why not come to the pictures with me, then? Not tonight, you'll need to let them know you'll be late, but tomorrow. Or – look, I've got an even better idea. Why don't you come back to the hostel with me for the night? We've got a good shelter in the basement and if there's no raid you can share my room.'

Irene stared at her. 'Is that allowed?'

Muriel shrugged. 'Who's to know? I've told you before, I have my own little flatlet on the top floor. I've been wanting to show you for some time. There's a lovely view over London. In any case, nobody's going to turn a visitor out in the middle of a raid. Why not come?'

'I'd really like to.' Irene gazed at her in excitement. 'Yes, I will. I'll tell Mum and Dad tonight.' She caught Mr Carter looking at her across the restaurant and scribbled hastily on her notepad. 'All right – I'll see you tomorrow.'

She hurried back to the kitchen, her heart thumping. She had never been invited to stay anywhere overnight before. Once again, she wondered why Muriel had singled her out for such flattering attention. Well, obviously because quality recognises quality, she thought with a tiny, nervous giggle. And Mum and Dad had seen it, too, when she'd taken Muriel home for Sunday tea. They'd approved of this friendship. They'd be pleased to know that Muriel thought enough of her to invite her to stay overnight, rather than risk trying to get home through an air raid.

The picture was quite good and there was no sound of planes or bombing. They came out into a night almost as quiet as in peacetime and strolled through the streets, arms linked.

'It's terrible to see all this damage,' Irene said. 'Thank goodness we haven't had anything round our way yet. It seems to be mostly the East End and the docks that are getting it. Not the nicer areas.'

'Well, Buckingham Palace has been hit,' Muriel pointed out with a smile. 'Or don't you consider that a "nice" area?'

Irene giggled. 'Oh, well . . . Did you see that picture of the King and Queen going round the bombed sites? She said she was *glad* they'd been hit – now they could "look the East End in the face". Seems a funny way to put it, doesn't it?'

'Especially when she's all dressed up in a nice smart coat and hat,' Muriel observed drily. 'I don't suppose we'll see *them* out in the street with nowhere to go, like some of the people she was talking to. They live in a different world, the royal family.'

Irene glanced at her in surprise. 'Don't you like the King and Queen?'

'Oh, they're all right, I suppose. They can't help being who they are – he was never meant to be king anyway, was he? It should have been his brother, and now he's been turned out of his own country and they're hounding him all over Europe. I call it a shame.'

Irene felt uncertain. 'But he could have been king. It was only because of Mrs Simpson—'

'Well, of course,' Muriel said distastefully. 'It's always the same. Men and their disgusting habits, they're the cause of half the trouble in the world.'

'What's the cause of the other half?' Irene asked, and Muriel laughed.

'Women who can't stop running after men, of course! Not like you and me.' She gave Irene's arm a squeeze. 'It's so much nicer to have a woman friend than a man, don't you think?'

Irene agreed. They were just passing Hyde Park, where Richard Godwin had tried to force himself on her that awful night, when she'd thought he was such a nice, refined sort of young man. It just showed that you couldn't trust any of them. It was much, much nicer to be with another woman.

They were almost back at the hostel when the raid started and they hurried inside. Girls and women were crowding down to the basement and Irene made to follow them, but Muriel held her back.

'There's no need. We can see from my window when they're getting near. So long as we don't put the light on, it's all right. You know half the time they don't know where the planes are going to come – it's a waste of time going downstairs till you've got to.'

They ran up the three flights of stairs and Muriel unlocked her door. It was the first time Irene had been there and she looked around with interest. It was smaller than she'd imagined, but she envied her friend the chance to have a room of her own, to be completely independent. I might think about moving somewhere like this, she thought. I wonder if they've got any vacancies here. It would be more suitable for a supervisor to have her own little flat than to be living at home with her parents like a child.

Muriel snapped off the light and took down the blackout curtain. They looked out over the shadowy roofs. The silvery net of searchlights moved ceaselessly across the black void, and somewhere a few miles away they could see the bright glow of fires burning.

'I'll make some coffee.' There was enough light coming into the room from the half-moon and the searchlights, and Muriel moved confidently about, filling the kettle and setting it on the little gas stove. There was a bottle of milk on the windowsill and she poured some into two cups and mixed it with some liquid Camp coffee.

They sat together on the edge of the bed, gazing out of the window. The noise was loud but the planes were clearly some distance away. Irene could see incendiary bombs coming down, already in flames, like bright, shimmering sparks. She watched, fascinated, as they fell on roofs or in the streets and were either hastily extinguished or set fire to their surroundings. She imagined the streets, out of sight from this high vantage point, filled with scurrying people – ambulances, fire engines, ARP wardens running to and fro, trying to regain order.

'It's quite exciting really, isn't it?' she said. 'Better than being down in a poky little shelter!'

'Oh, yes. As long as they don't get any closer, we're quite safe here.' Muriel slipped her arm around Irene's shoulder. 'I'm glad you're here. I worry about you when these raids are on.'

Irene turned her head in surprise. 'Do you? You worry about me?'

'Well, of course I do,' Muriel Chalk said, regarding her calmly. 'You're important to me, Irene. Didn't you know that?' And before Irene could reply, she leant forward slightly and kissed her on the lips.

Irene was too astonished to move. Nobody had kissed her on the lips since she was a small child – except for Herbert Lennox, and Richard Godwin, and she hadn't liked it then. Their mouths had felt wet and sloppy, or else too harsh, as if they were trying to eat her. Muriel Chalk's lips were dry and cool and gentle. It was nice.

'Oh,' Irene said when the kiss finished.

Muriel smiled, her teeth gleaming in the dim light. 'There. That's just to show you how much I think of you. Just to say we're friends. We are, aren't we?'

'Yes, of course we are,' Irene said.

'We trust each other, don't we?'

'Yes, of course we do.'

'Bosom pals,' Muriel said with a contented sigh, and laid her hand on Irene's breast. 'Funny expression, isn't it? But right, somehow, for women friends like us.'

Richard Godwin had done this, too, and Irene hadn't liked it at all. But again, it was different with Muriel. She was a woman herself, she had bosoms, too, there was nothing different about Irene's. It was just a nice, friendly gesture. It made Irene feel warm and because she wanted to make her friend feel warm, too, she laid her hand on Muriel in the same way.

'Oh, yes,' Muriel said softly, and let herself lie back on the bed, bringing Irene with her. 'Oh, *yes* . . .'

'I suppose people are being more careful with what they say in the restaurant these days,' Muriel observed as she and Irene sat having breakfast at her little table the next morning. They could have gone downstairs into the main dining-room, but Miss Chalk preferred to keep a few little stores, such as a packet of cornflakes and her own tea and coffee, in her 'kitchenette'. A gel needed a little privacy, she considered.

'Some of them are. Some of them are so free with their tongues, you wouldn't believe it.' Irene sat basking in the warmth of her friend's affection. Some of the things they had done in the night had surprised her, but it had all felt so pleasant and natural that she couldn't object. After all, it wasn't like a man touching you. 'There were a couple of sailors only yesterday, telling one of the other girls which ship they were off and when it was sailing and everything. I mean to say, you just don't know who might have been listening.'

'How foolish of them. I suppose they were from the Pool of London?'

'That's right. Merchant ships, going on convoy. I gave

249

her a sharp word in the canteen, I can tell you, but as she said, you can't stop people saying things when you don't know what they're going to say.'

'No, indeed. Well, it's just as well it didn't go any further.' Muriel poured Irene another cup of tea. 'I suppose they know they can trust Nippies.'

'It's not us, though, is it? It's whoever might be at the next table. I mean, if there'd been a fifth columnist sitting there drinking in every word and then going off to tell Hitler that the *Saucy Sue* was sailing at midnight on Friday with a big convoy and six destroyers – well, they'd have been sitting ducks, wouldn't they?'

'Is that what the ship was called?' Muriel asked, amused. 'The *Saucy Sue*? It sounds more like a pleasure steamer.'

Irene laughed. 'No, I don't know what it was called. But that's the sort of thing we hear all the time. They don't take any notice of all those posters about walls having ears and that sort of thing.'

Muriel got up briskly and began to clear the table. They washed up together and then set off for work, slipping down the stairs while everyone else was at breakfast so that nobody saw them go – not that it would have mattered, Irene told herself, but she just didn't fancy that nosy little Jewess, Etty, spotting her and blabbing all round Lyons. As Muriel often remarked, a gel liked a bit of privacy.

'When shall I see you again?' Muriel enquired as they parted at the corner of Oxford Street. 'I suppose you'll be going home tonight.'

'Yes, I told Mum I would.' Irene hesitated. 'You could come with me if you liked – come to tea and stop the night. Mum wouldn't mind you sharing my room.'

They looked at each other. Irene's heart was beating rather fast. Muriel smiled, a slow, cat-like smile.

'I'd like that, dear. But not tonight – I haven't got any of my things with me. Maybe at the end of the week, when we've got the next day off and don't have to get up early.'

'Yes,' Irene said, feeling a mixture of disappointment and delight. 'Yes, that'll be best.'

As it happened, Irene and Muriel hadn't slipped out of the hostel unobserved. Etty, coming out of her own room just as they turned the corner below, caught the briefest of glimpses of Irene's back, but it was enough for her to recognise her fellow Nippy and she felt a small shock of surprise.

Fancy Muriel Chalk smuggling Irene Bond in for the night! Obviously they'd been out together and come back here to save Irene the journey home. It seemed sensible enough, and although Etty knew you weren't supposed to have friends to stay overnight, Mrs Denton would probably have turned a blind eye – especially in the case of one of the businesswomen on the top floor. And it wasn't as if Miss Chalk was having a man in – the manageress of the hostel certainly wouldn't have allowed that!

Etty had her breakfast and set off for work. Like everyone else, she was getting used to picking her way through the bombed streets, but this morning there were no fresh obstructions and she was there in good time. She met Maggie in the cloakroom, already struggling into her uniform.

'Hullo, Et. How was it round your way last night?'

'Not too bad,' Etty said, taking her black dress from its hanger. 'We had to go down to the basement but there wasn't anything hit around us. It's just the noise, and all the vibration, but we're even getting used to that. I took my blankets and a couple of pillows and got quite a good night's sleep.'

'We copped it a bit,' Maggie remarked. 'Pub down the corner got smashed to smithereens. The landlord and his wife was blown right out of their beds on to the pavement.'

'No! Were they killed?'

'Not a scratch on 'em,' Maggie said cheerfully. 'Still

251

wrapped up in their blankets they were, like babies in a pram. Didn't do the pub much good, though. All the barrels were split and there was beer everywhere, all over the pavement. Nearly broke our Dad's heart to see it.'

Etty laughed and they finished dressing and went through to the restaurant. Everyone was there, and the customers were already trickling in. Maggie spotted the young soldier, Andy, and a couple of his mates, and went over to them.

'What you lot doing here? I'd have thought you'd be fighting for your country by now.' She surveyed them. 'Coo, you don't half look a mess – what's your sergeant going to say if you turn up for parade all covered in dust?'

Andy gave her a grin. He looked tired and his khaki uniform was smeared with dirt. Even his hair had cement dust in it.

'We've been on duty all night, standing guard over some of the shops to stop looting. And fighting the odd incendiary and that. We've got to report back to barracks in an hour's time so the sarge said we could have a few minutes to get a bite to eat.'

Maggie sniffed. 'And I dare say you'll get another big fry-up when you get back an' all. I've heard about the army food – bacon and eggs every day while the rest of us has to make do with Spam. Well, what d'you want this morning – because it's off!'

The boys laughed. 'Just bring us whatever you've got,' Andy said. 'We need something to keep body and soul together till we get back. We've been up all night and never had a bite pass our lips since yesterday teatime.'

Maggie didn't know whether to believe him or not, but she knew that an air raid didn't give teabreaks. She went back to the kitchen and loaded three plates with baked beans and toast, and carried it all back to them.

'Sorry you can't have eggs. It's the wrong time of year for birds'-nesting.'

'That's okay. You're a smasher.' Andy picked up his knife and fork and fell ravenously upon the food. 'Here, I don't suppose you'd like to come out for a bit of a drink tonight, before the fireworks start?'

'Me?' Maggie said, as if she'd never been asked out before. She felt an odd little twist of her heart. I ought to be able to say, no, I'm a respectable married woman, she thought, but I'm not. I'm a widow.

'Yes, you. We'll be round this way on guard again. I thought I might meet you when you leave work, we could have a bit of a natter – what d'you think?'

Maggie looked at him. She missed Tommy dreadfully and still cried herself to sleep over him at night. Nobody could take his place, but that didn't have to mean she could never go out with another bloke. Andy was only suggesting a drink, not even a whole evening. And he'd been up all night, doing his duty, and would be up all the next night, too, and the one after that . . . that's if he survived. Soldiers, as Maggie knew all too well, stood a high chance of being killed.

'All right,' she said. 'I'll see you at six o'clock round the back door. Only I can't stop long, see, me mum will be expecting me back home.'

She thought of him several times that day as she scurried about her work, serving customers as quickly as possible while still managing to keep a cheerful smile on her face and a merry word on her lips. She had steeled herself to remain cheerful no matter what she felt inside. All these people had problems as well – many of them had lost relatives and friends, and were just as unhappy as she was. It was up to everyone to keep cheerful, because if they didn't, they might as well ring up Hitler straight away and invite him over to tea.

There were several alerts during the day. The watchers on the roof reported a swarm of over a hundred German planes coming over, to be intercepted and turned back by

RAF fighters. However, only a few of the German planes were actually bombers and it looked as if their intention was to wear down all the British resources in preparation for the bombers which would follow. Even so, a few bombs were dropped and the staff and customers were forced to leave their tables and file down to the basement for shelter.

'Remember that the customers must pay for their meals before they go down,' Mr Carter warned the Nippies. 'We've had too many instances of people "forgetting" their bills and slipping away. You must give them the bill when you serve the meal – if they choose to leave the food when the siren goes, that's their choice!'

It all made the day's work much harder, and the situation in the kitchens was almost impossible. The cooks never knew whether they would be able to finish cooking food they had started, for as soon as the warning went they had to turn out the gas, and when they came back there might not be any to turn back on. Gas mains were fractured in almost every raid, and apart from the danger of explosion there was the worry of half-cooked and wasted food. Salads became the standby and there was always plenty of bread for sandwiches. While the gas was available, quick snacks like beans or cheese on toast were the most popular.

Maggie hadn't forgotten her vow to do whatever she could for the young soldiers and sailors whose last taste of home life this might be before they went into the fighting. When six o'clock came, she put on fresh lipstick, powdered her face from the little compact Tommy had given her and marched out of the Corner House to meet Andy.

He was waiting for her, looking better than this morning. His uniform had been brushed clean and he'd washed his hair and shaved. He looked a smart young 'Tommy Atkins' again, and he gave Maggie a quick, flashing grin as she approached.

'I was scared you wouldn't come.'

'I promised, didn't I?' she said. 'I always keep my

promises.' She tucked her hand into his arm and they walked off together along the ruins of Oxford Street.

'Well, this is one of the ruins that Cromwell knocked about a bit, and no mistake,' Maggie observed as they picked their way past the heaps of rubble. 'Look at poor old John Lewis's, it's been gutted. And Peter Robinson's have been hit, so someone told me today, and Selfridges copped it, too, only they caught it round the back more. There won't be a thing left standing soon.'

They found a pub down one of the side streets and went in. Andy ordered a beer for himself and a port and lemon for Maggie. She thought of the time she'd told the other girls she was pregnant and how Shirley had said she'd never drink port and lemon again if that was the effect it had . . . Her throat ached suddenly, and tears stung her eyes.

'You all right?' Andy asked quietly, and she nodded.

'It was just something – you know, you get sudden reminders. It's all right. Just something you got to get used to.' She picked up her glass. 'Cheers.'

'Cheers,' Andy said. They sat quietly for a few minutes, then he said, 'We've got a posting. We're going away soon.'

'Away?' Maggie felt a sudden, unexpected rush of anxiety. 'Where to?' She clapped a hand to her mouth. 'Oh – I suppose you can't say. I shouldn't have asked.'

'It's all right. We don't even know ourselves, really. I s'pose they think if they don't tell us we can't pass it on to anyone else.' He glanced at her. 'I'm looking forward to it, but I'm a bit disappointed, too. I was hoping you and me could have got to know each other a bit.'

Maggie looked down at the table. There were ring-shaped stains where people had put wet glasses. She bit her lip.

'I told you, I was married—'

'I know. I know about your Tom. But—'

'It was our first wedding anniversary, second of September,' she whispered. 'Just before the blitz started. We didn't even have half that time together – just a few weeks, that's all. I can't forget him.' She couldn't forget their baby either, she thought, little Noel who hadn't even had a chance to live. But she couldn't tell Andy about that.

'I'm not asking you to,' he said. 'I just want to feel – well, that there's someone who cares about me a bit, that's all. If you'd just come out with me these last few nights, before we go. And maybe write to me as well . . .'

'Oh, Andy,' Maggie said, her eyes filling with tears, 'of course I will. I'll come out every night till you go, and I'll write to you every week. How's that?'

He slid his hand across the table and laid it on hers. 'You're a smasher, Maggie. I knew it the minute I first saw you.' His eyes were very dark and she caught a glimpse of something that made her heart lurch suddenly. I can't be feeling like this, she thought, not so soon. And she remembered the feelings she'd had the first time she'd seen Andy and his mates.

You poor, poor loves, she'd thought then, and she'd wanted to gather them all into her arms and hug them. She'd wanted to look after them and love them, and give them something warm and close to remember when they were out there in France or Germany or wherever they ended up, so that they had some good memories to keep them going through all the awful times.

I can't do it for all of them, she thought sadly, but I can do it for Andy and maybe for some of the others from time to time. I can give them something to remember, like I gave my Tom. And he wouldn't mind. I know he wouldn't mind.

Chapter Fifteen

'I reckon we ought to go and shelter down the underground,' Sam Pratt said. 'They're letting people down there now and it'd be a lot safer than that doll's house they put up down the corner. And it's not all that far to get to our station. You could take your bits and bobs in our Queenie's little pram.'

'What's all this "you" business?' his wife demanded. 'You don't think I'm going down without you, Sam.'

'Well, you got to. I'm a firewatcher, ain't I, *and* in the Home Guard. I got to be on duty when there's a raid on.'

Ivy pursed up her mouth. 'That's different. I know you're somewhere nearby then, and you can pop your head in whenever you get the chance. I don't like the idea of being down in the tube, not knowing what's going on.'

'You'll go,' Sam said abruptly. 'I'm not having no argy-bargying about this, our Ive. This bombing ain't no party game and I wants me family safe. You can't get no safer than down there in the tube, and that's it and all about it.'

His wife knew that when he spoke like that, with not even one little rhyme, there would be no further discussion. She folded her mouth tightly and then said, 'And what about your ma? How's she going to get down all them steps, eh? Tell me that.'

'I'll carry her,' Sam said. 'I'll carry her meself. I'm having you lot safe, so just you make up your minds to it.'

He didn't have to carry Ada, however. The old woman, who had to be almost prised out her corner by the range, stamped the tip of her umbrella on the floor and refused point-blank to be lifted on her son's shoulders.

'Be carried like a baby? Not on your nelly! And you needn't look at me like that, Sam Pratt. You're still my boy, however big and ugly you are, and *I'll* be the one to say what I do. I've carried you in my arms often enough as a baby, I'm not ready to be treated like one meself!'

She shuffled through the door, head down and face glowering, and Sam looked after her helplessly.

'Blooming old bat,' he said. 'Obstinate as a mule – obstinate as a whole bloody *pack* of mules! I just wish old Hitler could come over and meet her, she'd soon put him right about a few things.'

'He'd never dare come within a mile,' Ivy said, watching her with admiration. 'D'you know, Sam, I haven't seen her move so fast for years. I reckon she's been having us all on, sitting there in that armchair pretending she couldn't walk.'

'Never mind that,' he said. 'You just get out there after her. And take all this gubbins with you.' He waved an arm at the pile of blankets and baskets that they'd put ready. 'You get off down that underground station. We've had a quiet weekend, but that don't mean Jerry's finished with us. If you ask me, it's just the lull before the storm.'

Ada only bothered with the tube once, however. The next evening she stayed firmly in her chair and refused to leave the house.

'We can't get her out for love nor money,' Maggie told the other Nippies. 'Says it's too noisy down there, what with people singing and dancing and the trains rattling in and out. Reckoned she was the only one got a decent night's sleep!' She chuckled, then said, 'Here, have you lot started to think about Christmas yet? There was dried fruit round our shop last week. Our mum got some suet from the butcher, too, to make a Christmas pudding and a bit of cake. No icing, but we're going to put a bit of white cardboard on top and we've still got the decorations we always use. She says we've all got to collect all our silver threepenny bits for the pud, too.' She took her purse out of her pocket and tipped the contents on the table. Three pennies, two ordinary threepenny bits, one silver one, a sixpence and three farthings with perky little wrens on the 'tails' side. 'There. That's another one, I'll keep that back.'

'One and sixpence three-farthings,' Etty said. 'You're rich, for a Friday!'

'Well, I haven't had to spend much this week,' Maggie said, and the others exchanged a swift glance.

Maggie had been out with Andy quite a few times now. They went to the pictures or dancing, and she let him cuddle and kiss her in the back row or in the dance halls. She knew he wanted more, and in a funny way she wanted it herself, but she couldn't quite bring herself to go 'all the way'. That had been for her and Tommy, and she was afraid that if she let another man make love to her she would remember Tommy at the most crucial, intimate moment, and feel all over again the anguish of hearing that he'd been killed. At the same time her body cried out for loving and she spent many restless nights just longing to feel a man's arms around her. Tommy's.

Or Andy's.

Or anyone's.

'I'd like to see Maggie take up with a nice bloke and be happy again,' Phyl remarked to Jo later. 'And that Andy does seem nice. But it's a bit soon after Tommy, isn't it? I mean, she was so cut up about him. I don't see how she can get over it so quick.'

'You know Maggie. She always did like a good time.'

'That's not a very nice thing to say! She's not a good-time girl.'

'I didn't mean that,' Jo said. 'I just meant – oh, well, she's sort of cheerful and happy by nature. I know she's still upset about Tom, but she's not the sort of girl to let anything get her down for long. Anyway, I don't suppose it's serious with Andy – he's going away soon.'

Andy had been expecting for weeks to go away, but it seemed now as if it was definite at last. He took Maggie to the pictures and they sat close together in the back row, kissing so much that they barely saw the film. Maggie felt dazed and light-headed. She knew this was the last time they would meet. It didn't seem right to let him go with no more than a few kisses and cuddles to remember her by. And she knew that she couldn't. She wanted to know everything about him. She wanted to feel a part of him.

They came out of the cinema and looked at each other helplessly.

'Where can we go?' he asked, holding her hands tightly. 'We've got to find somewhere.'

'There's still a few places in the park,' she whispered.

'It's so cold . . .'

'We can use your coat.' She touched his thick, khaki greatcoat. It was like a blanket, heavy and warm. 'It doesn't matter about the cold. We'll keep each other warm.'

'Oh, Maggie—'

'There's just one thing,' she said. 'I don't want a baby. You've got to be careful, Andy. I – I couldn't go through that again.'

'It's all right,' he said in a low voice. 'I brought something – just in case. I didn't want to take it for granted, Maggie, but – I hoped, you know.'

She grinned at him. 'So did I,' she said, and led him away from the cinema.

There were, as Maggie had said, a few places in the park, despite the gun emplacements and the barbed wire. She chose an area where she and Tommy hadn't gone, and they crept between some rhododendrons and found a little hollow, surrounded by roots and thick, shiny leaves. As Maggie lay down on the warm khaki coat she looked up to see the searchlights begin to sketch their network of thin, silver beams across the skies. With Tommy, she had seen the stars and the moon and thought them the most beautiful and romantic sight in the world, yet the silver filigree of the searchlights had its own silent beauty, and she was glad that it was different.

'Maggie, you're so lovely.'

'Don't talk,' she whispered, and drew his head down to hers. 'Don't talk, Andy. Please. Just – just *do* . . .'

Irene stayed at the hostel twice a week now, slipping in late at night and out again early in the morning. On Sundays, Muriel came home with her and stayed the night, sharing Irene's bed. She took the trouble to make friends with Irene's parents and they were rather proud of their daughter's new friend.

'It shows the kind of people she's mixing with these days,' her mother said. 'You know, I was afraid when she went to work as a waitress—' Mrs Bond never used the word Nippy '—that she'd only meet rather a common sort of girl. But some of the customers there are really quite a good class.'

'Muriel's a fine woman,' her husband agreed. 'She's got a good head on her shoulders. She understands a lot. We had a good talk the other evening, her and me.'

Irene's father wasn't as highly placed in the civil service as Irene liked to pretend, but you didn't have to be a 'high-up' to know quite a bit about what was going on, even if it wasn't your own work. As Irene liked to hint, he could tell quite a lot if he chose to but, of course, like all civil servants, he'd signed the Official Secrets Act and not a word would pass his lips. The other Nippies, taking this as just another of Irene's attempts to put on 'side', dismissed her words as boasts, but Muriel showed a flattering interest in his job and he enjoyed talking to her.

'You ought to think about joining the civil service,' he

told her. 'You could do all right. And it's good pay, even for women.'

'Oh, I don't think I'm an office person,' she smiled. 'I like my job as a buyer in the store. Of course, I wouldn't want to work anywhere common – like Selfridges, for instance, or Gamages.'

Mrs Bond, who had thought Selfridges the acme of style, immediately determined never to go through the big plate-glass doors again.

'I suppose you must meet a lot of very well-off people,' she said wistfully.

'Well, I don't deal so much with the *public*, you know. My work is mostly deciding what we'll have in the shop. Of course, I work in the best department – the furs – but it's not the same with this war. We can't get the imports, you see. We do still have a little mink and leopard, but I'm terribly afraid we're going to have to sell the cheaper furs like coney.' She shuddered delicately and smiled again at Irene's father. 'Perhaps if it comes to that I might think about joining you. It must be very interesting after all. I dare say you know a lot more than you tell us about what's going on.'

He puffed himself up a little and laid one finger along the side of his nose. 'Best not to say too much, eh? Not that anyone here's likely to give away any secrets.' He leant forward a little and everyone else did the same. 'It probably won't do any harm to tell you this much . . .'

As they undressed for bed that night, Muriel said, 'It was interesting, what your father told us this evening, wasn't it? About those ships.'

'I've never heard him talk so much about his job,' Irene admitted. 'Mum's not really interested and he's never bothered much with me. You won't repeat it, will you, Mu?'

'Of course not! Whatever do you take me for?' The older woman came over to Irene and laid a hand on her bare arm.

'You know I'm not the sort to go blabbing – not like those customers you were telling me about a while ago, talking about that convoy going from Pool of London.'

'That reminds me!' Irene exclaimed. 'I never told you – there was a ship got mined the day after that. I kept wondering if it was the same one. I mean, it makes you think that maybe there *was* someone in the Corner House itself, listening to what they were saying and reporting it to the Germans. Wouldn't it be awful?'

'Oh, I don't suppose it was the same one. And I don't think the Corner House has got spies – after all, if they'd talk about it there they'd talk about it in other places, too.' She laughed and slid her fingers down Irene's arm, making her shiver. 'Come on. Let's forget about spies and get into bed.'

Irene's face flushed, and she could feel the blush running down her neck and touching her breasts with colour. She hesitated. 'Mu, what we do – it's all right, isn't it?'

Muriel raised her eyebrows. 'Whatever do you mean?'

'Well, it seems a bit funny somehow. I mean, I like it,' she added hastily. 'You know I do. But I've never heard anyone talk about it – about girls being together, I mean. It's always men you hear about, wanting to do it with girls. Only that's different, of course, I know that, it's just—' She broke off, confused, and Muriel laughed.

'Different! I should just think it is. You wouldn't want a man doing things like that to you, would you?'

'Ugh!' Irene shuddered, thinking of Herbert Lennox's loose mouth and sweaty hands, thinking also of Richard Godwin's demanding caresses. 'No, I wouldn't.'

'Well, then. And you don't have all the risks either. You won't *get into trouble*.' She mouthed the words delicately. 'We're just friends, that's all, only better friends than most gels could ever be. What's wrong with a kiss and a cuddle? That's all it is after all.' She gave Irene a sudden sharp glance. 'Are you telling me you don't want to be my friend any more?'

'Oh, no! *No*.' Irene felt a sudden panic at the thought of losing Muriel's friendship. 'No, I couldn't bear that. I don't know what I'd do any more if I didn't have you. And it's all so nice and warm and . . . . sort of lovely . . . It was just . . .' She shrugged a little, helplessly. 'Just that – oh, I don't know *what* it was. I don't know what I'm talking about!'

Muriel smiled. She drew Irene over to the bed and sat her down. With swift, practised fingers, she unbuttoned Irene's bodice and slipped it from her shoulders, and then bent and kissed her breasts lightly. She slid Irene's knickers down and pulled them over her feet.

'Get into bed,' she whispered, 'and don't worry about it any more. It's all perfectly all right . . .'

'You sure they'll be all right, now? Winter's coming on and it was a bad one last year. I know it looked like something on a chocolate box when we were there in the summer, but it'll be a lot bleaker when the snow starts to fall. They couldn't get out for weeks last year.'

Alf Woods was fidgeting with the Sunday newspaper. Owen had come over for dinner and Alf had been on at him about the farm ever since he arrived. He'd been obsessed with it lately, nagging Shirley incessantly about what it was like there now, what Annie and Jack would be doing, worrying about whether they were safe.

'Of course they'll be all right, Mr Woods,' Owen said reassuringly. 'Uncle Dafydd and Auntie Mair are quite used to winters on the mountain. And they're safe from the bombs – isn't that the most important thing?'

'Leave Owen alone,' Shirley said, coming in with a tray of tea. 'Mum and Jack are a lot better off where they are than if they were here. And remember what Dafydd said – Jack had a smashing time in the snow last year, building

264

snowmen and igloos and playing snowballs. He loves it there.'

'I know, I know. I'm being selfish. I wouldn't want them back in London, not the way things are, but it still seems all wrong without your mother here. 'Specially with Christmas on the way. I just can't imagine what it's going to be like.'

He reached out for his tea and stopped suddenly, wrinkling his nose.

'There's a funny smell.' His eyes rolled a little in his head and then settled momentarily on Shirley's face. *Shirl, a funny smell – it's happening—*'

'Dad!' Shirley leapt forward and caught the tea as it slipped from his hand. At the same time, her father slid sideways in his chair, the Sunday paper rattling as he crushed it beneath his body. Owen sprang to break his fall and then jumped back as Alf's arms and legs went into spasm, kicking and punching wildly. The little table with the tray on it went over with a crash and Shirley cried out again. She grabbed a cushion and pushed it on to the fender to stop her father knocking his head against the hard brass bars, and stuffed a teaspoon into his mouth to stop him biting his tongue. Once again Irene's words came into her mind and made her shudder, but there was no time to dwell on them. Instead, she and Owen pushed the furniture back out of the way of the convulsing body, leaving Alf as much space to move as they could.

'Oh, Dad. Oh, God. Owen—'

'It's all right, *cariad*.' Owen's arms were around her, holding her close. They stood watching, helpless. 'He'll come out of it presently. He always does, doesn't he?'

'It's ages since this happened,' Shirley whispered. 'I thought he'd got over it. He was hoping to go back on the crane soon . . . Oh, it's not fair, Owen, it's not fair. Just because he got knocked down by a car one night in the blackout.' Her father's body was quietening down but an unmistakable smell filled the room. 'And now he's messed

265

himself. I know he can't help it, but – it makes him feel so awful, Owen, as if he was a baby again. I'd better put the kettle on again, ready to clean him up.'

Owen let her go and watched soberly as Alf lay still and then, slowly, came back to consciousness. As always, he was vague and bewildered, uncertain as to where he was and, when it finally dawned on him, disgusted with himself. He was still lying on the floor, his face turned into the cushion and sobbing like a baby, when Shirley returned with the bowl of hot water.

'It's all right, Dad,' she said softly, kneeling beside him. 'It's all right. Owen's going to go and get you some clean things, aren't you, Owen? And I'll just give you a nice wash. We'll have you better in no time. It's all right.'

Her father turned his eyes on her. They were bitter and angry.

'That's right,' he said. 'Talk to me as if I was a baby. It's what I am now, isn't it? A baby that can't control its own shit, having to be cleaned up by my own daughter. Well, when you've done that you might as well stick me in my pram and give me a bottle. It's just about all I'm bloody fit for now.'

It had taken weeks of hard persuasion to get Alice out into the country at last.

All the same old arguments had been trotted forth, on both sides. It always boiled down to Alice's safety against Robertson's. The little girl was convinced that without her he would either pine away or run off and never be seen again. In vain did her parents point out that they were quite capable of looking after one cat and that Robbie managed quite well when Alice was out at school or playing with her friends. Obstinately she insisted that he was only all right because he knew she'd be home that night. If she were to go, it would be quite different.

'Look, it was Robbie who found his way home when you

266

ran off that time,' Jo reminded her. 'You don't even know where you were when you lost him.'

Bill Mason got up from his chair and stood in the middle of the room. He glowered down at his younger daughter, curled up in her accustomed place on the floor. 'I've had just about enough of this. Now you listen to me, my girl. Rightly or wrongly, me and your mother have always tried to let you youngsters have your heads as much as is reasonable, we've talked things over with you and we've let you have your say. But when it comes down to it, we're responsible. *You* know what the bombing's been like. You've seen dead people being carried out of bombed houses, you've seen fires, you've sat in the shelter of a night and listened to the bombs. We've all seen it. And I'm not prepared to let you stop here and take those sort of risks any more, you understand? We're going down the offices tomorrow, all of us, and get your name put down for evacuation, and that's it and all about it.'

Alice stared back at him. Jo watched her and marvelled. I'd never have dared stand up to Dad like that when I was her age, she thought, seeing her sister's eyes narrow and her lower lip stick out. I hardly dare now.

'If it's that bad,' Alice said, 'why aren't you and Mum going out to the country? Why isn't our Jo?'

Bill gave a grunt of exasperation. 'It *is* that bad! You know it is! You've *seen* it. And you know we can't go. I've got me work to go to, and so've your brothers, and your mother stays here to look after us. That's our patriotic duty. And it's *your* patriotic duty to go somewhere where you'll be safe from the bombs.'

'Why? Why's it me patriotic duty?'

'Because when this war's over we're going to need young people!' her father shouted. 'Because there's more and more getting killed every day and *someone's* got to stop behind and clear up all the mess. And because if anything happened to you, our Alice, obstinate and headstrong as you are, always

267

wanting your own way and never thinking about anyone else and what they wants – well, if anything happened to you, I don't think me and your mother would ever get over it. Ever.'

His voice broke on those last words and he sat down again suddenly, as if his legs had given way, and covered his face with his hands. The family stared at each other, appalled, and after a few minutes Alice, her face scarlet, crawled over to him and put her hands on his knee.

'I'm sorry, Dad. I didn't mean to upset you. I never thought . . . Dad, don't cry. I'll go to the country. I'll leave Robbie here to look after you.' She tugged at his hands, trying to pull them away from his face. 'I said, I'll *go*, Dad, I'll *go*. I won't cause no more trouble, I promise. I'm *sorry*.'

Bill lifted his head and looked into his daughter's eyes. Grey like his own, set wide apart, they were clouded with anxiety. They filled with tears and her lip trembled.

Bill reached out a hand and ruffled her soft, gold-brown hair. His own eyes were brimming, too. Jo felt embarrassed – she had never seen her father cry, never thought he could do it. Men didn't. But that, she knew, just wasn't true. Anyone who had walked through a bombed street just as people began to come out of their shelters had seen grown men cry.

'That's all right, Alice, love. That's all right. We only want what's best for you, you know that, don't you? And we'll look after Robbie. We'd never let anything happen to that blessed cat.'

'And I'll try and get somewhere near you, if I can,' Jo put in. 'Soon as they call me up for the Land Army I'll tell 'em I want to be near my sister. You'll be all right, Alice, and so will Robertson.'

Alice nodded and sniffed. She looked round for the cat to gather him into her arms, but for once he was nowhere to be seen. She let go of her father's hands and picked up the little cloth bag she kept her knitting in.

'I don't suppose my sailor will mind if I don't finish his Balaclava quite as quick as I meant to,' she said. 'Only Robbie's going to need a new pompom to play with while I'm away.'

'Here's your little girl, Mr and Mrs Tawe. She's got her things with her. I'll be round in the morning to see that everything's all right.'

The billeting officer, who was tired and hungry after spending most of the day trailing a rag-tag of children around the village looking for foster-homes, disappeared, leaving Alice standing just inside the door of a small cottage. They heard her footsteps retreating rapidly along the rough, unmade lane outside.

For a moment or two, nobody moved. Alice gave a swift glance around the room, taking in the dim lamplight, the huge stone fireplace with a fire burning deep in its depths, the heavy beams in the ceiling. It was like something from a Grimm's fairy-tale, she thought, and the old people sitting in their armchairs were like trolls.

'Why, 'tis a liddle maid,' the old man said eventually. He was looking at Alice as if he'd never seen a little girl before. He had fluffy white hair round a pink, shining scalp, and patches of white hair like cotton wool on his cheeks. 'Look, Mary, 'tis a liddle maid been sent to us.'

'Why, so 'tis, then,' his wife said, as if she hadn't realised it for herself. She stretched a hand out to Alice, still standing a little nervously just inside the door. 'Come you in, my pretty, and let's have a look at 'ee. Look, Jan, look at her lovely hair, just like beech leaves it is.'

Irritated, Alice stepped forward. She dumped her little suitcase on the floor. Nice though it was to be admired, she was tired and hungry and she needed the lavatory.

'Good evening,' she said, as she'd been taught. 'My name's Alice Mason and I live in London and please can you show me the lav?'

'The lav? What be that, then, lovey?'

'The lav. The lavatory. The – the . . .' She couldn't think of any other words to describe it. Mrs Tawe's face cleared.

'Oh, you mean the privy! Why, 'tis out the back, to be sure. Here, my pretty, I'll show you. You'll need a candle.' She rose stiffly from her chair and bent to light a taper from the fire, then touched it to a stub of candle standing on the stone hearth. She handed it to Alice and then led the way out of the room by another door.

Alice found herself in the garden. This wasn't a surprise, for their own lavatory at home was outside, but she didn't expect to have to go all the way down the garden in the dark. And what dark it was! She had never seen such blackness. It was almost solid, like a thick black wall. She hung back, feeling scared and wondering how far down the garden she was going to have to go.

Something touched her face and made her jump. She held the candle up in a shaking hand and saw a few low branches stretching like fingers from a gnarled tree. She thought again about Grimm's fairy-tales, and stifled a scream. I want to go home, she thought, I want to go home to Mum and Dad and Robbie . . .

The old woman stopped suddenly and fumbled at something in the dark. The faltering candlelight showed a small stone building with an old wooden door that groaned with reluctance as it swung open.

'Here you be. The paper's on the nail there. Mind you don't set light to the cobwebs!'

She gave Alice a gentle push and shut the door. Alice was left alone in what appeared to be a garden shed. Nervously, she peered around in the flickering candlelight. The mention of cobwebs had unnerved her, and she stifled another little scream as she saw that there were indeed heavy grey hammocks draped in the corners. Whatever size spider made a cobweb like that? she wondered, and for two pins she would have backed out, but her need was too great.

The lavatory consisted of a large round hole in a plank of wood set across the back of the tiny building. A strong smell emanated from the hole and Alice looked at it with dismay. Was she supposed to actually *sit* on that? Suppose the spiders who had built those cobwebs were lurking in the depths? What on earth was in there, to make it smell so horrible?

Unwillingly, still frightened but too desperate to do anything else, she pulled down her knickers and edged on to the seat. It felt cold to her bare thighs and she couldn't sit properly on it and keep her feet on the floor at the same time, she had to let her legs dangle. She felt very vulnerable. And the smell was making her feel sick.

When she had finished, she reached up for the paper the old woman had pointed out to her. It was a newspaper, cut up into squares, and felt rough and unpleasant against her skin. She dropped it in the pan and stood up quickly, dragging her knickers up to her waist, and then looked for the chain.

There wasn't one. Alice looked everywhere, holding the candle up and steeling herself to peer into all the corners, but she could see no chain, or anything else that might perform the same function. In the end, hoping that the old couple wouldn't be too angry with her, she left the pan unflushed and let herself out into the garden again, gratefully breathing in the fresh air. Even the darkness, she thought, was better than the dreadful place she had just left. I'm going home tomorrow, she thought. First thing. I won't stay here. They can't make me.

Something brushed against her ankle and she let out a startled yelp. It was too much. She froze where she stood, imagining enormous spiders with long, furry legs.

There was a faint, mewling cry, a familiar chirruping purr, the kind of purr Robbie made when he wanted to be picked up. Alice felt her heart turn over. Robbie – *here*?

Unbelieving, she bent and held her candle nearer the ground. A shadow slipped quickly out of her vision. Her heart jerked and she felt a sudden rush of warm joy and hot, wet tears.

She knelt on the cold ground and whispered, knowing it couldn't be true, praying that it was.

'Robbie? Robbie, is that you? Have you come to find me? Have you come all this way and found me?' Her fear had evaporated. If she could just have her beloved cat, everything would be all right.

The cat came out of the shadows. It wasn't Robbie, she thought with bitter disappointment. It was nothing like him. It was black and white with an ugly, battered face and a torn ear. But it came to her trustingly as Robbie would do, and pushed its head against her and purred, and when she stood up it came with her, lifting itself against her legs, its paws upstretched, so that there was nothing she could do but pick it up and hold it against her chest.

The cottage door opened. Mrs Tawe came out with another candle and hobbled down the path.

'Be you all right, my dear? You've been a terrible long time down there. I hope you've not got a touch of collywobbles after the journey . . .' She caught sight of the cat, cradled in Alice's arms. 'Oh, you've found old Solomon. Well, better bring him in with 'ee, in the warm. He's an old fule, thinks he's a kitten still and stays out all night hunting if we don't get he in early, but he seems to have taken to you all right, maid. Now come along in, we'm letting in the cold.'

Talking softly in her warm, rich brogue, she ushered Alice and her burden back into the cottage. And suddenly it all looked different. Not like a Grimm's fairy-tale at all, but like something out of Enid Blyton. Warm and friendly and cosy. The cat wriggled out of her arms and went to sit in front of the fire, where it began licking its paws, and Alice sat down beside it, her hand stroking its cold fur.

'A drop of hot milk, that's what you need,' Mrs Tawe

said. 'And then it's straight to bed with 'ee. It'll all look better in the morning, you'll see.' She smiled and Alice smiled back.

They weren't trolls at all. There was nothing to be frightened of here. Nothing – except for the spiders in the privy down the garden.

Andy had gone away but there were other servicemen who came into the Corner House while they were on leave or waiting to be sent away, and somehow there always seemed to be one who gravitated towards Maggie's tables. Some were just like ordinary customers, pleasant enough and appreciative of Maggie's saucy manner, but obviously already attached to a girlfriend or wife back home. Others were cheeky and flirtatious, and obviously on the lookout for a girl who was available and 'easy'. But it wasn't those that Maggie was interested in.

Her eye was caught one lunchtime by a young air force corporal. He was fair-haired with very blue eyes, and when she came to the table to ask for his order he gave her a quick, upward glance and a shy smile.

'What's best today?' he asked.

'You'd be better to ask what's *on* today,' she replied crisply. 'It's not like the old days here now. Not but what you do get isn't just as good as always, or as good as the cooks can make it,' she added fairly.

'I've never been in a Corner House before,' he confessed, 'so I wouldn't know.'

Maggie looked at him. 'Never been in a Corner House? Where d'you usually go, then?'

'Well, nowhere. I've never been to London before, you see.' He had a soft, warm voice and a way of talking that Maggie could only describe as 'round'. Countryish, she decided.

'Where d'you come from? Somewhere in Devon?' she hazarded.

He shook his head. 'Cornwall. That's even further west. I live in Penzance. I don't suppose you've ever heard tell of it.'

'I haven't, but we hear more about places in France and Germany these days than we do about our own country. Now, look, the steak and kidney pie's good today, and there's lots of mashed spuds to go with it. It'll fill you up, if nothing else.'

'I'll have that, then.' He gave her that quick, upward glance again. 'I suppose you couldn't tell me the best place to go for an evening? I've only got a few days before I do my basic training and they say you don't get much chance of going to the flicks, or dancing or anything.'

Maggie felt an odd twist to her heart. 'I can tell you where to go, but it won't be much fun if you haven't got anyone to go with.'

The boy looked down at the table. 'I don't know anyone in London.'

Maggie looked down at his bent head, the shining fair hair, the nape of his neck. He didn't look much more than a baby, she thought. Poor little devil.

'You know me,' she said.

At long last, Jo had got her papers from the Land Army.

'You're really going,' Phyl said, sitting on the bed in their new lodgings. 'I can't believe it. It's going to seem so queer without you, Jo.'

'I know.' Jo was brushing her long chestnut hair. She paused to read the letter again. 'I've got to report to the office next Monday and they'll sort out the uniform and everything. But I don't think I'll be actually sent to a farm till after Christmas.'

'They're really throwing you in at the deep end, aren't they? A farm in January! I wonder if you'll stick it.'

'Of course I'll stick it!' Jo retorted, annoyed. 'I'm not going for a holiday. I know it'll be hard work, and cold and

274

dirty, but I want to do it. I'll never get a chance like it again.'

'Well, I know. I didn't mean you couldn't do it, Jo. I know *I* couldn't stick it, that's all. And it's going to seem so queer,' Phyl repeated. 'I mean, we've always been together.'

Jo dropped her brush and came to sit on the bed beside her. 'I know, Phyl. Ever since we were babies in our prams. We've done everything together.' She paused for a moment. 'It feels queer to me, too. Going off without you . . . To tell the truth, Phyl, I'm a bit scared. Suppose I'm not good enough? Suppose they don't like me?'

'Don't be daft! Everyone likes you! And how could you not be good enough? It's only digging and planting and looking after horses, and that sort of thing. Anyone could do that.'

Jo wasn't sure that 'anyone' could, but since she knew no more about it than Phyl she couldn't argue. She looked at the papers again. Now that they had come, she felt her confidence slipping away. After all, how *did* she know she would be able to stick at it – getting up early in the mornings, going out to milk cows (Phyl hadn't mentioned that possibility), digging for carrots or whatever you had to do . . . Jo found that despite having worked in a green-grocer's shop, and despite her father having an allotment, she was disconcertingly hazy about how such crops as carrots and potatoes were grown. Her panic grew the more she thought about it. It was all going to be very different from giving the baker's horse an apple when it came down the street!

'I wouldn't put it past 'em to send over twice as many bombers at Christmas,' Carrie Mason said dismally as she mixed her Christmas pudding. She and May had pooled their dried fruit and sugar to make a really good pudding for the whole family to enjoy, although with dried egg instead of fresh, and grated carrot and parsnips as well, it wouldn't be quite like a real pre-war Christmas pudding. With the rationing and shortages getting worse, it didn't look as if there would be much else. 'They'll want to make sure we don't have any fun.'

'They have Christmas as well,' Bill pointed out. 'Don't you remember in the first war they had a truce on Christmas Day? All the shooting stopped and the soldiers climbed out of the trenches and crossed the wire to no man's land and even had a game of football.'

'I know. I often wondered where they got a football from, in the trenches,' Carrie said thoughtfully. 'And what a shame they went straight back to fighting again next day. You'd think that once they'd shaken hands and had a game together, they wouldn't want to start killing each other. It seems to make it even worse.'

'Well, it's no use thinking about that now,' Bill said hastily, sorry he'd raised the subject. 'Let's just hope they give us a day off this Christmas.'

Carrie stirred for a few moments without speaking. Then she said, 'What about our Alice, Bill? What do we do about her at Christmas? I can't bear to think of her not being home with us.'

'Well, she's only just gone away, hasn't she? We can't bring her back too soon. It's not as if the bombing's got any better, really. I mean, it's eased off a bit but there's other places getting it bad as well, and they still come back to London and give us a bashing. We can't depend on them letting us off at Christmas.'

'No, but I don't like the thought of her out in the country without any of her family. It seems awful. And I'll miss her.' She bit her lip. 'The whole family's getting broken up, Bill. The boys joining up – our Jo going for a land-girl. There'll only be you and me left soon.'

'I know, girl. But we just got to put up with it, haven't we? And that old couple she's with sound all right. That was a nice letter the woman wrote you, Carrie.'

'It was. It was good of her to think of it.' Carrie smiled a little waveringly. 'And fancy our Alice having taken to their cat so well, too! I never thought she'd look at another one after Robbie.' She finished stirring the pudding mixture and began to spoon it into white china pudding bowls. She sighed. 'Well, we'd better send her as much as we can. Not that there's much in the shops for kiddies. No toys or dolls, nothing like that. I know what I could do, though, I could unpick that pink cardigan of mine she's always liked and knit her a new jumper.'

'*I* like that cardigan, too,' Bill said. 'I've always liked you in that.'

'Well, you'll just have to make do with thinking about it,' Carrie said with a smile. 'If our Alice has got to be out in the country, she's going to have the nicest present we can send her. We'll put together all our sweet coupons as well.' She scraped the last of the pudding mixture into the bowls and levelled off the tops. 'There. I'll put them to steam now. It smells good, doesn't it?'

'Nearly as good as pre-war,' Bill said. He got up and came over to his wife and put his arm around her shoulders. 'Don't think I don't know how hard it is for you, Carrie,' he said quietly. 'It's not what we wanted – the family all going off like this so young. But it's the same for everyone. We just got to make the best of it and all pull together.'

Carrie leant against him, thankful that he was still here, that he was over forty and thus too old to be sent away to war. 'I know, Bill. I know. And it'll come to an end someday. Things always do.' She turned suddenly into his arms and held him tightly, her voice choking. 'Oh, Bill – *Bill . . .*'

He held her close. 'I know, love. I know.'

An end would come, someday. But nobody knew what might happen before it came. Nobody knew how the families that were being broken up now would survive.

Nobody could look into the future and know just how it would be, when the war finally came to an end.

Muriel was going to spend Christmas with Irene and her family.

'I could go home to my own people, of course,' she said when they discussed it in a small teashop before going to the pictures. 'But I don't usually bother. It's a long way, and transport's so bad these days, and they're not really up to it, you know. It's better for them if I stay in London.'

Irene nodded. Muriel hardly ever spoke about her own family and Irene was vague even about where they lived. Somewhere in the north, she thought, although Muriel's accent wasn't particularly northern. She supposed Muriel had worked hard to get rid of it, and Irene was determined to do the same.

'I sometimes think I'd like to leave home,' she remarked. 'Be independent, like you. But Mum and Dad would have kittens.'

Muriel gave her a considering look. 'That's probably because they still see you as their little girl – they want to look after you. They probably wouldn't mind if they thought you were going to be with someone else, someone they knew and trusted.'

'No, probably not.' Irene made a little face. 'Trouble is, there's no one at work I'd want to be with and I don't fancy lodgings like that Phyl Jennings and Jo Mason have got. I mean, they say it's very nice and the woman looks after them all right but it's not that much different from being at home, is it? If I leave home, I want to be properly independent.'

'You would be if you shared a little flat with me,' Muriel said, spreading margarine on a scone.

Irene stared at her, not sure if she'd heard correctly. 'Share a flat? With *you*? But – but you've got a flat, up at the top of the hostel.'

'Well, it's not really a flat, is it?' Muriel said dismissively. 'A flat*let*. I have to share the bathroom. And I haven't got proper cooking facilities. No, what I'd like is a nice little place with its own sitting-room and bedroom and everything, somewhere we could shut the door and know it was our own. Self-contained. Wouldn't you like that, too?'

'Yes,' Irene said slowly, her face beginning to flush with excitement. 'Yes, I would. Oh, Muriel, wouldn't it be gorgeous? But could we find anywhere like that? I mean, just now with all the bombing – there's practically nowhere, surely.'

'There's always places. And now could be the best time. Plenty of people are leaving London to go to the country – they'll be only too glad of some rent. There's places to be snapped up for the asking.' Muriel's eyes gleamed. 'Tell you what, we'll start looking straight after Christmas. Don't say anything to your people, though, not till we know for sure. There's no point in upsetting them.'

Irene wasn't too bothered about upsetting her parents. She had never been especially close to them. Her mother had always been a little distant and her father cold. Irene was well aware that they both thought more of her younger brother than they did of her. She had been a disappointment – it hadn't been until he had been born that they'd got what they'd really wanted.

'I don't think they'll mind all that much, really,' she said. 'They just like to know what I'm doing and where I am, but if I decide to move out they'll have to put up with it. There's nothing they can do to stop me – I'm over twenty-one.' She turned to Muriel, her face alight. 'Oh, just think of being together all the time! Just *think* of it! Oh, I'd like to hug you, I really would!'

Muriel smiled. 'Well, we won't do anything about it just yet,' she decided. 'We'll get Christmas over first. At least it seems to be getting a bit quieter just lately – there haven't been nearly as many night-time raids just lately.'

'No, it seems to have been places like Liverpool and Manchester getting it most,' Irene agreed. 'Here, you remember what I told you about that ship that got mined after I heard someone talking about it in the restaurant? Well, there was another one last week! You know, I'm sure there's someone spying at work. There must be. And I've got a pretty good idea who it is.' She gave Muriel a mysterious look.

'Oh, I don't suppose there is,' Muriel said, pouring another cup of tea. 'After all, anyone who's going to blab will be doing it everywhere, not just at the Corner House. Anyone could've heard them. And you don't really know it was the same one, do you?'

'No, I suppose not. It just seems funny, that's all. Well, I'll tell you what – I heard another bloke talking about when his ship was going out only last night. It's sailing on the tide at two o'clock tomorrow morning, and I wasn't the only one who heard it either. That Etty Brown was waiting at the next table and she turned round and looked at me, so I know she heard. And if anything happens to the *Susan* – that's the name of the ship – I shall *know* it was her.'

'You won't really. He could still have said it somewhere else,' Muriel argued. 'You don't really think young Etty's a spy, do you? She's such a timid little rabbit.'

'She is, but that don't stop her being a Jew and it don't stop her being a traitor,' Irene said doggedly. 'I tell you, Mu, I'll be listening for the news to see if that ship does get attacked, and if it does . . .'

'What'll you do?' Muriel asked curiously. 'Go to the police?'

'I might. They probably won't believe me, though. Well, maybe I wouldn't do anything, not really. It's not worth all the bother, is it?' Irene said, airily dismissing the sailors who might be killed in such an attack. 'But I'd let her know I knew, that's all, and I might let Mr Carter know as well.

We'd be better off at Lyons without little Jew-girls like her.'

Muriel stirred her tea thoughtfully for a moment. Then she said quietly, 'No, don't do that. Don't mention it to Mr Carter – or anyone. Tell me if anything like that happens again.'

Irene glanced at her in surprise. 'You?'

'Yes.' Muriel hesitated. 'I shouldn't really be telling you this, Irene. We're not supposed to tell anyone – not even our nearest and dearest. But I'm not just a store buyer. I've got another job as well – one I'm not supposed to talk about.'

Irene stared at her, fascinated. 'You mean something secret? A Secret Service job?'

'Ssh.' Muriel glanced around them. The rest of the customers were shoppers, women with tired faces trying to scrape together a few little treats for their families for Christmas. 'Don't forget walls have ears, even in little teashops. Anyway, I can't say any more. Just pass on to me anything queer that you hear at work – or anywhere else, come to that. I'll be able to take it to the people who really know what to do.'

'Oh, I will.' Irene gazed at her, enraptured. 'Fancy you being in the – oops!' Her hand flew to her mouth and she giggled nervously. 'I nearly said it again! It's just that I never suspected!'

'No, well, you're not supposed to, are you?' Muriel said a little tartly. 'And we won't talk about it any more, if you don't mind. It's not something you need to worry about. Let's think about our little flat instead. And about the film we're going to see. Talking of which . . .' she glanced at her watch '. . . it's starting in twenty minutes! We'd better be off.'

She paid the bill and they hurried out. It was dark and cold outside and the bad weather had eased off. It was the sort of night there might easily be a raid.

281

However, once again London had a quiet night and the German attacks were directed at Manchester and Merseyside. It really did look as if even the Germans thought that the capital city had suffered enough.

Chapter Sixteen

The raid began at six o'clock in the evening.

Maggie was already on her way home from a Sunday afternoon shift. She had got a bus as far as Holborn and then they were turned off and told that was as far as it was going. There was some kind of obstruction down one of the streets a bit further on. Sighing, too tired and fed up to grumble, the passengers gathered their bags together and got off to stand in dispirited huddles while they decided what to do next.

'Well, it's shanks's pony for me,' one man declared. 'No use waiting for another bus. Too blooming cold to stand around here.'

'I've got miles to go,' a girl wailed. 'I can't walk all that distance, I've been on me feet all day. Maybe a few of us could share a cab – anyone else going my way?'

A few of them got together and started looking hopelessly for taxis. Maggie hesitated and then decided to follow the man's example. It wasn't all that far for her now. Walking would get her home just as quickly, and once she was there she could sit by the fire with Gran and her mum would make her a cup of tea.

She set off along Holborn Viaduct. A thin, bitter wind scoured the pavements and scraps of litter blew against her ankles. In the dismal, unlit streets Christmas already seemed far away. The restaurant had been quiet, as if people were too depressed to come out after the shock of the heavy raid following such a brief, tantalising peace. It was almost worse than if there hadn't been a truce, she thought. It reminded us what peace could be like.

She wondered what Mum would have on the go for supper tonight. Maggie had had her dinner at the Corner House, but that was hours ago and she was hungry again. And there was something about Mum's cooking, something warm and comforting, that made her feel like a little girl again, petted and looked after.

She thought about David, the fair-haired boy, and about Andy with his dark curls. I wonder if I'll see them again, she thought. I wonder if they'll ever come back to the Corner House.

They'd been so sweet. So tender and innocent. David had kissed her like a little boy, and then when she'd opened her mouth to him he'd almost recoiled in shock before she'd felt the fire run through his body. Even then, he'd scarcely known what to do at first and she'd had to guide him some of the way – but he'd soon got the hang of it, she thought with a grin, and once he'd got the idea there was no stopping him. Three times they'd done it that first night, and twice the night after, and then he'd gone off, confident and manly, his growing-up completed. She'd watched him go with a feeling of sadness, knowing that she would probably never see him again, knowing that, however short or long his life, he would never forget her.

Since then there had been two others. A young sailor in square rig, his face sore from a razor he'd only just begun to use, and a soldier who didn't look old enough to be into long trousers. They were both men, though, when Maggie finished with them, and she thought they would fight all the better for it. And they hadn't had to go to a tart either and pay for a few minutes up against a wall. They'd had some proper loving, some real warmth, and whatever happened to them now they'd know what it was like to be with a real woman.

And each time she thought of Tommy. As she lay in the darkness with an unfamiliar body wrapped in her arms, and heard the whispering voice in her ear, the urgent

284

murmuring of a boy coming to manhood, she thought of Tommy and she looked up at the stars above and sent her love to him. And as the young men sank against her breast, she stroked their heads and felt a huge wave of all-encompassing love for every boy who was going to war, for every young man who might never know what it was to love and be loved, and she thanked the stars for the love that she and Tommy had known.

It was Andy who had caught at her heart, though. Andy, the first of her 'boys'. Sometimes at night, when she lay alone and unable to sleep, grieving still for Tommy and their lost baby, his face would come into her mind as well and she knew that there had been something special between them, something that could, in another world, at another time, have turned into something more than a cuddle in the park. Baby-snatcher! she scolded herself. He was only a kid. They're all just kids.

Not all of them, though. There'd been that bloke this afternoon – a soldier in stiff, brand-new khaki like most of them were – who had a dark, angry face and eyes that burned. He'd spoken to Maggie as if he already knew her, and told her he was going away soon and his mate had told him there was this Nippy down at Marble Arch who was getting famous for giving a bloke a good send-off . . . Maggie hadn't liked his tone, or the things he was saying, and gave him an icy look.

'I don't know what you mean. I'm a good girl.'

'That's what my mate said. Very good, in fact.'

'Did you want to order something to eat, sir?' Maggie enquired coldly. 'We're quite busy today, so if there isn't anything you want—'

'Did I say that? I want the best you've got.' His eyes held hers and Maggie felt an odd little thrill. This bloke wasn't a boy, going off without knowing what it was all about, she thought. Without shifting his gaze, he reeled off a number of items on the menu and Maggie scribbled them down.

And that's all you're getting, *sir*, she thought as she flounced away to the kitchen.

'Coo-er, who's that you've got at your table, then?' Phyl whispered as they stood in the queue. 'Clark Gable?'

'Don't be daft. He's not a bit like Clark Gable.'

'You'd better take a closer look,' Phyl advised, loading her tray with sausages and chips. 'And think about getting your eyes tested. He's the best-looking chap to walk in here for weeks!'

Maggie wrinkled her nose at her and collected her own orders. She had two tables to serve before returning to him, and as she unloaded the trays she glanced at him under her lashes. Phyl was right. He was a bit like a film star, though she'd have said Stewart Granger herself rather than Clark Gable. As if he could feel her gaze on him, he turned his head suddenly in her direction and she looked away swiftly, feeling her cheeks grow warm.

When she brought his order, half expecting some more suggestive remarks, he smiled at her and said, 'Thank you'. She looked at him, hesitating, and his smile widened.

'Look,' he said, 'I'm sorry if I overstepped the mark, maid. I'm a bit nervous – only just got called up, never been to London before. And my pal did ask to be remembered to you – Davey, his name is, Davey Pascoe. I dare say you've forgotten all about him.'

'Davey?' Maggie echoed. 'Young feller with fair hair and blue eyes?' She thought of his baby face, his innocent kisses. 'No, I haven't forgot Davey. I liked him. How is he?'

'He's fine.' The soldier watched her set the plates and teapot on his table. 'He sent a message for you.'

'A message? What's that, then?'

The soldier glanced around. 'Not here. I'd rather tell you outside somewhere. Why not meet me for a drink after work?'

'I can't. I promised I'd go straight home after work. Mum worries if I'm late.'

'I didn't get the impression from Davey that you were tied to your mother's apron strings,' he murmured.

Maggie straightened up, her eyes furious. 'Now, look here—'

'All right! I'm sorry – I'm sorry. It's just my way when I'm nervous.' He didn't look at all nervous, Maggie thought, eyeing him dubiously. He didn't look the sort of bloke who ever got nervous. And she didn't believe he'd hardly ever been out of Cornwall. He'd been around, this one. 'Look,' he went on, 'forget I said that. If you can't meet me tonight, how about tomorrow? Tell your mum you'll be an hour or so late and I'll make sure you get back okay. How about that?'

'I don't know . . .' Maggie said doubtfully. 'I don't see why you can't tell me what Davey said here and now.'

'I just can't. You'll understand when I do tell you. Please,' he added, and she noticed how dark brown his eyes were. The burning look had changed to one of pleading. She hesitated a moment longer and then gave in.

'All right. Tomorrow, after work.'

'I'll wait for you,' he said, and smiled at her.

There'd been something odd about that smile, she thought now as she hurried home against the biting wind, but there was no point in worrying about that now. All Maggie wanted was to get home by the fire and get warm. And even as she thought it, the siren began to wail.

'Oh, *bloody* hell!'

Maggie broke her stride, hesitated for a second and began to run. A few moments later, breathless, she slowed to a walk. All around her people were scurrying for shelter and a warden waved a rattle in her face and shouted.

'Get under cover!'

'I can't! I live round the back of St Paul's—'

'Get under cover here!' he yelled. 'There's a shelter round the corner.' He was gone into the shadows, and Maggie was almost knocked over by a burly man shouldering his way down the street. She snapped angrily at him and then began to half run, half walk in the direction of home. I'm not going down any bloody street shelter, she thought furiously, I'm going *home*. And nobody's going to stop me.

The wail of the siren died away and the air was filled with the moaning throb of German aircraft. My God, she thought, they're here already, they're right overhead. Automatically, she looked up at the dark sky and its criss-cross of white searchlights, and as she did so an incendiary bomb landed a hundred yards up the street. The flames lit the buildings with a sudden flare of orange and Maggie jumped and flattened herself against a wall. A man running past shoved her roughly to the ground and she lay still, breathless, feeling the graze of the pavement against her cheek. As she looked up, another incendiary fell, a short distance nearer, and she cried out with fear.

'Get into a shelter!' The air throbbed with the noise of aircraft and there was a sudden roar of anti-aircraft fire. The incendiaries were falling thick and fast now, the sky raining fire, and already a building in the next street was going up. Maggie could see the flames, rising high into the sky, lighting the barrage balloons with a coppery glow. She heard the roar of a plane coming in low, beneath the balloons themselves, and ducked her head again. I've got to get home, she thought desperately, I've got to get back.

She ran down the road, her back tingling with fear as if the devil and all his horsemen were after her. Fire-bombs rained down. She juddered to a stop as one hit the pavement only a few yards ahead of her, then jinked round and saw another behind, and screamed as a third hit a wall close by. Already a man was diving out from a doorway, dragging a bucket of sand which he threw over the nearest ball of flame. He saw Maggie and yelled at her to help. 'The whole place'll go up if we don't put these buggers out! Get another bucket, quick.'

He turned back into the building and Maggie scurried

after him, finding herself in the foyer of a block of offices. Sandbags were piled around the doors and a row of red-painted buckets of water and sand stood along one wall. Following the man's example, she snatched one up and rushed outside to hurl it over the long tongue of flame already licking at the doors. The flames hissed angrily and she dashed back for another bucket. The man passed her with a fire extinguisher and started to direct the spray at the flames.

Maggie heard a sudden crash from above. She looked up, and saw to her horror that the high ceiling was on fire and burning debris already beginning to fall through. As the man tore back through the doors, his face reddened by the glow, she grabbed his arm and pointed upwards.

'Oh, my God,' he said. 'That's it, then. Get out – get out before we get burnt to death.' He put his hand between her shoulders and pushed her through the doors. There were flames spreading rapidly up the jambs and it was like going through an archway of fire. Maggie felt the heat as she stumbled out into the street, but when she saw what was happening she scarcely noticed it.

'Oh, my *Gawd*,' she said, momentarily transfixed.

It seemed as if the whole street were burning. The incendiaries had fallen everywhere and set fire to whatever they landed on. People were scurrying to and fro, screaming at each other and pitching sand and water on to the flames. Some had fire extinguishers, some had hoses. There were fire engines at one end, the firemen unreeling their longest hoses and aiming them at the conflagration, but anyone could see that they had no hope of dousing such an inferno. As Maggie and the man stood, transfixed, an entire wall, its windows all ablaze, leant slowly outwards and then crashed into the road as the firefighters scattered before it. A vast shower of sparks shot upwards and then descended like the biggest firework display anyone had ever seen, and the road was on fire from wall to wall.

'Get back. Get *back*. We'll be killed if we stand here.' The man dragged her roughly back down the street. 'God knows what happened to them poor devils . . . Where you goin', love? Couldn't you find no shelter?'

'I was going home. I live round the back of St Paul's.'

'Blimey,' he said. 'It don't look too good round that way.'

Maggie followed his glance. The whole sky was lit with a deep glow of crimson, as if painted with blood. You could see the barrage balloons like shimmering orbs of gold and red, gigantic Christmas baubles hung from a torn velvet sky, with the network of searchlights like tinsel woven amongst them. And you could see the planes, too, black and menacing against the gaudy backdrop.

The whole of the city was on fire. Flames leapt high above the skyline, so that the buildings showed in sharp black relief, momentarily obscured as masses of thick, billowing smoke drifted across their faces. The fire had taken hold on every side, and Maggie felt she was in the middle of a huge furnace, trapped amongst the blazing buildings. She gave a frightened gasp and looked with wide eyes at the man beside her.

'Bloody hell,' she said. 'What are we going to do?'

'Go down fighting,' he said grimly. 'I'm buggered if I let the Jerries fry *me* for breakfast.'

A shower of incendiaries fell not far away. None of them was large, they were just small, smouldering fires that could quite easily be put out but which would, if left alone, burn for a long time and set fire to anything they happened to land on. The greatest danger was in their sheer numbers and the fact that they might fall on roofs or in inaccessible places where they couldn't be checked.

Maggie and the man ran towards the bursts of fire. Every building had sandbags and buckets outside, and they snatched up what they could to smother the flames. Other people appeared to help them and together they worked to stamp out the blaze, but even as they did so more incendiaries fell, starting new fires, and a sudden huge tongue of flame licked along the wall beside them, illuminating the street with a burst of searing light. The sudden, fierce heat made Maggie jump back with a scream.

'It's no good! We'll never beat this lot . . .' The crowd dragged each other away, shielding their faces from the heat with their hands. Maggie could feel it scorching her skin even through her thick coat and scarf. She had lost her gloves, she realised, and her bag as well, the bag that had Tommy's photo and his last letter in it, but there was no time to think of that now. With the others, she scuttled out of range of the fire, only to find herself in the thick of another. I'm going to burn here, she thought despairingly, I'm going to burn to death. Oh, Tommy, Tom . . . where are you? Wait for me . . .

Her frantic thoughts were shattered by a huge explosion. Somewhere not far away, a high-explosive bomb had landed and blown a vast shower of debris into the air. The crimson glow of the sky was blotted out by a huge cloud of dust, smashed bricks and mortar and concrete, plaster, wood and glass – everything that went into a building, together with the bomb fragments and spikes of shrapnel that in themselves could kill, all sent skywards by the blast and spread over a wide area before falling back to earth, lethal weapons in their own right. A few scraps even reached Maggie and her companions, and they cringed and flung their arms over their heads in an attempt at self-protection.

'Blimey, what are they doing to us?' someone muttered. 'What in hell's name are they *doing* to us?'

Nobody answered. It was obvious what the enemy were doing. They were driving the capital city to its knees. They were preparing for invasion.

The raid ceased at ten o'clock but the fires raged on and every street was an inferno, filled with firefighters, with rushing ambulances, with crowds of people helping, searching, hindering. 'Where's my Joan?' 'Where's our Millie?' 'Can't you do something about *my* house? It's on fire and nobody's doing nothing . . . It's down the next street and there ain't been no fire engines nor *nothing*, it's all burning away . . .' 'It's gone, love. There's nothing we can do. It's all gone . . .' 'Where's our Millie?' '*Where's my Joan?*'

Maggie scrambled from one street to another, hardly knowing where she was in this unfamiliar landscape of fire and flame. This must be what hell's like, she thought, and wondered for a moment if she had died and this was her eternity. I haven't been that bad, surely, she thought in panic. I only wanted to give a few boys a good time before they went away . . . A gobbet of flame soared from an upper window above her head and fell at her feet, and she leapt back out of its way, fear rising like yellow bile in her throat. Oh, Gawd, she thought, oh, *Gawd* . . .

She turned a corner and halted, a gasp on her lips. She was on Ludgate, facing St Paul's Cathedral, and she could see the great dome itself, standing clear against the sky. Lit by the flames that burned all about it, silhouetted against the black and crimson clouds of smoke, it stood in the midst of the inferno, calm and untouched to the very tip of its topmost spire. Maggie stared at it and caught her breath in something very close to ecstasy.

'Gawd,' she whispered. 'Gawd . . .'

'What a sight, eh?' a man nearby muttered in her ear. 'What a bleedin' sight . . .'

Slowly, Maggie made her way up Ludgate. Buildings all about her were burning. Looking aside as she passed, she saw the interior of an office block, lit by flames, its opulent carpets a billowing sea of shifting, shimmering red and gold. The heat was intense. She could walk only along the centre of the road, and even there she was in constant danger of being struck by a fragment of blazing debris. The way was blocked every yard or two by mounds of rubble and splintered beams of wood, most of them ablaze. It seemed impossible that anyone could pass, yet there was nothing else to do, for if she turned to go back the way was blocked in just the same way and the fires burned just as fiercely.

Yet always ahead of her she could see the great dome of St Paul's, lit white and red and yellow by the leaping flames. At every moment she expected it to fall, or to suddenly fragment as a bomb burst it asunder. But no matter how many bombs fell about, no matter how high the flames might leap, it stood serene, looking down upon its smitten city with a calm that seemed to give hope to all who saw it. St Paul's Cathedral stood before them untouched, a symbol of faith, and to the Londoners there that night it gave renewed determination, renewed optimism. In the midst of the greatest air attack yet, this most recognisable feature of the city stood invincible, and therefore so did London, and so, too, did the people of London.

Maggie finally reached home at five in the morning. Bone-weary, her eyes reddened by smoke and searing light, her face scorched by the heat and her yellow hair blackened and singed, she stumbled round the corner, dreading what she might be about to see. As she came within view of the house, she stopped, her head turning slowly from side to side, trying to take in the scene before her and lay it as a picture over the vision she had always carried of her home.

It was still dark, yet the streets were uncannily light, illuminated still by the flames and the embers. The air was bitingly cold, yet heated by the fires. It might have been drizzling or even raining, but she couldn't tell; it might equally have been the spray from the hoses of firefighters that touched her brow and as quickly evaporated in the heat. Whatever it was, it hadn't been enough to put out the flames.

The street was devastated. From the little church at one end to the grocer's shop at the other, every single house had been destroyed. Gutted ruins, charred wood, splintered glass were all that she could see. The road was piled with rubble, a crater the size of a house blown about two-thirds of the way down. Another crater had been cordoned off, with a little crowd of soldiers gathered about it, and she recognised the signs of an unexploded bomb.

Where the Pratt house had stood, there was nothing but a huge pile of bricks and shattered glass and broken planks of wood. A crowd was gathered round, some on their hands and knees, hauling at the rubble. She could see her brother Jim amongst the workers. As Maggie approached, a man turned and saw her and came quickly to shield the sight from her gaze.

'Maggie! You wasn't in there, then?'

Dumbly, she shook her head. 'Who was? Me mum? Me dad? Gran?' Her voice shook and she tried to push past him. 'Where are they? Where are they, for Gawd's sake? We got to get them out—'

The man gripped her arm. He came from two doors down, a man called Bert Higgins who they hadn't much liked. 'You can't do nothing, Maggie. The wardens are there, diggin'. They'll get 'em out for you, don't fret . . . Didn't they usually go down the shelter?'

'Mostly they did, yes. Gran was fed up with it, though. And it started so *early* tonight.' Her tone was aggrieved, as if this hadn't been playing fair. 'I don't suppose they were prop'ly ready. And Dad was a firefighter. *He* wouldn't have been in there.' Her voice sharpened. 'Where is he? Where's me dad?'

The man looked unhappy. 'He was a bit hurt, Maggie, love. They took him to the hospital. But he'll be all right – I'm sure he'll be all right.' His grip on her arm slackened and Maggie pushed past, thrusting to the front of the crowd digging in the rubble. Somewhere beneath them she could hear a cry, a faint whimpering. They were alive. Someone was alive down there.

'Get them out! We got to get them out . . .' She was on

her knees beside her brother, scrabbling at the rubble. They were making a hole, she saw, slowly enlarging it until it was big enough for someone to go down. Me, she thought, it'll be me. I want to be the one to go down there and get me mum out and me gran and – and anyone else who's down there. Her mind flooded with pictures. Ginnie. Queenie. Billy. Evie . . .

A hand dragged her away. 'Get out of it, Maggie. This ain't no place for you.'

'I got to get them out,' she panted. 'Let go of me – I got to get me mum and me gran out of here.'

'Leave it to them as knows what they're doing,' the man advised. Blackened by fire and soot, he was unrecognisable, but she knew his voice. He was one of the Pearlies, a friend of her dad's. 'It's not safe for you, Maggie.'

'I don't care. I don't care about me—'

'It's not just you. It's them down there. You could loosen something and it could fall and – look, Maggie, do as I say, there's a good girl. We'll get 'em all out, don't you worry.'

Reluctantly, she retreated and sank down on a pile of bricks, watching anxiously. There were about half a dozen men, all digging carefully, removing bricks and lumps of rubble one by one and setting them aside. The hole was growing larger, soon someone would be able to get down. Now and then, during the occasional brief lull in the crackling of the fires further along the street, mixed with the noise of people, running and calling, rising above the racket of fire engines and ambulances, she was sure she could hear voices coming from down below. If only I could tell who it is, she thought, straining her ears. If it's Mum, or Gran, or our Ginnie. Or one of the others. Or even all of them, all shouting together.

Oblivious of the cold, unaware of fatigue or hunger or of her burning thirst, she sat watching as the dawn crept slowly across the sky, pallid beside the rage of the still burning fires, and laid a dull, grey light over the smouldering ruins of the city of London.

It was the second Great Fire of London.

That was what the *Daily Mail* said on its front page on the Tuesday, two days after the great raid. The Nazis had planned to start fires all over the capital before midnight. In only three hours, more than ten thousand incendiary bombs were dropped, and once the fires were raging the heavy bombers, carrying hundreds of tons of high explosives, arrived to complete the destruction. Lit by the flames, the barrage balloons shone like beacons and the bombers came snarling in below them. The City was to have been completely destroyed, paving the way, so the newspaper said, for the final and conclusive invasion of Britain.

As well as the dramatic front-page photograph of St Paul's, silhouetted against the flames and the billowing smoke, the newspaper carried stories of those who had seen the devastation, those who had been in the fires. There was a long list of the buildings that had been destroyed – St Bride's church, St Lawrence Jewry, St Andrew-by-the-Wardrobe, and the Guildhall itself – blackened skeletons, it said, shattered by the bombs and gutted by the fires.

It seemed as if half of London's history had gone with them.

And already the questions had begun to be asked. How could it have happened? Why had it been allowed to happen? The city was supposed to be protected – by the balloons, by the anti-aircraft guns, by the RAF itself with its fighters. How could the Germans, at six o'clock on a Sunday evening, have penetrated so far and so devastatingly?

Firstly, the paper said, it was because there just hadn't been enough fire-spotters. All buildings where thirty or more people were employed were required by law to provide a 24-hour watch for fires, yet on many of the larger buildings there hadn't been anyone at all. One fire-spotter told how he and his colleagues had watched in frustration as fires burned on the roofs of other buildings where there were no watchers. 'As soon as we'd dealt with our own we turned our hoses right across the street on the fires starting on another large building where more than a hundred people work.' They had dashed down the street and entered other office blocks to get to more fires, risking their lives to get to blazing roofs, but some had proved impossible to get into and they'd had to watch helplessly as the buildings smouldered and then burst into flames. And some firemen, making heroic efforts against terrible odds, had paid with their lives.

In Maggie's street, her father had been one of the firewatchers. He'd been putting out incendiaries as fast as they fell, until a bomb had struck a house halfway down the street and some falling debris had knocked him out. He'd been grabbed up from where he lay and a passing ambulance had been flagged down and rushed him to the first-aid post. From there he'd been taken to hospital and he was there in bed in a crowded ward when Maggie arrived, dusty and tear-stained, later that morning.

'Dad . . .'

'Maggie, love.' His eyes, almost the only parts of his head visible amidst the swathe of bandages, brightened. 'Thank Gawd you're okay. I was worried about you coming home in that lot . . . What about the others? They were supposed to be going down the shelter, only your gran was kicking up as usual.' His voice was weak and husky, as if his throat hurt. 'And our Jim. He went out firefighting. He's all right, ain't he? Nothing's happened to Jim? And the twins, they oughter bin with him, too. Are they all right?'

Maggie's eyes fell. '*Dad*—'

'What? What is it? What's happened?' He gripped her hand. 'Don't tell me – don't tell me they've gone. Not your mum. Not your gran. Not – not our Evie and Queenie – and the baby.' His voice was rising painfully, grating as if he had a throat full of broken glass. 'Tell me, Mags, for Gawd's sake, *tell me they're all right*.'

Maggie swallowed. Her own throat felt as painful. She shook her head and the tears began to fall. 'Oh, *Dad* . . .'

There was a moment's silence. Then he said heavily, 'It's all of 'em, ain't it? They've all gone.'

'No.' She shook her head blindly. 'No – not all of 'em. Mum's all right – a bit knocked about, but she's okay. And our Ginnie. And Gran – you wouldn't believe Gran. She come out swearing like a trooper. I've never even heard half the words she used. If Hitler'd been there waiting for her, she'd have torn him into little pieces, I'm sure she would. And Billy, he's all right, too. It was . . .' Words failed her again and she drew in a deep, sobbing breath. 'Oh, *Dad* . . .'

'It's our Evie, isn't it?' he said quietly. 'Our Evie. And – and Queenie? Our little Queenie?'

Maggie nodded. She closed her eyes and saw again the moment when they had finally managed to get the family out of the ruined house. Her mother, shaken and bewildered, bleeding from the temple, staring at Maggie as if she'd never seen her before. Her grandmother, wild-eyed and furious, cursing volubly through toothless gums, ready to attack any German who happened to be standing in the way. Her little sister Ginnie, pale and frightened under a thick coating of dust, but apparently unhurt. And her little nephew Billy, taken gently from beside his dead mother.

Evie had been crushed by a fallen beam. In the curious way that bombing could kill one person while leaving another unmarked, she had been cradling baby Freddy in her arms and the beam had missed him by little more than an inch. But her other child, little Queenie, also cuddled close to her mother, had received the full brunt of the beam across her own small head.

Maggie shuddered at the memory. She remembered the

looks on the faces of the rescuers as they dug down through the rubble. Bert Higgins, who had always been a bit of a pain in the backside, Bob Wilkins the Pearly – she'd seen the sick horror in their eyes. They'd glanced back towards her and she'd started up, wanting to know and wanting not to know, praying that it wasn't true, knowing she must see for herself. And they'd tried to prevent her, holding her back, shaking their heads urgently. Bert Higgins had put his arms around her in his efforts to stop her seeing what she had to see.

'No, Maggie. It won't do no good—'

'I've got to,' she panted. 'I've got to know . . . .' And she'd broken out of his arms and run to the edge of the hole and stared down.

'Don't look, Maggie,' he said, coming behind her, but it was too late and she turned away, knowing that she would never be able to get rid of the memory of her sister Evie, crushed beneath the beam, and her little niece Queenie, a mess of tangled yellow hair and white splintered bone, matted with blood and brains.

'Queenie,' her father whispered painfully. 'Our Queenie. My little princess.'

'Oh, Dad,' she choked, and brought his hand to her face and wept against it.

Chapter Seventeen

Maggie was given three days off to help sort out the family.
Her mother and grandmother, together with Ginnie, Billy
and the baby, had been sent to a church hall which was
mercifully undamaged and crowded with homeless families.
They made their home in a corner, surrounded by the few
possessions they had managed to save – a couple of china
ornaments, a few cups and saucers, a drawer full of cutlery,
some clothes so thick with dust that Ivy didn't think she'd
ever get them clean. Just bits and pieces, but now that they
were all they had left they had become precious.

They'd been given a few more things – blankets,
some tired-looking pillows, a jumble of clothes. We look
like refugees, Maggie thought, staring at them. We *are*
refugees . . .

And it wasn't just the living who had to be cared for.
There were the dead to think about, too.

There were too many of them for separate funerals. A
mass burial would be held later that week, though where
they would be put when so many churches had been
destroyed and so much land torn to pieces was another
question. But there were formalities to be gone through –
registrations, certificates, all the trappings of officialdom
which had to be observed – and only then could Evie and
her little girl go to their graves with all the rest.

It was a Pearly funeral. So many of the Pearlies had been
killed that all their families turned out in whatever dress
they could get together. Maggie's own costume had been
salvaged, along with her father's and mother's and Ginnie's

and even Gran's, in the old tin trunk in which they were stored. They put them on and marched with the rest into the streets, to follow the sad procession of coffins and pay their last respects. The streets, still heaped with rubble, were lined with people and the Pearlies walked with bowed heads, hearing the subdued cheers and whispers. So often, ever since they had first come into being through the work of young Henry Croft, the first of all Pearlies, they had been the ones to help the less fortunate. Now they were the ones in need of help and encouragement, and their neighbours were ready to give it.

'I tell you what, Maggie,' Sam Pratt said as they sat in their corner of the church hall when it was all over, 'you never know who your friends are till bad times hit you. That Bert Higgins, now, he's always bin a thorn in my side, but today he come up to me, good as gold, and give me a clap on the back and said anything I needed, I'd only got to ask. And he meant it, too, you could see that.'

'I know, Dad. He was ever so good to me, too, when I come down the street that morning.' The vision flashed before her eyes again and she gave a little sob. 'He's not such a bad sort, is he?'

They sat in silence for a moment. Sam had been let out of hospital in time for the funeral and didn't need to go back. He was still bandaged but Ivy and Maggie could see to that for him. He had made up his mind to go back to work tomorrow. There weren't enough blokes in the market now for him to swing the lead.

'So what we going to do now, ducks?' he asked. 'How do we find somewhere to live? You found out anything?'

Maggie shrugged. 'They're snowed under with people bombed out. And as fast as they find 'em somewhere, they get bombed out again. There's a woman down the end who's been bombed out three times – she says she's getting fed up with it! I dunno what we're supposed to do.'

'Well, we can't live in ruins. I been down to look at the

house before I come along here. There ain't nothing left of it, Mags! I never seen a place knocked down like it – it must've got a direct hit.'

'It was the house three doors down that got a direct hit. We just got the blast. The worst of it is that Gran *was* going to go to the shelter – she hadn't been kicking up at all, not after you went out. They were just looking for her teeth.' Maggie gave a wry little laugh. 'They won't never find 'em now!'

Her father gave a sudden exclamation and felt in his pockets. 'That's just where you're wrong, girl! *I* found 'em – sitting on top of a pile o' bricks, grinning at me, they were. I picked 'em up and forgot all about 'em – look.' He drew them out of his pocket and Maggie stared at them – the fearsome set of teeth her grandmother hardly ever wore, the rictus grin she had once suggested could be Britain's secret weapon against the Germans, the teeth that had somehow, miraculously, survived a blast that had killed her sister and baby niece . . . She shook her head blindly and burst into tears.

'Oh, Dad! Dad! It don't seem fair. It don't, really. It don't seem *fair*.'

Ivy, Ada and Ginnie were evacuated to the country, taking little Billy and baby Freddy with them. They went to Devon and were found a tiny cottage on a farm. They didn't want to go, but the shock of the bombing was still hanging about them, dulling their senses, and they went like lambs. Maggie and Sam went to the station to see them off.

'I never thought I'd end up being buried alive once, let alone twice,' Ada grumbled. You'd have thought that the experience of being bombed out would have subdued and aged her but instead it seemed to have given her a new lease of life. She was so furious with the Germans who had dared to destroy her home that if Hitler had been within range of her old black umbrella (which Sam had found not far away from her teeth) she would have beaten him about the head until he'd agreed to call off all his forces. And the loss of her granddaughter Evie and the little girl Queenie who had been the darling of the family had whipped up her anger even more. She glowered fearsomely from under her old black hat, and Maggie wondered what the country folk would make of her.

'You're not being buried alive, Gran,' she said. 'You're going to a smashing little cottage in the country. A lot of people would give their eye teeth to have a place of their own and not have to share.'

'I've give me teeth already, all the lot of 'em. It don't seem to have made no difference. What'll we do with ourselves out there? Tell me that.'

Maggie thought she would probably do more or less what she had been doing at home – sitting by the fire and complaining. But under her grandmother's basilisk-like glare, she dared not say so. Luckily, her sister Ginnie came to her rescue.

'Pick blackberries and climb trees,' she said. 'That's what Ellie Jones done when she was there. She told me.'

Ginnie was looking pale and her voice, usually so bright and full of enthusiasm, was quiet and subdued. The shock had hit her hard. She had been close to Evie and Queenie when the house had collapsed, and had felt their blood warm on her hand. She'd had nightmares every night since and wouldn't sleep on her own any more, and any loud, sudden noise made her jump out of her skin.

Maggie put her arm round her sister's shoulders. 'You're a brave girl, Ginnie,' she said. 'You'll be all right in the country. You'll help our Mum and Gran, won't you? You might even make some jam with them blackberries. You could send some back to Dad.'

Ginnie nodded. She was making huge efforts to hide her unhappiness, but Maggie knew she missed little Queenie desperately. She was holding Billy by the hand now, obviously determined to be a 'little mother' to him. Billy, at five years old, was a sturdy, pugnacious little boy, nothing like his fairy-like sister had been, and he would obviously have preferred not to have been clutched so tightly by the hand. In his other hand he carried a toy gun which Jim had made for him from a piece of wood, and he glowered at Maggie as if she were the enemy.

'I'm going to catch parachutists,' he said grimly. 'I'm going to catch Germans and shoot 'em dead.'

'You do that,' Maggie told him. 'And I'll have the parachute to make silk knickers with.' She looked at her mother. 'Take care of yourself, Mum. And write every week.'

Ivy tried to smile. 'I ought to be saying that to you. You'll go and see your dad regular, won't you, Mags? And our Jim and the twins? You know they're on about joining up now they're eighteen?'

'You can't stop 'em, Ma. They'll be called up soon enough anyway.' Maggie sighed. Jim would be going, too, and Etty wouldn't like that. And Evie's husband, Joe, had been in the army for the past six months. All the young men were going off to war, and everyone knew that a lot of them wouldn't come back. It didn't bear thinking about.

The station was packed with people – soldiers in khaki going back to barracks or camp, air force men in their blue-grey uniforms returning to their airfields, sailors in navy blue going back to sea. And evacuees like the Pratts, dressed in an assortment of clothes doled out by the WVS or salvaged from the wreckage of their homes, carrying their few possessions in old suitcases or shopping bags, looking bewildered and lost. Nearly everyone had somebody to see them off – a wife or sweetheart, a husband or father, a mother who couldn't believe that her baby son had grown into this tall, uniformed man who was going off to war.

The noise was deafening, and above it all Maggie heard the shrill whistle of the boilers as they made up steam, and then the huffing of the engines as they began to move. The guard blew his whistle and waved a flag and she gave her mother a hasty shove.

'Get aboard, Mum! You don't want to get left behind. Come on, Gran, up you go – and you, Ginnie. Bye-bye, Billy, take care of your grannies for me, there's a good boy, and don't forget that parachute.' She and Sam pushed them aboard and stood back as the doors slammed. Ada was already plodding along the corridor, making for the seats where they had dumped their bags, and Billy followed her, but Ivy and Ginnie leant out, their eyes suddenly brimming with tears. Ivy reached out a hand and Sam grabbed it and clutched it, his face red and crumpled.

'Oh, Sam – Sam . . .'

'Look after yourself, Ivy,' he choked. 'Blimey, I ain't half going to miss you, though.'

'Sam, I don't want to go without you—'

'Now, don't be daft. You'll be better out in the country, away from the bombs. You just enjoy it and make sure you get plenty to eat – why, you'll be as fat as butter when you comes home again. I won't hardly know you.' He reached up and gave her a smacking kiss as the train began to move slowly along the platform. 'Cheerio, Ginnie, girl. You do as you're told, mind.'

'Bye, Dad. Bye, Maggie.'

'Bye, Ginnie.' Maggie gave her sister a quick kiss, then just managed one for her mother as well before the train began to pick up speed and took them beyond reach. She stepped back and watched, her hand to her mouth, the tears blurring her eyes, as the train chugged away. Her mother's face was still visible, a pale blob, until the train finally disappeared round the bend.

There was a moment's silence on the platform, broken only by sobbing from some of the women.

Maggie turned to her father, a wry look on her face.

'Well, Dad, that's it. They've gone.'

He nodded and wiped his face and round bald head with a big red handkerchief. His usual cheery expression was gone, making him look like a woeful giant baby. He looked crumpled, as if someone had screwed him up like a paper bag and then just thrown him down in the street.

'Gone,' he repeated. 'Your mother and gran and Ginnie sent to the country, and me and Jim and the twins put to stop in a doss-house. Our Evie and my little princess dead, and the family all split up. Well, at least you've got somewhere decent to go, Mags, that's one thing. You'll be all right in the hostel along with young Etty.'

She nodded dispiritedly and they parted outside the station. It seemed strange to be going back to the Corner House after all that had happened – she felt as if she'd been away for years. But the warm greetings of the other girls lifted her spirits a little and she put on her uniform and went into the restaurant, determined to serve her customers as well as ever.

'That bloke's been in looking for you,' Phyl whispered to her.

'What bloke?'

'The one who looks like Clark Gable. He came in twice. He asked about you yesterday and I told him you'd got a bit of trouble at home.'

'Oh, him.' Maggie had forgotten all about the dark-eyed soldier with the message from David. It all seemed a very long time ago now. 'Well, I don't suppose he'll come in again.'

There was one thing about being a Nippy, she thought. It didn't give you time to dwell on your troubles. And one thing the war was teaching everyone was that they weren't the only ones who had troubles – whatever had happened to you had happened to other people as well, and sometimes worse. There were people Maggie knew who'd lost their whole families, right down to the cat, didn't have a soul left to call their own. She was lucky, really . . . Thinking these thoughts as she dashed between her station and the kitchens, she forgot again about the dark-eyed soldier and almost jumped out of her skin when she came to a halt beside one of her tables to find herself looking into those very eyes.

'So here you are at last, maid,' he said. 'Thought you were avoiding me.'

Maggie stared at him. 'Why on earth should you think that?'

'We had a date, remember? You stood me up. I waited a hell of a long time, too.'

'We had a raid,' Maggie said tersely. 'Our house was bombed and my sister and her little girl were killed. Sorry about the date, but I just couldn't get away, see?'

He was silent for a moment, his eyes on Maggie's reddened cheeks, then he said quietly, 'Sorry. I didn't know. It's been a bad few nights, hasn't it?'

'I've had better.'

'Well . . .' For a change, he seemed at a loss, staring at the table. Then he looked up at her again. 'Look, I know things have changed for you, but I've still got that message from Davey, if you're interested.'

Maggie bit her lip. She hadn't thought about the young servicemen and didn't know if she had the energy or the wish to get involved with any of them again. Too much had happened to her. She felt empty, hardly knowing how to share her grief out amongst all those who deserved it. I don't want to go back to that sort of thing again, she thought miserably. I'm sorry for the kids, but they'll have to find someone else to send 'em off happy.

But David . . . She couldn't help remembering his delight in her, like a child seeing heaven. That's what he'd called it. Heaven.

'I don't see why you can't tell me here,' she said, glancing around. 'Not that I've got time to stand chattering. We're busy.'

307

'That's why I can't. Look. We had a date the other day for after work. Can't we meet tonight? I'll wait for you.'

His eyes met hers. They were very intent. Maggie felt a twinge of unease. I wouldn't like to cross this one, she thought. He could be nasty . . . But he showed no signs of being nasty with her, and if all he wanted to do was have a drink and give her a message . . . And she would like to know how Davey was, she really would.

'All right, then,' she said. 'Out by the side door at half-ten. I'll see you there.'

For the rest of the afternoon and evening, she hoped that he wouldn't be there. Curious as she was to know what message fair-haired David had sent her, she really didn't want to start seeing men again. But nobody else seemed to realise that and she'd seen the floor supervisors giving her funny looks while they were talking. Once Miss Turgoose herself came and wandered around the restaurant, pausing as if to adjust some cutlery or examine a glass and seeming to hover as Maggie exchanged cheerful banter with a couple of young men. She had always done this, of course, but it seemed to Maggie that she spent more time lingering near her station than by anyone else's.

It couldn't be a coincidence either that Irene chose that moment to start passing caustic remarks.

'Turning Lyons into a you-know-what,' she muttered, just loudly enough for Maggie to hear as she passed by. 'I wonder the management puts up with it.'

A bit later on, Phyl caught her in the lavatories. 'You'll be getting the sack if you're not careful, Maggie. I saw Mr Carter watching you just now when you were serving that feller. These boys don't mean anything to you. Why d'you do it?'

Maggie was silent for a few moments. Then she said quietly, 'You're wrong, Phyl. They do mean something to me. They remind me of my Tom. He told me once, when a chap goes away he knows he's got a good chance of being killed and he just wants to know what it's like, see – being with a girl. He knows it might be the last chance he'll ever have.' Maggie turned and looked into Phyl's face. 'I think it's awful that these boys are going off to fight and be killed, and they haven't even had a chance to know what being a man really means. Well, that's where I reckon I can help them, see? I can send 'em off knowing what it's for and what to do with it. It makes them feel better – and it don't do me no harm either!' She gave Phyl a wry grin. 'Me and my Tom had a lot of good times together before we got wed as well as that little while we had after. And I'm glad we did. And I'm glad I been able to give these young blokes a good time, too – but to tell you the truth, I'm not sure I'm going to do it any more. I don't seem to have the heart for it now, not after what's happened.'

She turned away, and Phyl touched her arm comfortingly. 'So you won't be meeting that bloke after work, then, like he was asking you?' Maggie turned and looked at her, and Phyl grinned wryly. 'I'm sorry, I couldn't help hearing.'

'I'm meeting him because he says he's got a message for me from one of the others – the young, fair-haired one, Davey, he was called. But that's all. There's not going to be no hanky-panky.'

'Well, I should watch it if I were you,' Phyl said. 'He looks as if he could turn funny. I don't want to hear you've been found in an alleyway with your throat slashed!'

'That's a nice thing to say! Anyway, I won't be. It's just a quick drink, that's all, and as soon as he's had his say I'll be off. And that's it for me. A few nice quiet evenings at the hostel with Etty is all I want from now on. So you can stop worrying about me, and you can tell Lady Muck to keep her spiteful remarks to herself in future.'

Phyl gave her a smile. 'All right, Maggie. Don't get your rag out. You know it's only because we love you.'

'Lady Muck don't love me,' Maggie said tersely. 'Lady Muck don't love no one but her own nasty little self.'

Despite Maggie's hopes, he was there at half past ten, just as he'd promised. She gave him a smile but he just looked at her and held out his arm. Her heart sinking a little, Maggie took it. I hope he's not expecting the full works, she thought. I just don't feel up to it. Not tonight. Maybe not any night.

'So what's this message, then?' she asked, trying not to sound too impatient.

'Not so fast. You promised to come for a drink with me.'

'Oh, that's all right,' she said wearily. 'I don't mind having a drink. But I promised to go and see me dad on the way home, see, so I can't hang around.'

'And where's your dad live?'

'In . . .' Maggie bit her lip. 'In a working men's lodging-house with me brothers, since we got bombed out. Mum and Gran and my little sister were evacuated. Pity they didn't go sooner,' she added quietly.

The soldier said nothing. They walked swiftly down a side street until they came to a pub that was still serving. He pushed open the door and Maggie went ahead of him, shoving aside the blackout curtain. There were only a few people drinking – most were at home, waiting for the siren to go. The soldier bought a pint of bitter for himself and a glass of stout for Maggie and brought them over to a table.

'Happy days,' he said, lifting his glass. Maggie grimaced and said nothing. She wished he'd say whatever he wanted to say and get it over with.

Funny, really, she thought, watching him. Here she was out with a bloke who could pass for a film star, and all she wanted was to go home. If she'd had a home any more. Funny how you didn't realise how much your family meant to you till they'd gone.

'Seen enough, then?' the soldier asked suddenly, and she flushed.

'Sorry. Didn't mean to stare.'

'It's all right,' he said in a tone that made her want to hit him, 'I'm used to it.'

'My Gawd!' Maggie exclaimed. 'You don't half think a lot of yourself, don't you?'

'No more than I deserve,' he said, grinning, and again she wanted to smack his face, take that smug, conceited grin off it and make him smile on the other side. I dunno why I came out with him, she thought. He doesn't need me and I'm beginning to wonder if he really has got a message from Dave.

'Come on, then,' she ordered, 'spit it out. Tell me what Dave said and then I can go.'

There was a moment's silence. Then the soldier leant nearer to her. His eyes were narrowed and he looked suddenly frightening again. Maggie shifted her chair away a little.

'What did he say?' she asked again, wishing more than ever that she hadn't come. 'Look, I've done what you wanted, I've come out for a drink. Now you keep your side of the bargain.'

'Right, I will.' He paused, chewing his lip. 'Maybe it ain't quite the way you think. You see, the message isn't exactly from Davey himself—'

'I knew it.' Maggie scraped her chair as she made to stand up. 'You got me here under false pret—'

His hand shot out and gripped her wrist. Maggie almost cried out at the pain of his grasp. She sat down again.

'All right.' Her voice was shaking. 'So, if it isn't from Dave, who is it from? If there's any message at all,' she added scornfully.

'Oh, there's a message all right. And I'll tell you who it's from.' Another pause. 'It's from my sister.'

Maggie stared at him. 'Your *sister*? What the hell has *she* got to do with this? I don't even know your sister. Come to think of it, I don't even know your name.'

'My name don't matter. Nor does my sister's. What matters is that she was engaged to Davey – until he met you. And then what happens? You take him down the park behind a bush and teach him things our kid don't even know, and the next thing is he's breaking off the engagement, saying he's met someone else. A Nippy, down the Corner House. *You*.'

Maggie stared at him. 'He can't have said that. There was never nothing – I never said – I never even expected to see him again—'

'I don't suppose you did. Have your fling and then chuck 'em away, that's your style, ain't it? Never mind that a kid like Davey can't handle it. Never mind he might forget the girl he's got at home, the girl who's been his sweetheart since they was kids and promised to wait for him, the girl who writes to him every day, the girl he's bought a *ring* for. Never mind he might fall for you. You're not bothered, are you? You've got another bloke by then, another half-dozen. I know what you are – I've been watching you. Out with any Tom, Dick or Harry that gives you the eye. You're nothing but a common tart.'

'I'm not! It's not like that!'

'It is,' he stated. 'You've busted up Dave's life and you've busted up my sister's life, and I don't bloody see why you should get away with it.'

'But he never told me he was engaged – he never even hinted—'

'It wouldn't have made any difference if he had,' the soldier said, still gripping her wrist painfully. 'You just wanted a bit of fun and it wouldn't have made any difference if he'd been married with six kids.'

Maggie flinched. 'It *would*. I only ever—' She caught his sardonic stare and lowered her voice. 'I only ever went with chaps who'd never done it before,' she whispered. 'I just wanted to give 'em something to remember – something nice. And if they already got girlfriends and their

312

girlfriends won't do it – well, it serves 'em right if someone else will.'

'You're a slut,' he said coldly. 'You're in it for what you can get. And this time you're going to get a bit more than you bargained for.'

Maggie gazed at him. His eyes were hard, like stones. She read the intent in his look and jerked her arm away. Swiftly, she scrambled to her feet and made for the door. Two men who were coming in barred her way and she shoved them aside and ran, panic-stricken, into the street.

'Put that light out!' The blackout curtain had got caught up and yellow light streamed out on to the pavement. Maggie, running for all she was worth, glanced back and saw the soldier emerge, slamming the door behind him. In the sudden darkness, she stumbled and almost fell. His heavy footsteps sounded close behind and a moment later he was on her, dragging her into the mouth of a nearby alleyway.

'Let me go!'

'Not till you've given me what you give young Davey. And a bit more besides.' His hands were tearing at her clothes. She struggled, pushing and kicking, but she could hardly move in the confined space and he laughed nastily and pinned her against the wall. He dragged her skirt up round her waist and she felt the roughness of damp bricks against her skin. His hands were rough and brutal between her thighs, fingers probing. She gave a squeal of pain.

'You're hurting me.'

'Good,' he said brusquely. 'That's what I mean to do.' His body was hard against hers, thrusting her against the wall. Maggie screamed and instantly his hand was over her mouth. She felt something cold and hard in his palm. A knife – oh, God, he had a knife . . . She had a sudden sickening memory of Phyl's voice saying that she didn't want to hear Maggie had been found in some alleyway with her throat slashed . . . A thrust of searing, intrusive agony

313

jerked her buttocks back against the brick wall once more, and the soldier moved his hand from her lips to her neck, and covered her mouth with his. He squeezed her throat and she felt the cold blade once more, thin and sharp against her jaw. His saliva was bitter and his teeth bit into her tongue. Maggie tasted blood and gagged, knowing she was going to choke. The rapid, brutal thrusting of his body against and into hers became almost unimportant against the need to get some breath, the need to stay alive.

By the time he gave a final savage thrust, almost flattening her between the wall and his body, Maggie was only half-conscious. Before her popping eyes she could see nothing but a thick red mist. Her ears roared, and when she finally managed to take a breath it was sucked into her lungs with a desperate scraping, retching sound. He's going to kill me, she thought. I'm going to die in this alleyway and nobody's going to help me . . .

There was a moment's pause. Then the soldier grunted and dragged himself away from her, tearing her flesh as he did so. He stepped back and Maggie sank to the ground. She waited for him to kick or stab her. He had heavy boots, he had a knife. Nobody would see. In a moment, he would do it. She moaned.

He gave her a nudge with his foot and Maggie waited for the final blow.

'Just you remember that,' he said with a sneer, 'the next time some baby-faced young sprog asks you for a date. Just you remember!'

Maggie groaned and spat the blood feebly from her mouth. She heard him walk away, then turned her head and vomited painfully. She was sore all over. She lay in the cold, dank mud, waiting for the roaring to cease and the red mist to clear, and wondered if she was going to die. He hadn't needed to kick or stab her after all, he knew there was no hope. He could just walk away and leave her here to die, like a dog in the gutter.

Somewhere above her, she heard the rising wail of the air-raid siren, and then the familiar snarl of enemy aircraft. But Maggie was beyond running for cover.

Chapter Eighteen

These days, when someone didn't turn up for work, nobody knew what to think. Normally you'd just shrug it off – 'got a cold' or a headache, or the time of the month. But when you were in the middle of a blitzkrieg, it could mean a lot worse than a bad headache. It could mean being bombed out of house and home. It could mean being dead.

When neither Etty nor Maggie came in that day, the other girls looked at each other in dismay. Nobody liked to say what was in all their minds.

'Where was the raid last night?' Jo asked at last. 'Was it anywhere near the hostel?'

'Etty always goes into the shelter. She told me that weeks ago. Maggie would've gone with her.'

'But Maggie didn't go straight back after work last night,' Phyl said. 'She was going to meet that soldier who's been hanging round after her. The one that looked like Clark Gable. She told me they were going for a drink.'

'Oh, well, then,' Irene said with an unpleasant little laugh, 'we know what'll have kept *her*, don't we!'

Phyl turned on her. 'Keep your nasty remarks to yourself, Irene Bond. She told me definite she wasn't going for anything more than a quick drink. She's not interested in anything else, not since her sister and niece were killed. She didn't even want to do that, only he told her he'd got a message from someone else.'

Irene looked sceptical and turned away with a sneer. Shirley ignored her and said, 'That wouldn't account for Etty being late as well. They must be together.'

'So she must have gone back to the hostel,' Jo decided. 'If only we could find out . . . Isn't there anyone else lives round that way?'

'Jean does. The girl who works on the counter.' Shirley slipped across the dressing-room to where the Sallies were getting into their uniforms and came back frowning. 'She's in all right, and she says it wasn't too bad round their way. She doesn't think there was anything big like the hostel hit.'

'So why are they both late?' The girls stared at each other anxiously and then turned as Mr Carter came in for their inspection.

'Is everyone present?'

'No, sir, Maggie and Etty aren't here,' Jo answered as they lined up, some already holding out their hands to show their clean fingernails.

Mr Carter tutted. 'I thought Margaret had settled down after her days off. I know it's hard for her, but so many of us are having to cope with such tragedies these days. And Esther's usually so punctual.'

'Please, Mr Carter, that's why we think something must have happened to them,' Phyl said. 'We've asked, and there wasn't a big raid round their way last night so it must be something else.'

'Maybe a breakdown on the tube,' someone suggested, and there was a general murmur of agreement. 'Or a bus might've had to go a long way round.'

'I dare say that's all it is,' Mr Carter said. 'Well, we shall just have to cover for them.' He looked worried. 'At this rate, with half the Nippies leaving to join up and the other half never sure whether they're going to be here or not, we're going to have to think of another way of serving our customers. We simply can't go on like this.'

The girls stared at him. Their inspection over, they began to make their way through the tunnel to the restaurant. Jo turned to Phyl and said, 'What d'you think he meant by that? How else can we serve the customers? We've got to have Nippies.'

'I don't know. Unless he means they'd all have to line up for their food, like in a canteen.'

Jo hooted with laughter. 'What – carry their own trays? Don't be daft, Phyl! This is the Corner House. They'd never sink to treating customers like workers in a canteen. Why, it wouldn't be worth them coming here at all if they had to do that.'

They went to their stations. The previous shift of Nippies handed over to them and they began work. But all the time she was hurrying to and fro with orders and trays, part of Phyl's mind was worrying about Maggie's and Etty's absence. If they hadn't been bombed, what had stopped them coming to work today? A tube or bus breakdown, or blocked streets, might have accounted for it if they'd been on morning shift, but this was afternoon and they'd had plenty of time to set out early and get here. Those sorts of excuses, as Miss Turgoose had said a few weeks ago, just didn't wash any more.

'Something's happened to them, I'm sure of it,' she muttered to Jo when they finally went for their short teabreak. 'I didn't feel happy last night about Maggie meeting that soldier. There was something funny about him. I hope—'

'But that wouldn't account for Etty being late, too,' Jo argued. 'She'd have come in as usual, surely.'

'If Maggie hadn't come home all night? What would you have done if it had been me?'

Jo chewed her lip thoughtfully. 'Well, I see what you mean, but that's different. Maggie could've gone to see her dad and stopped the night over there. Etty would have thought of that and not worried.' She shook her head. 'No, that's not right either. She'd have expected Maggie to come in the morning . . . Oh, I dunno, Phyl, I dunno what's happened to the two of them. I guess we'll just have to wait and—'

318

'There they are!' Shirley had just joined them at their table. She set down her tray of tea and pointed at the canteen door. 'Well, there's Etty, anyway. I dare say Maggie's coming, too – found a ladder in her stockings probably!'

They laughed, relieved, and then their laughter faded as Etty came slowly across the room to greet them. Her face was white and drawn, her eyes rimmed with red. And there was still no sign of Maggie.

The girls fell silent as she reached them. She stood looking from one to the other, tears trickling down her pale, thin cheeks, her mouth trembling.

'Etty?' Jo whispered at last. 'Etty – what is it? What's happened?' And, after a pause which seemed to go on for ever, 'Where's Maggie?'

'Oh, Jo – Phyl – Shirley . . .' Etty paused and gulped. Her face crumpled. 'It's awful. Maggie – Maggie—' Sobs choked her and she screwed up her eyes and shook her head. The girls glanced at each other in consternation and Jo pulled out a chair for Etty to sit on. When she made no move, Phyl pressed gently on her shoulder until she sank down. She leant her elbows on the table, covered her face with both hands and wept.

'Tell us, Etty – for God's sake, tell us what's happened,' Phyl begged, her voice rough-edged with panic. 'Please. Please.'

Etty shook her head and continued to sob for several minutes. Gradually, the sobs became shudders and the shudders hiccups. At last, she was able to lift her tear-sodden face and look up at them again.

'Just tell us what's happened,' Shirley said gently. 'Is Maggie – is she hurt?'

Etty nodded, her lips trembling again.

'She – she's not . . .'

There was a moment's breathless hush. Then Etty's face seemed to disintegrate, like a jigsaw that has been lifted up

319

so that its pieces gradually fall apart. She looked from one to the other and then buried her face in her hands once more.

'Oh, Jo, Phyl, Shirley,' she cried again. 'It's awful . . . What's happened to Maggie . . . It's just *awful* . . .'

Etty had known that Maggie wasn't coming straight home after work. She watched uneasily as her friend went off on the arm of the tall, good-looking soldier. Like Phyl, she was unhappy about the life Maggie had been leading, but she didn't like to say anything about it. Maggie was a married woman – well, a widow, sadly – and that put her into a different position. It wasn't for someone like Etty to reproach her.

Still, even Etty was aware that Maggie was playing with fire and, like Phyl, she had a nasty feeling that this one might be the one to set the flames going. He wasn't a boy, still wet behind the ears, he was a man who'd been around. You could tell that at a glance. Maggie might be walking straight into trouble.

Etty went back to the hostel on her own. As she walked in the front door she saw Muriel disappearing upstairs and wondered who was with her. Probably Irene, she thought. Thick as thieves those two were, and good luck to them. They deserved each other.

She went up to the room she now shared with Maggie. Mrs Denton had been only too pleased to take another resident when Pat and Cora had left, and Etty could hardly believe her luck in having her best friend to live with her. Of course, she reminded herself, her good luck came from Maggie's tragedy, and she must never forget that. But at least it meant that she could be on hand to comfort her friend when she woke in the night from a bad dream, or lay grieving for her husband and baby. It meant she could be a real friend to the girl who had looked after her when she'd needed it.

I wish she was here now, Etty thought, getting undressed

by the flickering light of the gas mantle. I wish she'd come home with me instead of going off with that soldier. He had mean eyes . . .

She got into bed and lay awake for a while. Then, as usual, the siren sounded and with a sigh she got out again, wrapped her coat around her, pushed her feet into her shoes and made her way downstairs to the basement.

Maggie wouldn't come now. She'd have found shelter somewhere else.

The policeman arrived just as Etty and the rest of the hostel inmates were sitting down to breakfast.

Everyone looked up with concern. It wasn't unknown for bad news to come for one of the girls these days – usually by telegram, but sometimes brought by a policeman just like this one, his expression inscrutable beneath his tall helmet. The girls and women waited as he tucked his helmet under his arm and approached Mrs Denton. She was already on her feet, equally anxious.

The two of them muttered together for a few moments and then the hostel manageress came over towards Etty's table. Etty felt her heart catch and her breath stopped. She stared up at the serious faces.

'Esther. Come into my office a moment, would you?'

Numbly, Etty rose and followed her. She heard the buzz of conversation break out, high with relief, agog with curiosity. The policeman closed the door behind her and Mrs Denton motioned her to sit down in the small wooden chair by the desk. She knew before anyone spoke that it was about Maggie.

'What is it? What's happened?' She stared at them. 'It's Maggie, isn't it? She never came home last night. Did she get caught in a raid?'

'Not exactly,' the policeman said. 'Well, she did in a way, miss, but she didn't get hurt. Lucky not to, as well, seeing as where she was found—'

'Where she was found? What d'you mean, found? Is she hurt? She – she's not *dead*?'

She hadn't wanted to say the word, but it seemed to burst from her mouth like vomit, impossible to hold back. She stared wildly from one to the other and began to get up. The policeman touched her shoulder and she sat down again, slowly. 'What's happened? Where is she?'

'She's in hospital,' he said quietly. He didn't have a Cockney accent like her own, he sounded as if he came from somewhere in the north, like the newsreader Wilfred Pickles on the wireless. 'Nay, don't panic, she's going to be all right.' It took Etty a moment or two to understand that what sounded like *reet* meant *right*. 'Aye, she's a strong lass, she'll get over it.'

'Apparently she was attacked, Etty,' Mrs Denton said. 'She was found lying in an alleyway. She was there all night as far as anyone can make out, so she was very cold, but she's not too badly hurt. She'll have to stay in for a few days but the doctors say she'll be back with us by the end of the week.'

'Oh, poor Maggie!' Etty felt the tears well up. 'Oh, she's had so many awful things happen to her.' She looked up at the policeman. 'Can I go and see her? Which hospital is she in?'

'Aye, you can see her, and happen you can help us with a few questions, too. Where she was off to last night, who her friends were, that sort of thing.' He nodded towards Mrs Denton. 'I'll take the young lady along now, if that's all right with you. Or mebbe you want to finish your breakfast first?' he added.

Etty shook her head. 'I'd nearly finished anyway. Let's go. But will they let us in this early? Don't hospitals only have evening visiting?'

'They'll let us in,' he said, a trifle grimly. 'There's a few things we want to know about what happened to your friend last night, Miss Brown.'

Etty shook her head, bewildered, then ran off to collect her bag and coat. The policeman walked her swiftly through the streets to the hospital and then through endless corridors. She thought of Shirley coming here when her father was ill, and of Maggie having to identify her sister's body and little Queenie. The tears came again and by the time she reached Maggie's bedside she was weeping with terror.

'Oh, Maggie – Maggie! Whatever happened to you?' Shocked, she stared at her friend's bruised and battered face. Maggie had a swollen nose, a black eye and a nasty cut down one cheek. There was a bandage round her head and another round one arm. 'Who did it?' Etty whispered. 'Who did all that to you? Was it – was it that soldier?'

'Him that looked like Clark Gable, yes.' Maggie's lips were swollen, too, and her voice slurred. 'Turned out a right bugger, he did.' She was as white as the sheets that covered her, and she sounded sick and exhausted. 'Oh, Et, I made a proper fool of meself, going off with him.'

'Maggie. You poor, poor thing.' Etty sat down and took her hand. She stroked it gently. 'Where else do you hurt? What did he do?'

'What didn't he do?' Maggie tried a rasping laugh. 'Half killed me, that's what he done. Held a knife to me face – near enough choked the living daylights out of me – and fucked me nearly senseless.'

'Maggie!'

'Well, he did. That's what he done. Raped me, if you want a different word for it. I don't care what you call it, it hurt just the bloody same.' She turned her head on the pillow and Etty stared at her, horrified. It could hardly have been worse. Raped, almost murdered, left to die in a cold alleyway in the midst of an air raid . . . She felt a surge of rage against the good-looking soldier. If he dares to show his face in the Corner House again, I'll kill *him*, she thought furiously. I will, straight.

The policeman touched her shoulder again. 'Reckon she's asleep now, lass. Come and answer a few questions, now. Do you know who she meant?'

Etty nodded. 'He's a soldier,' she said, following him into the corridor. Nurses and doctors passed them all the time, dashing from one patient to another. Casualties must have been coming in all night long – people with burns, blast injuries, shrapnel embedded in their flesh . . . 'He's been in a few times, looking for Maggie. He wanted her to go for a drink but she wouldn't at first, said she didn't feel like going out with men for the time being . . . She'd just lost her sister and baby niece, you see . . . Anyway, last night she said she would but she told me she wouldn't be late, she *promised* . . .'

'I reckon she meant to keep that promise, too,' the policeman said, writing down what she had told him in his notebook. 'I reckon she was right not to want to go.' They talked for a little longer and then he rose and said he was going back to the station now but he'd be in touch again, they'd be wanting to talk to Maggie again when she felt a bit better. 'And I reckon you might as well go off to work,' he said to Etty, looking down at her kindly. 'Best recipe for shock, that is – work and a few of your mates around you. You can come back and see your friend this evening, when you knock off.'

Etty nodded numbly. She wanted to go back and sit with Maggie, but she knew she wouldn't be allowed to. Hospital visiting times were strict. Half an hour each evening, and no more. She'd only been allowed to see her now because the policeman had insisted.

'I'll have to go and see her dad and brothers first,' she said dully. 'I'll have to tell them what's happened.'

The policeman helped her to her feet and they walked together to the entrance. He looked at her again. He looked like a father, Etty thought, the sort of father she'd always wished she had. For the first time in a very long time, she

324

wondered just what her own father really did look like and where he was now.

She would never know that. But Sam Pratt was as good as a dad to her, and tonight she would have to be strong, so that she could be a daughter to him, while his own daughter lay in a hospital bed, put there by the brutality of a man who looked like Clark Gable.

Chapter Nineteen

'I'll kill him,' Sam Pratt said. 'I'll bloody kill him. I'll have his guts for garters.' He looked fiercely around the room of the hostel where he and his three sons were now living. It was bare and unhomelike, with two sets of iron bunks, a battered old sofa and a cheap wooden table with four chairs. There was a small table in the corner with a gas ring balanced on it, where Sam and the boys could make a cup of tea. Their meals were taken either in the hostel dining-room or brought home wrapped in newspaper from the fish and chip shop.

The twins had already been sent to shelter in the underground for the night, and Sam and Jim had been just about to go themselves when Etty had arrived with her news. The policeman had obviously been only too thankful to be relieved of this task, and Mr Carter had allowed Etty to leave work early.

'Only if I don't do it first, Dad,' Jim told him. 'But first we got to find the bugger.' He looked at Etty. 'What's his regiment? What unit's he in?'

She shook her head helplessly. 'I don't know, Jim. He was just a soldier.'

'Well, next time he comes into the Corner House—' Sam began, but Jim interrupted him.

'He won't show his face there again! He wouldn't be such a fool. I don't suppose he'll go anywhere near Marble Arch. You given the rozzers his description, I suppose?'

'They've been in and out all day, talking to us all,' Etty said wearily. 'Trouble is, we got no proof it was him. It could've happened after she left him. All we know is she was going to have a drink with him, but she didn't want to so she might just as well have gone off on her own straight after. It could've been anyone, and even if they do find him he'll deny it. Who's to say any different?'

'The police are no good,' Sam said disgustedly. 'It's not that they wouldn't try, but like you say they'd have nothing to go on. No, Jim, I reckon it's our job to sort the bastard out. Knocking our Maggie about like that!' His face clenched like a fist with his anger. 'I'll give him what for, see if I don't!'

'I don't think any of us'll ever see him again,' Etty said despairingly. 'Like Jim says, he'll keep out of the way from now on. Oh, it just ain't fair!'

The words were scarcely out of her mouth when the building was rocked by an enormous explosion. The three of them dived for the floor and Jim dragged Etty under the table and threw himself on top of her. All around them they could hear the splintering of wood and shattering of glass, and then there was another tremendous crash that sounded as if the roof were falling in.

'My Gawd!' Sam cried. 'The whole place is coming down! Etty – are you all right? Jim, are you all right?'

'We're not hurt, Dad,' Jim said breathlessly. 'Whatever it was, it's not in here. But we'd better get out all the same. You'll have to stop down here in our shelter, Etty.'

They hauled themselves out and looked at each other with frightened faces. Miraculously, the gas light was still on but the teacups had been shaken to the floor and lay in smithereens. Sam started to push the others towards the door.

'Come on, you two. Etty, you get down the shelter fast as your pins can carry you. Me and Jim'll have to get out and do our bit of fire-watching – it sounds as if this is going to be another big 'un.'

They could hear other explosions now, and see the flames

already beginning to lick the skyline. From the window, Etty caught sight of fire raining down as the incendiaries dropped in huge numbers. She grabbed Jim's hand.

'I'm not going down no shelter. I'm coming to help.'

'You can't—' he began, but she was already on her way down the stairs.

'I can! We've been trained for it. Just show me where the fire buckets are and the hoses. I'll show you what Nippies are made of!'

There was no time for argument. Together, they flung sand and water over the flaring incendiaries, stamping out the sparks and even once throwing a coat over an obstinate flame. It'll never be the same again, Etty thought, shrugging it back on, but at least it did the job . . . The Germans must be able to look down and see us all scurrying about like ants, she thought grimly, and spared a moment to look up and shake her fist at the planes so high above. She felt as if she had been lifted outside herself, all the anger and distress of the past twenty-four hours coalescing in white-hot fury.

'Bastards! Bloody bastards!' But there was a strange elation in her fury, an excitement that gripped her as well as rage, and she laughed as she stamped out yet another fire, kicking the sparks as if she kicked at the enemy himself. 'That's for *you*, Ribbentrop! And *you*, Rommel! And *that* one's specially for *you*, Adolf bloody Hitler, and I hope you shove it right up your nasty little *arse*!'

'Etty!' Sam was shaking her arm. 'Etty, come and help – there's someone trapped over here, I can hear them yelling out.' They ran across the road, heedless of the danger, to the huge pile of rubble that was all that was left of a row of houses. Sam was right – there was a voice calling for help and already a small crowd of wardens and soldiers was digging frantically in the ruins.

'We've got a bit of a hole here,' one of the ARP men shouted. 'Someone small might be able to get down—' His eyes lit upon Etty. 'You, girl, reckon you can get down there, see what's what?'

Etty stared at the hole that had been cleared amongst the fallen walls and splintered wood. Dark, narrow, filled with dust, it looked as if it might cave in again at any second. But from somewhere below she could hear the voice calling out again for help, and as well as that she could hear a faint crying. There was a baby down there.

'There's a kid,' Sam said, and Etty heard his voice shake and knew he was thinking of Queenie.

'It's all right – I can do it.' She scrambled over the pile of broken bricks. 'How deep is it?'

The man shrugged. 'Gawd knows. It was a cellar, see, so it should be about four or five foot, but the blast might have made it deeper. We'll hold on to you, girl, don't worry – we won't let you fall. Here, better take off your coat, it'll only get in your way and you don't want to spoil it, do you? And take this torch.'

The cold night air blew through her jumper and touched her skin, but Etty shivered once and then forgot about it. She knelt beside the hole, peering down into the darkness. The voice sounded a little louder.

'Help! Help us, for God's sake! My baby's hurt – and our Gran, she's in a bad way. And I can't get Uncle Bert to say nothing, he won't move . . . Help us, someone, for God's sake, *help* us . . .'

Etty lowered her legs into the hole. The ARP man and a soldier held her by the waist and lowered her down, leaning down themselves to let her go as far as possible. It was narrow, so narrow that the rough, broken edges scraped her sides as she went. She stretched her toes out, feeling for a floor, and to her immense relief felt something solid. Cautiously, she waited till she was sure she was standing on firm ground and then called up to the men to release her.

'Oh, thank God,' a voice said, close beside her. 'Thank God you've come. My baby – my baby – I can feel summat wet, it's blood, I'm sure. And Gran – and Uncle Bert, they're hurt bad . . . Are you a nurse? Can you help them? Can you get us out?'

'I don't know. I'm not a doctor or nothing like that – I was just the smallest person, the hole was too small for anyone else . . .' She flashed the torch about and discovered herself to be in a small cellar, its walls broken and half its ceiling tumbled in a pile in one corner. The joists of the floor above hung splintered and broken, looking perilously close to falling in. One more explosion nearby, she thought, and the whole lot's going to cave in . . .

The family was huddled in another corner. The woman who had been calling out was sitting against the wall, cradling a baby in her arms. She looked about twenty, no older than Etty herself, and she was filthy with dust, her clothes torn. Her eyes were wild with fear and her lips were loose and trembling.

Next to her was an old woman. She looked as old as Maggie's grandmother and wore much the same kind of black frock, with a collar that had once been white. But she didn't look as if she was going to come out of the hole swearing, like Maggie's gran had done. Her face was grey and her eyes rolled in her head, and with her hands she made little clutching movements. She didn't seem to be injured – at least, there was no blood that Etty could see – but she was clearly, as the girl had said, in a bad way.

The man, Uncle Bert, lay sprawled in the middle of the floor. For a moment, Etty was sure he was dead, but as she shone her torch on him he stirred and began to sit up, holding one hand to his head. He looked round the cellar, bewildered, for a moment, started to say something, then made a choking sound and was sick on the floor.

'Oh, Uncle *Bert*!' the girl cried with a mixture of reproach and relief.

Etty hesitated, not knowing what to do. The man seemed all right, apart from being sick. He was groaning and

330

retching, but he didn't seem to have anything broken, and although there was a dark trickle on his temple he didn't seem badly hurt. She remembered the baby and turned back quickly to the girl.

The baby was a few months old, also covered in dust except where its mother had tried to brush the dirt away from its small face. It lay quiescent in her arms, its face white. Its thin wailing had faltered into silence and it looked very still. There was a thick patch of dark blood oozing from its scalp and Etty knew with a sinking heart that if it wasn't dead, it was not far off.

'Can't you get us out?' the girl asked in a whisper.

'I'll see.' She stretched up into the hole. A ring of anxious faces peered down at her. 'There'a a mother with her baby, and an old woman and a man called Bert. I don't think there's anyone else . . .' She glanced fearfully at the pile of debris in the corner. 'They're hurt – the baby's bad, I think – and the old woman. And Bert's been – sick—'

'Bin knocking back the booze, I dare say,' the ARP man said cheerfully. 'Don't you worry, kid, we'll have 'em out in no time . . . Can you pass the baby up, d'you think? There's an ambulance down the street, we can get it off to hospital in two ticks. Careful how you lift it, now.'

Etty didn't need to be told to be careful. She looked at the girl, who was staring down at the white little face. 'They want me to pass the baby up. They'll get it to a hospital.'

The girl gasped and clutched the little body against her. 'Without me? I might never see him again.'

'You will. Of course you will. They'll be able to look after him there.' Etty sat down on a fallen floorboard beside her. 'He needs to be in hospital.' She looked doubtfully at the still face and blue lips. 'What's his name?'

'Stephen. Stevie, we call him. He's my first.' Her face shook. 'His dad was in the navy – he was torpedoed . . . I can't let Stevie go, he's all I got left.'

'He'd be better in hospital, honest.' Etty gave the girl a swift glance. 'Here, you aren't any bigger than me, they ought to be able to get you out as well. Then you can go with him.' She was sure the baby was dead. 'I'll shout up and tell 'em that's what you want.'

'Will you stop here, then? With Gran and Uncle Bert? I couldn't leave 'em all on their own.'

'I'll stop here,' Etty promised as another explosion shook the earth and a few more scraps fell from the ceiling. 'Don't you worry, I'll look after them.'

She stretched up the hole again. 'The mother wants to come, too. She's no bigger than me. If I pass the baby up first, can you lift her up as well? Here,' she added, turning back to the girl, 'what's your name?'

'Annie. Annie Baker. You'll be careful, won't you?' she asked, relinquishing the tiny body with reluctance. 'You won't drop him?'

Etty took the little bundle. She could feel no movement of breathing, but perhaps babies' breath was so light you wouldn't feel it anyway, through all the shawls and blankets . . . She held it up and one of the men reached down long arms and took it from her. There was a moment of panic when she wondered if he had a proper grip, and then the baby was lifted from her arms and handed on to someone else.

'Now the mum. Come on, girl, let's have you out of there. Get you both off to the first-aid post, see what they can do . . . That's it, reach up and we'll pull you out like a cork popping out of a bottle . . . Annie, is it? Come on, Annie, there's a good girl, *up* you come. Pull, now – pull – and *hup* she rises!'

Etty found herself alone in the cellar, with the old woman and the groaning man. Suddenly at a loss, she turned and flashed the torch over them. The old woman was crying softly and the man was sitting up, holding his head in his hands. The cellar stank of dust and blood and vomit.

332

Etty sat down beside the old woman, where the girl had been, and took hold of her hands.

'Are you all right? Are you hurt? Tell me.'

The old woman stared at her. Her eyes were rheumy and old, the brown of the pupils melting into the yellowed whites. Her mouth shook constantly.

'Annie? Is that you, Annie?'

'Annie's gone to hospital with the baby. My name's Etty. I'm going to stay with you till they can get us all out.'

'Annie?' the old woman repeated perplexedly. 'Our Annie's gone to the hospital to have the baby? I thought she had it, in our back room . . .' She peered again at Etty. '*You're* our Annie. What you doing, having some sort of game with me?'

'No. I'm Etty.' She stroked the wrinkled hands. 'Tell me if you're hurt.'

'I don't know what you're doing,' the old woman said fretfully. 'Pretending you're not Annie . . . And why can't we go upstairs? I don't like it down here. I want to go to bed.'

'There's been a raid. A bomb. They'll get us out soon and you'll be able to go to bed. They'll find a bed for you somewhere.' Though God knows where, she thought.

'I want to go to bed *now*. Get our Annie, she'll tell you. I go at eight o'clock on the dot, every night, I has to, the doctor said . . . Where's the doctor? Where's our Annie? Who are you?'

'I'm Etty,' Etty said patiently. 'Annie's gone with the baby. With Stevie.' She became aware of the man. He had been sick again and lay moaning on the filthy floor. 'Are you all right? Bert? Are you hurt?'

'Course I'm bleeding hurt,' he growled, and struggled back to a sitting position. 'It's me head . . . Oh, my Gawd, I feel like bloody death . . . What's up with Ma?'

'She's just frightened,' Etty said as calmly as she could. It was beginning to seem like a nightmare, a nightmare that

333

would never end. 'Let me see your head.' She thanked God for the first-aid classes Lyons had insisted that everyone attend, and shone the torch on the trickle of blood. 'It doesn't seem to be too bad. It's stopped bleeding. But there's a huge lump, and a bruise.' The lump was, in fact, the size of an egg, already purple, and seemed to be getting bigger as she watched. 'You might have concussion,' she said doubtfully. 'You'd better not move too much.'

'Christ, girl, I ain't going nowhere! Who're you, anyway? How d'you come to be here?'

'I was the only one small enough,' she began to explain again, and stopped as a voice called down the hole. Letting go of the old woman's hands, she crawled back across the floor, feeling the vomit sticky under her hands and knees. The smell made her want to retch herself, but she held back and stuck her head up towards the fresh air. A head and shoulders were silhouetted against the red glow of the sky.

'You okay down there, love? How's the old woman? And the feller?'

'Not too good,' Etty said. 'I don't think she's hurt but she's wandering a bit, and he's had a nasty bang on the head. He's got a lump and a bruise and he keeps being sick . . . Can you get us out yet?'

'Doing our best, love. Here. There's someone wants to speak to you.' The head disappeared and was replaced by another. To Etty's astonishment and relief, it was Jim's voice which spoke next.

'Etty! Etty, love, are you all right? What the hell did you go down there for?'

'I was the only one—' she started again, but he broke in before she could finish.

'They're trying to make the hole bigger. But you could come out now. They got that other girl out all right. Give me your hand, Et – let me get you out, for God's sake. It's dangerous down there. If there's another blast—'

'I can't,' Etty said. 'I can't leave them.'

'Someone else'll go down,' he said urgently. 'One of the ambulancemen – or an ARP. They're trained for it, Et.'

Etty glanced around her. In the dank, rubbled cave of the cellar she could just make out the white faces of the man and the old woman. They were staring towards her. As she watched, the old woman reached out a quivering hand and croaked, 'Annie. Annie, come over here, love, come and give me an 'and, for Gawd's sake . . .'

'She thinks I'm her granddaughter,' Etty said to Jim. 'I can't just go off. She's hurt and frightened. She doesn't know what's happening.'

She let go of his hand and crawled back across the slippery floor. The torchlight was growing weak, flickering in the stinking darkness. Etty found the crumpled heap of clothes and put her arms around the quivering body.

'It's all right, Gran,' she whispered. 'It's all right. Annie's here. Annie won't let nothing happen to you—'

The crash seemed to come from somewhere deep in the earth, something so deep and thunderous it was felt rather than heard. In the tremulous light, the walls turned to liquid and fell towards her, and she staggered back with a scream and slipped in the pool of vomit to fall headlong on the littered floor. She felt the body of the man beside her, and the soft thud and weight of the old woman on top, and then her eardrums seemed to burst and the sound of crashing bricks and mortar and cement and wood and glass mingled with the roar and pounding of her own blood.

Etty didn't return to the hostel that night, neither did she go to work next day. She spent the hours first at the local first-aid post and then at the hospital, surrounded by people in beds, on trolleys, on makeshift mattresses on the floor, people who were bandaged, in splints, in traction, people who slept or lay unconscious or who were awake and silent, or groaning and raving. It was another sort of nightmare, she thought, and wondered how many sorts there were and if they were going to have to live through every single one before this awful war was over.

Sam had been hit by a piece of shrapnel and his head was bandaged again. He sat beside Etty while it was being done and joked that he might as well wear it permanently, to save the nurses the trouble. A tin helmet would be more use, the nurse told him tartly, and asked where his had gone, and he said he hadn't seen it since the night they were bombed out and did she want him to go and look for it now?

Jim was scratched and grazed from digging after the cellar had caved in for the second time. His fingernails had been almost torn from his fingers and his hands were bandaged. He had a black eye that he couldn't account for at all, and at some point he'd had a nosebleed as well and the traces were still on his face. His hair was grey with dust and at a quick glance he looked about seventy.

Etty was finally found a bed and lay in it, pale and still. She'd had a bad knock on the head, the doctor had told them, but otherwise she was all right. She'd been very lucky indeed.

The old woman and Bert had both died.

'What about the baby?' Jim asked in a hoarse whisper as he and his father sat beside Etty's bed. Jim was stroking the thin, still hand with his bandaged fingers. He never took his eyes from Etty's face. 'What happened to the baby?'

Sam shrugged. 'Not heard a thing. Could've gone to a different hospital, see. They was just taking them anywhere they could last night, there was ambulances everywhere. I dunno where they went.'

Jim nodded. He knew that they would probably never find out. People came and went in the raids, you saw them for a few minutes, you shared some of the most important moments of their lives with them, and then they disappeared and you never heard of them again. There wasn't

336

even time to try. You couldn't go all over London, from hospital to hospital, asking for a baby called Stevie and its mother.

A nurse came past. She paused and stooped, studying Etty's face. She held the delicate wrist and counted, her eyes on the ward clock.

'Is she going to be all right?' Jim asked her, without taking his eyes off Etty's white face. 'Is my Etty going to be all right?'

'Course she is,' the nurse said stoutly. 'Your Etty's not going to give in that easy. She's a heroine!'

'She is, that.' Sam nodded vigorously and then winced. 'Going down that hole like that – dunno as *I'd* have done it.'

'Course you would, if you'd have been the only one what could've done it. So would your boy here. What you got to understand, mister,' the nurse said, 'is that you're *all* heroes and heroines. You're Londoners, see? Cockneys, like me. And Londoners can *take it*, isn't that what they're always saying?'

'So they say, girl. So they say.' He looked again at the bed. Etty's body was so small and thin, she made scarcely a mound under the blankets. 'But we ain't half had to take a lot just lately. I dunno how much more we can take.'

The nurse looked at him soberly. She wasn't much older than Etty herself, and she looked tired. She must see things like this every night, Jim thought, and worse. Things like that baby Etty passed up which everyone could see was dead, and the poor mother. And people who were torn to bits yet still just about alive. She knew just how much Londoners were being asked to take.

He was about to speak when he felt a faint a pressure in his hand, as if Etty was trying to move her fingers. He looked quickly back at the pillow and was just in time to see the pale blue eyelids flicker and catch a glimpse of dark brown eyes fixed upon his face. He gasped and leant closer.

'Etty. *Etty*. It's me, Jim. Can you see me? Can you hear what I'm saying? Oh, Etty . . .'

'Jim,' she breathed, her voice no more than a thread. 'Jim . . . what happened? Where am I?'

'You're safe,' he whispered joyfully. 'You're safe and you're going to be well again. And listen – you're in the same ward as our Maggie, and when she wakes up in the morning they're going to put you together. That'll be a bit of all right, now, won't it just?'

She stared at him uncomprehendingly, then seemed almost to shrug and closed her eyes again. Jim looked up appealingly at the nurse.

'She's all right,' the girl said, grinning at him, almost as pleased as he was himself. 'She's all right. She'll go to sleep now. And I got to go. Look, you can stay here a bit if you want. Nobody's going to take no notice, we're too busy to worry about a few extra bodies. Get yourself a bit of kip.'

Jim and his father looked at each other. Sam hesitated, then shook his head.

'It's a bit quieter out there now, by the sound of it, but the all-clear ain't gone yet and I dare say there's still plenty to do. You stop here along of Etty, Jim, but I'd better get back to me duty.'

Jim didn't even flicker. 'I'll come, too.' He bent and kissed Etty gently on the cheek. 'So long as I know she's all right. You heard what that nurse said – we're heroes. Well, we'll be better heroes out there than sitting here safe and warm in hospital!'

Chapter Twenty

'Thank God it's not too far to be able to hop on a train and come up to London to see you,' Nick said as he and Jo wandered hand in hand along the Embankment one day towards the end of January. 'I'd go mad if we couldn't get a bit of time together, Jo.'

'I'm just glad to know you're safe,' she told him. 'Every time I hear the sirens go, I think of you, being scrambled. And I can't forget that time you had to bale out. Honestly, Nick, it goes right through me, that awful wailing noise, and knowing you're probably already up there, trying to fight them off.'

'I scored two hits this week,' he said proudly. 'Sent 'em right down into the drink. That's another two crosses on the old crate.' He grinned at her. 'You don't need to worry about me, Jo. I'm a good flyer and the Spit's a smashing plane. I can make her just about sit up and beg now. And it's wizard being able to put her through all her paces, 'specially at night when there's a full moon. Honestly, I wish I could take you with me – not to fight, of course, but just for the ride. You'd enjoy it.'

Jo rather thought she would. She glanced up now, trying to imagine what it must be like to be in a tiny aeroplane high above London, gazing down at the city. It would have been wonderful before the war, she thought wistfully, before all the bombing had destroyed so many of the old buildings. You must be able to see for miles and miles, like looking down on a living map. And at night, when all the street lights had been on, it would be like fairyland.

It wasn't like fairyland now, though. It must look more like a demolition site.

They paused on Westminster Bridge and gazed at the damage done to the Houses of Parliament during the raid in the first week of December. The tower of Big Ben and some of the windows and old stonework had been knocked about a bit, but tarpaulins had been draped over some of it and temporary repairs carried out to make it safe.

Jo shivered. 'It's freezing. Let's go and get something hot, Nick. There's a teashop down the road, we'll go there and get a bowl of soup or something.'

They walked away from the river, but as they turned the corner they were brought to a halt by a barrier stretched across the road with a small crowd of soldiers gathered in front of it. Jo groaned.

'An unexploded bomb, I suppose. Honestly, you can't get anywhere these days without going all round the houses to get there.'

One of the soldiers turned and grinned at her, and she saw to her astonishment that it was Mike. They stared at each other for a moment.

'Mike! What on earth are you doing here?'

'I might ask you that. Finishing these buildings off, of course – they're too dangerous to leave standing, see, so we're going to have a bit of fun with them.'

'Fun?' Jo said. 'You mean you're knocking them down?'

'Blowing them up,' he corrected her. 'It'll be good practice for when we finally get over to Germany. We can have a go at their buildings then.' He winked at Nick. 'I hear your lot're doing a bit of damage over there already.'

'Tit for tat,' Nick agreed. 'It's only fair. Give Hitler a taste of his own medicine. I'm not on bombers myself, mind. I wouldn't want to give up my little Spit, she's like a little mosquito, dodging about. Great fun!'

Jo looked from one to the other. 'Fun! *Fun*! You two talk like a couple of little boys. It's not fun. It's awful. Killing people – doing all this damage.' She looked again at the ruined buildings, buildings which had stood for a hundred years, two hundred years, and were now being smashed to smithereens. 'You're like little kids with sandcastles,' she said bitterly. 'You ought to think about what's been happening to people like Maggie and Etty. They're only just out of hospital, both of them.'

She made to move on, but Nick laid his hand on her arm. 'Let's stop and watch, Jo. It'll be interesting.'

'It'll be horrible,' Jo said, but she stayed by his side. Mike moved away, intent once more upon his job. The soldiers waved them back a bit, and they and the small crowd that had gathered stepped a little further away. There were several small boys, jigging from foot to foot with excitement and doing their best to get under the barrier, a knot of old men in scarves and a couple of housewives with shopping bags. They'd be better off queueing for today's rations, she thought.

The buildings were several tall office blocks with shops on the ground floor. You could see they were unsafe – their walls bulged dangerously out over the pavement and there were concrete beams and lintels hanging by little more than a thread. Even Jo could see that it would be impossible to rebuild them as they were, but it seemed a dreadful shame to just destroy them. This war's not going to leave anything of London as it used to be, she thought sadly. All these old places that have stood here for years and years – *hundreds* of years – just wiped away in a night. It's not right.

Mike and two or three other soldiers were kneeling on the road, doing something to some long planks of wood. It looked as if it was delicate work, and they were obviously taking great care over it, but you couldn't really see what they were doing. Jo craned her neck but still couldn't quite make it out.

'They're laying a charge,' Nick said. 'They're going to blow it up, like Mike said. It's going to be quite a sight.'

341

'Is it safe to stand here? We won't get hit by bricks or anything?'

Nick shook his head. 'We're far enough away, they'll have made sure of that. See, that wire leads to the fuse and when they press the plunger it sets it off. It's a controlled explosion – not like a bomb. Look, they're just about ready.'

Jo watched, fascinated despite her revulsion. The soldiers had completed their preparations and retreated from the bulging walls. They had built a barrier of sandbags and they crouched behind it. The soldiers by the barrier waved at the crowd to get back again, and one of them grabbed a small boy by the ear and gave him a hefty push.

'How old are you?' he demanded pugnaciously. 'Thirteen? And d'you want to be fourteen? Get over there, then!'

A man in the crowd reached out an arm and hauled the boy close to him, holding him there firmly. The crowd fell silent. Jo felt for Nick's hand and held it tightly. It seemed strange to feel so nervous, she thought, after all the real bombing. Like everyone there, she had seen explosions caused by bombs and parachute mines, she had seen buildings shattered. Something like this ought to be nothing out of the ordinary at all. Yet, because you knew what was going to happen, because you *knew* that those bulging walls were about to be blown down, you couldn't help feeling a strange excitement, a thrill of anticipation—

Her thoughts were shattered abruptly as the charge ignited. The bulging walls shivered and seemed to hover for a moment, as if undecided. Then the masonry at their foot gave way, like knees buckling, and all the way up there was a ripple of movement as the shock slid like a wave to the top. Almost slowly, almost gently, the walls slithered in a heap and settled in a cloud of red and grey dust to a pile of rubble on the pavement.

There was a moment's silence and then a small cheer

from the watching crowd. The soldiers turned and grinned, like performers receiving their applause. Mike sketched a salute through the cloud of dust.

Jo and Nick looked at each other.

'I can't see anything to cheer about,' Jo said. She was near to tears. 'I used to to walk down that street regular, when me and Phyl came down this way for a walk. I always liked looking at those places. There were nice carvings over the doors. Now they're gone for ever, they'll never be the same again.'

'Well, don't blame us,' Mike said. 'Blame Hitler. He's the one that started it all. If it wasn't for him, we'd still be selling suits in Burton's, and your Nick'd be getting promotion at Lyons. Mind you,' he added thoughtfully, 'it wouldn't be half so exciting.'

Jo stared at him. Then she turned and looked at Nick, whose lips were twitching into a grin.

'Oh!' she exclaimed. 'You're hopeless, the pair of you. You really are just like little boys!'

In between demolition jobs, Mike snatched an hour to see Phyl whenever possible and they, too, like Jo and Nick, walked the streets to be together, or sat in cafés or sometimes, if he had long enough, went to the pictures or a dance.

'I thought we'd have been married by now,' he said one day, sitting with his cold hands wrapped round a large mug of tea. 'We've been talking about it for getting on for a year, and we still haven't managed to set a date.'

'I know. I keep thinking about it, too.' Occasionally Mike managed to wangle a 24-hour leave pass and Phyl would come and stay at his parents' home. They'd managed two whole nights on the Put-U-Up in the last six months – nights when, miraculously, Mike's leave pass had coincided with a quiet night over London. But even then it wasn't easy, for at any moment the siren might go and the whole family come tumbling down the stairs, and there was always a debate about whether they'd go down to the shelter anyway, just in case. Any lovemaking was an anxious, hurried affair, and Phyl felt more miserable and frustrated afterwards than she had before.

'It's the married men get the leave passes mostly,' he told her. 'D'you know what we've been told? It's their duty to get their wives pregnant, so there'll be more youngsters to keep the population going after the war! So they send the married blokes home as often as they can, just to give 'em a chance!'

'It seems a cold way to look at it,' Phyl said doubtfully.

'Well, after the last war there weren't that many men left, I suppose. And then there was that big flu epidemic. They don't want the country to be left with just women and old chaps. Anyway . . .' he squeezed her against him '. . . what it means is that they're only too pleased for more blokes to get spliced, and I reckon we ought to take our chance while we've got it.'

'Get married, you mean? Now?'

'Yes. Well, as soon as possible. We were talking about a special licence, weren't we? Let's see about getting one, Phyl, and then we can just go ahead. We don't want a big wedding, do we?'

'No-o. I suppose not. I'd want a white frock, mind.'

He grinned wickedly. 'D'you think you should?'

Phyl blushed. 'If I don't, our Mum'll want to know the reason why! And then there'll be bridesmaids and a cake and all that . . . And getting the church booked. There's still quite a lot to arrange.'

He made a face. 'I thought we could do it in a registry office. Just nip in and out, us and a couple of witnesses.'

'Mike! You don't mean it! Mum'd never forgive me, and nor would the rest of the family. It's got to be a church wedding.' She frowned thoughtfully. 'I could borrow a frock, perhaps. There was one of the Sallies got married a little while ago, I could ask her, only she's left now and I don't know where she is . . . There's just no materials in the shops these days, that's the trouble.'

'Does it have to be a white frock?' he asked. 'I mean, everyone knows you can't get the stuff, so why not wear something else? A suit, perhaps.'

'Well, I suppose I could . . . But I always wanted to be married in white, Mike. I mean, it's a girl's one big day. You want something to remember.'

'I'll give you something to remember,' he whispered, 'but you won't be wearing a white frock – or any frock!'

'Mike!' Phyl glanced around the café, her colour rising again. 'Honestly, if you go on talking like that there won't be any wedding at all. I don't know why I ever went out with you in the first place, I don't really.'

'Yes, you do,' he said, unwrapping one of his hands and laying it on hers on the table. It felt warm from the tea, warm and big and comforting, and a little thrill ran through Phyl's body as she looked into his eyes and saw the darkness of his pupils. 'You know exactly why you went out with me, and why you keep on going out with me, and why you're going to marry me. It's because we love each other and we want to spend the rest of our lives together, and for all I care you could get married in a boiler suit, just so long as you're my wife. So let's make it soon, Phyl, please and never mind about white frocks and bridesmaids and cakes. We don't know how long we've got before I get sent away again. Let's get that licence and get on with it.'

Phyl bit her lip. The tears came to her eyes and she looked down and stared at their hands, entwined on the table. Then she looked back at him and nodded.

'Yes,' she said. 'Let's.'

Maggie and Etty were back at the hostel after a few days. Etty hadn't been badly hurt but the doctor was concerned that she might have had concussion and kept her under observation. She came back looking pale and thin, and Maggie, who had more or less recovered from her own bruises, put her straight to bed.

'I'll tell Mrs Denton I'm bringing all your meals up on a tray. And all the girls want to come and see you. You're a heroine, you are.'

'Me?' Etty shook her head painfully. 'Don't talk so daft, Maggie. Of course I'm not.'

Waking to find Etty in the next bed to her in the hospital had shaken Maggie back almost to her normal self. The shock of what had happened had almost overwhelmed her at first, but she'd told herself robustly that she'd only got what would have come to her in the end anyway, one way or another, and she'd been lucky to get out of it alive. No more going with servicemen, she thought. If they want it so bad, they can use the proper girls for the job. She had recognised, too, that it had been partly to assuage her own grief that she had offered herself so freely. Now she knew that you couldn't get over it that easily, and she felt guilty at having tried. My Tom deserves to be mourned properly, she thought. No more short cuts.

'Don't be daft,' she told Etty. 'You blooming well are a heroine. Getting that woman and her baby out and then stopping down there with that old man and woman. I don't know that many girls who'd have done that.'

'Of course you do,' Etty said. 'Anyone would. You would, or Jo, or Phyl, or Shirley, or any of them. People are doing braver things than that all the time.'

'I know one who wouldn't,' Maggie said darkly. 'Irene Bond.'

Irene had kept aloof from the cluster of Nippies, Trippies, Sallies and other Lyons staff who had gathered round Maggie as news of Etty's heroism had spread round the Corner House. Everyone had wanted to know what the shy little orphan girl had done, and how badly she had been hurt. Irene, however, had ignored the excitement and had

346

sat in a corner, smoking through her long green cigarette holder and reading a magazine.

'She wouldn't lift a finger to help anyone else,' Maggie said. 'Selfish cow.'

The other girls at the hostel all came in to see Etty and Maggie and some even brought little presents – a lace-edged hanky, a small bar of chocolate or a tiny bottle of scent. Maggie, who knew they didn't know all the details of her attack, felt as if she were there under false pretences and diverted attention to Etty, who was overwhelmed with all the attention, and even smiled at the girls who had bullied her. Only one person didn't come, and that was Muriel Chalk.

'She's another cat,' Maggie said. 'But what d'you expect? She's thick with that Irene, isn't she? I've seen the two of them sneaking up to her "flatlet" – as if anyone else cares what they get up to!'

'What do you mean? What could they get up to?' Etty asked curiously, but Maggie just laughed. 'You don't think they're spies, do you?'

Maggie's laughter turned to a hoot. 'Cripes almighty, Etty, you'll be the death of me, you will really! *Spies!* Our dear Lady Muck and her fancy friend? Oh, dear, oh, dear!' She sat on the plain wooden chair by Etty's bed and shook with laughter.

Etty closed her eyes. She was tired after all the visitors and didn't really care about Irene and Muriel Chalk. All she wanted to do was get better and go back to work.

Mr Carter was waiting for her at the door of the dressing-room when she went back a few days later. He came forward and shook her warmly by the hand, then led her in style through to the restaurant.

'Here she is,' he said proudly. The restaurant was not yet open and there were girls everywhere, laying tables, polishing cutlery, wiping down the legs of tables and chairs and filling salt and pepper pots. They all stopped what they

347

were doing and looked around as Mr Carter led Etty up on to the little dais where the band played.

'Here's our Etty. Our little heroine.' He smiled round at them all. 'You all know what she did and I know you're just as pleased as I am to see her back at work. And there's something else I know, too.' He beamed at them while Etty stared at the floor and wondered whether, if she prayed hard enough, it might open up and swallow her for ever. 'I know that there's not one amongst you who wouldn't do the same. Because Etty's a Nippy, and that's exactly what Nippies are like – always ready to help. So I'm going to ask you all to give Etty the applause she deserves, but remember while you're doing it that you're also applauding yourselves. The Nippies of Lyons' Corner Houses!'

He let go of Etty's arm and began to clap, and everyone in the room joined in. Someone shouted, 'Three cheers for Etty! Three cheers for all Nippies! Hip, hip . . .' And they all yelled, 'Hooray!' The noise was tremendous. Etty stood scarlet, almost in tears, and then Mr Carter lifted his hands for silence.

'Thank you, girls. And now let's get back to work. The queue's almost up to Trafalgar Square!'

They laughed at this and turned back to their work. Maggie bustled up to the platform and helped Etty down. Mr Carter gave them both a kind smile.

'Don't do more than you feel like today, either of you,' he said. 'As soon as you start to feel tired, you tell me and I'll get someone else to cover your tables. We mustn't overwork you on your first day back!'

Maggie nodded briefly. She was determined not to feel tired. Etty gave him a smile and hurried to her tables. On the way, she passed Irene.

The green-eyed girl curled her lip.

'Think you're the cat's whiskers now, I suppose,' she muttered as Etty began to sort her cutlery. 'Well, it don't cut no ice with me. As far as I'm concerned, you're still a mealy-mouthed little Jewish bastard, and nothing's ever going to change that!'

Phyl found out about the special licence and got the papers. It was happening a lot these days, the clerk told her, with so many men going away at short notice. She went round to the local church and saw the vicar but to her dismay he said he couldn't fit her in for a fortnight.

'I've just got too many weddings to do,' he said. 'And funerals, too, I'm afraid. And there are sick people to see and relatives, and services to hold. I'm very sorry, my dear.'

'It's not just that,' Phyl said. 'I don't really know when my fiancé can get leave. We were hoping you could do it at short notice.'

He shook his head. 'The best thing you can do is tell me when he can get leave and see if I can squeeze you in then. I'll do my best, but that's all I can say.'

Phyl went home and told her mother what he'd said. May looked disappointed.

'It's not very satisfactory, is it? We can't make any arrangements. There's all the family to invite, and the frocks and all that . . . We want it to be a *bit* special.'

'I know, Mum. So do I. But it's the way it is now, isn't it? There's lots of girls having to get married quick, like this.'

'Phyl! Don't say it like that – have to get married quick! It makes it sound so hole and corner, – as if you're – you know . . .'

'In the family way,' Phyl said with a grin. 'Well, you don't need to worry about that, Mum, and anyone who thinks I might be will find out soon enough that I'm not. Look, we can't afford to worry about what other people think and we can't afford to wait to have a big white wedding like pre-war. We just want to be married, and if we've got to do it quick with just the family there, that's the way it'll be. So get your best frock out of mothballs, ready!'

The other girls were determined that the wedding should

not be a hole-and-corner affair. 'We're all coming,' Maggie declared. 'Don't matter when, don't matter where, we're coming. We're not missing a party!'

'I don't think there'll be a party,' Phyl began, but Maggie gave a hoot of laughter.

'No party! Of course there's going to be a party! We'll all bring something – sausage rolls, cheese straws, jellies and custard, and we'll bring a few records as well and have a dance in the street. No party! Don't talk daft, our Phyl.'

'How can we dance in the street?' Phyl asked, laughing. 'There's a blackout, remember?'

'We'll dance in the dark, then. But if we're lucky the Jerries'll provide the lighting, same as they been doing for the past five months. Can't see 'em letting a chance like that go by.'

Phyl began to feel as if she were being swept along on a tidal wave of enthusiasm and delight. A party was just what they needed after months of bombing, and a wedding was the best excuse you could ever have. For the next few days, tea and lunch breaks were filled with excited chatter about weddings past and future, hats and frocks and hairstyles, honeymoons and wedding cakes.

'I wonder if Lyons will give you a cake, like before the war?'

Phyl nodded. 'Mr Carter's already said so.'

'What about your frock? My sister got married last year – you could borrow hers, only she's five foot ten.'

Phyl, who had never made it past five feet two, rolled her eyes. 'What am I supposed to do, pin it up behind my ears?'

'What about a bouquet? There's no flowers about.'

'I'll use a sprig off the old Christmas tree and some decorations,' Phyl said, so straight-faced that they almost believed her.

'What about the *honeymoon*?' they breathed.

'And that's summat I'm *not* telling you about,' she declared, pushing back her chair. 'You'll have to use your own imaginations.' And she walked off, ignoring the hoots and catcalls which followed her across the canteen.

'It's lovely to see Phyl so happy,' Shirley said, watching her wistfully. 'Remember when she and Mike stopped seeing each other? I've never seen anyone so miserable.'

'She tried her best to hide it,' Jo agreed, 'but you could see it in her eyes. And it was all through that Irene, you know, she got it in for Phyl and she did her level best to make everything go wrong for her.'

'Didn't work, though, did it?' Maggie observed. 'It went wrong for catty Irene instead. I dunno what it was happened, but she went all quiet for a while. Wasn't she knocking about with Phyl's other boyfriend for a time? That Richard Godwin, from Coventry Street Corner House?'

'That's right,' Shirley said. 'I saw them dancing out at the club at Sudbury. Really making up to him, she was, and then it all seemed to stop. She came in one day looking really upset and wouldn't talk to anyone. He doesn't go there now.'

'Too good-looking, that one,' Maggie declared. 'Smooth. I didn't like him.'

'I don't know that Phyl did either, all that much,' Jo said. 'Not when she got to know him. She told me once, when all the other blokes were talking about being called up, that he didn't believe in it. He said he wasn't going to volunteer.'

'Well, some people don't,' Shirley said fairly. 'Conscientious objectors. I know someone who's a Quaker, and he's like that, he had to go to a tribunal and they sent him to prison but now he's out he's allowed to work on a farm.'

'No, I don't mean like that,' Jo said. 'He just said he wouldn't fight. He wanted to get on in his job and he didn't see why someone he's never seen in a country he'll never go to should make any difference to that.'

'Sounds ideal for Irene,' Maggie said, and they all laughed.

351

Irene heard them laughing. Irritated and impatient with all the talk of weddings, she had sat on her own in what was becoming her favourite corner. She glanced across at the other girls with dislike and lit another cigarette, fitting it into the green holder and thinking about Muriel.

They hadn't managed to find a flat yet, and Irene was beginning to think they never would. There seemed to be hardly any point in looking when the city was being bombed to bits. As fast as we find a place, it'll be blown up, she thought despondently. But she was getting fed up with having to go home to Mum and Dad and Bobby every night, except for the few when she slipped in to stay with Muriel, and wished she and Muriel could do something so that they could be together all the time.

'Couldn't I come and live at the hostel?' she asked as they lay on the bed in Muriel's room. 'If one of those other women were to move, we could have a flatlet each and make it like one. Think of all the room there'd be!'

'I can't see them budging,' Muriel said. 'They're like limpets. But if someone from downstairs moves out, you could have that room.'

Irene stared at her. 'What good would that be? I want to be with you!'

'I know. And so you would be. We could use another room as a little sitting-room. Or just store things in it. That would make more space in my little domain.' Her eyes gleamed. 'It would do for the time being.'

'Yes. Yes, it would. But is anyone likely to move out?'

'Not that I know of, but as you know I don't mix a lot with the other gels.' Muriel thought for a moment, then gave her a sideways glance. 'Unless you could persuade those two friends of yours – the Nippies.'

'Maggie and Etty? They're no friends of mine!' Irene caught her look and laughed. 'But you're right – if we could get them to move out, we could take their room over. But I thought it was a three-girl room?'

'It is, but the other gel's moved out now – she's joined the WAAFs, silly little monkey. It's a nice big room, Irene.'

'It's a wonderful idea.' They gazed at each other. 'But how can we persuade them to go? That Maggie's only just moved in.'

'Well,' Muriel said, 'I'm sure we can think of something. You work with them every day, Rene. You're the one with the opportunities.'

Irene thought about it. She'd done her best to get Phyl into trouble at one time and had been warned by Mr Carter as a result. She didn't want to get on the wrong side of him again. But if she could just get rid of Etty and Maggie – at work as well as in the hostel . . .

'I'll do something,' she promised. 'I'd do anything to be with you, Muriel. You know that.'

Muriel smiled. She wrapped one arm around Irene and kissed her on the mouth.

'I know you would, Rene. I know you would.'

Chapter Twenty-One

Preparations for the wedding went on. May had found an old dance frock of her own in cream satin, and together she and Phyl decided that it could be altered a bit to make a nice wedding dress. 'It's lucky you take after me,' she said with a smile. 'I can't see Jo fitting into one of her mum's old frocks!'

The remark gave Phyl an idea, and as soon as she was back at the digs with Jo she said, 'Why don't you and Nick get married at the same time? Make it a double wedding? The vicar wouldn't be able to say he couldn't do you then – it can't take much longer to marry two lots!'

Jo, half in and half out of her skirt as they got undressed, stared at her. 'Nick and me were going to wait till after the war.'

Phyl, already in her pyjamas, bounced on to her bed. 'You might wait a long time, then. And anything could happen while you're waiting. Why don't you talk to him about it, Jo? There's still time for you to get a licence.'

Jo thought about it. It was true that she and Nick had been finding it more and more difficult to part after their snatched meetings. If they were married, she might be able to move down to the station to be near him. They could rent a little flat or a couple of rooms somewhere. It would mean leaving Lyons, but she was going to do that anyway when she went into the Land Army . . . The thought brought her up short.

'I've volunteered. I might be sent away myself.'

Phyl wrinkled her nose. 'Well, that applies to me, too, I

suppose. Will they still call up married women? I don't want it to look as if I'm trying to get out of doing my duty.'

'I think they're still taking ones who haven't got a family,' Jo said. 'And girls get married after they've joined up, don't they? But if I was sent off to the north of England and Nick's still down near Chichester, there wouldn't be much point in being married.'

'Oh, I think you'd find there was a point,' Phyl said, straight-faced. 'Look, Jo, that's going to happen anyway. You'll get sent where you get sent, it won't make any difference whether you're married or not – except that if you are, they might try to keep you near him. You do want to be married, don't you?'

'Oh, yes,' Jo sighed. 'More than ever. And if the war does go on for years, I don't know how we're going to wait.'

Phyl was silent for a moment or two. Then she said quietly, 'You don't have to wait, you know.'

'What do you mean?'

'Well – you know. To be together. Not married but, well, as near as makes no difference.' She was looking down, pleating the bedspread with her fingers as she spoke, but she looked up then and caught Jo's eye.

Jo flushed. 'Look, Phyl, you don't have to tell me anything. I mean, obviously I've guessed, but—'

'Guessed what? How have you guessed?'

'Well, it's been obvious from the way you look when you've stopped the night over at Mike's place. You're different, Phyl. You keep going off in a dream. It's as if you know something the rest of us don't – a sort of secret.'

Phyl blushed and laughed. 'Well, I suppose I do in a way. And I'll tell you this, Jo – it's a rather nice secret!' She grinned wickedly and then said, 'You're not too shocked, are you? I mean, we all know Maggie and Tommy did it before they got married, and I bet she's glad they did now. And that's why Mike and I decided to take the plunge, too. We thought he might go away and never come back, and we'd never know . . . And we *are* getting married.'

'I know. I'm not shocked – not much, anyway. But I wouldn't like to see you go the way Maggie's been going, Phyl.'

'I won't do that. I don't know how she can – I couldn't bear to do it with anyone but Mike. But Maggie seems to think she's doing something good – giving them something nice to remember.' Phyl shook her head, then bounced like a child on her bed. 'Anyway, that's not the point. The point is, why don't you and Nick get married with me and Mike? We've always done things together, haven't we? It'd be lovely to do this together, too.'

'You wouldn't want us to go on honeymoon together as well, would you?' Jo enquired innocently.

Phyl made a wry face. 'Chance'd be a fine thing! Can you see any of us getting time to go on honeymoon? I'd be happy just to have that ring on my finger, Jo, and know that Mike was my husband.' She giggled. 'Sounds funny, doesn't it – husband? And me a wife. I don't even feel grown-up yet, not properly.'

'That's because you're not.' Jo pulled on her pyjamas and sat on the bed, brushing her long chestnut hair. 'Oh, Phyl, you're right – it would be lovely. But what could I wear? I'll never fit into one of my Mum's old dresses like you can with yours.'

'This is where we came in,' Phyl laughed. 'Don't worry, Jo, we'll find you something. But you'll do it? You'll talk to Nick?'

'I'll do better than that – I'll write to him tonight, and post it in the morning. Then we can talk properly next time he comes.'

'Well, you haven't got much time,' Phyl warned. 'Mike's scared all the time they'll get sent away before we get the arrangements made, and he won't want to hang about

356

waiting for you and Nick. You've probably just about got time to get the licence.'

Jo wrote her letter and posted it on the way to work next morning. The reply came the same day, but not in the way she had expected.

'Nick!' she cried as she came out after her evening shift. 'What are you doing here?'

'Wangled a few hours off.' He stood smiling in his RAF uniform, his dark, curly hair gleaming in the weak February sunshine. 'So I came straight up to see my future wife.' He pulled her into his arms and gave her a smacking kiss.

'Nick! Did you get my letter?'

'I certainly did.' He drew her hand through the crook of his arm and they set off along the street. 'And I couldn't wait to come and tell you what I thought about it.'

Jo stopped and looked at him anxiously. All around them, the big stores stood in various states of damage – broken windows boarded up, walls cracked, roofs with gaping holes. The demolition men and the army had done good work in making it all safe, but there were huge gaps where whole buildings had been demolished and she remembered the day she and Nick had watched it happening.

'You're not cross, Nick? You didn't mind me writing like that?'

'Mind? Why on earth should I mind?' He pulled her close again and gave her another kiss, a tender, more lingering one that sent thrills of delight coursing through her body. 'We're engaged, aren't we?' A gang of men working on a building across the street gave shouts of encouragement and wolf-whistles, and Nick turned and grinned and waved at them. 'I think it's a wizard idea. I just wish it had been mine!'

'Well, it was Phyl's really. But it would be nice, wouldn't it – a double wedding? I know we said we'd wait, but—'

'But that was a daft idea,' he interrupted. 'Well, maybe not daft at the time, but it feels like it now. I think you're

357

right. We shouldn't waste time. The only thing that worries me . . .' He paused and Jo looked at him anxiously.

'What? What worries you?'

'The thought of you being left a widow,' he said soberly, and Jo gasped. 'Look, I know I've always said nobody's ever going to get me, but d'you know what? Practically every bloke I started off with in the squadron's bought it now, one way or another. There's not one left that started off with me. There's only two still left alive – one's old Ted Buller who lost his arm, and the other's Algy Brownlow who went crackers and tried to hang himself. It's not very good odds, Jo, you've got to realise that.'

Jo was silent. She had never seen Nick look so serious. He talked very little about what happened to the rest of the squadron, only mentioning occasionally that one of the others, one whose name she might know, had 'bought it', and then his voice was so casual she wondered sometimes whether it affected him at all. And in his swaggering confidence he had never given a hint that he felt himself to be at all vulnerable.

'If anything happens to you,' she said at last in a low voice, 'I'll have lost you just the same. And I'd rather be a widow than just a fiancée.'

'Yes,' he said, 'and I'd rather leave you a widow's pension than nothing at all.'

They stood still for a moment, just outside Selfridges, staring unseeingly at the windows with their criss-crossing of bomb protection. Jo leant her head against his shoulder.

'Shall we do it, then, Nick? Shall we get married with Phyl and Mike?'

'We'll get married,' he said positively. 'If we can do it with Phyl and Mike, we will – but if we can't, we'll do it just as soon after as we can. Now we've decided, I can't wait, Jo. I want you to be my wife – as soon as possible.'

They kissed for the third time. There were no catcalls, no wolf-whistles. The men across the road had gone back to their work and had no time to watch young lovers. The hurrying crowds, on their way home to their teas and tonight's air raid, swirled around them like a wave. Jo and Nick noticed none of them.

They were in their own world, cocooned in each other's arms, warmed by their love for each other, and if anyone had asked Jo then if she knew what it was like to fly, she would have answered yes. And Nick would have told her she was right.

'*Two* weddings?' May and Carrie exclaimed in unison, their expressions so alike with shocked delight that their daughters burst into laughter. 'My goodness, you two don't half spring some surprises!'

'Come on. Mum,' Jo said, grinning all over her face, 'you can't pretend you didn't see it coming. Me and Nick have been engaged long enough, after all.'

'Well, I know that, but I thought you'd decided to wait. It isn't because you just want to steal your cousin's thunder, I hope?'

'Mum! What an thing to say! Anyway, it was Phyl's idea, not mine. But me and Nick think it's a pretty good one.'

'And what about Mike?' May asked. 'Does he get any say in it?'

'If I think it's a good idea, he does, too,' Phyl said demurely, and the rest hooted.

'Easy to see who's going to wear the trousers in your family,' her father said. 'I feel sorry for the poor bloke already. Maybe I ought to give him a few hints on how to control his wife.'

'Well, I shouldn't think that'll take long,' Bill Mason observed. 'Neither of us has ever learned how to control ours. If he can get the upper hand over your Phyl, I reckon we'll be going to him for advice!'

'I think that's a really mean thing to say, Dad,' Jo declared. 'Phyl's like a little lamb when she's with Mike.

She *is*,' she insisted as they all roared with laughter again. 'Anyway, the point is, we're all getting married together so you'd better get your best suit out and polish up your shoes.'

'It's for your benefit really,' Phyl declared. 'So you don't have to worry about two new outfits and all. I mean, we're only thinking of you.'

'Well, that ought to go down in history,' her brother Norman said, coming in from the scullery with a towel in his hands. 'Not that I'm saying you're selfish, of course,' he added as Phyl threw a cushion at him.

'*You* won't be coming at all, if you can't get more oil off your hands than that,' she told him severely. 'Call that a wash? You're not going to be one of *my* bridesmaids, I can tell you that for a fact!'

'Crikey, I *am* disappointed,' he said, rolling his eyes and looking exactly like her for a moment. 'I've been looking forward to wearing a pink frock and all.'

'All right, that's enough larking about,' his father said. 'We've got a lot to sort out and not much time to do it in. What are you women planning for a reception?'

Carrie looked worried. 'What can we plan? We stand all day in a queue as it is, just for our daily rations. There's nothing in the shops for things like wedding receptions. You practically have to go down on your knees for an egg these days.'

'Lyons will give us a cake,' Jo said. 'So you don't have to worry about that.'

'No, but what can we do for the meal? I'd say ham salad but we'll never be able to get ham for all those people, and there's no salad about at this time of year. I just don't know . . .' The familiar little crease of worry appeared between her brows.

'Ask everyone to bring their own sandwiches,' Norman suggested flippantly. 'At least you'll be sure they're all getting something they like.'

'Don't be daft,' his mother said sharply, but, always the

more optimistic of the twins, she turned to Carrie and said, 'Mind you, he's got a point. There's no harm in asking people to contribute a bit. Nobody'd mind these days, and after all it's only family we're asking, isn't it?'

'And our friends,' Phyl said. 'People like Maggie and Shirley and Etty. And a couple of the girls we used to know at school. Pam Nash and Jennie Kilburn, they were our best friends, we ought to ask them.'

'Didn't you know?' Carrie asked. 'Pam's gone into the WRAC and Jennie's a Wren. Well, she is,' she protested as they all laughed. 'It's not my fault it sounds funny.'

'Well, the Nippies, then,' Phyl said. 'We've got to ask them.'

Carrie did a rapid count in her head and said, 'With the aunties and uncles and your granny and grandad, that makes twenty-four people. Well, that isn't too bad. I dare say we can squeeze them in if we use both houses. One for the girls to get ready, the other for the party. We'd better use yours for that,' she said to her sister. 'You decorated your front room just before the war started and it looks better than ours.'

The preparations went on. There was a new sort of cold meat in the shops – Spam it was called, and it wasn't bad at all. You could have that with some salad, if there was any salad, but it could go equally well with some boiled potatoes and a few slices of bottled beetroot. Or there was corned beef. It wasn't exactly a feast, but everyone would understand.

'We can do quite a lot with what we've got,' May said as she and Carrie pored over lists and ration books. 'You can make winter salads with shredded cabbage and grated carrots, and some chopped apple and potato. And I got this recipe off the wireless the other day, look, for an almond tart. You use semolina and almond essence and I bet nobody'll even know the difference. We can make a bit of a spread, Carrie.'

'Some of those recipes are quite good,' Carrie agreed, brightening up. 'I like the ones Elsie and Doris Waters do. All right, we'll do spuds and cold meats and beetroot, and maybe a vegetable flan to go with that, and then some almond tart and a trifle. We'll need stale cake and a tin of fruit if we can get one.'

'Stale cake? Cake never gets the chance to go stale in our house! I'll have to make one 'specially and hide it. Here, what about your Alice? Is she coming home for the wedding?'

Carrie wrinkled her lips. 'Me and Bill are still talking about it. He says he won't have her home while this bombing's still going on, but she'll be so disappointed to miss it. I don't reckon she'll ever forgive us – but you know what she is, get her back with that cat and we'll have the devil's own job making her go away again. I don't know what to do.'

'Better disappointed than bombed,' May said, and Carrie nodded.

'That's what Bill says. But, of course, you know what'll happen – we won't be bombed and then she'll always be able to point her finger at us and say we should have let her come. I don't know what it is about that child, May, but she's always wanted her own way. All kiddies want their own way, of course, it's natural – but most of 'em'll give in after a while. But not our Alice. She just keeps on and on till she gets it.'

'Still, she did go away in the end.'

Carrie nodded again. 'Yes, and she seems to have settled down all right. The old couple are kind to her and she seems to have got nearly as fond of their cat as she is of Rob. And I suppose that'll mean more tears when she has to leave *him*!'

The sisters looked at each other and gave rueful sighs. There was no doubt about it, bringing up children wasn't the easiest job in the world – and being at war didn't make it any easier!

*

362

Alice had indeed settled down better than anyone could have expected. The Tawes had taken her to their hearts and although Solomon would never replace Robbie in her heart, he had become her constant companion in just the same way as the ginger cat at home. He sat beside her on the old settle as she ate her meals or did her schoolwork, he came with her into the garden where she helped old Mr Tawe dig vegetables, he waited for her at the rickety wooden gate when she came back from morning school. And he slept on her bed at night, a large, weighty lump that seemed to get heavier and more immovable as the night went on, so that Alice had to curl herself around him.

There were a number of evacuees in the village and they had school in the mornings while the local children went in the afternoons. The evacuees had their own teachers, too, who had come with them from London. There was constant friction between the evacuee children and the locals, who viewed them with suspicion and found their ways strange.

'Never slept in a bed, that's what mine told me,' one of the women declared as they gathered on the village green to swap experiences. 'Use a mattress on the floor, she said, three of 'em together. And there was nits in her hair, too, took me best part of a fortnight to get rid of 'em.'

The other women nodded knowingly. They'd had to deal with nits as well, and fleas and worse. Quite a few of them complained of bed-wetters, especially among the boys, and the woman billeting officer looked tired and harassed as she went round checking on them all.

'It's not really their fault. They've all experienced the bombing, and they've been taken away from their homes. It's no wonder they're a little upset.'

'A *little* upset?' another woman exclaimed. 'The little tacker I've got hasn't stopped crying in three weeks. I don't know where all the tears come from, I'm sure I don't.' She sighed and shifted her shopping bag to the other arm. 'I've said it before, and I'll say it again, five year old be just too young for a kiddy to be took away from his mummy.'

Fights frequently broke out between the village children and the Londoners. Each considered themselves superior to the others, and nobody was going to give way. One or two managed to make friends, but after the first skirmishes and a few stern lectures from their respective teachers, the two factions settled down into an uneasy truce.

Alice took no notice of any of them. The Tawes had a grandson two or three years younger than herself, whose father had joined the army and whose mother had had to go and look after her own parents in another village. While she was away, he came to stay with his grandparents, sleeping in a tiny cupboard of a room off the kitchen. Ossie was an outsider, too, not fitting into either group, and after an initial wariness he and Alice made friends. Soon the three of them – Alice, Ossie and the cat Solomon – were inseparable.

'He'm proper ugly,' Ossie said as they sat by the log fire one day, regarding the big black and white cat washing his paws.

'He's got a beautiful soul, though,' said Alice, who had read this phrase in one of Jo's books. 'Looks aren't everything.'

'That's right, maid,' Mrs Tawe said from her armchair where she sat knitting. Everyone you saw knitted these days and even Alice was working on a long, multi-coloured scarf, using any bits and pieces of wool that she could beg. ''Tis only skin deep, beauty is.'

Alice sat gazing into the fire. She had had a letter from Jo that morning, telling her about the wedding. It had been a very apologetic letter, explaining why Alice wouldn't be able to be there, but Alice thought otherwise. She had already counted her small stock of money, saved from the penny-a-week pocket money she received, and wondered how she could find out what it would cost to go home on the train.

Ossie shook his head when she asked him.

'Never been to Lunnon, maid. I've been to Exeter, though. Them've got trains there.'

'I know that,' Alice said impatiently. 'That's no good anyway – Exeter's in the opposite direction from London. There's a station in the next village, isn't there?' Sometimes she thought Ossie was a bit dim.

'Ah, so there is, but I don't know where the trains go. Time I went there, they was going to Penzance, and that's in Cornwall.'

'Well, they must go in the opposite direction as well. Otherwise Penzance would be full of trains. Look, Ossie, can't you find out for me? See if someone'll tell you when the trains go to London and what it would cost. They'll be suspicious if I ask.'

'I'll try,' he said doubtfully, but when he came back with the information Alice's face fell.

'I haven't got that much money. I've only got five shillings with my Christmas money from Auntie Joan.'

'I've got three and sixpence,' he offered helpfully. 'You could have that.'

Alice stared at him. 'You wouldn't give me all that! It's a lot of money, Os.'

'Doesn't matter,' he said. 'You can have it.'

Alice chewed her lip thoughtfully. Eight shillings and sixpence might be enough to get her to London, or at least a good part of the way. But the memory of her experiences when she had run off with Robbie just before the war began made her cautious. She didn't want to get lost again.

'I'll need ten shillings at least,' she said. 'There's buses and trams at the other end, too. And there's coming back . . .' Her voice trailed away as she thought of being at home again. At home with Robbie. Would she want to come back, even to big, ugly Solomon and Ossie, and Mr and Mrs

365

Tawe and their funny little Grimm's fairy-tale cottage? Perhaps Mum and Dad would let her stay this time. They hadn't been bombed, after all.

Ossie wasn't so dim after all. 'You've got to come back again, mind,' he said. 'I won't give you the money if you don't come back.'

'But this isn't where I live. I'll have to go home some time.'

He looked obstinate. 'Not till the war's finished. That's what our teacher said. None of the evacuees are going home till the war's over, you're here for the – the darnation.'

'*Duration*,' Alice said automatically. 'Yes, but once I'm home they might want me to stop. I mean, they must have missed me ever so much.'

Ossie set his mouth in a line. 'I'll miss you ever so much too, and it's my money.' He looked at her.

Alice met his eye and recognised an obstinacy as immovable as her own. She was surprised. Until now, she'd always been able to get her own way by just sticking in her heels and refusing to budge. Even her father had usually given in to her in the end. But Ossie wasn't going to, she could see it in his eyes, and although it annoyed her to be beaten by a boy nearly three years younger than herself – and a country boy at that – she knew he wasn't going to budge either. And it *was* his money.

'All right,' she said, and reached out to pull the big black and white cat into her arms. 'I promise I'll come back . . .'

Chapter Twenty-Two

Irene stayed apart, as usual, from all the excitement. It had been bad enough, she thought, when that fat tart Maggie had got married – and look what *that* had led to! – but the fuss over the cousins' double wedding was twice as bad. Well, you'd expect it to be in a way, but that didn't make it any easier to put up with. Every teabreak was taken up now with chatter about frocks and bridesmaids and flowers, until Irene just wanted to be sick.

'And we all know what's really at the back of it,' she told Muriel as they had supper in Muriel's room one evening. 'They're not really thinking about frocks and flowers and stuff at all – well, they are, but it's the honeymoon they're most interested in, only none of them has got the face to say so. It's what's going to happen that night they're really getting all worked up about.' She made a face. 'Disgusting, that's what it is.'

She thought fleetingly of the times when she had woken in the night as a child and heard strange noises coming from her parents' bedroom – the pleading voice which hadn't sounded a bit like her mother's, yet must have been, and the deep groans which must have been her father. She'd always been afraid that she would wake in the morning to find that some dreadful tragedy had taken place and they were both dead – but to her surprise, they'd always seemed perfectly normal. Now she understood what had been going on, and the thought of it made her shudder.

Since knowing Muriel, she hadn't thought of those times so much, but the everlasting chatter about weddings

367

at work had brought it back to her mind and increased her distaste.

'I agree.' Muriel poured two cups of tea and lifted hers, elegantly crooking her little finger. 'No better than animals. I mean, we all know it has to happen – or none of us would be born, would we? – but to make a meal of it like gels do these days, well, it's not ladylike.' She smiled at Irene. 'I must say, I'm glad you're not like that. You've got a proper respect for yourself.'

'I should hope so.' It was a proper respect that had made Irene spurn that oily Herbert Lennox's clumsy advances, and fight off Richard Godwin from Coventry Street Corner House when he'd got fresh. Irene had been surprised by Richard – he'd been so suave, so sophisticated when they'd gone out together, yet that night he'd been no better than the sweaty Herbert Lennox and had threatened to turn even nastier. I had a lucky escape that night, she thought, but at least it cured me of wanting to go out with men.

'All the same,' she said, continuing her thoughts aloud, 'I suppose we'll have to get married one day. So long as we can find chaps who'll respect us.'

Muriel lowered her cup and stared at her. 'Have to get married? Whatever do you mean?'

'Well, you know,' Irene said, not noticing her reaction. 'We'll need husbands, won't we, to provide a good home and all that? I mean, I don't want to be a Nippy all my life, and even if I get promoted to be manageress – which I will be before long, you can be sure of that – I shan't want to go on till I'm old like Miss Turgoose and the others. And I suppose we'll want babies, too. One, anyway – don't know as I'll want more than that.'

'A *husband*? *Babies*?' Muriel echoed, as if they were extinct species. 'Rene, have you gone out of your mind? What about *us*?'

'Well, what *about* us?' Irene looked at her, noticing her

scandalised expression for the first time. 'It won't make any difference to us, Mu. Why should it? We'll always be friends.'

'I thought we were a bit more than friends,' Muriel said in a tight voice.

'Well, so we are. Lots more.' Irene gave her hand a squeeze. 'And we always will be. Nobody's going to come between us, Mu.'

'No? You think you can get married and have a husband and he won't come between us? You think we can go on being – being close, like we've been all these past months, and be together, and he won't mind? You think he'll let us go on sharing a bedroom?'

'Well, no. Not all the time, anyway.' Irene looked uncomfortable. 'Tell you the truth, Mu, I hadn't really thought about it all that much at all. I mean, it wouldn't be for years anyway, and I wouldn't want anyone who was too interested in – well, all that lovey-dovey stuff. I was thinking of someone older, more or less past it.'

'You said you'd want babies.'

'Only one. And if we were lucky, we'd only have to do it the once. I could still see you as often as we do now.'

'But what about our flat?' Muriel's voice rose. 'What about all our plans? Didn't you mean *any* of it?' Her face was white, the flesh around her lips tight and working. Irene looked at her, suddenly frightened, and gripped her hand more tightly.

'Of course I meant it, Mu! I meant all of it – I *want* us to be together, I want us to have our flat and everything. But . . . I never thought it'd be for ever. I thought one day you'd want to get married yourself. People *do*.'

'Not all people.'

'But how could we live? Without a man . . . You know what sort of wages girls get. I mean, you've got a good position, but I'll never be able to earn that much. Not even as a manageress. The women always get less than the men,

369

you know that. Women *have* to get married, if they want a decent home and enough to live on.'

Muriel was silent for a moment or two. Then she withdrew her hand and said coolly, 'I'm sorry. It seems we've misunderstood each other.'

Irene stared at her. 'What do you mean? How have we? Why are you looking—at me like that? Mu—'

'I thought we were really close. I thought we were more than friends.'

'We were. We *are*. Mu, I'm not talking about getting married *now*. You know I don't want to. I don't want to ever, if I can help it. But I don't know what else we can do. I've always thought everyone did, eventually.' She gazed pleadingly at her friend. 'If I could stay with you for ever, that's all I'd ever want. I just don't see *how*. Mu, please don't be angry with me. Please don't look at me like that. I'd do *anything* to be with you, you know that.'

Muriel looked at her steadily for a few moments, as if to test the sincerity of Irene's words. Then she smiled, and Irene relaxed and almost burst into tears.

'All right, Rene. Don't look so tragic. As I said, it was just a misunderstanding. Everyone has them from time to time.' She played with Irene's hand for a moment. 'You see, I've always believed we'd spend the rest of our lives together, Rene. It never even occurred to me that you were thinking it would only be for a little while. It never struck me you might be thinking about marriage and babies. After all you've said about your friends at work—'

'They're not my friends!' Irene burst out, her voice trembling with tears. 'I work with them, that's all – and I hate all this talk about weddings. You know that. And I – never realised you were thinking about a whole lifetime. I . . . didn't think you liked me that much,' she finished in a whisper.

Muriel laughed and gave her hand a pat. 'Silly gel! Of course I like you *that much*. Why, I'd have thought you'd know that without being told. Now, let's stop all this silly talk about getting married. I can earn enough for both of us, so as soon as we've got our little home together you can stop work and just stay at home, if that's what you want to do. Or perhaps I could find you a position in the store. Once the war's over, of course.' She smiled, and Irene felt a great tide of gratitude wash over her. 'How does that sound?'

'Oh, Mu . . . It sounds lovely. Really lovely.' Irene blinked hard and then wiped her eyes with her free hand, laughing shakily. 'I'm being silly! I just can't help it – I feel so happy. And – and I meant what I said, Mu. I'd do anything for you. Anything.'

'Silly gel.' Muriel smiled again. 'You don't have to do anything at all. Just be yourself. And tell me some more of those stories about your customers at work and the things they say. You know I like hearing about them. And it's time you took me to see your people again. You know I enjoy talking to your father, about his work and so on. So nice to talk to an intelligent man who's not going to get any silly ideas.'

'Oh, yes,' Irene said gratefully, 'of course you can come over again. Come to tea on Sunday. Dad was telling us yesterday about how our pilots can see in the dark – it's supposed to be a secret, but he told me and Mum, in confidence, of course, and made us swear not to tell another living soul.' She glanced about, almost as if Hitler himself were about to leap out of Muriel's wardrobe, and whispered, 'It's carrots. They eat loads and loads of carrots and the vitamins help them see in the dark. It's true! Vitamin A, I think it is.'

'Carrots!' Muriel said with a laugh. 'Oh, Irene, you'll be the death of me . . . Carrots indeed!'

The weddings were set for March the fifteenth. The vicar grumbled a bit because he already had five weddings that day, but Phyl opened her big brown eyes very wide at him and he gave in, hardly knowing himself why he did so. She skipped all the way down the street beside Jo, who felt like skipping herself but knew that her lanky figure would look just too ridiculous.

'We can really get things started now. We can do the invitations and everything.'

None of the preparations would take very long. That was one thing about rationing and shortages, it cut down on all that. The girls could stay at their digs and go to work each day knowing that their mothers had everything well in hand.

Nick wangled an afternoon, and hitchhiked to London, arriving at the Corner House just as Jo came off her shift. He caught her in his arms and waltzed her down the street.

'Two weeks from now and you'll be my wife! And I've got news for you.'

'What? What news?' Jo tried to stop him whirling her around. 'Nick, stop it, people are staring at us! What's the news?'

'I've got us somewhere to live! It's not married quarters, it's just two rooms in a house on the edge of the airfield. It's a big house,' he added. 'A sort of country manor. The people that live there are letting out half a dozen rooms – it saves them having to take in evacuees, I suppose. I've been to look – they're smashing, Jo. A big room with a bay window looking out over the garden, and a smaller room for a bedroom. And we can use the main kitchen, there's a rota so everyone gets a fair turn. I'm going to see about furniture. There's a place in Chichester where you can get second-hand stuff, they said they might have some beds coming in soon. That's all we need to start with, isn't it – a bed?'

'I don't know what you mean, I'm sure,' Jo said primly, then her smile broke through and she laughed and hugged him. 'Oh, Nick, it sounds gorgeous. But what if I get my Land Army papers?'

'Well, you can probably get them to give you a place nearby. You might even be able to work in the gardens at the house, they've all been dug up for vegetables. And then we can be together all the time.'

'Well, whenever you're not flying.' Jo's face sobered. 'That means I'll know whenever you go up, Nick.'

'I'll fly over and waggle my wings at you,' he declared. 'That's what a lot of the blokes do. They do it when they come back, fly over their quarters and waggle their wings so their wives know . . .' His voice trailed away and Jo glanced at him anxiously.

'What's the matter, Nick? You've gone all quiet.'

'Oh . . .' He shook himself and gave her an odd, twisted little grin. 'It's just that old Lofty Short used to do that. He got spliced about a month ago and they had a little place on the other side of the 'drome. Tiny little cottage, just about big enough to swing a cat, so long as it was only a little one.' He fell silent again.

'And?' Jo prompted him. 'Tell me, Nick.'

'Well – it was just that he used to fly low over the cottage when he came back and waggle his wings to let Lorna – that was his wife, nice girl, dark-haired, a bit like your Phyl – to let her know he was safe home. Only, on Tuesday, he didn't.'

'Didn't what?' Jo asked, her heart cold, knowing the answer.

'Didn't come home safe. Didn't come home at all, as a matter of fact. Bought it over the Channel. One of the other blokes saw him go down.'

'Oh, Nick,' Jo said quietly.

'I didn't mean to say anything,' he said ruefully. 'Didn't want to spoil the day.'

'That poor girl. Only married a month.' She looked at him, her face full of fear. 'Nick, don't let it happen to you!'

'Don't worry!' He forced a laugh. 'I take great care not to let it happen to me. I mean to see this war out to the bitter end.' He squeezed her waist. 'And I want more than a month of married life!'

He had to go back soon after that. It had taken him most of his few hours off to reach London and it would take him as long to get back. He was on duty that evening and had to be ready to scramble as soon as there was an alert. Reporting late would mean jankers, but it would also mean the loss of a sortie and perhaps a German plane getting through that wouldn't have got through, and bombs being dropped that might not have been dropped. No pilot could forgive himself for that.

Phyl was able to see more of Mike, since he was still in London working on demolition and repair of bombed buildings. He also had to stand guard over shops and houses that might be looted – every bombing raid brought its gang of scavengers who picked through the ruins to gather up anything they could find. Sometimes it was just a few kids, looking for souvenirs, or an old woman who picked up a battered saucepan that nobody seemed to want, but often it was real looting – men and women who clambered over the heaps of debris, scrabbling to take away armloads of clothes or crockery or bits of furniture. It was Mike's job to stop them and make them put it back, and then get a policeman to arrest them.

'It's there for anyone,' a young woman, with yellow hair and fingertips stained brown from nicotine, told him, struggling as he gripped her arm. 'Whoever lived there don't want it no more – they're dead and buried, you can see that.'

'They could as easy have been in the shelter, safe and sound,' Mike told her, so disgusted that he had to restrain himself from slapping her face. 'In any case, it's not yours. It's stealing.'

'It ain't stealing! I found it. That's not stealing.'

'It's stealing by finding and you can get six months hard for it, and I hope you bloody well do.' He marched her off to the police station and gave her to a bobby. 'Here's another one, sarge, and you can chuck the book at her. She'd take the rings off a dead woman's finger, this one would!'

At the end of the week, his words were to come sickeningly true. The following Saturday saw the most vicious raid London had received since the beginning of January. More than a hundred tons of high-explosive bombs were dropped on the city, hitting many of the railway lines and stations, but there were two targets which were especially shocking.

One was the hit on Buckingham Palace. The bomb struck the North Lodge and killed a policeman. There were three huge craters in the forecourt, and the great decorative orbs were knocked from the gates. The palace was beginning to look battered and wrecked, no longer fit for a king, but all London knew that this wasn't going to deter their monarch. The King and Queen had already declared that they didn't mean to leave England, and as long as they stayed, the country felt somehow protected from the worst of the war. It was almost like being a child and knowing that as long as your parents were there, nothing could really harm you.

'And it makes just about as much sense,' remarked Bill Mason, who knew only too well that being a parent – or, presumably, a king – didn't automatically make you invincible. 'But anything that can make folk feel a bit better these days has got to be better than nothing.'

The other target of the raid was in Coventry Street. When the Nippies arrived at work and heard that a restaurant in Coventry Street had received a major hit, they immediately thought it must be the Corner House. Mr Carter quickly reassured them.

'It wasn't ours, although I believe there was some damage – windows shattered and so on. It was the Café de Paris. It got a direct hit – there were a lot of people killed and injured.'

'The Café de Paris?' Jo exclaimed. 'But they said that was

the safest restaurant in London. It's all underground, isn't it?'

'That's right.' Phyl had gone pale. 'It was such a posh place, too,' she said, as if this ought to have protected it from bombs. 'Ever so expensive. Just think of all those smart people being bombed, just like anyone else.'

'I went there once,' Irene said, and they all turned to stare at her. 'Richard Godwin took me.' She couldn't help looking at Phyl when she said this. 'I don't suppose he ever took you there.'

'No, he didn't,' Phyl said tersely. Her most painful humiliation had been the night when she had met Richard and Irene at one of the Sudbury dances. 'Not that I'd have enjoyed it. I'm too common, and I'd rather be with Mike any day.'

All the same, she felt anxious about Richard. Mr Carter had said there had been some damage to the Corner House, and since it stayed open all night there might easily have been some casualties as well. She waited for news, and when it came she felt as if she'd known all along.

'There were three people hurt and just the one killed. A blade of glass came through and pierced his chest. He died instantly.'

Mr Carter made the announcement just as they were preparing to go home and Phyl felt the tears come to her eyes. She'd almost fallen for Richard Godwin. His kisses had been like champagne, she remembered, and he'd been so good-looking and so well mannered. But he'd thrown her over for Irene and in the end she'd been glad she'd never let him have his way. Now he was dead, stabbed through the heart by a sword of glass.

Suddenly, she wanted nothing more than to be in Mike's arms, held close in that comforting bear-hug of his, exchanging kisses that weren't like champagne at all but were much more solid, and in the end much more exciting because there was real love in them. But Mike was on duty, as he always was immediately after a raid, and she didn't know where.

In fact, he was at the Café de Paris itself, where he'd been directed as soon the restaurant had been hit. The unit was on standby, ready to go to the nearest fire, and were off the minute the news came through, driving through the streets in an army firefighting vehicle, hardly aware of the roar of planes and the screaming of the bombs. It was all part of the job, a job they'd become accustomed to in the past few months, and if they couldn't do the job they'd been trained for – to go to war and fight – this was the next best thing. They could fight fires.

The fires at the Café de Paris were quickly dealt with. The bomb had been a high explosive, not an incendiary, and any fires that had started had come from kitchen equipment. Fat fires were always the worst of these, and the fastest spreading, for fat had its own ignition point, when it would explode, sending gobbets of fire in all directions, but tonight these were swiftly put out. All the same, the damage was appalling.

'My God,' Mike said when he saw it, but there was no time for more. Bodies lay everywhere in the rubble, sprawled amongst smashed furniture, shattered crockery and glass, a mess of food and drink and blood. People were trapped beneath fallen walls and beams, some moaning and screaming for help, others horribly still. Mike saw a famous actress, her blonde hair matted with blood, her gold dress torn almost off, one arm ripped away from her body. Her blue eyes, which he had seen so often gazing from the screen at the pictures, stared sightlessly at him from a face that was almost untouched, save for the mess of blood and bone of her skull. Near her was a woman in a fur coat, crying and gurgling as blood welled from her mouth and spilled over the silver mink, and quite close lay a waiter, his black jacket grey with dust, his silver tray still clutched in a torn hand.

Glass crunched underfoot and chandeliers lay in a million glittering shards. It was difficult not to slip on spilled food and sometimes what you took for a pool of blood turned out to be wine seeping from a broken bottle, or vice versa. As always, there was the danger of electrocution from wires that might have been laid bare, always supposing the electricity was still working, or the peril of a gas explosion from a broken main.

The work of saving the injured, releasing them from their jagged prisons without causing further harm, and of lifting out the dead and laying them in a quiet corner for removal, went on throughout the night. At some point the raid stopped and the all-clear sounded, but Mike didn't notice it. His face blackened by smoke and dust, his eyes rimmed with red, he realised that the grey, cold light of dawn had come and he could see. He found he didn't much want to see.

It was the worst he had encountered yet, and just as if that wasn't bad enough, there were the looters.

They came with the dawn, slipping as silently as the grey light into the ruins. At first they looked like shadows, flickering past just out of your line of vision. And then you could see them moving over the rubble, turning things over, lifting something here, laying it down again, transferring another into the sacks that they carried . . . Mike stared at them and then went over quickly, his hand on the butt of his rifle.

'Here! What d'you think you're doing?'

One of them lifted her head and stared at him. With a shock, he saw the yellow-haired woman he'd taken to the police only last week.

'You again!' He grabbed her arm and she twisted away, spitting and swearing. 'What the hell d'you think you're doing? You ought to be in jail!'

She peered more closely and then gave a cackling laugh. 'If it ain't little Tommy Atkins! Why ain't you fightin' for your country? Tha's what you oughter be doing, not badgering honest citizens what are only trying to do our patriotic duty.'

'Patriotic duty' Mike echoed. 'How d'you make that out, then?' His glance fell on the sack in her arms and he jerked it away from her with one hand. It gaped open. 'Look at that! Bottles of champagne! How's that your patriotic duty, eh?'

'They tells us to save, don't they? They tells us to waste not, want not. Well, I ain't goin' to see all this lot go to waste, not after all I bin through.' She twisted away from him. 'Go back to your sentry-box, soldier boy, and play with your little gun, why don't you? It might go off bang, if you're lucky.'

'I'm taking you to the sergeant,' Mike said grimly. 'He'll see the police get you, and this time they'll put you where you belong. I told you before, looting's an offence. It's a crime.'

The yellow-haired woman pushed her face close against his. 'Oh, it is, is it? An' what was done to me ain't, I suppose. Shall I tell you what they done to me, soldier-boy? Shall I tell you what I suffered? I been bombed out three times – *three times*. I lost everything I ever 'ad – *everything*. I lost me mum and dad, me little sister and me Auntie Enid what I used to go to tea with after school. I lost all me clothes and me necklaces and me earrings and me new lipstick. I lost me bed and the teddy bear me dad give me when I was six, and there wasn't *nothing* left of our house, nothing at all. It was just a pile of rubble.'

She turned and gesticulated at the wreckage of the Café de Paris. 'Look, I seen the people what come here. They had it all. They had money and houses and cars and fur coats – everything. All right, so they bin bombed as well now, but they ain't going to miss a few bottles of booze, are they? They ain't going to miss a few rings and

379

necklaces, not where they're going. And the ones that ain't dead, they got plenty more at home. It don't matter to them.' She drew her hand from her pocket and Mike saw the glitter of a diamond necklace. 'I 'ad one looked just like this. It come from Woolworths. My sweetheart give it me, just before he went to sea. He was in the first ship that got torpedoed by the bloody Germans. An' then I lost that, too.' She lifted her head suddenly and her eyes met Mike's. 'Don't you tell me looting's a bloody crime,' she said quietly.

Mike stared at her. He felt helpless. The woman had been stealing and it was his duty to report her, but her words had struck him to the heart. He thought of Maggie, losing her sister and her baby niece, of Etty down in the hole with the old woman. Neither of them had gone looting, but neither had lost everything they owned, everyone they loved.

He glanced swiftly around and let go of the woman's arm. He gave her a shove.

'Get out,' he said. 'Get out of here fast, and don't come back. And if I ever see you again, hanging round somewhere there's been a raid, I'll give you in charge, straight I will. Now *scram!*'

The woman gave him an unbelieving look. Then she took a step closer. For a moment he thought she was going to kiss him, but instead she drew back her head and then brought it forward savagely and spat directly in his face.

'That's just in case your precious sarge sees you!' she muttered, and gave another squawk of laughter. 'Goodbye, soldier! And don't worry – you'll never see me again, not if I sees you first!'

She was gone, slipping away like the shadow she had been when he first saw her. Mike, standing suddenly alone amidst the dusty ruins, felt a mixture of disgust and pity. She was off her head, he thought, as he wiped his face and then turned to go on digging at the rubble to salvage whatever could be found. She'd been sent right round the bend by this bloody war. And she wouldn't be the only one either. She wouldn't be the only one by a long way.

Chapter Twenty-Three

'It's nearly the middle of March,' May said in despair when Phyl rushed home the week before the wedding to make sure the preparations were still going ahead. 'We've been bombed every night, more or less, since the beginning of September. That's six months. How much longer are they going to keep it up? There'll be nothing left of London by Easter.'

'We're giving as good as we get,' Phyl said. 'And we're shooting down lots of their planes. They'll give up in the end, they got to.'

'Someone's got to,' May said, but she didn't sound very hopeful and Phyl gave her mother a sharp look. It wasn't like May to be pessimistic. She was usually the brighter and more cheerful of the twins. But when Phyl looked carefully she could see shadows beneath her eyes and a dull look to her skin and hair.

'You look tired, Mum. It's not too much for you, is it, getting ready for the wedding? I don't want you to wear yourself out over it.'

May gave her a smile. 'It's not the wedding, Phyl. I'm glad to have something nice to think about for a change. It's just that I'm so tired. I feel so tired sometimes, I could just sit down and cry. I'd like to sleep for a week and not have to worry about bombs again, ever. I'm tired of going down the shelter every night and listening to the planes and the bombs and never knowing what we're going to come out to, whether the house'll still be standing, who'll have been killed . . . Last week I was stood in a queue with that girl of

Martha Stubbs, you know, the one what had the baby, and the next morning I heard she'd been indoors getting a jug of cocoa when a bomb dropped and all they could find was little bits . . . It's horrible.'

Phyl gazed at her in concern. She had never heard such an outburst from her mother before. But there was nothing she could say to reassure her. The experiences May was talking about were common to everyone in London and the great cities now. Everyone knew people who had been killed or injured, or had lost members of their families or friends. Everyone was worn out with it, and how they kept going nobody really knew.

'It'll be over one day,' she said helplessly. 'It can't go on for ever.'

'So they tell me.' May was silent for a moment, then she gave a sigh and visibly pulled herself together. She gave Phyl a smile, a pale shadow of her usual bright look but a brave effort just the same. 'Well, we'd better get on with what we were doing. This won't buy the baby a new bonnet. Oops!' She giggled suddenly and covered her mouth with one hand. 'That's not the right thing to say, in the circumstances!'

Phyl laughed, thankful that her mother was able to make a joke. She picked up the sewing they'd been doing, making alterations to the frock May was going to wear. It was her only silk one, a few years old now but still in good condition, and May had been putting a new white collar on it.

'This is nice. It suits you. Is Auntie Carrie wearing hers, too?'

May shook her head. 'She thought about it, but she said the brides' mothers ought to look different, so people would know which was which. And it seems a bit hard on the boys, finding themselves with two mother-in-laws! The worst bit's been trying to get new stockings, they're like gold dust. Your auntie stood three hours in a queue the other day to get us a pair each.'

'Well, at least she did get stockings when she got to the top of the queue,' Phyl said. 'I know a girl thought she was queueing for stockings and when she got to the top she found they were selling dishcloths. Is everything else ready, Mum?'

'I think so. The dairy's promised us some eggs so we can make some sandwiches and the baker's going to let us have enough loaves. We gave up the idea of a sit-down meal, there just isn't enough room, and you can make stuff go further in sandwiches. Friday's going to be a busy day, getting it all ready. You'll be home then, won't you?'

Phyl nodded. 'Mr Carter says I can have the whole weekend off, from Friday till Monday. Oh, Mum – just think, in two weeks' time I'll be a married woman!'

May smiled. 'I know. Doesn't seem possible, does it? It only seems a little while since you were a tiny baby and now here you are, getting ready for your wedding. Oh, Phyl—' Her voice broke suddenly and tears came into her eyes as she reached out for her daughter. 'I hope you're going to be happy. I really do. This wedding – it's not what I ever thought it would be. Getting married in the middle of all this bombing, no home of your own to go to, not even knowing when you'll be able to settle down into a proper married life. But if you do as well as me and your dad, you'll be all right, and that's the best thing I could wish for you.'

'Thanks, Mum.' They held each other close for a moment and then May broke away and her voice held its old brisk cheerfulness as she picked up her needle and thread. 'And if you've come home to help, you can do your father's shirt for me. It needs its collar turning and I just haven't had time to settle down to it. It's over there on that pile.'

Phyl made a face and then grinned. Turning collars was her least favourite job, but at least her mother sounded her normal self again. And with her wedding only a few days away, even turning a shirt collar could be a pleasure.

*

Alice and Ossie counted out their money. Together with a rather thin, wide penny that Ossie's cousin had put on the railway line one day and a silver threepenny bit saved from last year's Christmas pudding, it came to nine shillings and ninepence farthing. It would be enough for the fare to London with some left over for buses.

'Will it be enough to buy a return ticket?' asked Ossie, whose knowledge of train travel had grown in the past few weeks.

'Oh, yes.' Alice wasn't sure it would be, but she wasn't going to let Ossie's doubts stop her now. She was going to her sister's wedding and that was that. 'Anyway, if Dad's so keen on me being out here he'll pay the fare back.'

Ossie stared at her suspiciously. 'You promised you'd come back.'

'I will. I promise I will.' She stroked Solomon's back. 'They won't let me stay in London, not with all the bombs. And there's our tadpoles anyway.'

Ossie had shown Alice a pond where frog spawn lay in huge jellied masses, like sago pudding. Fascinated, she'd insisted that they gather up great scoops of it in a bucket and bring it home, where Mr Tawe let them put it in a half of a beer barrel from the village inn. Only a week ago the first tadpoles had wriggled free of their glutinous womb and were now swimming like minute whales around the edges of the barrel. Alice and Ossie watched them every day, counting each new infant. To begin with they'd given them names, but since neither of them knew hundreds of names this idea soon went by the board. Only Tarzan and Goliath, the two largest, survived as individuals.

'I've got to see them get their legs and turn into frogs,' said Alice, who was still not entirely convinced of the truth of this story. 'They won't do it while I'm away, will they?' she added anxiously.

Ossie shook his head. 'They take weeks. I had one once never did it, he only ever got his back legs, never had no arms at all. Grandad said he wasn't getting enough meat.'

Alice decided to go to London the day before the wedding. She could be there by evening and nobody would send her back until Sunday at the earliest – probably not till Monday. She could see the wedding and have two whole days with Robbie. It seemed so long since she had seen her beloved ginger cat and she was sure he must have missed her as badly as she'd missed him.

I might even bring him back with me, she thought. He'd like the train.

As if in answer to May's prayer, the second week of March was a quiet week as far as bombing went, in London at least. It wasn't so quiet elsewhere and Phyl was afraid that Mike would be moved out of London to help with demolition in one of the other battered cities. With only a few days to go before the wedding, she was gripped by a superstitious dread that something would go wrong. She told Jo as they got ready to go to work on Thursday, but her cousin laughed at her.

'Don't be such a twerp, our Phyl! What's going to go wrong now? Everything's fixed.'

'Anything could happen. You know that. I just feel – well, me and Mike, we nearly lost each other through that Irene and I'm scared we'll lose each other now. There could be a bad raid. He's out in them all the time, fighting fires and getting people out of bombed houses.' Phyl sat on her bed, her brown eyes wide and anxious. 'I've just got this horrible feeling, Jo – a sort of premonition.'

Jo sat beside her and put her arm around Phyl's shoulders. 'Stop worrying. Nothing's going to happen to Mike. Or to you. This wedding's going to happen, and you're going to be Mrs Mike Bennett – whether you like it or not!'

'Oh, I'll like it all right,' Phyl said shakily. 'You don't

386

have to worry about that. I'm just scared stiff something's going to go wrong.'

'Well, it's not. It's my wedding as well, don't forget, and *I* haven't got a premonition.' Jo gave her shoulders a squeeze and a little shake. 'Stop looking so down in the mouth. What's brought this on anyway?'

'Well, Mum was a bit down when I saw her last week and I suppose it's affected me a bit. I started thinking about it all in the night. All the people we know who've been killed or bombed out. It's like the world's coming to an end sometimes.'

'Phyl! Don't say such things. Of course it's not coming to an end. It's going through a rough patch, that's all. Look, there've been wars before and I suppose there'll be wars again. There'll always be people like Hitler getting power somewhere. But they don't ever win, not for ever. And apart from all that, if we don't both get married on Saturday the vicar'll never speak to us again!'

Phyl laughed and stood up. 'Okay, Jo. You're right. I'll stop making a fuss about nothing. Anyway, we'd better get our skates on or we're going to be late for work.'

It was no longer a good excuse that you had to pick your way through ruined streets or come round a longer way, or that your bus or tram didn't run that morning. It was the same for everyone, the girls were tartly reminded, and if there was a raid in your area you were just expected to start out a bit earlier in the morning. However, since there had been few bombs dropped on London that week, most of the girls managed to get in on time. Phyl and Jo arrived first and took off their coats quickly before hurrying through the tunnel to the main restaurant, where they began sorting out clean cutlery and laying their tables.

Shirley came in looking better than she had for weeks, having managed several nights' good sleep. Her father hadn't had a seizure for a fortnight now and they were beginning to dare to hope he was getting over them. Irene, as usual, passed them without a glance. Etty scurried in looking anxious and Phyl paused in her task of filling salt cellars and glanced at her curiously.

'What's the matter, Etty? You look a bit het up.'

Etty paused and glanced about her before answering in a low voice. 'It's Maggie. She never come home last night.'

Phyl rolled her eyes. 'Oh, not again. Surely she wasn't going out with some bloke, not after what happened before.'

'I don't know. She never said nothing. I thought she'd gone round to see her dad and she'd be back by ten, but she never come. I was awake till two o'clock and then I couldn't help going to sleep, I was so tired. I thought she'd be there when I woke up, but she wasn't. I didn't know what to do, Phyl.'

'I don't know either. I can't believe she'd have been that daft again . . . Couldn't she have gone to see her dad like you thought, and stopped the night there?'

'No. Jim was with me, see, and he went home about half past ten. If Maggie'd stopped over there he'd have made her let me know somehow, or he'd have come back himself.'

'And how long would that have taken? You'd have been in bed by then, and how d'you think he could have let you know? Throw stones at your window? Honestly, Etty, I bet that's what she did and she'll be here in a minute right as ninepence.' She didn't tell Etty the other possibility in her mind – that Jim might not have made it back to the hostel. You just didn't know what might happen these days, but there was no sense in scaring the poor kid any more than she had to.

Etty shook her head doubtfully. She had what Phyl would have called a 'premonition' that all was not well. Maggie was flighty, everyone knew that, and since Tommy had been killed she had gone off the rails a bit, but she hadn't looked at a man since she'd been attacked that night. She hadn't even liked going out on her own, and Etty had quite expected Jim to escort her back home. And there'd

388

been no raid to use as an excuse. People often did stay out if they were caught in a raid, they had to find shelter and it might be hours before they could get home, but London hadn't been raided all week.

The morning wore on. The girls finished their tasks and went back to the dressing-room to change into their uniforms. There were the usual panics over buttons that had unaccountably come loose during the night and ladders in precious stockings. Mr Carter came round as usual to inspect their hemlines with his torch, making sure that everyone's petticoat was the right length under their skirt. The Nippies went into the canteen to have their own lunch before the restaurant opened. And still Maggie hadn't arrived.

'Something's happened to her,' Etty said, almost in tears. 'I know something's happened to her. Maybe I ought to go to the police station.'

The other girls were worried, too. Maggie had never missed work before. When Mr Carter came on to the floor, right in the middle of lunch when the Nippies were at their busiest, they looked at him in alarm and then glanced quickly at each other over the heads of the diners. He beckoned to Etty, who was hurrying back to the kitchens with an order for shepherd's pie and peas. Her heart in her mouth, she went over to him.

'Come into my office a moment, Etty,' he said. His voice was grave but kind and Etty's heart sank right down into her stomach. It was the oddest and most frightening feeling she'd ever known. She followed him and stared in terror at the two men who were waiting there.

They were big men, both of them, at least six feet tall and broadly built with muscular shoulders. They wore dark suits and carried trilby hats. They looked huge in Mr Carter's office and she knew at once that they must be policemen – and, since they weren't in uniform, very high-up policemen.

'What is it? What's happened?' Her voice came out in a croaky sort of squeak. 'Is it Maggie? Has she been hurt again? She – she's not . . .' Her voice refused to say the word and she trembled all over.

'Sit down, Etty, and don't look so frightened.' Mr Carter put his hand on her thin shoulder and pressed her into a chair. 'The gentlemen just want to ask you a few questions.'

'Questions?' Etty gave him a frightened look. 'What about? Where's Maggie?'

'Don't worry. Maggie's quite all right. She's not hurt and she's quite safe. She's helping the police.' Mr Carter gave the men an apologetic look. 'I'm sorry, perhaps I shouldn't have said that.'

'It's all right, sir.' It sounded funny, the man calling Mr Carter 'sir' when he must be so much more important. Etty continued to feel frightened. What had Maggie done? She shrank into her chair and cast an agonised glance at Mr Carter.

'Don't worry,' he said again, and then fell silent as one of the men made a small gesture. He gave Etty an intent look. He had a big, square face with a lined forehead and heavy black brows. His eyes were so dark a brown they were almost black and Etty was terrified of him.

'Now then, Miss Brown. I understand you live at the GFS hostel in Brownbridge Street.'

'Yes,' Etty whispered.

'You've lived there quite a long time.'

'Yes.' What could all this be about?

'And your friend Margaret Wheeler – Maggie – recently came to live there too.'

'Yes.' So it *was* about Maggie. 'What's happened to her? *Please* tell me.'

'We'll come to that in a minute. How long has Maggie Wheeler been living at the hostel with you?'

'A few weeks. Since her home was bombed. Her sister and her sister's baby were killed. Maggie's mum and gran and her other sister were evacuated and her dad and brothers live in a men's place now. And the girls in my room had both moved out so Maggie came to be with me. She's my friend.' She raised her eyes to the men's faces. 'She was the first proper friend I ever had.'

The other man was just as big, but he looked friendlier, as if he was used to cuddling people. He looked like a father or an uncle. His hair was a lighter brown, cut very short but with a bit of a curl to it, and his eyes were grey. He gave her a smile and Etty tried to smile in return but her lips wobbled and refused to move.

'Please tell me what's happened,' she said in a low voice. 'Maggie never came home last night. I've been worried stiff. She was hurt a few weeks ago – a soldier—'

'Yes, we know about that. And you've no need to worry. Maggie was with us,' the friendly man said. 'She was quite safe. But there were reasons why we couldn't let anyone know.'

Etty stared at him. Maggie had been in the *police station*? But why – whatever could she have done to get arrested and kept in a cell all night, and why couldn't they have let her know? Hadn't they even let her father know? She opened her mouth but before she could say a word the dark man was speaking again.

'Did Maggie often come home late at night, Miss Brown?'

The truth hit her like a blow. They thought Maggie was a tart – a *prostitute*! They'd been watching her, seen her going into the park at night with all those different boys, the young airmen, the soldiers in their stiff new uniforms, the occasional sailor in his square rig. They'd arrested her for soliciting.

'No!' Etty cried. 'You've got it wrong! Maggie wasn't like that – she never took money, never. She didn't even want them to give her presents – she did it for *them*. She said it was all wrong, young chaps like them being sent off without

391

ever having a chance to know what – what it was like. And it was only since Tommy got killed. She wouldn't *never* have gone with anyone else while he was alive, *never*.'

The men stared at her. Mr Carter's face turned a deep red and as the two policemen glanced at each other Etty could have sworn she saw their lips twitch. You stupid fool, she berated herself, you stupid, *stupid* fool. Now I've really let the cat out of the bag. I ought to have kept my big mouth shut. I ought to have said, no, she never came home late, we were always together, she never went with other men. Now she'll go to prison and it'll be all my fault.

The dark man leant across Mr Carter's desk.

'Let's forget about Maggie for a moment,' he said. 'Let's talk about some of the other girls in your hostel. You're friendly with some of them, too, aren't you? You've known them a long time. And isn't there another of your Nippy friends who goes there quite a lot? Irene Bond, is it?'

'Yes, she comes to see Muriel Chalk,' Etty said, bewildered by the turn in the conversation. 'But she doesn't *live* there. She just comes to tea and if there's a raid she might stay the night, but that's all. And she isn't really a friend of mine, nor of Maggie's. She doesn't like any of us all that much.'

The policeman nodded. 'All the same,' he said, 'we'd like to have a chat with her as well.' He glanced up at Mr Carter. 'Perhaps you could get someone to take Miss Brown to the canteen for a cup of tea,' he suggested. 'I can see she's feeling upset and worried. It'll help calm her nerves. And then I'd like to see Miss Bond, please.'

His voice was perfectly ordinary, Etty thought as she followed Miss Forton, one of the floor supervisors, upstairs. But there was something in it that told you he was used to being obeyed. A sort of steeliness that glinted from his eyes as well. The sort of man you wouldn't want to cross.

Surely, she thought, they wouldn't make all this fuss about someone they'd picked up for going with men in the park. It must be something to do with the hostel, although what it could be she couldn't even begin to imagine. But why else would he want to know about the other girls, and ask to talk to Irene, even though she only came as a visitor?

The most frightening question of all came back into her mind again. Why had they taken Maggie to a police station and kept her there all night?

And why had he sent *her* upstairs to the canteen, with someone to keep watch on her – almost as if he didn't want her talking to anyone else?

Chapter Twenty-Four

The other girls watched in surprise as Mr Carter came out into the restaurant again, his face serious, and called Irene into his office. Phyl and Jo, who were both standing at the till, looked at each other and Shirley came over to them.

'He says we've got to cover their tables. He looks ever so stern.'

'What's going on?' Phyl whispered, glancing around the busy restaurant. 'We're run off our feet as it is.'

'Well, we'll just have to run a bit faster. What's happened to Etty? Is it about Maggie not coming in?'

Shirley shrugged. 'I don't see how it can be, do you? Irene wouldn't be involved in anything to do with Maggie. Or Etty. Anyway, Etty's gone up to the canteen with Miss Forton. I saw them on the stairs.'

'Gone to the *canteen*? But it's the middle of lunchtime!'

'I know. But we'd better get on or we'll be the next ones in trouble.' Shirley picked up her order pad and hurried off to a table which had just been filled by the seater. There were new customers at one of Etty's tables, too, she noticed. If she and the others didn't get a move on, there would be complaints to add to the day's troubles.

Irene walked into the office with her head up, looking down her nose. Her expression changed when she saw the two policemen and she sat down rather suddenly, glancing at Mr Carter with an expression half accusing and half fearful.

'What's this, then? What's been going on? If it's anything

to do with that Maggie Pratt, I don't know anything about her.'

'I thought the name was Wheeler,' the dark policeman murmured. 'Isn't she married?'

Irene flushed. 'She's a widow. But she was only married a few months, we never had time to get used to it.'

'Perhaps she didn't either.' There was a small pause. 'Is there anything you'd like to tell us, Miss Bond? Mrs Wheeler's quite safe, by the way, she's been with us in the police station all night.'

Irene stared at them, baffled. The two men remained silent, watching her. Then she burst out, 'She's nothing but a tart, that Maggie Pratt. She goes with men all the time. They've only got to come in here and give her the eye and she's off like a b—a lady dog, I mean,' she amended primly. 'And she's no taste. They're just boys, all of them. She doesn't care, she'll go for anything wearing trousers. She's bringing Lyons right down into the gutter and I'm not sorry you've caught up with her.'

The men said nothing, but watched with interest as Irene, scarlet with anger, finished her tirade. Then the dark one said, 'That's all very interesting, Miss Bond, but it's not what we asked you in here to talk about. We want to know a little about the hostel, where Mrs Wheeler and Miss Brown live. I understand you visit there from time to time.'

Irene stared at him. 'Yes, I do. I've got a friend there. What about it?'

'We just need to know a few things, that's all,' the grey-eyed man said pleasantly. 'You know what they say, Miss Bond – or might I call you Irene? The onlooker sees most of the game. I shouldn't think there's much misses your eyes, is there?'

Irene transferred her gaze to him. He was much nicer than the dark man, she decided. He looked the sort of man you could talk to. She smiled a little, feeling more comfortable, and nodded.

'I'm pretty sharp,' she allowed. 'My dad always says I could've made a good detective if I'd been born a boy.'

Henry Bond thought Irene could have done any number of things, if only she'd been born a boy. Her appearance as a girl had been the greatest disappointment of his life, and he'd never let her forget it. Irene had spent all her twenty-two years trying to atone for her mistake.

'I'm sure you could,' the grey-eyed man agreed. 'So you'd be able to tell us if there was anything suspicious at all going on in the hostel.'

Irene stared at him. 'Anything suspicious? I don't understand.'

'Well, anyone behaving suspiciously. In an odd manner. Skulking about, say, listening to other people's conversations. Slipping out at odd hours to meet mysterious people. Someone who perhaps isn't very friendly with the other inmates of the hostel.'

Irene shook her head. 'I don't know anyone like that but, then, I don't really know the other people very well. Just my friend, Muriel Chalk, and Maggie and Etty. *They* behave oddly enough, mind. Etty's never had all that many friends – well, she's a Jew, you know – and Maggie's always coming in late and getting Etty to let her in. I reckon you've got the right one already, you don't need no one to tell you that.'

'The right one? The right one for what?'

Irene stared at him again. 'Well, for whatever it is you're talking about. Acting funny. Listening to other people and nipping out at all hours – well, that's Maggie Pratt all over, isn't it?' She chewed her lip and then burst out again. 'It's spying, isn't it? She's a fifth columnist. I knew it! I always knew there was something about her! And Etty Brown's her accomplice. Well, it's plain as the nose on your face, isn't it?'

The men looked at her.

'Well, isn't it?' she repeated, a little uncertainly.

The grey-eyed man leant forward again and rested both his arms on Mr Carter's desk.

'Let's just have a chat about some of the other people in the hostel,' he said smoothly. 'Just to make sure. Now, to start with, tell me about your friend Muriel Chalk . . .'

Alice and Ossie left the cottage early. They told Ossie's grandparents that they were going for a walk and felt, virtuously, that they had told the truth. They went for a walk to the next village, where the railway station was.

The weather was typical of March, warm when the sun was out and bitingly cold when a cloud blew across. The clouds were dark and grey, full of rain, and when you looked west across the distant shadow of the moor you could see sheets of it falling like curtains, blotting out the shape of the hills. Sometimes, in the opposite direction, there was a rainbow.

It took them about an hour and a half to reach the station. There was a porter on the platform and a man in the little ticket office where all the parcels were sorted out. He peered at them through the little glass window.

'Lunnon? Both of you?'

Alice began to say no, but Ossie forestalled her. 'What's it cost, mister?' He had his money clutched tightly in one fist. He had refused to give it to Alice before they'd left.

'Four shillun and threepence each. That's single halves. You'd want to be coming back, so that'd be—'

'No,' Ossie said. 'Alice's mum and dad will pay for us to come back.'

'*Ossie!*' Alice cried. 'I never said—'

'Two singles to Lunnon, then,' the ticket man said, and stamped out the little slivers of green cardboard. Ossie handed over the money and received the tickets in return. He gave Alice a glint of triumph and marched past her on to the platform.

'What did you do that for?' Alice hissed, catching up with him. 'I needed that money—'

'I never been to Lunnon,' he said. He strode along the platform. There were flowerbeds all along the side of it, which had been the stationmaster's pride and joy until he'd had to dig up all the flowers and plant vegetables instead. Now they were neatly dug and raked, and little labels showed that seeds had been planted where potatoes and cabbages had already been harvested. A large black cat sat in the middle of the platform, washing itself industriously.

'I'm going to work on trains when I'm growed up,' Ossie said. 'I'll be an engine driver to start with and when I'm too old like Mr Potter I'll have my own station and grow things. Or I might be a signalman and live in a box up the stairs and work the points.'

'You took the money I was going to use,' Alice said angrily. 'I was going to get a return ticket.'

'I didn't know you would. I thought you might stop in Lunnon.'

'I *said* I'd come back.' Her face was red with exasperation and annoyance and she wasn't far from tears. 'I *said* it.'

Ossie looked at her, and once again she recognised an obstinacy as great as her own.

'Anyway,' he said, 'I wanted to come. I never been to Lunnon and I wanted to see the station there and the big trains.' He drew the scrap of green cardboard from his pocket and regarded it with satisfaction. 'And now I'm going to.'

Etty didn't come back to the restaurant that day. After she had been to the canteen she disappeared and the other girls had no idea where she had gone. Neither was Mr Carter any the wiser. He looked drawn and anxious as he went about his work, and when Miss Forton returned she was tight-lipped and unapproachable.

'Irene's gone, too,' Phyl whispered. 'I don't understand

398

it. What have they all been doing? I can't imagine anything that Maggie and Etty and Irene would have been doing together.'

'It must be a mistake, whatever it is,' Shirley agreed. 'Someone's got it wrong. They'll all be back tomorrow, you'll see.'

Phyl wasn't so sure. Her premonition seemed to be coming true. Not that Maggie's or Etty's disappearance could actually prevent her wedding taking place, but it was all so queer that you just didn't know what might happen. She slept fitfully that night, starting up every hour or so with the conviction that something had occurred – the air-raid warning sounded, or a bomb dropped nearby. But Jo was peacefully sleeping in the other bed and there was no sound of hurrying people, no shouting or crying outside. It was almost uncannily quiet when there were no raids, she thought wryly, and tried to go back to sleep.

'You're looking tired, Phyl,' Jo said with some concern, looking at her shadowed eyes as they sat down to breakfast. 'You're not still worrying about that premonition of yours, are you?'

'I don't know what it is.' Phyl stirred restlessly and poured hot water and milk on to her Weetabix. 'I just feel all at sixes and sevens. I couldn't sleep properly at all last night.'

'Phyl, you've got to snap out of this. You're getting married tomorrow, remember? Mike isn't going to want a bride with a long face.' Jo leant over the table and gripped both Phyl's hands in her own. She stared into her cousin's face. 'Nothing's going to go wrong,' she said forcefully. 'Tomorrow's our wedding day, yours and mine. We've always done things together, haven't we? Well, we're going to do this together. We're getting married and *nothing's* going to stop us.'

Phyl gazed at her. Her lips trembled and she looked ready for tears. 'Jo, I can't help—' she began, but before she could go any further there was a sharp ring on the doorbell. They stared at each other and held their breath.

Their landlady's footsteps sounded, going along the passage to the front door. They heard the door open, a murmur of voices, and a moment later she was in the room, holding out a small brown envelope. Phyl reached out a shaking hand, but the woman shook her head and held the envelope out to Jo.

Jo was white. Slowly, she let go of Phyl's hands and took the envelope. Her fingers trembled and fumbled at the flap but she got it open and drew out the scrap of paper with its words stuck clumsily on it. She stared at them.

'What is it?' Phyl's voice was husky.

Jo's face flooded suddenly with brilliant colour. She looked angry and exasperated and almost hysterically amused. She flung the scrap of paper on the table and then snatched it up again, staring at the words as if they might somehow have changed.

'It's history repeating itself, that's what it is! It's that blasted kid, determined to get her own way as usual. It's our flaming *Alice*.'

'*Alice*?'

'Yes. She's done it again, Phyl. She's run away from that nice old couple what've been looking after her down in Devon, and she's come to London for our wedding. Walked in last night, cool as you please – and brought her own boyfriend with her to top it all.' Jo shook her head. 'When I *saw* that brown envelope . . . . I'll kill that kid, scaring us like that. I'll flipping *kill* her!'

'You mean she's at home now? She got back all by herself? But what boyfriend? Alice is too young for a boyfriend.'

'Oh, I know who he is,' Jo said, beginning to laugh. 'He's the old couple's grandson. Ossie, he's called, and he's three years younger than our Alice and tricky as a barrel-load of monkeys, from what I hear.' She gave her cousin a broad grin and Phyl couldn't help smiling back and instantly felt better. 'This is what your premonition's been about, Phyl. You said something terrible would happen, didn't you? Well, I can't think of anything more terrible than our Alice and a boy called Ossie creating mayhem at our wedding!'

By the time Maggie and Etty were allowed to go back to the hostel, everything was over.

'I had to report it, didn't I?' Maggie said as they sat in their room, still feeling shaken by the events of the past two days. 'I mean, we all know what can happen. All those posters . . . When I come back late the other night and saw that light flashing from the top window, I knew someone was signalling. I knew it had got to be reported.'

'That man with the nice eyes said Muriel Chalk had been signalling for weeks and no one noticed,' Etty said, marvelling. 'She'd been getting information from all sorts – people in the store as well as Irene – and passing it on. He said she could have been responsible for quite a lot of ships getting sunk. It doesn't bear thinking about.'

They continued to think about it, nevertheless. Irene had been arrested as well as Muriel, and had tearfully denied everything, but eventually admitted to telling Muriel little snippets of overheard gossip about ships leaving the Pool of London, or soldiers passing odd remarks about their units' movements. She had never seen any harm in it, she'd said, it had just been something to say, chatter between friends. Reminded that this was exactly what the posters warned against, she looked sulky and insisted that she'd *known* she could trust Muriel, they were friends, *close* friends.

'How close?' the grey-eyed man said, not so nicely now. His eyes were like cold steel and Irene flushed scarlet and burst into tears again.

'We were going to get a little flat together. We were going to stay together.'

'Well, if you want to stay with your friend now you'll

have to do it in jail,' he told her brutally. 'She'll be there for a long time and you'll be lucky if you don't end up there, too. *And* your father – I gather he's been spilling a few beans as well.'

Irene almost screamed at this. She wept and tore her hair and beat her fists on the table, but the man took no notice. He went on asking questions and making notes until Irene was no more than a wet, sobbing heap and none of her fellow Nippies would have recognised her for the smart, sharp-faced girl they knew so well.

The Corner House buzzed with rumours. Phyl and Jo, working their last day as single girls, felt mildly aggrieved that Maggie and Etty had stolen their thunder, but the scandal was too great for them not to join in. Eventually Mr Carter came into the canteen as they ate their lunch and called sharply for silence.

'I want to hear no more talk about what's been happening. Margaret and Esther will be back at work on Monday and nobody is to question them about it. Remember that it's idle gossip which has caused all this trouble, and we want no more of it. There's to be no further discussion, either in the Corner House or anywhere else.'

'Will Irene Bond be coming back, too?' someone asked, and there was a gasp and a smothered, nervous giggle from several people. Mr Carter looked annoyed.

'I don't know what will be happening to Irene. I doubt if the police will take me, or any of us, into their confidence. You don't seem to realise, girls, that all this is extremely serious. I don't believe for a moment that Irene meant any harm, but harm has almost certainly come of her carelessness and she'll have to be punished for it. Let's just make quite sure that nobody else at Lyons goes the same way. And remember what I said – not another word.' He gave them all a long, severe stare and then turned and walked out of the canteen.

There was a moment's silence, then a buzz of chatter.

402

'I've never *seen* Mr Carter look so cross,' Phyl whispered. 'All this has really upset him.'

'Well, I'm not surprised,' Jo said. 'I feel horrible about it myself – as if I've touched something dirty, just by knowing Irene Bond. I hope she doesn't come back.'

'Well, we'd better do as he says,' Shirley observed, 'and not talk about it any more. And why should we, anyway? We've got a wedding to think about – *two* weddings!' She glanced at the canteen clock. 'Look, Phyl – Jo – it's two o'clock. This time tomorrow you'll be walking up the aisle together!'

Jo laughed with excitement. 'So we will!' She looked at her cousin and gave her a broad grin. 'And I reckon enough's happened now for all the premonitions in the world to have come true. We shan't have to worry any more – there's nothing else *can* go wrong . . .'

403

Chapter Twenty-Five

It was Saturday morning at last. There had been no real raids on London all week, no more than a stray bomb here and there. For once, Londoners were left in relative peace.

Jo and Phyl had gone home on the Friday evening, straight after work. With Etty, Maggie and Irene all absent, there was far too much work for them to be given the afternoon off, as Mr Carter had intended. But as soon as the afternoon rush slackened off, he told them to slip away, and they were home by six.

The first person they saw was Alice, who came running out of the front door to meet them. She was wearing a green jumper and skirt that Carrie had made for her last year and Jo was taken aback to see how short the skirt was. She stopped and gave her sister a severe look.

'What are you doing here? You're supposed to be in the country. And you've grown.'

Alice grinned cheekily. 'I wanted to be at your wedding. It's not fair, leaving me out of everything. And there's been no raids this week so I don't see why I shouldn't stay for a bit. I want to show Ossie round London.'

Jo glanced past her at the small boy in thick knickerbockers and a jersey with a hole in. He looked up from beneath a thatch of straw-coloured hair, totally straight and sticking out in all directions. He look a bit like a scarecrow, she thought, and wondered if he was coming to the wedding, too, and if he had anything else to wear.

'This is Ossie,' Alice informed them. 'He lives with me

and Granny and Grandad Tawe. They're his granny and grandad really, but I'm allowed to call them that, too.'

'And did they know you were coming to London? And bringing Ossie with you?'

'Not till they found my note,' Alice said cheerfully. 'But they won't mind. They let us do mostly what we please.'

'I bet they do!' Phyl muttered with a chuckle in her voice. 'Your Ally hasn't changed, Jo.'

'More's the pity,' Jo said, but she bent and gave her little sister a hug. 'I'm glad you're here,' she said. 'It wouldn't have been the same without you. And it's nice to see Ossie, too. Come on, let's go and tell Mum and Dad we're here.'

'The wedding cake's come,' Alice told them, jumping up and down on the doormat. 'It's in Auntie May's house, in the front room. That's where the party's going to be.'

'Oh, let's go and look,' Phyl exclaimed, and they hurried into the house next door. There was the usual flurry of greetings and then they went to see the cake. It was in pride of place in May's front room, right in the middle of the sideboard and surrounded by presents.

'Oh, how *gorgeous*,' Phyl breathed, gazing at it in delight. 'Three tiers and all! And look, Jo – there are *two* little brides and grooms on top! One's me and Mike, the other's you and Nick.'

Jo chuckled. 'They've even made one of the brides tall and the other short! So there'll be no argument over who's which.'

May and Carrie had been slicing bread all day for the sandwiches. They put the loaves together again and wrapped them in sheets of greaseproof paper to keep them fresh for tomorrow. In the morning, one of the boys would be sent to the grocer's shop for Spam and other ingredients, and Alice was to go to the dairy for eggs and butter. Carrie and May had been saving the family's ration for weeks.

'Look at all these presents,' Phyl said in awe. 'I never expected anything like this.'

405

'Everyone in the street's given you something,' May said, coming in with Carrie. 'It's not all new, but you can't expect that in wartime. But you'll have enough to get you started when you get your own places.'

The girls looked rueful. Only Jo was likely to have her 'own place', when she moved down to the aerodrome as soon as the rooms Nick had found were ready. Till then, she was staying on at the Corner House. Phyl was also staying on, but the only home she and Mike would have would be back here in her own bedroom whenever he had a weekend pass. And they knew that he must be sent away soon. The army couldn't stay at home indefinitely.

'It's not just Europe,' he'd told her the last time they'd met. 'It's Africa as well – and maybe even Japan. The way they're going into China, they'll have to be stopped as well. We could be sent anywhere.'

Carrie had made supper for both families in her house, so that May's place could be kept clean and tidy for the next day. The families crowded around the table and helped themselves to cottage pie. There wasn't much meat in it, but Carrie had made a layer of mashed swedes and carrots as well as potato, and there was plenty of cabbage, so it was tasty and filling. For afters, she'd done a huge bread-and-butter pudding.

'Bread and marge, really,' she said. 'And I had to throw the dried fruit in from the top of a hill. It's not like a pre-war pudding.'

'It's good for a wartime one, though,' Bill said loyally. 'You're a good cook, Carrie. You manage well on what we get.'

Alice and Ossie sat together at one end of the table. Small as he was, Ossie had a huge appetite and passed his plate back three times for extra helpings. Carrie looked at him in amusement.

'I'd rather feed you for a week than a fortnight,' she observed, piling his plate with more pudding. She'd been dismayed and exasperated to find him and Alice on the doorstep, but she hadn't been really surprised. It stood to reason that Alice wasn't going to miss the wedding without a fight, but Carrie hadn't expected her to bring Ossie as well. But although Alice hadn't said so in as many words, she'd got the idea it hadn't been Alice's plan and she found the thought of a little boy managing to beat Alice at her own game rather entertaining. And she liked him, with his shock of fair hair and his big blue eyes and cheeky grin.

'We've got a cat, too,' he told her. 'Solomon, he's called. And we've got newts and tadpoles in the pond. And ducks and chickens and my grandad's got a cow, too, she's called Bluebell. She lives with a bull sometimes.'

'She's going to have a calf,' Alice joined in. 'She's having it in May and then we'll be able to get milk from her.'

Ossie nodded. 'She's getting fat already,' he said to the table at large. 'That's because the calf's inside her, getting big.'

'Oh, really,' Carrie said faintly. Like most city mothers, she hadn't told Alice the 'facts of life' yet, and it came as a surprise to find that her innocent daughter probably already knew quite a few of them. Country children were very different, she thought, watching Ossie unconcernedly finishing his third helping. It was all right for them to know such things, but she really hadn't meant Alice to know for another few years yet.

Well, it was all part of the war, and there were other things to worry about now. Like whether there would be a raid tonight and whether they should go down to the shelter or go to bed and hope for the best.

In the end it was decided that they should go to bed but if there was an alert everyone was to go down to the shelters. There were still a few last-minute details to decide and the families sat round Carrie's table making the final arrangements. By ten o'clock they were saying goodnight.

Mike and Nick, both on duty tonight, would be at the

church. They had each put in for a 72-hour pass, and if nothing happened they wouldn't have to be back until Tuesday. Nick had arranged to take Jo down to Bognor, and Mike and Phyl were going to his auntie's house in Wiltshire. The girls, hardly able to contain their excitement, said goodnight at the front door.

'Just think,' Phyl said, looking up at the stars, 'this time tomorrow . . .'

'Don't!' Jo said, poking her in the ribs. 'I'm feeling nervous already. Just let's think about the wedding.'

'You'll be all right,' Phyl advised her. 'Just relax and let yourself go. It's nice.' She rolled her eyes and grinned cheekily, and Jo gave her a reproving look.

'You're a wicked girl, our Phyl. You didn't ought to be getting married in white at all!'

'Shush – don't let our Mum hear you say that. She'd kill me if she knew.' Phyl glanced around, then leant closer. 'I tell you what, Jo, I'm not sorry at all that Mike and me have done what we've done. I'm glad. And I don't see anything wrong with it. All the same, it'll be nice to be married and not have to pretend any more!'

'Well, I'm going to bed now,' Jo said, turning back into the house. 'See you in the morning, Phyl, all ready to put on our frocks. Oh, I can't *believe* it's really going to happen!'

'Nor can I,' Phyl said, suddenly sober. 'I really did have a feeling something was going to go wrong, you know.'

'But nothing has. So you must be feeling better now. And next time you have a premonition, you just tell it to go away, see!'

Phyl nodded. But after Jo had gone indoors she lingered for a few moments, gazing up at the darkening sky. I *still* feel worried, she thought. It *hasn't* gone away. And there's still time for something to go wrong.

She shivered, and turned to go indoors.

When Maggie and Etty returned to the hostel, they discovered that their popularity had disappeared.

'We've had police here all day,' Mrs Denton told them stiffly, meeting them as they came in. 'Turning the place upside down, they've been. I told them all my residents are respectable girls and women, but they took no notice. And the questions! I've never been so humiliated in all my life, never.'

'It's not our fault,' Maggie said defensively. 'I only did my patriotic duty—'

'Patriotic duty! Muriel Chalk's a refined businesswoman – not like some of the common ones we've had coming here lately,' Mrs Denton snapped, forgetting that a moment ago she'd said they were all respectable. 'Mentioning no names, but there was something fishy about that business of you landing up in hospital a few weeks back, and don't try to say there wasn't. I never did believe you were hurt in a raid.'

'Well, I'm not telling you any different,' Maggie retorted furiously. 'The police know what happened and there's no need for you to poke your nose in. And if it's Muriel Chalk's sort you want, you'd better write to Hitler and ask him to send you a few more spies!'

'*Maggie!*' Etty tugged at her arm frantically. 'You know we weren't supposed to say anything—'

'I'm not. Mrs D. might be an old cow but she's not a fool. She knows what all those questions were about.'

Mrs Denton was looking more like a turkey-cock than a cow. She seemed to swell before their eyes, her face turning bright crimson. She took a deep breath, spluttered a bit and then said in a tight voice, 'I think you'd better go and pack your chattels, Mrs Wheeler. And you may as well go with her, Miss Brown. I'm beginning to think the other girls were right in the first place. Your sort only brings trouble.'

Etty turned white. Maggie, angrier than ever, took a step forward but Etty gripped her arm and hauled her away.

'Don't let's have any more trouble. Please. Let's just do as she says and go. I've always hated it here anyway.'

'That's all very well, but we got to have somewhere to stop, Et. And you can't chuck us out without notice,' she added to the manageress, 'so there. You got to give us a week. Come on, Et. We won't have no trouble finding somewhere better than this hole.'

They walked stiffly up the stairs to their bedroom. Maggie closed the door behind them and leant against it, looking suddenly tired. Etty sank down on one of the beds and looked up at her woefully.

'Oh, Maggie. Whatever are we going to do?'

'I dunno, Et.' Maggie came and sat beside her. 'I honestly don't know. But it don't make a lot of difference. We'd have had to move soon anyway. At least, I would.'

'You would?' Etty stared at her. 'Why?'

'Because I'm up the spout,' Maggie said flatly. 'In the family way. Got a bun in the oven. I'm having a baby, Et, and I don't even know whose it is!'

For March, it wasn't a bad day at all.

The showers of the past week still persisted, with a heavy burst of hail just before breakfast, but the sun came out soon afterwards and a rainbow adorned the sky with a frieze of brilliant colour. It was a good omen, Jo said, looking out of her bedroom window, and nothing could possibly go wrong now.

Breakfast was a hasty affair, with people snatching at Weetabix or cornflakes when they could and washing their own bowls in the sink, while May and Carrie spread slice after slice of bread with margarine and waited impatiently for the boys to come back with the Spam. Bill and Stan, together with Freddy and Norman, went up to the off-licence at the pub and came back with a couple of crates of beer and some lemonade, and at the last minute Phyl and Jo went to the flower shop to collect their bouquets. They were simple affairs, not so much bouquets as bunches of spring flowers – daffodils and narcissi with a sprig or two of cherry blossom, and a posy of primroses for Alice. They looked bright and pretty and Phyl declared that she wouldn't have wanted a posh bouquet of exotic flowers anyway.

'These are lovely. It's like a dream, Jo.'

They came back down the street, stopping every few steps to be congratulated by neighbours who wanted to wish them all the best. At two o'clock, when the taxi came to take them to the church, the same neighbours would be out in force to see the brides leave, and again when they came back. You couldn't have a 'quiet' wedding in Woolwich!

'If it wasn't for the blackout, we'd be having someone's piano out in the street later on, too,' Phyl said wistfully. 'Like Maggie's wedding reception, remember?'

Jo grinned. 'I'll never forget that day. We thought we weren't going to make it, didn't we, what with our Alice running off like that? And she's done the same thing this time, only in reverse. Little monkey!'

'Well, I don't blame her. I wouldn't want to miss it either.' Phyl laughed at herself. 'I hope Maggie and Etty will be able to come, though. There's no reason why they shouldn't, is there?'

Jo shook her head. 'They'll be here. And Shirley. They're all going straight to the church. And talking of the church, we'd better get our skates on, Phyl, or we're never going to be ready in time!'

They hurried down the street, waving at bedridden old Mrs Perkins who was already stationed by her window ready to see them off, and burst into the Masons' house where Carrie had an extra plate of sandwiches to see everyone through till the reception.

As soon as they came through the door, they knew something was wrong.

'What?' Jo demanded, stopping dead in the doorway. 'What's happened?'

Carrie and May were sitting by the table in the back room. Their faces were pale. Behind them stood their husbands, and out in the scullery the girls could see their brothers, apparently at a completely loose end, as if they had nothing to do and all day to do it in. On the rug, crouched with Robertson between them, sat Alice and Ossie.

The silence was unnatural. The girls stared at the solemn faces and Phyl felt a cold hand of fear grip at her heart.

'What is it?' Jo asked again, her voice rising. 'Why are you all looking like that? Mum – Auntie May – *whatever's happened*?'

Carrie stepped forward. 'There's been a telegram, love,' she said, and held out the scrap of rough, brownish paper.

'A telegram? For me?' Jo stared at it as if it were a snake. She made no attempt to take it from her mother. 'What does it say? Have you read it?'

'We had to open it,' Carrie said apologetically. 'The boy wanted to know if there was a reply. Your dad said we ought to—'

'What does it say?' Jo whispered, and then in that high, panicky voice again, 'Mum, tell me what it says! For God's sake—'

'It's Nick. It's from his parents. He was shot down last night. He's—'

'*Shot down?* But there was no raid last night. How could he have been shot down?'

'There was no raid over London, love.' Her father moved to her side and put his arm around her shoulders. 'But there was a raid over Glasgow. All the squadrons along the south coast were scrambled. They didn't intercept many, but Nick got tangled with one and they both went down apparently. At least he gave as good as he got,' he added wryly.

Jo stared at him, unbelievingly. She groped for something to support her and he steered her to a chair and sat her down. Her mother got up and put both arms around her.

'Jo. Oh, Jo, love—'

'But it can't be,' Jo said. 'It can't be true. Not Nick. Not my Nick.' She turned and stared at Phyl, standing white-faced with shock beside her. 'It was you had the premonition,' she said almost accusingly. 'It wasn't me at all. It was you. *Your* premonition. Not mine.'

'Jo—' Phyl began, but Carrie interrupted.

'Jo, listen to me. It's not as bad as you think. He's not dead. He's still alive – a fishing-boat got him out of the sea and took him to harbour. He's in hospital now.'

Jo leapt to her feet. 'He's in hospital? Why didn't you tell me? Why did you let me think he was dead?' She dropped the bouquet she had been holding. 'I've got to go to him. Where is he? Mum – Dad – *Phyl*—'

'Wait a minute, Jo. His mum and dad are going down straight away. They're catching the train from Waterloo at two o'clock. They'll meet you there and you can all go down together. You've just got time to get changed – your suitcase is packed, ready . . .' Carrie's voice faltered. Jo's case had been packed for a honeymoon, not a hospital visit. 'I'll pack some of these sandwiches for you.'

Jo stared at her wildly. Then she looked at Phyl.

'Phyl, the *wedding* . . .'

'We'll call it off,' Phyl said quickly. 'We won't have it without you and Nick. We'll wait till – till he's well again.' She knew as she said it that to wait might be to miss her own chance. If Mike were to be sent away, the opportunity might not arise for months. Maybe even longer. The tears sprang to her eyes and she blinked them away angrily. It wasn't fair. Nothing was fair these days.

Jo hesitated, then shook her head.

'No. You mustn't do that. You have your wedding, Phyl – all the arrangements are made and it wouldn't be fair to put everyone off now. You have yours, and I'll ask the vicar

413

to squeeze us in next Saturday. Nick's sure to be fit by then.' She turned back to her mother. 'I'll wear my going-away costume and I'll take enough sandwiches for Nick's mum and dad, if that's all right. They'd have been coming here anyway . . . I'll send you a telegram as soon as I see how he is. And I'll find somewhere to stay down there for a day or two, till I know he's better.' She gave a crooked smile. 'You know what he is – nothing gets him down for long!'

She ran up the stairs and they heard her moving swiftly about as she changed from her old skirt and jumper into the grey costume with the nipped-in waist that she had meant to wear to go on honeymoon. The family looked at each other and Phyl, still white-faced, sat down in the chair Jo had vacated.

'It's my fault,' she said shakily. 'If I hadn't had that premonition—'

'Don't talk so daft!' Her father's voice was sharp. 'It's nothing to do with premonitions. That's silly talk.'

Phyl began to cry. 'Oh, Dad, you don't know. I've felt all along something was going to go wrong. Mum, we'll have to call it off – I can't get married without Jo. I just can't!'

'You can,' Stan stated. 'You can and you will. There's all the family coming, and your mates from the Corner House, all expecting a bit of happiness to brighten up their lives, and you're not letting them down. Where's the sense in it? It's not going to help Jo or Nick, now, is it? Jo's right – there's no point in putting off the whole thing. There's nothing we can do but go ahead without her. Don't you reckon so, Bill?'

Bill Mason nodded, and the twins glanced at each other and sighed their agreement. The occasion would have lost half its joy, but there was no sense in letting it ruin everyone else's day as well. That would be just giving in.

Jo came running down the stairs in her grey suit. Her face

414

was pale but her eyes were bright and determined. She gave them all a swift glance.

'I don't know what you're all doing, standing about like stuffed dummies,' she said in a brittle voice. 'You've got a wedding to get ready for, haven't you?'

'Oh, Jo,' Phyl said, getting up to give her cousin a hug. 'Jo, are you sure?'

'I'll come with you,' Carrie said suddenly. 'I can't let you go on your own.'

'I won't be on my own. Mr and Mrs Laurence are going, you said that. They won't want a crowd of us at the hospital. I'll be all right, Mum.'

'I'm coming with you to the station all the same,' her father said, fetching his coat from the back of the door. 'I'll get your ticket and all that, make sure you meet the Laurences all right. I'll be back as soon as I've seen her off, Carrie.'

There was a brief silence. They all looked at each other. Jo's eyes filled suddenly with tears.

'*Mum . . .*'

'There, there,' Carrie choked, throwing her arms around her daughter and patting her on the back. 'He'll be all right, Jo. I'm sure he'll be all right.'

'I don't know what I'll do if he isn't,' Jo gasped. 'I just don't know *what* I'll do.'

'Come on,' said Bill from the doorway. 'We'll miss that train if we don't get going. I'll see you later, Carrie – maybe at the church. Don't wait for me.'

'No. No, all right.' They crowded to the door to watch father and daughter hurry up the street, and then filed quietly back indoors.

'Well,' Carrie said in a subdued voice, 'I suppose we'd better do as he says and go on getting ourselves ready. Phyl, I am sorry. It's an awful thing to happen. But at least he's alive. That's the main thing. He's alive and he'll get better and, as Jo says, there's no point at all in you putting off your

415

wedding. And you'd better stop crying or you'll have red eyes to greet your new husband!'

Phyl sniffed and nodded and tried to smile. She got up from her chair and stood irresolute for a moment, her eyes on the bunch of spring flowers she had carried so proudly home. The other bunch lay discarded on the table.

'If we're going to have the wedding after all,' Alice remarked from the floor, 'can I carry our Jo's bouquet instead of that bunch of primroses?'

Chapter Twenty-Six

The little church was buzzing with rumours. The boys had gone round to act as ushers and make sure people sat in the right seats, but Bill and Stan had impressed upon them that they weren't to say too much about what had happened to Nick. Just that he couldn't be here after all because of what Bill called 'the exigencies of the service'. Neither Eric nor Ronnie could get their tongues around that, however, so when people asked them they just shook their heads and mumbled that they didn't really know.

That didn't help at all, of course. And as the church filled, it began to be noticeable that none of Nick's family had come either. People looked at each other and whispered. Had Jo been stood up at the altar? Had *Nick* been stood up at the altar? Had they had a row and was the wedding off? If so, would Phyl and Mike still go on with their own vows?

'Course they will, you twerp,' a cousin hissed. 'We wouldn't be here otherwise, would we? *Someone's* got to get married.'

Mike was in a fever. Nick ought to have been here by his side. He tried without success to catch one of the boys' eyes, and eventually left his position in the front pew and marched down the aisle, watched by everyone in the place. He grabbed Ronnie's sleeve.

'Where's Nick? What's going on? And where are Freddy and Norman? They're supposed to be our best mans – *men*.'

Ronnie looked embarrassed. 'Dad told us not to say too much. He didn't want to upset everyone—'

'I'm upset already! I'm supposed to be getting married in a quarter of an hour's time and half the guests aren't here and neither is the other bridegroom nor the best men.' It still didn't sound right. Irritated, he went on, 'Come on, Ron, out with it, what's going on?'

Ronnie glanced around as if he were afraid that spies might be lurking behind one of the pillars. 'Nick's been shot down. He's okay—' as Mike began to exclaim in dismay '—at least, as far as we know. He's in hospital somewhere or other and Jo's gone down to see him, and so've his mum and dad. So it'll be just you.' He grinned. 'Unless you don't want to go it alone!'

'Don't be daft.' Mike stared at the younger boy. Ronnie was twenty now and waiting for his own call-up. ''Strewth, that's a facer. Poor old Nick. But . . . if he was shot down—'

'Ssh.' Heads were craning their way. 'Dad said not to let the cat out of the bag. He's going to tell the vicar and he'll say something, but they don't want any fuss because of Phyl. She'll be here in a minute. Here's our Norman, so you've got your best man anyway.' He slipped away from Mike and greeted a couple more guests, people he had never seen before in his life, and shoved them into a pew without even asking which side they were on.

Mike stood irresolute and didn't move until Norman gripped his arm and walked him back up the aisle.

'Try and look a bit more pleased about it, can't you?' the best man muttered. 'The way you're acting, it looks as if I've got you under arrest.'

'Ron's just told me about Nick. Don't you know any more than that? Was he hurt? They get burnt, these pilots—'

'All we know,' Norman interrupted, 'is that he got involved in a dogfight and both the planes went down into the sea off Dover. There was a trawler nearby and it fished him out.' He grinned. 'That's good, isn't it – a trawler,

418

fishing him out? Anyway, he's being sewn up or whatever they need to do, and our Jo's going to send a telegram the minute she knows any more. She reckoned she'd be there in an hour or two so we'll know before you and Phyl go off.'

'What a flaming mess,' Mike muttered, staring at the altar. 'Poor old Nick. Why'd it have to happen last night of all nights? There wasn't even a raid round this way, it was all up in Scotland.'

'There's always a few raiders trying to slip through. Or maybe it was someone got lost in the dark – didn't eat enough carrots! The thing now is for you to forget all that and concentrate on you and Phyl. She's a bit upset – she'll need you to hold her up.'

Mike sighed and nodded. The day seemed to be turning into a shambles. No double wedding, no Jo beside her cousin and best friend, and half the guests missing . . . He glanced behind him and saw to his surprise that quite a lot of Nick's family were there after all. They were all looking anxious but they smiled at him and he felt cheered. It was nice of them to turn up when they didn't even know him or the rest of Jo's family.

He could see Maggie and Etty now. They were sitting a few rows back on the bride's side. They were dressed in their best, with little hats on, but they didn't look as happy as they should. They'd heard about Nick, too, he guessed. Maggie looked as if she'd been crying and Etty was white. Perhaps there'd been more news – worse news.

There was movement at the back of the church. The vicar was there and when Mike turned his head he could see Jo's dad talking to him earnestly. Then the door opened and he saw a flurry of colour as the bridesmaids arrived – Mike's own sisters and Nick's, and little Alice in her best frock, with a posy of primroses.

The organ began to play softly. Trembling, Mike got up and stood beside Norman, his eyes fixed on the altar.

The notes changed. He remembered suddenly Maggie's

wedding eighteen months ago, when they'd whispered the rude words to 'Here Comes The Bride'. It ought to be 'brides' today. What *had* happened to Nick? You couldn't be shot down into the drink and not be hurt . . . .

Norman nudged him sharply in the ribs and he turned to see Phyl coming towards him on her father's arm. Stan Jennings looked grave and Phyl's face was hidden by the veil she wore, but as Mike gazed at her he forgot Jo, forgot Nick, forgot everything but that this was his Phyl, coming to marry him, coming to be his wife. His heart seemed to swell and rise within him and the smile that broke over his face seemed to lighten up the whole of the church.

The wedding went off without a hitch. There was no fumbling for the ring, no mistakes made in the words, no tripping over long dresses or tantrums by small children. They sang 'All Things Bright and Beautiful' and Phyl, who had wanted 'Through The Night of Doubt and Sorrow' just because it was her favourite hymn, was glad that she'd been persuaded against it. It would have seemed cruel to Jo and Nick. But as they sang Jo's choice, 'Love Divine, All Loves Excelling', there were tears in everyone's eyes, even the men's.

It seemed all wrong to be the only ones signing the register and Phyl wept in her mother's arms for a moment, thinking of Jo and wondering what she would find when she reached the hospital. But May patted her shoulders and then handed her back to Mike.

'Buck up, Phyl. Put a smile on your face, now. You've just got married, remember?'

'Yes, try and look a bit pleased about it,' Mike said, repeating Norman's words, and Phyl laughed shakily and walked out of the vestry on his arm with her head high and a look of joy upon her face. There was an audible sigh of relief from the congregation and they all smiled back. Phyl's radiance touched them all, despite the anxiety, and the chilly March day was warmed by the happiness in her face.

Mike and Phyl had a taxi to take them back to the house, but the rest of them walked. It was only two streets away, and they were soon there, being handed glasses of sweet sherry or beer. They stood about, discussing the wedding and wondering what was happening down at the hospital, and then Phyl's father shouted for silence so that he could make a speech.

'We all know that this ought to have been a double wedding,' he said. 'A double wedding and a double celebration. Well, it wasn't to be and we all hope young Nick isn't badly hurt and we hope he'll soon be on the road to recovery. And then we'll finish the job! We'll be asking you all back for part two.' Everyone laughed. 'But since young Mike here wasn't so quick off the mark and walked into the trap my daughter set for him—' a squeal of indignation greeted these words '—then it's my very pleasant duty to ask you all to raise your glasses and drink to *one* happy couple at least. To Phyl and Mike.'

'Phyl and Mike,' they all repeated, and held up their glasses. 'To Phyl and Mike. A long and happy life together.'

'For they are jolly good fellows,' Norman struck up, and they all joined in, 'For they are jolly good fellows. For they are jolly good fe-ellows. And so say all of us!'

Phyl stood close beside her new husband, smiling through her tears. He bent towards her and she lifted her face for his kiss. Everyone cheered and she rested her head on his shoulder, blushing furiously. The party broke up again into conversation and the two newly-weds looked at each other.

'Happy?' Mike whispered, and Phyl nodded.

'As happy as I can be. There's only one thing missing, and you know what that is.' Mike nodded, and Phyl's eyes filled again with tears as she said quietly, 'I hope he's all right, Mike. I hope to God Nick's all right.'

The train journey seemed interminable.

Jo sat in the corner of the compartment, staring out of the window. She saw nothing of what they passed – the ruins of bomb damage, the static water tanks, the barrage-balloon sites, the fields of cows and sheep, the farms and villages. She was scarcely aware of Nick's mother opposite her, gazing just as unseeingly out. She barely noticed his father, trying to comfort them both, with little success.

'If he's badly hurt,' Mrs Laurence kept saying brokenly. 'If he dies . . . My Nick. My boy. I won't be able to bear it, George. I won't.'

'He's not going to die, Mary. Not our Nick.'

Jo heard the words as if through a muffling fog. She wanted to believe them, but her mind kept being invaded by pictures from the night when she and the other Nippies had been called to Cadby Hall, to take trolleys of food out on to the railway platform. She remembered the long, long lines of soldiers coming off the trains, wet, dishevelled, bandaged. She remembered Mike, coming to their trolley, telling them about Tommy Wheeler, Maggie's husband.

Maggie hadn't been able to believe that her Tom could have been killed. Neither had any of the rest of them. But he had been, and look at poor Maggie now.

All through the journey, Jo thought about the wedding. She hoped Phyl was going on with it. It would be stupid not to. At the same time, she was bitten with anguish that it was going on without her and Nick. We ought to be there, she thought. It was our wedding, too. He ought to be in the church with Mike. I ought to be with Phyl now, getting ready. Now we ought to be at the church – walking up the aisle – saying our vows – signing the register. Now I ought to be Mrs Laurence. I ought to be a married woman, along with Phyl. It isn't fair. It just isn't fair.

The train took up the rhythm. *It just isn't fair, it just isn't fair, it just isn't fair* . . . Once she had heard it, clacking away beneath her, she couldn't get it out of her head. *It just isn't fair, it just isn't fair, it just isn't fair* . . .

'I can't bear it,' Mary Laurence said again.

'Look, Mary, he's alive. He didn't get killed. Hold on to that. Whatever happened to him, he's alive and he'll get better. And we'll see him for ourselves soon. Then we'll know.'

'Oh, George . . .' Mary Laurence turned her face into her husband's shoulder and shook with tears. 'Oh, George . . .'

They reached the station at last. They didn't have to go as far as Dover; they could get out at a small village station near the hospital. They stood on the platform, feeling the chilly March wind blow through them, and looked uncertainly about. The train disappeared round a bend but Jo could still hear the clacking rhythm. *It just isn't fair, it just isn't fair, it just isn't fair* . . .

'Will there be a taxi?' Mary Laurence asked doubtfully. Her husband walked past the little ticket office and glanced up and down the village street. The station master who had taken their tickets came out and asked where they wanted to go. The hospital, he said, was half a mile along the road. You couldn't miss it. There'd be a bus in about ten minutes.

'We can walk it in that time,' Jo said anxiously. She knew she could never stand still waiting for a bus for ten whole minutes. 'Let's walk.'

Mrs Laurence looked down at her shoes. She was dressed, like Jo, in a smart costume, ready for the wedding. The groom's mother. Her shoes weren't made for walking along country roads.

'I don't know . . .'

'Please,' Jo begged. Her own shoes weren't much better, but she didn't care as long as they got her there. 'It's only a ten-minute walk.' She was already on her way. 'The bus might be late. It might not come at all. *Please.*'

They set off along the lane, walking rather more slowly than Jo wanted to. Mary Laurence wasn't used to walking far, especially in her best shoes which pinched her toes and had higher heels than her others. She hobbled along, clinging to her husband's arm, and by the time they reached the hospital gates she was sure she had a blister. But, like Jo, she hardly noticed the discomfort. In a few minutes she would see her son. She would know then – they would all know – just what had happened to him.

'He'll be all right,' George Laurence kept repeating. 'He's our boy. He'll be all right.'

He's got to be all right, Jo thought, remembering Mike's face as he told them about Tommy and feeling sick. He's got to be all right.

The hospital was a country house, requisitioned for the war. It was bustling with hurrying nurses and doctors walking briskly to and fro in white coats. Jo and the Laurences hesitated in the door and were taken up the stairs to what had once been a large drawing-room.

They stopped at the door and looked at each other.

'I'm afraid,' Mary whispered. 'Oh, George – I'm afraid . . .'

Jo was shaking. She felt hollow inside, as if her stomach had fallen away somewhere. Every nerve felt as if it were standing erect, like a million tiny hairs sticking out of her skin. She felt that now she had stopped she would never be able to move again, never go through that door, never see what had happened to Nick on the night before their wedding day.

The nurse paused with her hand on the doorknob. She looked at them gravely.

'I'm afraid you may have a shock when you see your son.' She was speaking to the Laurences, as if Jo weren't there. If we were married, Jo thought, it'd be me she'd be telling. *It just isn't fair* . . . 'He was rather burnt. He's quite heavily bandaged.'

Mary Laurence gave a little gasp of horror and Jo felt as if the whole world had fallen away from around her. She put a shaking hand up to her forehead. Dimly, she was aware of